THE RED BRANCH

Note

Chapters from Orpen's memoir and the Coda are written with British English spelling.

Chapters from the memoir of Ophelia Williams are written with American English spelling.

Also By Myles Dungan

Land is all that matters (2024)

The Forgettables (2023)

The Great Irish History Book (2022)

Four Killings (2021)

On This Day, Volume 2 (2017) (Collected *Drivetime* columns)

On This Day, Volume 1 (2015) (Collected *Drivetime* columns)

How the Irish Won the West (2014)

If you want to know who we are (2013)

Mr. Parnell's Rottweiler (2010)

Conspiracy: Irish Political Trials (2009)

*The Captain and the King: William O'Shea,
Parnell and Late Victorian Ireland* (2009)

The Theft of the Irish Crown Jewels (2003)

They Shall Grow Not Old (1995)

Irish Voices from the Great War (1993 & 2014)

Snuff (with Jim Lusby) (1992)

Distant Drums (1991)

Dungan's narrator, Robert Emmet Orpen, is an engaging and often very witty character in this thrilling tale set in old San Francisco.

—Arthur Matthews, co-creator of *Father Ted*

The combination of a dynamic narrator with a vivid recreation of 1880s San Francisco makes *The Red Branch* compulsively readable.

—John Boyne, *The Boy in the Striped Pyjamas*

The Red Branch is a wonderfully inventive, vigorous and exciting fiction woven out of the facts of the Irish republican movement on the west coast of America in the nineteenth century. The narrative is positively symphonic, and teems with memorable characters and colourful action. The character of our hero, Robert Emmet Orpen, is as intricately fashioned as his highly resonant name. A splendid read.

—John Banville, Booker prize-winning author

Myles Dungan's magnificent *The Red Branch* introduces us to Robert Emmet Orpen, an Irish man from Kells Co Meath who started out in the Dublin Metropolitan Police and then to the London Met before landing in the Wild West of 1880s San Francisco where he is charged with infiltrating the infamous Knights of the Red Branch, a supposedly benevolent organisation. Here, he comes across knaves and rogues as villainous as himself though perhaps not quite so eloquent. Dungan's use of language and wordplay although light in tone, displays an extraordinary talent; plotting is watertight and characterisation is rich and vivid. A totally absorbing and highly amusing caper.

—Liz Nugent, *Strange Sally Diamond,*
Irish crime novel of the year 2023

With humor, wit, and *savoir faire*, Irish historian Myles Dungan plunges us into San Francisco's Barbary Coast of the 1880s, complete with Irish/Chinese rivalries, corporate greed, and political shenanigans—all within a crime-espionage-double-murder-mystery page turner. BRAVO!

—Judy Irving, director of *The Wild Parrots of Telegraph Hill*

With the keen eye and dark snark of a hard-assed Dashiell Hammett gumshoe, Myles Dungan's fresh-off-the-boat Irish detective Robert Orpen prowls the streets of 19th century San Francisco seeking the source of explosives destined for domestic terrorism back home. It's a city still rough around its Gold Rush edges and churning with the racial tension and violence Dungan invokes as if he had lived there himself. Like the portrait that Dorian Gray keeps locked in the attic, *The Red Branch* reveals through Orpen's walks and encounters a reality masked by the city's narcissism.

—Gray Brechin, *Imperial San Francisco*

Myles Dungan has crafted a detective story that deserves to sit next to the best of Raymond Chandler. San Francisco of 1883, an infant city marred by corruption and criminality, comes alive from the Tenderloin to Chinatown to North Beach in this riveting, fast-paced read. Laced with humor, clever turns of phrase, and a panoply of richly drawn characters, this novel is not easy to put down.

—Matthew Spangler, playwright, *The Kite Runner,*
The Beekeeper of Aleppo, and *The Tortilla Curtain*

THE RED BRANCH

Myles Dungan

Etruscan Press

Etruscan Press
Wilkes University
84 West South Street
Wilkes-Barre, PA 18766
(570) 408-4546

Wilkes
University

www.etruscanpress.org

Published 2025 by Etruscan Press
Cover design by Logan Rock
Interior design and typesetting by Andrea Reider
The text of this book is set in Minion.

First Edition

17 18 19 20 5 4 3 2 1

Library of Congress Control Number: 2025944688

Please turn to the back of this book for a list of the sustaining funders of Etruscan Press.

This book is printed on recycled, acid-free paper.

'We are constantly deceiving each other—saying to each other things that are not, counter-combining, counterplotting and of course, as a consequence, counteracting each other in many ways.'

—Fenian leader John O'Leary,
*What Irishmen Should Know and
How Irishmen Should Feel*, (Dublin, 1886)

To the amazing women in my life, Nerys, Teri, Fiona, Amber, Lara, Gwyneth, Sadie, and Sophie, one or two of whom found their way into this fiction. And to the elder Dungan boys, who also feature.

ACKNOWLEDGMENTS

The Red Branch would not be *The Red Branch* but for the support and the interventions of my literary agent, Jonathan Williams. Throughout the lengthy process of writing and revision his good humoured and telling observations, and his faith in the original material, turned a promising piece of writing into something that (I hope) is more well-wrought. As did the input of my Etruscan Press editor, and honorary Cavanman, Philip Brady. His gratifying enthusiasm for the draft despatched across the Atlantic in the spring of 2024 did not blind him to the residual faults of the work. His telling comments and suggestions have produced a far better outcome, and I am undyingly grateful for his backing and his advice. As I am also to Amanda Rabaduex and Pamela Turchin of Etruscan Press for the multiplicity of parts they played in bringing this work from 'page to stage'. A process which must have put significant demands on their patience, dedication and versatility. As always, my heartfelt thanks go out to the central Williams in my life, my wife Nerys, who has been hearing about the unreliable narration of Robert Emmet Orpen for far too long now.

CHAPTER ONE

FROM THE UNPUBLISHED MEMOIR OF ROBERT EMMET ORPEN

12 October 1883 – The Embarcadero, San Francisco—early evening

'Were you coming for the other one, Skullcrusher?'

It was the last thing the cross-eyed lowlife heard as he staggered back into the Bay. When he went under, he looked aggrieved. Reproachful. Face like a clenched fist. As red as a slapped arse. Maybe it was the jolt of the icy water. More likely it was the certain knowledge that he couldn't swim. He may have mentioned it once or twice as he floundered. I think he was expecting me to rescue him. Not the brightest light in the firmament.

De profundis clamavi ad te, Domine.

I nearly broke my hand with the blow that sent Ollie 'Skull-crusher' Madden to his appointment with Neptune. I can almost feel the pain in my knuckles still, fifty years later, but it was well worth it. Madden and I had form, so this was a rematch. In a grimy Dublin back alley two years before, the decision had gone his way. As we squared up, I followed his eyes. Not a profitable exercise when you're trying to divine the intentions of an astigmatic. That cost me my left ear. I looked on a little too passively as a leering Madden swallowed it. I was so disengaged that I missed the wind-up for the right hook that broke my nose.

Perhaps some of Madden's chagrin at the prospect of death by drowning was because I weighed one hundred and seventy pounds in heavy brogues, and he had the heft of a Barbary Coast whorehouse. He sank like a turd in a privy. Just so much unassimilated waste.

Who knows, he might well have mastered the front crawl, and the capricious currents of the Bay, and made it across to the Marin Peninsula. Perhaps he bought a vineyard in Sonoma and settled down to a life of improving viticulture. No one would have recognised him anyway. The water of San Francisco Bay is so frigid that his eyes would have uncrossed as he floated. His desperate gurgles of 'Riley, Riley' gradually grew fainter as he drifted away from the wharf into the enveloping darkness.

I'll get back to Doghouse Riley in a minute. First, I probably need to explain why I was doing the *danse macabre* with Skullcrusher.

I had barely arrived in San Francisco after an interminable train journey from the east coast. I had just shaken off *rigor mortis* and was two hundred yards from the railway station when I spotted my escort. They were as inconspicuous as shite on sawdust, so bad at what they were supposed to be doing that I assumed they were unconcerned about being detected. Madden was wearing a manky top hat that you could spot a mile off. I'm a bit hazy about some of what happened next. But even after more than half a lifetime I still remember that clownish hat.

At the time, I knew San Francisco about as well as the already thinning patch of hair on my pate. But rather than prolong the charade, I followed my nose in the direction of the nearest available body of water. The Bay smelt as if it hadn't been taken out and cleaned in a while, so that bit was easy. It turned out to be a good move too.

As Madden floated off to whatever destiny the waters of the Pacific had in mind for him, I turned towards Riley with a lighter step. I ignored Doghouse's heart-rending profanities. He'd been stupid enough to bring a knife to what quickly turned into a gunfight. What can I say? His second must have not got the message. I figured that his distress was probably on account of the bullet lodged in his shoulder. It was a flesh wound, but don't believe everything you read about the mild discomfort of superficial injuries. This one seemed to be causing Riley all the anguish I could have wished for him.

But when I heard the first police whistle, I thought it might look better if I was discovered ministering to Riley in his agonies. So, I inserted my index finger in the gaping wound left by the passage of the bullet, leaned into him, and asked courteously (and perhaps a tad too cheerfully), 'Who sent you, you bastard?' As I expected, I got no usable information, just some more eye-popping obscenities. But I was happy enough with that. My vocabulary was profiting, and it didn't really matter. I already knew who had sent him.

I removed the offending digit as the first curious, blue-uniformed San Francisco policeman showed up and almost fell over Riley in the preternatural gloom.

The police officer—another Irishman as it happened, name of Tracy, Rory to his friends, broad-shouldered and a bit cranky, but not a bad sort as it turned out—had come from the direction of Market Street. In explaining the painful tableau being enacted on the pier—painful for Riley at least—I may have tried to suggest to Tracy that I had merely chanced upon this stricken citizen and offered my assistance. Tracy was unimpressed. He was quick to identify the hapless victim though. When he recognised the distressed Doghouse, his face was suddenly suffused with an expression of blissful contentment.

His look of amused scepticism at my cock and bull story was strangely enhanced by the fact that his eyes were of different colours—one green and one blue—and by Riley's indignant barking. 'That bastard Orpen shot me,' Doghouse croaked, indicating with an unsteady hand that I was Nemesis, not the Good Samaritan. Both of us, as it happened, neglected to tell Tracy about the aquatic Madden, whose mortal remains were probably halfway to Angel Island by then.

When Tracy insisted on searching me, he found the revolver. He sniffed the muzzle. I thought I detected the merest glint of approval in the green eye. The blue was unwaveringly neutral.

'That bastard … shot me.' Riley rasped between theatrical groans. 'Him. Orpen.'

'Shut up, Doghouse,' Tracy snapped.

Riley subsided and resumed his braying, *sotto voce*. Tracy returned his attention to me. His thin smile grew a little plumper. His glee had now reached the blue eye as well.

'While you have done the community a great service, young man, I'm obliged to ask why exactly you shot that parcel of Tipperary trash?'

'So, where are you from yourself?' I deflected, with practiced affability. But Tracy wasn't having any of the 'old sod' guff.

'I'd prefer if you'd just answer the question. Why did you feel the need to put a bullet into that animal? And why did you miss all his vital organs while you were at it?'

I bent down and picked up the knife with which Riley had been expecting to skewer me. Tracy took a precautionary step backwards.

'He came at me with this,' I told him.

'Proper order so. He's handy enough with one of those.'

He produced a small notebook from under his helmet and began writing but made no effort to relieve me of the knife. Something about the man suggested that this wasn't a mere oversight. He finished making his note, licked his pencil—in that unconventional order—and looked at me squarely. 'However, I do need to know who you are, what you're doing here, why you are carrying a weapon, and why your first instinct was to come up with a fairy tale about being the Angel of Mercy to that nauseating rodent in his hour of need.'

A sudden surge of weariness wafted over me. Or perhaps it was delayed grief for Skullcrusher.

'North or South Riding?' I inquired.

Tracy looked perplexed. His eyebrows parted company from the bridge of his nose. The blue eye darkened to a vivid indigo.

'Riley,' I explained. 'You said he was from Tipperary. It's big, so it's divided in two. Which is how you would have found me if our friend there had been just a wee bit handier with the knife.'

That sparkling piece of repartee merely extracted the scathing grunt it deserved. I had only one arrow left in my quiver. Something I learned once from an Italian music teacher bored with my faltering arpeggios. I stretched out with my right hand towards his left temple. Before he had time to recoil, I produced a silver dollar from his ear and presented it to him between my thumb and forefinger.

'Prego!' I announced, with affected triumph. It was what Signor Balotelli always exclaimed when he produced a farthing from where my left ear used to be. Tracy's blue eye now matched his uniform.

'Really? You wouldn't be trying to bribe a police officer, now, would you?'

I would. But his demeanour suggested that such an admission would be the wrong approach. I pirouetted.

'And what hope would I have with such a paragon of virtue?' I replied.

'Not a jot.' Tracy was clearly an aficionado of what is known in Ireland as *plámás*, 'flattery' being woefully inadequate to describe its syrupy character. His contempt for conjuring, sycophancy and corruption broke the spell. He pointed to the revolver.

'You won't mind if I hang on to this?'

'Not at all,' I assured him.

'And you won't mind coming along with me.'

'I'd be happy to. You seem like a thoroughly good sort.'

'I'm famous for it.'

'What about me?' whined Riley. 'I'm dying here.'

Just then another dark blue uniform appeared out of the mist. Darragh Somethingorother I seem to recall. Or don't, as it happens. Another fine Celtic policeman. Tracy commended the soul of Riley into his hands and started walking. He motioned me to follow. As I did so, I slipped the knife into the pocket of my jacket. When we passed its prostrate owner, I couldn't help noticing—alerted by the poor man's renewed shrieks—that Rory Tracy gave Doghouse a crafty kick in the crotch.

Scotland Yard, London, 9 August 1883

If you know anything about Ireland, you'll probably assume, with a name like Orpen, that I am from a wealthy Protestant family. A cherished member of the 'filthy fucking landlord class', to use an enlightened neighbour's colourful description. If I share the additional intelligence that I'm from just outside the town of Kells in County Meath—a rickety forty mile coach ride north-west of Dublin (these days the road is paved)—you'll already have conjured up a vision of a big house surrounded by rolling grassland, vast undisciplined trees, condescending thoroughbred horses in well-appointed stables, a small legion of forelock-tugging flunkies, and China tea on the lawn. And that's where you'd be well off the mark.

I'm Protestant all right, and there was once plenty of money in the extended family, but I wasn't born into the well-manicured, planter sub-clan. Fifty acres and four bedrooms near Kells, that was our lot. More than decent by Irish standards. Certainly not eligible for any monetary assistance from the Association for the Relief of Distressed Protestants. Unwarranted opulence, according to some of our more covetous Roman Catholic neighbours—and I can see their point. They spent the Land War of the 1880s courageously reading the local paper to see if someone had finally burnt us out, so that they could pick through the embers and move their beasts onto the ravaged property.

There was once an estate, but three generations of Orpens had steadily caroused their way through most of it before I was born. Our farm—they were called 'holdings' because you were expected to cling to them tenaciously—rather more compact than in the halcyon days, still provided a decent living for a family of five. This was reduced to four when my mother died of my father's apathy and her own tuberculosis. I was eight years old at the time. I suppose I should be grateful that my father never remarried. I cultivated an imaginary mother for a while, but she left us when I was twelve. My father drove her away too.

I was the second son, so whatever few acres that survived my father's love affair with his claret decanter were already destined for my older brother Daniel. Daniel O'Connell Orpen. I'm Robert Emmet Orpen. My mother, a Roman Catholic, wore her heart on the birth certificates of her sons, and of her only daughter, Grace O'Malley Orpen. She wasn't partial to the English, and she passed that antipathy on to me. I was perfectly willing, however, to allow them to pay my wages. It would have been churlish to do otherwise.

My older brother was sufficiently robust for me to renounce any jealous anticipation of his premature demise. I wasn't getting a single blade of grass. This meant that I could safely choose my own path in life. I'm not entirely sure why I should have become attracted to the prospect of a career in law enforcement. I suppose I just like to poke my nose into other people's business.

I survived three years in the Dublin Metropolitan Police, then accidentally fell into the London equivalent. I was briefly attached to 'G' Division in Dublin Castle under its canny Superintendent, John

Mallon, an Ulster Roman Catholic who specialised in exasperating the Irish Republican Brotherhood.

Now, if I were a religious type, I would offer up an occasional prayer to the intermittent resourcefulness of the IRB. Their trade, which mostly involved blowing things up, afforded unrivalled opportunities for a young Peeler on the make. *Carpe Diem*. I'd started out my professional life on the hardship detail, working the seedier Dublin pawnbrokers, checking for stolen goods. But I managed to catch Mallon's eye by ratting out several impious colleagues who were being rewarded for turning a blind eye to some heavyweight tardy drinking on lightly licensed premises. That was how I became profitably acquainted with the muscular vanguard of *Erin go bragh*.

My usefulness to Mallon, although he chose to remain studiously unaware of it, was indirectly related to my expertise at poker. This was the only life skill that I ever acquired from my father. We played together regularly until I reached the age of fifteen and began taking money from him. He always claimed that the cache of bottle tops I earned each night was merely a cache of bottle tops. I thought otherwise and settled our nightly account by accessing his ill-concealed and dwindling stash of banknotes when he would finally pass out on our shabby second-hand *chaise longue*.

In Dublin I managed to parlay my proficiency at cards into a small but highly serviceable cadre of informants. I called them my Secret Service, which was probably treasonable. I amassed this seedy gaggle of stool pigeons by getting them heavily in my debt. I was hard to read. A demeanour of dull impassivity can be lethal at the card table.

Mallon never inquired too closely about the source of my more useful nuggets of information. These concerned the domestic and social arrangements of much sought after Fenian *banditi*. You'll forgive me if I take issue with the DMP Standing Orders and Regulations, where it explicitly states that 'tap room information is rarely worth much'. If there are serious losses at cards involved, I'll take tap room scuttlebutt anytime.

I also have good reason to be eternally grateful to the Swedish gentleman who invented dynamite. Gunpowder's loss was my gain. At the time the Fenians were introducing Mr. Nobel's discovery to numerous public buildings in England. A few well-placed Brotherhood devices and, for me, London beckoned. Who was I to decline such a pressing invitation? In return for waging ceaseless warfare on 'Fenian fire' I rapidly rose to the vertiginous heights of Detective Sergeant in the Met. But for the enthusiasm of the IRB for remodelling English cities, I might still have been a uniformed constable in Dublin, developing fallen arches while trying to avoid the beady eye of Superintendent Maher of 'C' Division.

Thus it was that on a hot August day in 1883, I was summoned to the office of 'The Gosling', a ubiquitous but virtually undetectable phantasm.

His actual name, or at least his most consistent alias, was Major Nicholas Gosselin. Originally of Cavan extraction—a disagreeable fate I escaped myself by less than ten miles of soggy real estate as the crow flies—he had acquired certain skills not derived, *in rerum natura*, from his Irish nativity. Among the attributes bequeathed to him was a pair of exceptionally tight lips and a remarkable capacity to conceal his past and present. He had been old-school Army, before being seconded to the Special Irish Branch in Scotland Yard. That much and damn all else, we knew.

The 'Branch' was Sir William Harcourt's sleight of hand. It was the Liberal Home Secretary's way of facilitating the smooth transfer of blame for his failure to stop the Fenians from planting bombs wherever they were minded to. At first, when they were just practising, they had managed only to make some loud and alarming noises amongst a family of street bins. But Harcourt could see what was coming and had the wit to graze the scapegoat where everyone could see him. That was the genesis of the Branch. So, when the Bold Fenian Men went on to ignite the green upholstery of the House of Commons itself, someone quite a few rungs lower than the Home Secretary was to blame. I should add, by way of a footnote, that, happily, none of our beloved legislators was hurt when the bomb went off in the Palace of Westminster. The street bins, on the other hand, suffered acutely.

I had a sense that Gosselin wasn't even supposed to exist. Dolly Williamson—Chief Inspector Adolphus Frederick Williamson to a bottom feeder in the Met like me—was the putative head of the Irish Branch. But that didn't fool anyone. The Gosling was really in charge. He was an almost mythical mammalian life form situated in the food chain somewhere between the chameleon and the Cheshire Cat, yet entirely devoid of the latter's capacity for grim merriment. Gosselin was never known to crack a grin, but he did blend in like the fabled lizard. His appearance helped his anonymity. I met him on several occasions, but for the life of me I can't remember what he looked like, bar some dim memory of a head of hair that reminded me of King Charles I. I've never seen a single photograph of the man. He was spectral. He must have done someone's bidding, but it certainly wasn't Dolly's.

His office was sparsely furnished. It looked as if it could have been casually abandoned to the enemy—a besieging force of Foreign Office dogsbodies, for example—without consequence. There was a small cherry-wood desk in the middle of the room, with two chairs on either side. And an inkwell. No pen, no paper, no blotter, just an inkwell filled to the brim. On the wall the only adornment, if it can be so described, was a portrait of Queen Victoria. The Empress of India, clad in her mandatory capacious black, looked her usual glum and censorious self. It was an ideal setting for the Gosling: impersonal, devoid of character, and uninformative.

Gosselin wasn't alone that day. He sat behind the cherry-wood desk. Standing across from him, ignoring the second chair, smoking a cigar, and looking his dapper self, was another ghost, Robert Anderson. He was a Dubliner, but not of the kind you'd find quaffing porter in a Thomas Street tavern. Although they were both Irish by birth, Gosselin and Anderson were not potatoes and buttermilk Irish. They belonged to that class of Anglo-Saxon Hibernian who had chosen their tribe by jettisoning the letter 'r' from the alphabet, spawning the type of oick who called me 'Wobert'. Though not Gosselin and Anderson, you understand. We were not on a first name basis.

I have no idea if Anderson was the ascetic sort, but he certainly looked it. He was a sliver of dour Puritanism whom I suspected of secretly sporting Scriptural tattoos. Lots of pointing fingers, Gothic script and warnings of imminent perdition. He was Oliver Cromwell in a high stiff collar and dark greatcoat. He looked like a fractious street preacher who had left his Bible at home, and he offered visible confirmation that to be a true aristocrat in the Department for the Interdiction of Deranged Irish Rebels, you had best be an unhinged Irishman yourself. He was then in his middle years, gaunt to the point of the skeletal, razor-featured, and sporting a beard that was already dappled with grey. While there was a wraithlike serenity about Gosselin, Anderson was a metronome set to *presto*.

I was offered the vacant chair, which I accepted with considerable misgivings. I assumed I wasn't there to receive a medal or a commendation. Gosselin remained seated, but Anderson paced. He looked at me with undisguised distaste, clearly making an instant decision to take an instant dislike.

'Chief Inspector Williamson permits you to cultivate that mane of hair?' Anderson sniffed, by way of introduction. The hirsute Gosselin looked suitably peeved. In response, I lifted a masking lock from my face and revealed the spot where my right ear had once lurked.

'C.I. Williamson doesn't like my disfigurement upsetting the criminal classes.' I paused before adding a 'sir' after a satisfyingly subversive interval. Anderson's lip curled perceptibly, and he resumed pacing around the airless room. It was early August, and the weather had been freshly imported from Calcutta. I began to perspire within minutes of taking my seat. Neither of the phantoms looked even vaguely moist or uncomfortable. Anderson's only concession to the stifling humidity was to unbutton his coat. Apparitions obviously don't sweat.

It was Gosselin who began to deal the cards. 'I suppose you are wondering why you're here?' he inquired, with a studied lack of interest in my wonderment.

'You've been recommended to us,' the pacing Anderson observed.

Gosselin's face clouded. He was clearly displeased that it was Cromwell who had chosen to puncture the suspense.

'By Chief Inspector Williamson?' I asked. Gosselin ignored the question after exchanging a furtive glance with Anderson. I deduced that Dolly had not been taken into their confidence.

Gosselin studied me sternly for a moment. 'I'm told you are someone who is prone to affect airs and graces—'

'—with a mutinous tendency towards independent action,' added Anderson.

'Stand-offishness is not something we encourage in the Special Irish Branch,' Gosselin continued.

'Nor is insubordination.' Anderson was not about to see his gripe relegated to the minor placings.

I engineered a momentary pause in this deluge of deprecation by staring blankly at an imaginary spot on the wall behind Gosselin. Years of dealing with my father's irritation had taught me that a few seconds of eloquent silence, just when you felt a compulsion to speak, often produced desirable results. Anderson blinked first. He was a fully committed vacuum filler. Not even the most blatantly self-serving muteness stood a chance in the face of his garrulity. 'I suppose it could work in his favour,' he offered, 'that he has an extra layer of varnish, I mean.'

'I suppose so,' Gosselin conceded without enthusiasm. I was now being discussed by two senior policemen as if I was a tin of paint.

'No doubt San Francisco will scour some of the glaze,' Anderson observed exultantly.

'You're going to California,' Gosselin interposed curtly. Once again Anderson had jumped a fence out of sequence. Mute, inglorious, melting, I waited for the Gosling to elaborate.

But it was Anderson who broke into my reverie. 'You don't seem very pleased,' he remarked. He looked aggrieved, although, since this was his default expression, it was hard to know if I was the cause. He turned to Gosselin. 'Are you sure we've got the right man? I was told Orpen was quite clever for his age.' I longed to puncture his disdain by asking him to choose a card from the pack in my pocket and then produce it from his sphincter. But I wasn't that good yet, and I was certain it would not go down well.

Gosselin ignored Anderson's interruption. 'To San Francisco,' he said dully, conscious that Anderson had already tipped the cat out of the bag.

'A veritable Gomorrah I believe,' Anderson said, asserting his proud Puritan credentials.

Gosselin attempted to open a desk drawer. The operation did not proceed smoothly. It was the only time I ever saw the man at a loss. He tugged at the recalcitrant drawer, causing the laden inkwell to bounce ominously. Just as Anderson was showing embarrassing signs of offering assistance, the Gosling somehow managed to jerk open the drawer without spilling the contents of the inkwell. He produced a manila envelope and handed it to me. 'All the details are here,' he muttered through clenched teeth.

I handled the envelope gingerly, as if it was contaminated. 'Might I ask what is expected of me, sir?'

Gosselin reached back into the open drawer and removed a newspaper clipping. This time, for some idiosyncratic reason, he handed it to Anderson, who passed it on to me in what seemed like a well-rehearsed Masonic ritual. The clipping read as follows: 'Safety Nitro Dynamite: The Best of High Explosives, Extra Strong Blasting Powder, which Has No Equal for Bank, Stump or Wood Blasting: Manufactured by the Safety Nitro Powder Company, San Francisco.'

Gosselin said, 'Thanks to a timely raid in Ealing we were not obliged to discover if the product lives up to the claims of the advertisement. As you can see, the Safety Nitro Powder Company is based in San Francisco. We happen to have an extremely effective and resourceful infiltrator who usually keeps us informed about the activities of the IRB in that city. Up to now, the armchair rebels there have been gratifyingly ineffectual.'

'So, it was your man who saved the day, sir?' I thought I should display some interest in proceedings.

'No, it was not. And thereby hangs a tale.'

Anderson stopped pacing for long enough to give his next interruption additional weight. 'Are you familiar with the name Dan Horton?' he asked.

'My aged grandmother is familiar with the name Dan Horton.' I responded, before remembering to whom I was speaking. I pressed home my disadvantage. 'He was recently canonised by the *New York Times*, wasn't he ... sir? "The West Coast O'Donovan Rossa". That's quite a distinction in Republican circles. It situates him somewhere between an Archbishop and a Cardinal in the Fenian hierarchy. Is Horton supplying dynamite to Rossa?'

'No, he isn't,' Gosselin replied, recapturing the initiative. 'He's the effective and resourceful infiltrator.'

Had it not been for the soporific atmosphere, I am sure I would have betrayed my surprise at this piece of intelligence. Gosselin looked archly at Anderson. 'At least he was,' he added. 'Of late, he seems to have taken a vow of silence.'

Anderson trumped the Gosling's archness with a frosty stare. 'We need to find out why,' he said, emphasising every syllable and sounding like my old Latin teacher.

'To be frank, Orpen,' Gosselin said, 'my fear is that Horton has decided to go native again. Mr. Anderson, however, takes a more charitable view.' Mercifully, Gosselin's icy smile lowered the temperature of the room. 'While I'm touched and consoled by his faith in his informant, the possibility that Horton has defected, or returned to the pack, diminishes the value of the intelligence he has been supplying for, at least, the last two years.'

Both contending spectres studiously avoided each other's gaze. The Gosling was serene, but the agitated Anderson looked like someone who wished there was a weapon to hand with which he could smite the Cavalier. When *in extremis*, Calvinists are prone to smite.

Anderson broke the silence. 'I still have confidence in Horton's *bona fides*. I feel the Major underestimates the difficulty of becoming an "untraitor" having once betrayed a cause.'

Grateful for Anderson's hostage to fortune, Gosselin resumed the tutorial. 'The IRB in San Francisco operate under the aegis of an apparently benevolent fellowship called the Knights of the Red Branch. Banquets, hideous concerts, nauseating recitals of mawkish poetry, and St. Patrick's Day parades, that sort of thing. We want you to insinuate yourself into their activities, find out what, if anything'—here he paused and stared at Anderson—'has happened to Horton and put a stop to the exportation of dynamite from California.' He made it all sound like a dull Sunday school picnic with pink fairy cakes.

Anderson took up the refrain. 'I'm sure the Americans would much prefer to use the explosives themselves, for building longer railways and flooding the world with even more silver.'

I must have looked dubious because Gosselin addressed me sharply. 'You seem sceptical?'

'Well sir, I'm honoured to be entrusted with the task, of course.' As a matter of fact, I was just intrigued. I loathe the word 'honour' though I'm expected to use it a lot—Americans can't even spell it properly. 'But I'm astonished to hear that Horton is, or was, on *our* side. You might just as well have told me that Rossa himself was a closet royalist collecting dynamite for a fireworks display to mark the Queen's jubilee.'

'Your surprise is not unwarranted, assuming Mr. Anderson's confidence is well founded.' There was an audible 'harrumph' from the corner of the room. 'Horton is not quite the dragon he appears to be. A leaky investment portfolio has left him a little short and obliges him to join forces with St. George. Or obliged at any rate.'

Anderson, who suddenly stopped pacing, now proffered an inscrutable nugget of his own. 'Of course, Horton is not our only Trojan horse. A bird never flew on one wing,' he said, looking exceptionally pleased with this potpourri of metaphors. Gosselin shot him an admonishing glare. Anderson returned it with interest and resumed his tour of the room.

'Think of yourself from this point onwards as a moist sponge,' the Gosling said enigmatically. Though I was baffled by this remark, I attempted to look as if we were completely *ad idem*. 'You must squeeze out your past and soak up another identity. Assume a new and plausible persona. Ingrain the details. Your well-being will depend upon it.'

I could see from his irritated tracking of Anderson's movements that the latter's constant motion was now beginning to get under Gosselin's skin. I calculated that by the end of our meeting, Anderson would easily have covered enough ground to fulfil the conditions of a minor pilgrimage, assuming Puritans countenanced such Papist rituals. Without pausing in his circumnavigation of the room, he picked up a book from an otherwise bare shelf and began to study it closely. As luck would have it, it was a Bible. He leafed through the volume while Gosselin was speaking. As the latter warmed to his theme, Anderson suddenly interrupted his flow.

'Ah! How singularly appropriate. 23:4,' he intoned, holding the volume aloft by way of confirmation. The Lord himself, and the Gideon Society, had clearly spoken. We both stared at him, equally perplexed. I thought I could hear Gosselin's teeth grinding. Anderson was oblivious. He was protected by his public-school insouciance, moral superiority, and a lifetime of selective deafness.

'Psalms, 23:4,' he explained. '"Yea though I walk through the valley of darkness I will fear no evil, for you are with me. Your rod and your staff they comfort me". A succinct summation of Sergeant Orpen's mission, don't you think?'

Treating the interruption as if it had been a piece of carefully rehearsed dialogue, Gosselin turned back to me.

'Which reminds me,' he said, 'unlike that worthy pilgrim, I'm afraid we are most definitely *not* with you. Should you be apprehended in any setting that might cause embarrassment to Her Majesty's Government, you are traversing the valley of darkness entirely unaccompanied.'

'And the rod and staff?' I inquired.

'Feel free to draw whatever weaponry you think will come in useful. Good day, Sergeant Orpen.'

Neither Gosselin nor Anderson offered to hold the door for me as I left with my instructions. Neither did they wish me luck. I reckoned such an egregious failure of good manners gave me *carte blanche* to do things my way, whatever it might say in the manila envelope, or the Book of Psalms.

12 October 1883: San Francisco Hall of Justice, late evening

There being no further reason for dissimulation, the moist sponge sat reabsorbing his own past in an interview room in the Hall of Justice off Portsmouth Square. I could safely squeeze my assumed identity—conscientiously assimilated over a long weekend—down the toilet. I had, in the argot of the London underworld, already been 'well and truly rumbled, mate'.

Now, most lasting friendships begin effortlessly. Two people meet, there is an immediate *frisson*. Result, enduring intimacy. But with Detective Sergeant Thaddeus Kelly of the San Francisco police, it was more friction than *frisson*. I'm sure his mother must have loved him deeply, but I simply couldn't imagine anything other than maternal affection having entered his mansion, and, even then, by means of a gap in the privy door.

I suspect he loathed me before we had even met, based on information received. For my part, I gave the infant relationship my best shot, but it was to no avail. We were destined to be Cain and Abel from the outset. While I do not want to appear any shallower than is strictly necessary, Kelly's physical appearance was what first put me off. If I tell you that he was a weasel, you probably don't need to hear any more. Long neck and body, short legs, beady eyes. His disposition was pure weasel as well. With more than a hint of stoat.

We didn't get off to a good start when he walked into the small windowless room, accompanied by Tracy, and began a red-faced harangue against me for my assault on a solid citizen like Mr. Christopher Riley—that, apparently, being Doghouse's given name. He demanded to know what I had done to rouse such a placid soul into a display of violence. I was taken aback at his highly original approach. Kelly's sainted version of Doghouse was of a paragon clothed in the raiment of a docile Quaker, or a senior officer in the Salvation Army. Therefore, reasoned Sergeant Kelly, he must have been brutishly provoked to have felt the need to lay hands on me. When I protested that it was I who had been the victim of a gratuitous assault, Kelly guffawed. The chortle was merely a prelude to a cuff across my face from the back of his hand. He was a married man, and it was his left hand, so that added injury to injury. I tried to leap out of my chair and get my fingers around his scraggy throat, but the estimable Tracy—all grizzly bear to Kelly's weasel—managed to restrain me, while simultaneously remonstrating with his superior. My interrogator's face remained a bright pink, but soothed by Tracy, he gradually slipped into neutral.

Kelly and I would become better acquainted as time went on. I would discover that, where he was concerned, serious crime in San Francisco was always susceptible to simple solutions, viz, a convenient male Chinese, between the ages of ten and seventy, within a radius of half a mile. The application of gentle pressure—of the type to which I had just been subjected—would quickly lead to a confession. This radical technique often operated in reverse as well. Whenever Kelly came across a Chinese—Californians called them Celestials—in what he deemed to be 'the wrong place', i.e. anywhere other than Chinatown, he would immediately go in search of a crime, with his prisoner in tow.

'I could just let you off I suppose,' he blandly declared in his dulcet Cork accent. Was he suddenly changing tack under pressure from Tracy? Alas, no. 'A few words in the right ears and five minutes after leaving this building, you'd be swinging at the end of a rope somewhere south of Market. Natural justice.'

'That's not going to happen now, is it, Sergeant,' Tracy interjected. 'That's not how we do things here ... anymore.'

'That'll be all Tracy,' snapped Kelly. 'You can be on your way. I don't need any help from you.'

'You did a minute ago,' Tracy observed wryly. He looked as if he was conducting an internal debate. The devil's advocate won out and he decided to follow orders. With a worried backward glance, he left the room. Tracy obviously knew how these things worked, but he probably hadn't forgotten that I still had a knife in my pocket, should the need arise. 'You might need that silver dollar now,' he observed enigmatically to no one in particular, as he took his leave.

Kelly turned his attention back to me. He stalked the room for a while, surveying me from a few menacing angles. Presumably this was intended to add an element of tension and foreboding to the interview. I took the opportunity to inspect the cuticles on my right hand. They needed care and attention.

'What's your name, fella?' Kelly finally asked.

I was pleased that he hadn't bothered to ask Tracy, or even the stricken Doghouse. I mulled rapidly over a few interesting possibilities. The one that managed to elbow the other contenders out of the way belonged to a class bully at Westminster school whose stubby fingers I'd once had occasion to break when they came about an inch too close to my face.

'Plantagenet. Darcy Plantagenet,' I heard myself responding. Even as I spoke, I was dismayed at my own brazen audacity. 'At your service. Might I ask whom I have the honour of addressing?' I had already anticipated his response. He didn't let me down.

'You might not. What sort of a name is that? Plantagenet!'

'Ancient. And highly coveted, I believe. Kingly.'

'Not in San Francisco, it's not. We don't like kings here, or airs and graces.'

I'd never have thought Thaddeus Kelly and Major Nicholas Gosselin to have had much in common, but there it was again.

'And neither do we like smug English bastards shooting one of Sheriff Newman's best men.'

'I'm Irish as it happens.' There was another guffaw from Kelly, but this time he kept his fists to himself.

'Irish? Are you deluded? With a name like Plan-bloody-tagenet? In a pig's arse you're Irish. The man you shot, now there's a decent Irishman.'

I stretched and yawned, though I was feeling neither stiffness nor fatigue. Not that I was unduly concerned, but I was perplexed as to why there had been no reference so far to the fate of that other timorous

Irish plaster saint, Oliver 'Skullcrusher' Madden. However, I wasn't inclined to enlighten this polecat. Doghouse could break the news. I was surprised that he'd kept the information to himself thus far.

Just then the door opened and out of the corner of my eye I could see that a uniform had entered. This livery had an immediate effect on Kelly, so I assumed that it was not Tracy returning to the fold. It was as if Kelly had suddenly developed a puncture. He seemed to get smaller, rapidly deflating from weasel to ferret. An authoritative and sonorous voice uttered some welcome words in a distinctly north of England accent.

'I'll take it from here thank you, Sergeant Kelly. You can go.'

I was expecting, at the very least, a 'But, sir ...' from Kelly. The protest never came. There was a baleful glance all right, but it was in my direction. When Kelly turned to face the owner of the *basso profundo*, his face was the Sea of Tranquillity. He almost curtsied as he walked past my redeemer. I had been rescued by someone of consequence.

The welcome interloper introduced himself as Isaiah Lees, Captain of Detectives and late of Preston, Lancashire. I began to wonder, did any member of San Francisco's finest hale from California? Lees's rescue mission, it later transpired, had been prompted by a visit from Grizzly Tracy. I felt a wave of gratitude towards cuddlesome bears washing over me. Tracy had obviously reported to Lees on the bewildering apotheosis of Doghouse Riley. Only Kelly, it transpired, seemed capable of looking past the thuggish qualities of the man and seeing the Christ that lay buried deep within the Christopher. Lees was clearly as enamoured of Doghouse as was Rory Tracy. He had come to inspect me for himself.

'May I ask your name, stranger?' the newcomer inquired amiably. If Kelly was a weasel, Lees was a unicorn. He was a soft-voiced and rangy man in his forties with blue eyes that heralded misfortune for anyone who might presume too much upon his goodwill.

The effulgent but improbable Darcy Plantagenet sidled off into the shadows of the Westminster school privies—his natural habitat. He would re-emerge in due course, but his immediate presence would not have impressed this mystic equine intelligence. One whiff of old Darcy P. and the magical horn would engage.

'Robert Emmet Orpen is my name, sir. Thank you for asking.'

'May I be allowed to make a further inquiry? Are you involved in law enforcement? A Pinkerton agent perhaps?'

'Why would you think that, sir?'

'Because I'm not accustomed to being called "sir" by civilians. And Tracy was impressed by the highly efficient manner in which you dealt with the village idiot, Mr. Riley.' He pronounced the word 'Mister' as if it was liable to induce a bilious attack.

He didn't know the half of it yet. But the sad tidings of the probable demise of Skullcrusher could wait still longer. I contemplated barefaced denial, but the disconcertingly knowing glance of the man before me was extremely persuasive.

'No, not a Pinkerton, sir. Detective Sergeant, London Metropolitan Police.'

'I see. I assume you're not here on vacation.'

'Not entirely, sir, though I hear your city is both charming and hospitable.'

'Hmm. You've been seriously misled in that case. Intelligence-gathering must be in decline since my last visit to Scotland Yard.' Having cast aspersions on the city that paid his wages, he continued. 'Is there anything we can do for you? To make your stay more …'

I thought he was going to say 'pleasant?'

' … productive?'

I wasn't expecting that.

'A brief chat with the British Consul General would probably be helpful,' I suggested.

'I'll see to it. You may need this, by the way.' He handed me back my revolver. 'Tell me: are you capable of being discreet? I ask because your introduction to our city suggests otherwise.'

'I am the very soul of discretion, sir. I have medals to prove it. But obviously, I never wear them. That would be indiscreet.'

'Ah! A sense of humour. You may need that as well. Hell, hath no fury like a Newman thwarted.'

'Newman?' Even as I appended the question mark, I was aware that Lees could see through me like a threadbare cotton shirt. He smiled indulgently. His nonchalance suggested that I was entitled to at least some pretence of ignorance. After all, I wasn't having a good night. And we'd only just met. I was surely justified in some display of coquettishness. 'Come back here tomorrow and we'll talk,' he said. 'In the meantime, try and steer clear of Sergeant Kelly. He can be very excitable.'

'The left side of my face concurs, sir. Might I ask for one further misdemeanour to be taken into consideration?'

'Go on.'

'I'm not suggesting that you drag San Francisco harbour but, were you to do so, you might find the mortal remains of one Oliver Madden, late of Dublin, Ireland. I don't think he floats. He and I —'

'So that's who it was. Tracy had his suspicions.'

'He was a witness to that part of the fracas as well?'

Lees nodded.

'And chose not to intervene?'

Though my question was posed in the spirit of inquiry, not reproach, Lees looked a trifle vexed.

'Professional courtesy, Sergeant Orpen. You seemed to be getting along just famously. He was ready to intercede if required. But had he been forced to do so, I fear Mr. Madden would still be with us. I think Tracy displayed admirable restraint in the circumstances.'

'Admirable,' I agreed, mentally blessing my Grizzly Guardian Angel once more.

'Anyway, thank you for your candour, Sergeant. Nothing to worry about for the moment. If Madden resurfaces, we can always charge you with manslaughter.'

He was smiling, but I wasn't sure if he was joking.

CHAPTER TWO

ORPEN

12 October – late evening

As already mentioned, I harbour a patently unsupportable prejudice against upper crust Englishmen in general, but particularly—and irrationally—for those whose names end in a vowel. Too much Latin affectation, I suppose. So, I was sceptical when the gangly Kenneth Haddo, Her Majesty's Consul General in San Francisco, introduced himself. To my surprise, he turned out to be a moderately decent sort. As a mid-ranking Foreign Office diplomat, he was inevitably destined for a baronetcy were he to rise anywhere above the middle ranks of the service, but, unlike others of his ilk, he didn't behave as if he had already been knighted.

Despite the spareness of his physique, Haddo had an overweening lassitude about him which I normally associate with the more corpulent model of bored aristocrat. He was a fat lethargic man, inside the body of a whippet. He had been forewarned of my impending arrival but had only a vague sense of my mission. Gosselin viewed the Foreign Office, and all its burrows, as a bothersome and wholly unnecessary evil. But whatever scraps of knowledge Haddo had managed to acquire had injected an unwonted energy into his actions. The San Francisco gendarmerie was subjected to an aerial bombardment of *noblesse oblige*, and, after my colloquy with Lees, I was extracted as expeditiously as possible, lest some unfortunate 'accident' should befall me at the Hall of Justice.

My faithful ally, Tracy, was on desk duty as I took my leave. He was dealing with a gratingly intoxicated citizen in evening dress. Mr. Tuxedo was in full pugnacious flight when Tracy wheeled around and shouted to someone behind him.

'Fallon, get them apples out of Number Three, we're going to need the cell.'

From somewhere within, a lilting Mayo accent responded. ''Tis all right, Rory. They're safe. Collins and me is after eatin' dem.'

'Good work, boy.' By the time Tracy had turned back to face the future occupant of Cell Number Three, Tuxedo had fallen asleep in mid-rant. He was still upright. When Tracy spotted me leaving, he shouted after me, 'Goodnight now, Mr. Plantagenet. And don't be pullin' at any loose threads out there.'

Haddo and I drove straight to the Consulate just off Union Square. It was an early example of California baroque with at least one offensive turret too many. It was almost midnight when we got there, so we had the rococo building to ourselves. En route, I had regaled him with the tale of my unexpected *Céad Míle Fáilte* from Madden and Riley.

Haddo wouldn't hear another word from me until the first cup of reviving tea had been consumed in an appreciative silence. It was the last decent cup of tea I would drink until my next visit to the Consulate. After it had scalded my tongue, I elaborated on the fireworks with Doghouse and the tango with Skullcrusher. I may have exaggerated my personal *élan* while understating the role that sheer luck played in the affray. Haddo clucked sympathetically. When I'd finished, he had only one word to add to the narrative.

'Newman.'

'Newman,' I concurred. There it was again.

I have been dancing around the figure of the San Francisco Chieftain of Clan Newman for too long. Best to fill you in at this point. I had, as you will recall, tried, and failed, to convey the impression to Lees that I was unfamiliar with the name. In fact, he had loomed large in the contents of that manila envelope.

Among the Irish of the city and county of San Francisco, Newman was the counterweight and sworn rival of Dan Horton, despite avowedly sharing much of the latter's undying love of Old Ireland and hatred of Blighty. He was a High King who had been born of Alexander the Great and schooled by Machiavelli. He was capable, ruthless, but, above all, pragmatic. He might order the removal of your fingernails if he felt it was essential to good business practice but—assuming you subsequently co-operated—he would have them presented to you in the form of a fetching pendant by way of apology for the inconvenience. He was that uniquely Irish American political creature, the 'Boss'. This was a transatlantic euphemism for the ugliest gargoyle atop a totem of municipal corruption. He was a debased godhead to whom the high priests of local politics offered tribute.

However, unlike many another 'Boss', Newman had himself sought and achieved elective office. Most of his peers were shrinking violets or blushing Venus flytraps. They were far too diffident to offer themselves for the consideration of municipal voters. Newman, however, lacked such becoming modesty, and had served two terms as San Francisco County sheriff. He stood in the interest of that fragrant political flower of nativist bigotry dubbed the Workingmen's Party of California, dedicated to the extirpation of all things Chinese from the city, the state, the nation, the globe, our local solar system, the Milky Way, and probably the next world to boot.

During his tenure, he distinguished himself, and pleased his constituency immensely, by jailing numerous Chinese men. This was for the unconscionable crime—ingeniously manufactured by a municipal fiat—of occupying a living space smaller than five hundred cubic feet. While they were lodged at Newman's pleasure in the County Jail, he then ordained that their traditional plaited hair—their 'queues'—be cut off. Newman was not a believer in subjecting the objects of his antipathy to mere official indignities when he could add a personal humiliation of his own devising.

By the time I got to San Francisco, he was between totem poles. He had opted not to stand for a third term as sheriff. As proprietor of the Emerald Brewing Company, he was concentrating on building up his profitable and opportune business. Opportune because he was also solidifying his base in the Third District for a run at the Board of Supervisors—the city's supreme municipal authority. A limitless supply of beer can be a useful tool in an election campaign, especially amongst the loyal Irish voters in the Thirsty Third.

There were eleven supervisors running San Francisco. Most had the morals of a crocodile and the sensibility of a vigilante. Some had even functioned in the latter capacity during the early more lawless days of the city. Newman, a past master in the art of chicanery, would find his natural home in such a cesspit.

His feud with Dan Horton for hegemony among the Knights of the Red Branch was atypical. Most serious disagreements with Newman tended to be quickly settled in his favour. The dénouement usually involved the tragic passing of his antagonist. Or the painful loss of certain useful appendages. But Horton had managed to weather his adversary's hostility exceptionally well. Newman was deterred from indulging his natural vindictiveness by his rival's almost sainted status within the wider Fenian family. However, had the conspiratorial John Devoy, *doge* of Clan na Gael in New York, known that Horton was playing footsie with Sir Robert Anderson, Newman would have been encouraged to give free rein to his talents for defenestration and dismemberment. Haddo was well-informed on the state of relations between these two Celtic chieftains and supplied any gaps in my knowledge. He was unaware, however, of Horton's enlistment in the service of Her Majesty—now in some doubt—and I chose not to enlighten him.

Before the delightful tea had much opportunity to grow chilled, Haddo indicated that it was time to depart. Although it was late, his urgency suggested that he still had places to go. For my part, all I wanted was a room where I could sit and think about my predicament without running the risk of a reunion with Thaddeus Kelly's wedding band. I wasn't sure exactly what business Haddo was about at that late hour, but whatever it was, he intended to pursue it using some of my funds. To my surprise, just before we walked out of the Consulate, he asked casually if he could borrow some money. The sudden summons to the police station meant that he had come out without any cash of his own. In the circumstances, I could hardly refuse.

In return for my $50, I was given a piece of paper with the address of a lodging house. The name of the proprietor, Bella La Peur, suggested a character from a fatuous Gothic novel. The address was, I gathered, somewhere in North Beach, a neighbourhood which, whatever its distant maritime pretensions, was now at a considerable remove from sand and sea. With the dispatching skills of a post office sorter, and an implausible display of energy, Haddo procured a cab and sent me on my way.

I was driven through streets with which I would later become all too familiar. At the time they were as mysterious as the source of the Nile, although considerably less pristine. What can you say about the mewling puking infant that was San Francisco half a century ago? A stench of corruption and an aroma of criminality hung over the city, like one of its ubiquitous fogs. All sorts of reptiles and scorpions thrived in this miasma, from the lowliest pimp to the most acquisitive councilman on the make. At least the pimps robbed and cheated one sucker at a time. The politicians, albeit with a winning smile, collectivised the practice of rampant theft. The scale of their cupidity was breathtaking. The more capable ones could relieve you of your large intestine and you would never feel so much as an itch.

By the time San Francisco and I intersected, it had progressed from being a compact wooden walking city—prisoner of gold—to a sprawling brick metropolis, spawn of silver. The arrival of the cable car had opened the hills, and the millionaires had moved up in the world, building Gothic palaces above the fog. First, they robbed the city blind, then they offered burnt sacrifices to the God of Respectability and demanded that the *hoi polloi* curb their own intemperate ways. Gratifyingly, the lower orders generally had the moxie to advise their betters that they should insert their reforming zeal where the sun declined to shine.

So that night, and every night, this 'off the peg' city was alive and in motion. It was a card sharp, a loan shark, a thimblerigger, and an assassin. It was *The Canterbury Tales*, teeming with alluring transients on unsavoury pilgrimages. You could perfume the hills, coves, and sandlots of San Francisco, but the underlying stench would still be the same. It was dog food. And catnip. For all its degraded delinquency, it had a crazy energy that made it paradoxically alluring. It pampered the fortunate and devoured the meek. The earth was all they would inherit, while having their faces rubbed in it. My tryst with this wondrous tart of a city had just begun.

It was only when I got to the address written on the scrap of paper—it was on the corner of Green Street and Grant Avenue, then known as Dupont—and paid off the cab, that I realised, with equal parts amusement and chagrin, that Haddo had directed me to a whorehouse. Either he had a highly developed sense of humour, or he saw nothing amiss in lodging me in a brothel. Regular business, as it transpired, was conducted only at street level, leaving the second-floor rooms available for other activities, such as housing junior officers of the London Metropolitan Police in dubious battle with the

Irish underworld of Northern California. The proprietor, Madame La Peur—if the assumed name was designed to inspire trepidation, it was wholly successful—proved to be a formidable lady of generous proportions with threatening hair and merciless gunmetal eyes.

My tenancy was not a foregone conclusion. First, I was obliged to face an inquisition. Madame La Peur—there was no evidence of a spouse, but you would never have dreamt of calling her 'Mademoiselle'—was not about to release one of her rooms to just anyone. Abandoning her regular clients to a scantily clad subordinate, she led me into her private parlour. This was adorned, incongruously, with a portrait of Pope Leo XIII blessing pilgrims. Despite my congenital agnosticism—on my father's side only—I took this as a good omen.

Bella questioned me closely, in a French accent that was decidedly *faux*, as her pale flesh flowed over a plush red sofa. From some remote region of her capacious clothing a large and decidedly ugly brown and black tabby cat sidled into view. I am not partial to cats at the best of times. Unfortunately, the antipathy is not mutual. Cats appear, for some mystifying reason, to be enamoured of me. I am a feline patron saint and they are my disciples. Before I could direct the animal back towards its mistress with a surreptitious kick, it had jumped onto my lap and was purring vigorously.

'That's Grisel. He seems to have taken to you,' Madame La Peur observed, her tone indicating that she was besotted with this rotund beast, whose immense frame mirrored her own. 'Grisel is short for Griselda – zere was some confusion when 'e arrived as to what sex 'e was,' she explained, as if I should care deeply.

I assured her that the moggie's feelings of affection were returned with interest. This, they were not. Nobly concealing my aversion for felinity, I sat on tenterhooks with Grisel in my lap for the remainder of the interview. While Bella went through the rules of occupancy, I passed the time speculating vindictively on how excellent a meal an animal of his girth would afford diners in Chinatown, just a few blocks to the south. Grisel responded to these hostile vibrations by malevolently digging his claws into my crotch. Only the prospect of having to forego my accommodation prevented me from cursing the vile animal and heaving him through the open window. Pope Leo XIII watched enigmatically as I bit my tongue to avoid crying out. Virtue was rewarded. My invocation of the name of Kenneth Haddo secured the lodgings.

'Ah, so you are acquainted with Monsieur 'addo. Why did not you say so? *Un gentilhomme absolu*. Always pays 'is bills on time.' I thought it was an intriguing and highly original definition of a gentleman, and not one to which your average clubbable and raff-ish Londoner would have subscribed. I hazarded an educated guess, armed with this new information, as to where my $50 was currently being spent.

When she showed me to my room, having first coolly relieved me of a week's rent in advance, the stairs shook as if in the throes of one of those periodic San Francisco earth tremors. My accommoda-tion turned out to be comfortable without being plush. The wallpaper was gratifyingly plain, the mattress was encouragingly pliable, and if anyone wished me ill, they would first have to negotiate passage past the ample Bella La Peur and the malevolent Griselda. After that they would only have to contend with my Colt and Doghouse's knife.

The room gave onto the street below via a small veranda. I later discovered that a prior tenant, a Teutonic type named Kahn, weeks in arrears, had mysteriously 'fallen off' that same balcony. He had survived the fall but had then been floored by the descent of his loaded trunk as he rose groggily to his feet. I may not have behaved like a choirboy during my first visit to San Francisco, but I never fell behind in the rent.

13 October – early morning

The San Francisco Police Department was like a small, agitated nation state within the borders of a much larger anarchic kingdom. It was Jonah in the belly of the whale.

The hostile desert around this oasis was run by the avaricious Forty Thieves. And there were plenty of Ali Babas among the members of the force itself. They had the 'open sesame' to unlock the treasure of the Thieves and divert a reasonable proportion into their own pockets. Some were even more rapacious than the Thieves themselves, but not at the very top of the greasy pole. Perched there, above the forces of law and ordure, were two citizens above suspicion. One was a moral philosopher, the other a bare-knuckle pugilist. But, like dark chocolate and salt, they complemented each other.

The warrior was Police Chief Patrick Crowley. Crowley had the deportment of a prizefighter. He might have been named for an Irish saint, but there was nothing beatific about him. His nickname—'Crowbar'—had less to do with alliteration than with literality. He was a mobile wrecking ball who favoured demolition over debate. You could fortify the doors of your brothel, deadfall, or opium den all you liked, you could even bring in engineers who would design an entrance to your premises with a guarantee of inviolability, but if Crowley wanted to get inside, then you'd best just open up. Even if the door was unlocked, he might well decide to kick it down anyway, just for practice.

The logician was Isaiah Lees, thoughtful, solicitous, diplomatic and painstaking. He had about him the air of an Aquinas. Our second interview began with an amiable disavowal on his part. How was I to know he was being disingenuous?

'You are aware, of course, that I can't help you in any way, especially since you haven't taken me into your confidence on the nature of your mission.' He made no effort to conceal a telegram on his desk, at the end of which I could clearly make out the name 'Williamson'. We were both sipping from beakers of tea in his office. I could lie, and claim that this was a thoroughly pleasurable experience, but the tea was execrable, and well he knew it. He was English, after all. The inability to make a decent cup of tea is a point of pride with Americans. While I was in San Francisco, in the interests of self-preservation I was forced to develop a taste for sour coffee (taken with three sugars) which I have never been able to shrug off.

'Is this where you advise me to set sail immediately for "merrie England", sir?' I asked.

'That is, lamentably, the only course of action open to me.'

'I understand completely, sir.'

I began to regret having allowed Madame La Peur to finagle a week's rent in advance. I hoped Haddo had invested my $50 judiciously. While nothing would have persuaded me to seek the return of my deposit from Bella La Peur, I was not in the least intimidated by Her Majesty's Consul General.

'Unless …' he tailed off enticingly. Lees eyed me sharply. He looked as if he was about to ask the impossible. I was prepared to concede anything short of the unthinkable.

'I believe Chief Crowley would listen favourably to a request from an officer of Scotland Yard to be allowed to study San Francisco policing methods, and to be assigned, for a brief period of observation, to a senior member of our force. I think I could take such a proposal to him. I believe he would be suitably flattered that Scotland Yard had begun to sit up and take notice of our unique *modus operandi.*'

I wondered what Dolly Williamson would make of one of his sergeants studying at close quarters the value of the battering ram when dashed against reinforced metal doors, or the efficacy of the butt of a Colt revolver when introduced with blunt force to the base of the human skull. My eye fell on the departmental escutcheon atop the desk of the Deputy Chief. This boasted a profusion of feathers atop an open fire. I mentally substituted an image of crossed crowbars rampant on a bed of opium pipes.

'An intriguing suggestion, sir. I am sure that Scotland Yard has much to learn from Chief Crowley's methods,' I lied. I may even have crossed my fingers behind my back, an infantile approach learned in years of mendacious interactions with my father. 'Might we consider this a formal application for secondment?'

'Won't you have to consult your superiors?' I could not dismiss another compelling image. Gosselin with raised eyebrows rampant on a creased forehead.

'I believe, in this instance, sir, that I have plenipotentiary powers.'

'Excellent. That's settled then. I'll introduce you to one of our senior officers. Sergeant Wellington Campbell should fit the bill, and you can begin your period of secondment. Campbell is about to take charge of the Chinatown detail. We don't permit our officers to spend too much time there. It makes them more susceptible to … compromise.' There was a beat, but he, nonetheless, carried off the euphemism for 'bribes' with aplomb. This was one of the reforms Lees had introduced, with Crowley's approval. Regular rotation through the city's various precincts made suborning an officer of the law less attractive. There was no point in wasting money purchasing police 'protection' if the protective policeman wasn't going to be around for long enough to ward off more than a couple of fellow grifters.

'Sergeant Campbell is also something of an expert on the activities of our local Fenian brethren.' He looked at me meaningfully as he pronounced the 'F' word. 'Not that they are engaged in any blatant criminality—at least not for the moment—but we like to know what they're up to. Campbell has a network of …' here he struggled with his vocabulary to find an alternative to the word "spies", '… associates, who keep him well informed. I think you will find observing the activities of Sergeant Campbell very productive.'

There are more descriptive words I could use to characterise my internship under Wellington Campbell.

Lees then sent for my new mentor. Nothing could have prepared me for the ceremony that ensued. Whatever the circumstances, Wellington Campbell always made a point of entering a room in the manner of a fox invading a chicken coop. There might be a rooster to contend with as well, but that was a minor inconvenience. I am almost certain that he had to stoop before stepping through the door frame of the Captain's office. He was in his early forties and was enormously tall, with a frothy mane of explosive hair that added to his already impressive height. He uttered only a single word when we were formally introduced by the Chief of Detectives, a pretentious and mocking 'Enchanté', elongated to an unreasonable length in a sonorous Southern drawl, and accompanied by a low bow.

Having lit the fuse, Lees then retired, or more precisely, dismissed us from his office and instructed us to get to know one other better. Campbell took this as his cue to invite me to a nearby bar. There was, however, one peculiar preliminary, the first of many.

'Tell me, how do you spell "felonious"?' Campbell drawled. I scrutinised him for a moment, but he was a study in guilelessness. Was this some sort of bizarre induction? I spelled it out for him, too rapidly at first, and had to repeat myself.

'Are you certain? There aren't two 'l's'? As in 'fell over'? I assured him there was only one 'l', as in 'felon'. He brightened, nodded, added something to a notebook he was carrying and shoved it into an inside pocket.

'Heavenly. Shall we go?'

I followed him out of the building.

The man in whose shadow I was now expected to loiter had clearly not been briefed by Lees. He seemed to accept at face value the notion that a Scotland Yard detective would want to study the ways, moods and caprices of the San Francisco Police. Furthermore, he saw nothing untoward in having been chosen as an exemplar of all that was best among the ranks of San Francisco's finest. Campbell, I would quickly learn, shared the world with creatures he considered to be far less gifted than himself, an inability to spell words like 'felonious' notwithstanding.

The three things that struck you immediately about Wellington Campbell were his immense height, the dapper nature of his appearance, and the implacable Southernness of the man. He was elegantly dressed for a plain clothes policeman and clearly took considerable pride in his personal appearance. A strong face, with piercing blue eyes, was partially concealed under a soup-strainer of a moustache. This, oddly, failed to match the colour of his hair. While the generous tresses—somewhat in the style of a Custer or a Hickock—were a vivid chestnut, his bushy moustache, though predominantly brown, was generously flecked with red.

But, when you studied the man in any depth, you kept coming back to his stature. He was verging on the monumental. I'm half an inch the wrong side of six feet in height. The wrong side for a policeman at least. Campbell towered over me. He had a square head and square shoulders. If he wasn't a policeman, he could easily have found work as a steamroller.

But not even his height offered a hint of the length of his stride. With each step he consumed acres of the ground beneath his feet. While he seemed to move quite effortlessly, it was, in my experience, almost impossible to keep pace with the man.

Yet, I was to find that he also had a stillness about him which could be utterly disconcerting. He would suddenly lapse into immobility, silence and contemplation for no apparent reason. When this period of intense meditation ended, he would usually return to the world of conversation and movement with some perplexing and unsettling *non sequitur*. He would then invariably bestow a withering look on the imbecile who had been unable to follow him to the terminus of his silent train of thought, as if he always required to be accompanied by his own personal C. Auguste Dupin. An innate ability to ratiocinate (Poe's word, not mine, I prefer 'deduce') was essential around Sergeant Wellington Campbell. Some of this I quickly observed for myself. I had, after all, been sentenced to a period of scrutiny and surveillance, so why not start with my mentor? The rest, his Southern manners, mercurial disposition, and eccentricities, would become familiar over a longer spread of time.

Although largely unacquainted with the many regional variations of the American accent, even I was aware on our first meeting that Campbell's attenuated drawl marked him out as a Southerner. San Francisco was a new city where many of the inhabitants had not yet lost the accent of the place of their birth. You could easily identify an Irishman, a German or an Italian from their unique articulation of the English language, or their continued use of their mother tongue. Campbell was an American, but there was no mistaking his distinctiveness within that highly inclusive definition. He was a Virginian and very proud of his origins. He had miraculously emerged from the Civil War without so much as a scar. No visible blemish at any rate.

He would occasionally volunteer snippets of information about himself as we became better acquainted. He told me once that, despite his allegiance to the Confederate cause, he had no love of slavery. But this antipathy was overwhelmed by his loathing of Yankees. 'I was a bit like Kansas,' he confided, '… conflicted.'

He had left the South soon after the war ended—I later discovered why—and begun to wander. 'I decided not to wait around to be reconstructed,' was his pithy explanation. He had originally come west to try his luck in the Nevada silver mines, but the Comstock lode was never quite extensive or generous enough to intersect with any of his meagre and unproductive claims. Hungry, and fed up, he started wandering again and, like so many failed miners, con artists, hookers and ne'er-do-wells, he had moved as far west as it was possible to venture, and then stopped. That brought him to San Francisco.

We left the Hall of Justice and walked along Stockton Street—an arrow through the heart of Chinatown. We might as well have been in Shanghai for all the European faces we saw around us. To my Occidental eyes the Celestials all seemed to dart and scurry. As we strolled through their kingdom, the contrastingly languid Campbell talked incessantly about the advantages of policing over mining.

'For one thing,' he said, 'you don't have to stand up to your testicles in freezing water. Generally.'

Just as we approached the intersection of Stockton and Jackson, Campbell spotted someone, or something, in the middle distance. He abruptly abandoned me, walked across the street, picked up a piece of loose cobble, stepped up to a large unkempt man with his back to the human traffic, and hit him an unmerciful dunt on the side of the head. He then casually dropped the brick and recrossed Stockton as the man sank to his knees. Before I could question him about the curious interlude, he had picked up the thread of our conversation.

'Furthermore, I haven't given a single thought to fluctuations in the value of precious metals for years.'

Nothing was ever said about the apparently unprovoked assault. I began to wonder exactly who it was that Lees had appointed as my nursemaid. And why.

One thing you quickly noticed about Campbell, after his accent and his altitude, was his exaggerated courtesy—random assaults in Chinatown notwithstanding. It was carefully cultivated and utterly contrived, but it was still courtesy, in a town that didn't habitually trade in the niceties of human interaction. I imagined he would call you 'sir', and even beg your pardon for any offence caused, as he slipped a knife under your ribs. His 'old world' good manners put him at an immediate advantage. Everyone with whom he came into contact for the first time underestimated him because of his studied politeness. That's how it was in a town more familiar with unstudied malice.

Later I would discover a brooding, moody side to the man, but that did not manifest itself on our first meeting. One distressing attribute, if I can call it such, that did impress itself upon me at an early stage, was his fondness—when he wasn't smoking a cigar—for the most noxious type of cigarette it had ever been my misfortune to inhale at one remove. To this day—despite the passing of five decades—I can still smell the acrid aroma and see the blue haze. He told me they were Turkish. Turkish they may well have been, a delight they were not.

As we walked, Campbell, to my immense satisfaction, and probably in deference to my nationality, began to expound on the life and times of some of the less wholesome Irish denizens of the city, Horton and Newman included. I feigned ignorance of the subject, and he warmed to his theme. Horton, he informed me, was still an active Fenian, but latterly his focus had been on his struggle with Newman, and, consequently, on saving his property from incineration.

As for Newman himself, his run for the Board of Supervisors was apparently prompted by the fact that the previous incumbent in the Third electoral district had developed an unwholesome streak of honesty. He had somehow acquired religion. As soon as Jesus entered his life, he had taken to publicly handing back his backhanders, a palindromic activity frowned upon among the better class of political delinquent. He had been advised to resign by his highly indignant constituents and patrons. When he declined to do so, his house had mysteriously caught fire. Later his business premises met a similar fate. As a hedge against his own immolation, he had recently announced his retirement from politics to spend more time with his family. This was an essential precaution against their own spontaneous combustion. In the absence of an alternative trustworthy dupe, Newman himself had taken up the mantle.

Campbell's relentless stride finally relented outside a decrepit building on the north side of Pacific Avenue, at Sullivan's Alley, between Grant and Stockton. We were on the western edge of the infamous Barbary Coast. Although I was then a newcomer to the city this district's lethal reputation had preceded it. The Barbary Coast was a neighbourhood where even Crazy Horse and the victors of the Little Bighorn would have ventured only with extreme caution and a commandeered Gatling gun. At first, I didn't recognise the establishment outside which we had halted as a bar. It looked like a condemned doss house in the last stages of dereliction. Only a mosaic of placards on the door, including one that flaunted the virtues of Candidate Newman, and another, advertising a forthcoming recital by 'the city's finest diva, Caroline Schroeder,' suggested that something other than demolition lay in its stars. The opera poster seemed ludicrously incongruous, given what was in store for any *aficionado* when the door of this down-market gin palace was opened.

'Welcome to The Billy Goat,' Campbell said as we entered. He indicated the glorified shanty with a theatrical flourish. 'That's not what it's actually called but I'm not fond of its proper name myself.'

'Which is?'

'The Bull Run. Ned Allen—he's the owner—refuses to call it 'The Manassas' just to antagonise me. He claims to have fought there, obviously as a Yankee, hence the damned name. But I doubt it myself. He won the place a few years ago in a card game and rechristened it.'

Not even the smell of pipe and cigar smoke could subdue the overpowering aroma of sweat, urine, spittoon, congealed sawdust, and flat beer, which assaulted the unsuspecting drinker who ventured past the outer portal of the Bull Run/Billy Goat into the Stygian gloom within. All it lacked was a three-headed dog and a ferryman.

I was immediately introduced to the 'Yankee bastard' (Campbell's affectionate description, not mine) who had had the temerity to call his bar after the first great skirmish of the Civil War. Not to the satisfaction of Campbell, of course. The enduring Union and the late Confederacy could agree on little or nothing, not even the names of the battles they had contested. The Union called them after the nearest river, the Confederacy after the nearest town.

Ned 'Bull Run' Allen—originally an industrial product of the city of Boston—was a truly enormous and muscular man in an incongruous snow-white ruffled shirt. However, the shirt wasn't the first thing that caught my attention. That was drawn immediately to his monstrous nose. The best thing you could say about it was that, because of the sheer physical vastness of its owner, it had never been broken in a fight. His bibulous habits also meant that its natural colour more than matched his thatch of red hair. To conceal this awesome ruddiness, he had taken to glazing it—the nose, not the hair—with flour. This caused it to resemble a steak just before it was placed on a hot griddle. Many a surprised and unsuspecting customer had paid a high price for staring a moment too long, in awed fascination, at this eighth wonder of the world.

Ned Allen, it transpired, was himself a cross between Socrates and P.T. Barnum. On being introduced to me, he identified a sucker, and quickly tapped into a vein of patter that I guessed was well-rehearsed.

'You might ask, sir, what am I selling here?'

I was pretty sure I knew already. It didn't take an acute sense of smell. From this opening gambit, he was quickly into his stride.

'Now you, probably being the prosaic type, would answer "liquor". Well, that's where you'd be wrong. What I've got going here is something much less prosaic than that. I'm selling dreams … a tapestry of dreams.'

I looked around, hoping to locate the ornate textile in question. The only wall hangings were a pair of translucent curtains clinging precariously to a distorted horizontal rod. They were on their last warning, threatened with relegation to the status of dishcloth. The only dreams in evidence were those of an old crone fast asleep at the bar with her mouth open and a steady line of drool dripping onto the counter of Ned's Palace of Fantasies. Unable to locate the poetry in all of this I felt that the fault was probably mine and experienced the debilitating burden of my own prosaic nature pressing down upon me.

'Yessir … dreams.' Here the proprietor paused for long enough to allow Campbell to order drinks. I was perturbed when he demanded 'two *delirium tremens*, Ned.' Seeing my concern, he told me, 'They're not nearly as dangerous as they sound,' and winked. I was relieved when 'Bull Run' Allen poured two beers and placed them in front of us. Surely such a banal beverage posed no threat to body or soul. Whatever about the latter, I was soon to discover the effect of this brew on the former. While it was as flat as Nebraska, it had a kick like the recoil from a taut suspension cable. I did mention something to Campbell about breakfast, or the need for food of some kind, but I took the hint when his only response was a look of puzzled scorn. As he drank his beer, he began smoking one of the most noxious cigars within whose jurisdiction it has ever been my misfortune to stray. It wasn't one of those small slim athletic-looking cigars either. This was the William Howard Taft of tobacco products, oversized and rotund around the middle. It would probably take longer to smoke down to a stub than it had taken to grow the raw material.

After a few mouthfuls of his *delirium tremens*, Campbell became professionally Southern again. He offered an improbable explanation for his original decision to become a San Francisco policeman.

'Y'understand that it was the only force in the country at the time,' he said, tongue firmly embedded in cheek—at least I hope it was, 'with uniforms of Confederate grey. I had barely made myself indispensable when they changed to damn Yankee blue. I thought seriously about taking myself elsewhere but by then I was ill-equipped for any other occupation in any other city. And, at least, I had only to look at the damn uniforms, I didn't have to wear one. That straw would have broken this Virginia camel's back.'

We hadn't been drinking very long when the door of the saloon opened, and a posse of men entered. I could see Campbell studying them closely in the large mirror behind the bar while we continued our conversation. His drawl seemed to become even more pronounced. I would later recognise this as a sign of rising but well-disguised tension. Under his breath and behind his beer, he muttered, 'As it happens, we've just been joined by Sheriff Newman and some of his loyal band of brothers. A rare treat.'

I looked at the newcomers and wondered which was Thomas Newman. It didn't take long to figure that one out. He was the small bulbous-eyed circular man buying the drinks and doing most of the talking. He was the candidate after all. I noticed that all the members of his rapt and captive audience ordered whiskey. Ned's best whiskey, imported from County Cork, had a well-deserved reputation for excellence. It was also rather pricey.

Newman had clearly been making a campaign speech. He brought his declamatory tone into the bar with him. The accent was located somewhere between Killarney and Tralee. Purest and deepest Kerry.

'You see, boys, the Exclusion Act doesn't go nearly far enough,' he proclaimed. By adding two superfluous vowels, something I didn't think possible, he drew out the word 'exclusion' as if it caused him personal offence. 'We've only managed to keep even *more* Chinese vermin from crawling all over our city. The job is half-done. We need to get it finished.'

There were a few strangled 'Hear hears' from a couple of the more conscientious members of his travelling circus. They'd obviously been expecting more time to enjoy their liquor before being pressed back into service as the resident claque.

'If this was a self-respecting city,' Newman continued, 'there wouldn't even be a Chinatown. It would have been razed to the ground and the lice that inhabit it would have burned along with it.'

This time the rabble was better prepared. The approbation was louder and more full-throated. The encouragement caused Newman to warm to his subject.

'We need to give Johnny Chinaman something to think about, boys,' he fulminated. 'Something other than fireworks and laundries. We need that overcrowded abomination to become an inferno.'

'It's not easy settin' fire to a laundry, Tom,' observed a Neat Whiskey.

Newman glared at the man who had spiked his rhetoric. The sceptic quailed, withdrew from the field, and retreated into his amber tinted nectar. The peeved demagogue was about to relaunch when the saloon door opened. Campbell had remained silent during Newman's harangue. As he turned slightly to identify the newcomer, I noticed his body stiffen. I sensed trouble in the offing.

'Horton,' muttered Campbell. His right hand went straight to his jacket pocket. From the corner of the room, I thought I heard a stray pin drop. Campbell stood up from the barstool with unhurried deliberation and beckoned me, with his eyes, to do likewise. Horton, who was accompanied by three dour and threatening presences, broke the silence that had marked his entrance. The opening gambit was predictable and prosaic.

'I heard you were in here, Tom,' Horton began. 'But even if I hadn't, I'd have noticed the smell.' This introductory pleasantry was greeted only with a slight narrowing of the eyes on Newman's part. Several of his supporters, not all of whom were hired hands, looked distinctly uncomfortable.

'I have a message for you,' Horton continued. 'From New York. From the boss … Devoy himself. He's disappointed in you, Tom. He thinks you're distracted. Our struggle isn't your struggle anymore. He's on his way here to see for himself. And when he gets here, he won't be happy with the way you're cosying up to Nob Hill.'

In the short silence that followed, I thought I noticed a couple of Whiskey and Waters sizing up how long it would take them to abandon Newman and get to the door. One of them, a particularly weedy type, was already surreptitiously moving in that direction. By my reckoning, Newman could count on the muscular intervention of no more than three members of the *Uiscebaugh* coterie who had been enjoying his hospitality before Horton's interruption. So, the sides were even. Newman broke the silence.

'Is that a fact now, Dan? Well, you can tell that shrivelled fanatic Devoy that I couldn't give a flying fuck about his desolation. This is San Francisco, not New York. We have our own rules here. So even if Rossa himself makes the trip to shove a stick of dynamite up my arse, I'll be ready for him.'

'I'll be sure to let them both know,' Horton sneered. 'I've no doubt they'll be rightly impressed by your patriotism.'

'It's always "Erin go bragh" with you, isn't it, Dan? You need to spend less time thinking about the "old sod" and more time helping us grab our share of this one.'

'And how do you propose to do that, Tom? By licking all the knobs on Arse Hill?'

'It's only a temporary little arrangement, Dan. Right now, we have similar interests. After Johnny Chinaman is kicked out, they'll wade back into us. But we'll be ready this time. *Tiocfaimid aniar aduaidh orthu.* We'll catch them by surprise.'

'I know what it means, Tom. *Tá Gaeilge agam.*'

'It's just good politics. Wasting money on dynamite so that our patriotic brothers can blow themselves up. That's sentiment.'

As if on cue, the entire building, the entire world in fact, suddenly began to shake. A spittoon, perched precariously on the bar counter, gave up the ghost and succumbed to the combined forces of gravity and vibration. A Brandy and a Whiskey clung to each other as if their embrace somehow halved the chances of death by misadventure. I'd read about these occasional San Franciscan entertainments. We were in the throes of an earthquake. I expected immediate panic to set in and for everyone to head for the only exit. It wasn't as if the Billy Goat could survive a strong tremor, or even a gentle Zephyr for that matter. It didn't look as if the original architect had bothered with much protective brickwork in the construction of Ned Allen's 'Theatre of Dreams'. While that was a consoling thought, I wasn't disposed to take too many chances. There might still be a stone lintel around somewhere with my name on it.

It was only when I started to move towards the door that I noticed something odd. Other than the bonded Brandy and Whiskey, nobody was paying a blind bit of heed to the vibrations. To my astonishment, the only acknowledgement that the end was nigh was of the kind you might accord the passing funeral of a total stranger. There was only a barely perceptible display of respect for the awesome forces of nature being unleashed. Ned Allen casually extended a hand to prevent a bottle of execrable gin tumbling off its perch. A beer drinker at the far end of the bar raised his glass from the counter to avoid spilling even a hint of amber nectar. After about twenty seconds of communal shuddering the bizarre sense of seasickness passed. The floor was no longer in motion. The tremor moved on towards Oakland. The Brandy and Whiskey separated with grunts of mutual embarrassment. Obviously, I had a lot to learn about San Francisco and *sang froid*.

Horton, unfazed, was the first to return to the offensive. 'What about loyalty ... family ... history?'

'Now you're talking like a priest,' Newman responded. 'Your family is right here. In San Francisco. There is no history either. No past. Let go of it. It's time to stop paddling upstream.'

'Seize the day, is that it?'

'We need to seize every bloody day, *a chara*.'

'I'm no friend of yours, Newman.'

Another tense silence followed. I watched Campbell intently. As the temperature rose, he had his back to the two antagonists. He was keeping his powder dry. He didn't want to be recognised before everything kicked off and we had to intervene. I wasn't sure whose side we'd be on when that happened. When it came to it, neither was I certain that I'd be on the same side as Campbell.

A minor bloodbath was averted by a loud cough from Ned Allen. His appearance had changed. He was now fingering the butt end of an elegant walnut lever action Spencer repeating rifle, which he'd produced from God knows where. He wasn't pointing it anywhere in particular, but he didn't need to.

'Thank you, gentlemen,' he said, in a voice that barely rose above a threatening whisper. 'I've heard enough for one lifetime – take it outside please. I don't want my premises in flitters.' It struck me forcibly that a good fight could only improve the appearance of his saloon, but there is no accounting for maternal instinct.

Horton eyed the carbine, then studied Ned for a moment, looking for any sign of a sweat breaking out on the proprietor's upper lip. When he was satisfied that not a single pore would open this side of closing time, he made to leave.

'Fair enough, Ned. There'll be no trouble. Come on, lads.' With that he and the other three horsemen of our near Apocalypse withdrew. After waiting for a minute or two, Newman nodded curtly towards Ned and he and his crew followed Horton's platoon. I walked as far as the open door and looked up and down the street outside. Satisfied, I went back to the bar. The Spencer rifle had been returned to barracks. The old crone chose that moment to wake up and give me a toothless and charmless smile.

'Did they go in opposite directions?' Campbell inquired.

'Yes.'

'Heavenly.' Campbell beckoned to our innkeeper. 'Two more DTs, Ned.'

CHAPTER THREE

ORPEN

13 October, late afternoon

The ghosts of hundreds of ships haunt San Francisco Bay. They were abandoned when their crews lit out for the California gold fields in 1849. Over the years they've been scuttled, caught fire, were raided for their lumber, burnt at Candlestick Point— that's how it got its name—acted as land fill, or were used as the basements of buildings when the city started to advance from Montgomery Street to the new shoreline on the Embarcadero. Their skeletons lay underneath the fabric of the city. Ghostly galleons.

Or so, at any rate, a well-lubricated Campbell told me as we walked uncertainly uphill along a chilly California Street. I had finally managed to extract my new Virginian friend from Ned Allen's tavern by late afternoon. It was the first of many shifts we put in together in the Bull Run/Billy Goat. I had succeeded in persuading him that I was keeping pace with his drinking while consuming only four bottles of Delirium Tremens to his eight. As any grifter will tell you, deception and misdirection are vital constituents of self-preservation.

Walking uphill in the crisp October air sobered us both. We strolled aimlessly through waves of worker ants going about their afternoon business. Campbell's height, stride, and flowing locks attracted enough attention to make me glad we were not on our way to commit a crime. As we approached the intersection with Kearny Street, I was sufficiently in possession of my faculties to notice a black and gold carriage come hurtling towards us, heading down California Street from the general direction of Nob Hill. I was studying, but not really taking in, the elaborate crest that adorned the door of the vehicle when my attention was drawn instead to its sole occupant.

The carriage was forced to slow down just as Campbell and I neared Kearny. My eyes met those of the fair-haired and fair-skinned passenger. While no longer youthful, she was still captivatingly beautiful. She also looked terminally bored. She caught, and deflected, my gaze by briefly rolling her eyes at my impudence and then transferring her attention to nothing in particular in the middle distance. The encounter was fleeting but my interest was piqued, not least because I had an odd sensation that I had seen this woman somewhere before. After the carriage had passed, I noticed that Campbell was eyeing me with some amusement.

'I wouldn't if I were you,' he drawled. The second 'I' was closer to an 'Aah'.

'You wouldn't … what … if you were me?' I inquired with mock innocence.

'Lust after Caroline Schroeder. Having gone to a lot of trouble to acquire her, the lady's husband would be apt to disapprove. And he is a man of considerable wealth and influence in this city. Up there.'

He pointed towards what remains the steepest incline I have ever seen in a populated area. Outside of St. Patrick's Hill in Cork at any rate. Nob Hill was, literally and metaphorically, breathtaking. It could have been a minor peak in a modest range of mountains. Its manses were protected by the simple device of making the approach to its riches and delights as physically intimidating as possible. Nob Hill's protective sentinel was a daunting gradient of around twenty-five percent. And, if you managed to get to the top, there were plenty of other guard dogs waiting for you there.

It turned out that the higher you went in San Francisco, the more rarefied the society, thanks to Mr Hallidie's invention of the cable car in the previous decade. This ingenious form of locomotion—I am still baffled as to how it actually works, something to do with steel cables and extreme optimism—allowed the rich to isolate themselves on their very own Mount Olympus. If you had a residence on Nob Hill (I have often wondered when the preliminary 'S' was dropped) you were among the gods of San Francisco. You dwelt with the Crockers, the Huntingtons, the Floods and sundry other Pharisees. Gold, silver, banking, railway tracks, stock manipulation, even horticulture, could propel you towards those exalted heights. Nob Hill was the home of the San Francisco Brahmins. However, as you descended and approached Chinatown, the Barbary Coast, and the waterfront, you entered Dante's ninth circle of Hell, home of the *hoi polloi*. The oligarch's map of San Francisco displayed the contours and the streetscapes of Nob Hill and nearby Rincon Hill. The intervening landscape was dismissed with the legend 'Here Be Monsters.'

'Caroline Schroeder,' I repeated. 'Where have I come across her before?'Campbell pointed to a poster in the window of a haberdashery we were passing.

'Her name is everywhere writ,' he intoned histrionically. 'Which befits her status as an operatic demi-goddess. A diva, if you will. An English rose.' I remembered the handbill on the door of the Bull Run. 'But abandon hope, my young Irish friend. The lady is taken. A few years back, Schroeder watched her perform in our own humble Opera House when she was a humble Caroline Edwards and pursued her all the way to New York. He somehow managed to persuade the lady that her future lay back here, among the Argonauts. Is it any wonder the man is a millionaire? I can only assume he promised her a storehouse of gold and a throne beside his own in the Governor's mansion in Sacramento, because that's where Schroeder intends to abide when his ship comes in.'

Campbell then did a trick I was to see him perform effortlessly on several occasions. Taking a match from a box in his pocket, he lit it off the sole of his shoe. Although I wasn't a smoker – I still believe it to be a disgusting and unhealthy habit – I envied him that skill. But could he make a coin disappear down his sleeve? I could. Still can.

After he spoiled the effect by lighting another of those hideous Byzantine cigarettes, we turned right, onto Stockton and were back in Chinatown. As we walked through the realm of the Celestials, Campbell nodded occasionally to well-dressed, sober looking Chinese men. Some returned his greeting, albeit surreptitiously. Others darted furtive glances in his direction before slinking into doorways or down alleys that were unaccountably dark, despite the time of day. I gathered that Campbell was well-known in Chinatown, and even well-respected by its more law-abiding, but understandably circumspect, citizens.

'Captain Lees tells me you're moving back to this patch soon,' I ventured.

'Replacing the omnipotent Sergeant Tedious Kelly. Apparently, he's established a new force record for kickbacks over the last six months. I don't know how I'll begin to compete. I make it a policy to accept gifts only when it would be insulting to refuse. I hear you and he became acquainted last night.'

'I'm not sure either of us profited from the experience.'

'That's refreshing. Kelly usually manages to profit from every experience. I also hear that you put a bullet into Doghouse Riley. Somewhere painful I trust?'

'He seemed to think so.'

'Heavenly! I'm surprised you didn't encounter his travelling companion as well, an overlarge piece of shit by the name of Madden. Skullcrusher to his friends. The two are usually inseparable.'

I sensed I was being played, but my native contrariness asserted itself and I decided not to acknowledge that my first noteworthy act on being introduced to San Francisco was to reduce its population. Campbell kept fishing anyway. I could see he suspected that my encounter with Doghouse had not been a regrettable accident.

'It's none of my business, I know, but how did your path cross with Riley's in the first place?'

'He wanted me to part with my wallet. At least that was what I assumed when he pointed a knife at me and said, 'Hand over your fucking wallet, dandy.'

'Dandy indeed? Were you sporting a top hat at the time? The knife I have no difficulty believing. He specialises in disembowelment. Theft! Now that's odd. I've never known Doghouse to stoop to robbery. With him it's carve or starve. He's pure killer, a professional. I really feel for the poor man if he's been reduced to common theft. And the next time I see Oliver Madden, I must ask him why Boss Newman gave him last night off.'

All this was said with a distinctly knowing grin. My own fixed smile was sickly by comparison. Campbell enjoyed my obvious discomfiture for a few moments and then demonstrated his blithe indifference to the fate of either Madden or Riley by changing the subject. He began a discourse on Chinatown, the thrust of which was that its evil reputation was largely unwarranted. He then proceeded to contradict himself by enumerating the tongs, triads, highbinders and Hatchet Men who controlled the lucrative trade of this displaced Oriental purgatory.

'You really don't make it sound terribly benign,' I suggested.

'It isn't, if you're a Celestial. But Chinese thugs only prey on their own. The tong lords reckon it's not advisable to punish *gwailos* for any transgressions. They don't want to unleash the enduring spirit of the old Vigilance Committee.'

Given its history of what is euphemistically called 'local democracy', San Francisco should probably offer an annual Vigilante of the Year award. On two notable occasions, the running of the city had been taken over by anxious citizens who expressed their support for law and order by hanging people of whom they didn't approve.

'They even organise Chinatown tours these days,' Campbell continued, bristling with feigned indignation. 'Would you credit that? They bring in curious travellers, take their money, and then scare the hell out of them with stories of highbinders eating wildcat meat before going into battle. Then they take them to ersatz opium dens to give them a good story to bring home. It's all entirely bogus. The poor dupes never come within a waft of the real McCoy.'

The more he talked about tongs and the *boo how doy*—Chinese assassins—the happier I was because it meant that we were getting further away from any discussion of the heart-rending injury to Riley, or the mysterious fate of the misplaced Oliver Madden.

At the corner of Stockton and Broadway we parted company. He headed west, I continued north, towards Château La Peur, haven of the louche and weary traveller. Should I ever come into possession of a vineyard, I propose to call the most successful vintage after my first San Francisco lodgings.

I strolled past my bordello. I had an errand to run before I took my life in my hands and attempted to eject the feline *chevaux de frise*, Griselda, from my bedroom. I walked along Grant as it narrowed on its progress towards the northern shoreline of the city. The closer I got to Telegraph Hill, the more interested in my well-being the female inhabitants of the streets seemed to become.

There's a piece of doggerel that fits the bill—a history of San Francisco in four lines.

The miners came in forty-nine,
The whores in fifty-one.
And when they got together
They produced the native son.

Things had changed by the time I got there. San Franciscan prostitutes would have had status in the boomer society of the Vigilance Committee days—the 1850s. With so few women around, the miners, traders, thieves, sailors, murderers and shopkeepers—even some of the self-righteous religious zealots—couldn't afford to ascend their high horses and disparage the harlots. They were a pretty cosmopolitan lot back then. A red-light League of Nations. Most of them seemed to come from France, or at least they pretended to. They brought their *maquereaux* with them. Anywhere else—except maybe New Orleans—they would just have been called 'pimps'. In San Francisco, they were 'macks'. Not that the name-change purified them. A pimp is a pimp in any language. As generous as a devout Puritan, as trustworthy as a startled rattlesnake. Then, and now, the women did a lot of their business around Telegraph Hill. Bella La Peur didn't approve, of course. There are hierarchies in every profession, and she was at the apex of hers. Bella's girls got to work indoors.

The ladies of the night were not quite as visible by the time I arrived in San Francisco, though you didn't have to go too far to find them. Some of the senior members of the sorority had, however, done well for themselves. There were, after all, still twice as many men as women in the city. Some had made a pile of money and spent it on large piles of their own. Few of them made it to Nob Hill unless they buried their past so deeply that only a coal miner could chisel it out. But one or two did. Campbell would occasionally raise his hat to a woman passing by in a well-appointed carriage and announce that he had once arrested her for soliciting. But now she had a Nob Hill banker or a Rincon Hill judge for her mack. While most of them ignored him, a few—the feistier ones—would flash a knowing smile in his direction.

The sun had now set as I wandered the bustling streets of North Beach. Twilight brought out the worst in the city. There was an implicit curfew at play, but in San Francisco it brought the bad guys *onto* the streets. It was a free city; you could go anywhere you wanted anytime you wished. You just had to be prepared to make your case to a man with a knife if you wandered into the wrong parish. And in San Francisco there were more of those than there were lines in *Paradise Lost.*

As I approached the junction of Filbert and Grant, I spotted what I'd come for. Out of the shadows a woman approached, warily at first. She was young, that much you could tell in the darkness.

'Hello there,' she said awkwardly. 'Do you want to spend some time with a friendly stranger?'

14 October, morning

When I woke up, I wasn't sure which was worse. Was it the feeling that the army of General William Tecumseh Sherman was pursuing a scorched earth policy inside my brain? Some headaches begin at the frontal lobes. This one started below the knees.

Or was it the sight of my self-appointed familiar, the hellcat Griselda? He had been patiently dogging my fitful sleep—assuming a cat can dog—and was staring at me as if he was waiting for breakfast to finally stir.

Either way, both sensations were eclipsed by the unholy banging at my door. Somebody wanted to send me to hell with burst eardrums. It was like that scene from *Macbeth*, the one with all that knocking at the gate, with me cast in the role of Duncan. I thought I recognised the voice, though I tried to pretend otherwise.

'Orpen, get up. I want to talk to you.'

It was a splenetic Thaddeus Kelly. A courtesy call? Hardly. He didn't sound very courteous. Petulant, I would have said. Bordering on the fractious. I had no idea how he even knew where to find me.

'Open this door now or I'll kick it down.'

I was sorely tempted to encourage this act of wanton destruction just to see how he would cope with the wrath of Bella La Peur, and the retribution of Griselda. Instead, I unlocked the door tamely. I tried a cheery 'Good morning, Sergeant' but it came out as a gruff and hostile 'G'mun, san't.' Even at my most ebullient, it would have been difficult to dial up much enthusiasm for the presence of the dour and grim-faced Weasel. But I was not within spitting range of ebullience. Kelly was unimpressed by my obvious state of physical debilitation. The quality of mercy was strained.

'What the hell is wrong with you?' he said. I'd like to add 'compassionately' but that would be stretching credulity.

'*Delirium tremens*,' I offered. I essayed a dry retch to strengthen my argument. My punishment for sharing a dozen bottles of the brew with Campbell, despite my minority stake in the partnership, had been temporarily postponed. The effect of Ned's fine beverage mimicked the delayed action of a stick of dynamite with a long fuse. Kelly looked on dispassionately. Scanning the room, his eyes lit on my jacket, which was neatly lying in a heap on the floor beside a pair of abandoned trousers adorned with a soft moist buff-coloured substance. I had no recollection of having removed either garment the previous night. I could hazard a guess as to the origin of the colourful gunge. Kelly bent and picked something up. He came back into view clutching Doghouse's shiv.

'What's this?' he demanded triumphantly.

I thought about telling him that it was a knife, but a dim memory of our first tryst caused me to reconsider. I could not be sure that he wouldn't use it there and then. 'A gift from an old friend.' I replied, with as much nonchalance as I could muster.

'Where were you last night?' he hissed. In my delicate state, it sounded like an escape of steam from a stationary Central Pacific train.

'And what business is that of yours?' I replied. Another piece of advice. When *in extremis*, always answer questions with a question of your own.

As it happens, it wasn't me who posed the question. It was on its way to my lips but because it had to negotiate a thick fog, and a swamp full of alligators, it didn't quite emerge before its vicarious introduction to the conversation from the bedroom door. Our heads swivelled in that direction. I imagine Kelly's got there a lot more quickly than mine and inflicted less damage in the process. There stood a welcome Wellington Campbell, left hand on hip, feet a shoulder length apart, with his right index finger pointing at a disgruntled Kelly. Behind him I could see a few of Bella's less in-demand employees using their downtime to observe proceedings with sniggering curiosity.

'What are you doing here?' Kelly grunted, putting as much venom into the inquiry as a Black Mamba who has been denied his lunch by the arrival of a King Cobra.

'I might ask you the same question,' Campbell responded, just a tad loudly for my liking. I feared that precedent and principle would now force Kelly to raise the volume even further. My nerves were already screaming for a John Field nocturne and a lengthy period of recuperation in the South of France.

'In case you hadn't heard, Dan Horton was carved up last night. I want to know where this lackey of the Famine Queen was when it happened.'

'And when was that?' asked Campbell.

'I just said. Last night.' Kelly addressed Campbell as you would a small child who has thrown up on your carpet. Campbell responded in kind. He spoke with studied deliberation, almost spelling out each word. If the condescension didn't work, I was sure the oily courtesy probably would.

'Can't you be more specific? It gets dark between five and six p.m. these days. That's a lot of night to account for.'

'How the hell do I know? The body hasn't been examined yet.'

'So, what you're saying is he could have been dead for a week. I believe this gentleman got here only yesterday. That would seem to eliminate him.' I thought it wise not to remind Campbell that Horton had looked rudely healthy in the Bull Run Bar the day before. He had hardly been dead for a week.

'I'm saying nothing of the kind, Campbell. Don't put words in my mouth.'

'I wouldn't dream of putting anything of mine in your mouth. Certainly nothing of any value. Where, as a matter of interest, was the body found, and at what time?'

'Chinatown. A waste lot on Stockton and Washington. An hour ago. Not that it's any concern of yours.'

'Oh, but it is, my friend. And you'll be delighted to hear that I can immediately relieve you of the burden of this investigation. You will recall that I resumed my duties in Chinatown as of this very morning. I'm touched by the interest you appear to have taken in my case, but I'll pursue it from here.'

The Black Mamba's lunch was now vanishing down the King Cobra's throat. Kelly looked as if someone had just slapped him across the face with a dead fish. To his credit he recovered himself quickly. He took a deep breath and was about to launch into a diatribe. Campbell cut him short.

'Don't waste words, Kelly. Nob Hill beckons. Enjoy the Promising Land. Go forth and kiss some rich ass. Make yourself indispensable.'

'Fuck you, Campbell.' Kelly decided that gave him the last word, and he left. If you can leave a room darkly, then that's what he did.

'Expressed with your customary verbal elegance, sir,' Campbell called after him. 'I just wish I had a fraction of your astonishing gift for repartee. And I wish I had some of the gifts you'll be taking with you after six months in Chinatown.' The latter barb was added *sotto voce*. In view of my fraught nerves sotto voce was good from my perspective.

Campbell turned to me. 'You look like you've been in the ring with Gentleman Jim.'

'If you mean as his spittoon, then I concur.'

'*Delirium tremens* would appear not to entirely agree with you. You need more practice.'

I silently gagged at the prospect. He pointed to Griselda, still recumbent on the bed and inspecting us both with culinary intensity. 'Is that your cat?' he asked.

'He's very much his own cat. I'm staff.'

'Heavenly. Now then, in the interests of what Lees called "inter-jurisdictional co-operation" yesterday, I assume that I'm expected to invite you to the scene of the preliminary lying-in-state of the late Daniel Horton. I'm afraid I cannot supply the gentleman's middle initial. You Irish persons don't seem to set much store by such graces. Shall we?'

Anything to get away from the hungry green eyes of the watchful Griselda.

My third walk through Chinatown with Campbell, in contrast to the first two, was conducted without any violence towards unwary bystanders, and in almost total silence. Campbell was too preoccupied even to salute passing Celestials—much, I imagined, to their relief.

The entrance to the unused lot where Horton lay 'a-mouldering' was on Washington Street. It was somewhere between an alleyway and a fully-fledged thoroughfare, close to the hustle and bustle of Stockton, where the Celestials bought and sold all manner of food, drink, and indeterminate products, to one another. Before Kelly had abandoned the crime scene for our little *tête à tête*, he had left two constables to guard Horton's body. They had done their jobs well and had also managed not to attract too much attention to the location of the corpse. A guttural exclamation from Campbell in a language I didn't understand, and the last few curious Chinese onlookers quickly scampered to get away.

It didn't take a seasoned veteran to figure out that Horton had been knifed to death. He was dressed in a white shirt, lying on his back, chest bloodied, and his body was covered in stab wounds. I could see why Kelly had been so childishly excited at finding Riley's shiv on my bedroom floor. His eyes were still open. I don't normally find this too disconcerting except that, as you walked around the body, you got the sense that your movements were being tracked from below. The expression on the dead man's face was blatantly disparaging. Since our acquaintance had been less than slight, I decided not to take it personally.

Campbell set to work, and I watched, quietly impressed by his efficiency. Minute investigation was never my forte, but I could admire the work of a craftsman. Only once did he seek my assistance. That was to help him turn over the body so he could look for injuries to the victim's back.

'I hate knives,' he said. I was sure Horton couldn't have agreed more. 'You can never properly tell one from the other,' he observed to no one in particular, 'but a good bullet wound is a giveaway.'

I took the bait. 'And how does a bullet betray itself?' I asked with genuine curiosity. He looked through me as if he'd forgotten I was there, before getting me back into focus.

'I must introduce you to Jimmy Vernon sometime,' he said, quite jovially for a man examining an object in the first stages of decomposition. 'He's a local gunsmith who swears that if you give him a bullet from a body, he can match it up with a gun. Provided, of course, you can find him the gun.'

It was all just a little too preposterous, and I succumbed to temptation. 'And if we had eggs, we could have bacon and eggs for breakfast … if we had bacon.' I regretted my bravado when he lapsed into a sour silence. Americans have never really taken to being joshed.

Campbell stalked the mortal remains of Dan Horton for a few more minutes, narrowly avoiding a collision with a wooden beam protruding from below an upstairs window. 'Upstairs' in Chinatown was closer to the ground than in the Occidental part of town, and Campbell was almost tall enough to stretch from floor to ceiling.

'As you can see, he's been stabbed repeatedly.'

I presumed this was for my benefit, in case I was the type who had difficulty identifying a turd in a shitstorm. But he didn't address himself directly to me. It was as if he was dictating his thoughts to some concealed amanuensis. Was I supposed to be taking notes?

'He has … half-a-dozen wounds to his arms.'

He paused, reached into his pocket, and took out a small claspknife. Opening it, he inserted the blade delicately into one of the gaping wounds on the torso. It absorbed the entire length of the blade. I began to feel slightly squeamish. I wasn't used to this line of work, but I suppose Horton was past caring. Campbell then repeated the process on one of the arm wounds. The knife penetrated no further than half an inch.

'It could be that more than one weapon was used,' he continued. 'The wounds on the torso are much deeper than these here … on the arms.'

Word of Horton's tragic demise had already begun to spread among the insect community. Bloated flies floated by. Campbell brushed off the most persistent offenders. The rest he scattered by lighting one of his gargantuan cigars. The bluebottles and I retired to a safe distance. The flies were more fortunate, however, because I was summoned back almost immediately to help Campbell turn over the body. As he surveyed Horton's back, he took a long drag from the cigar. A dollop of flaky ash fell on the corpse. Nonchalantly, he brushed it away. He made a cursory inspection and motioned me to return the corpse to its original position.

'He was attacked by someone facing him. There are no wounds on his back,' he observed. I didn't demur, as this would have involved breathing. He sucked in another generous mouthful of burnt tobacco, waited for it to become familiar with his lungs, and then exhaled.

'And he wasn't murdered here.'

This was news to me. I could see that I was going to have to hold the front page. In response to my quizzical expression Campbell pointed towards two long parallel ridges that had been scored in the dust; they ended at the heels of the dead man's shoes.

'The body was dragged from the street. So, if there *were* two killers, only one of them brought him here. The body could have come from quite a distance away.'

I didn't follow his logic. 'And you say that because …?'

My question disturbed his reverie. He looked at me as if he had just become conscious of my presence. For a moment I thought he was going to ask me for identification.

'If two men had carried him,' he finally replied, with a shrug, 'one would have been at the shoulders and the other at the feet. There wouldn't be any drag marks. There would also be two sets of footprints, probably facing in opposite directions. Here we have one set, walking backwards, almost obliterated by the rut created by Horton's heels. So, he was either murdered out on the street and hauled in here, or he was killed somewhere else, lifted onto a cart or a dray, driven here, and then heaved out and dumped. Whoever dragged him in here was probably quite small in stature, judging by the boot size.'

He opened the clasp knife again and set it down alongside the clearest of the footprints. 'It's no more than a size eight. I'd put my money on a seven. But he was still strong enough to heave a grown

man at least …' he looked towards the street and did a mental calcu-
lation, '…thirty yards?'

To confirm this, he paced out the distance to the pavement on
Stockton, tracking the drag marks. I followed him. Out in the street
he glanced right and left, as if he was looking for someone, and then,
obeying some inner whisper, he gazed upwards, abstractedly. A lone
white cloud, looking decidedly sheepish, straggled across the face of
the sun. It lingered for a while, as if trying to glean information from
the scene below, and then continued its journey eastwards. It would
burn up over the Bay. Campbell watched it for half a minute. Then he
shook himself back to life

'And where is his jacket?' he asked. 'Was he walking around in
his shirt last night?' I thought it was unlikely. October days were mild
enough in San Francisco, but the nights were chilly.

'So, he was murdered somewhere else and brought here. Agreed?
It wouldn't be the first time someone was killed, and then deposited
in Chinatown. I sometimes wonder if *gwailos* with a body to dispose
of believe that Celestials have a taste for human flesh.'

He surveyed the street again, and then returned to the body.
Only now did he attempt to close Horton's eyes, but the dead Irishman wasn't quite ready to stop haunting us with his reproachful
stare. Campbell tried twice, but the eyes kept opening. Finally, he
took a handkerchief from a jacket pocket and placed it, almost rever-
ently, on the dead man's face. It felt good not to be subjected to that
disparaging glare any longer.

Campbell knelt beside the corpse for a few moments before
pointing towards Horton's right wrist. 'Do y'all notice anything else
… about the sleeves?' he asked. I looked closely but couldn't see whatever it was that Campbell had spotted. Reluctantly, I admitted defeat.

'Where are the cufflinks?' he asked. He was right. I had been
too preoccupied to notice. I was more concerned with how Robert
Anderson was going to take the news that Horton was definitively

hors de combat. I imagined Gosselin breaking it to him with all the pious sincerity of an undertaker.

I studied the left wrist. There was a jagged tear where the cufflink should have been. When I pointed this out, Campbell nodded distractedly. He was searching the dead man's trouser pockets. From the right pocket he pulled out a white envelope. I could make out Horton's name inscribed on the front, in what looked like a woman's hand. There was, however, no accompanying letter. Campbell put this, almost absent-mindedly into the same pocket from which he had extracted the handkerchief now covering Horton's face. Why toss away a letter and retain an envelope, I mused?

Then something else attracted his attention. Horton had not been wearing a collar when he died, and his shirt had been open at the throat. Campbell unbuttoned the shirt and carefully opened the ripped and bloody garment. The more enterprising and avaricious of the flies rejoined us. As the bare torso was exposed all I could see from where I was standing was caked blood, from the multiple stab wounds, on a hairless chest. Without touching the encrusted flesh, Campbell traced something with his index finger. He then repeated the gesture, his finger still hovering over Horton's body. He seemed to be drawing the letter 'H'.

'Do you see it?' he asked, pointing at the torso. 'It looks to me as if he's been sliced up. You can see the outline, right there. He's been branded.' Slowly and painstakingly, he refastened the buttons.

When he stood up, he suddenly clapped his hands together. I thought he was summoning one of the uniforms, until the squashed remains of a careless fly spilled onto the ground at our feet.

When Campbell had seen enough, he arranged with one of the two constables for the corpse to be moved to the morgue. A dray, drawn by a bored looking horse who had obviously seen it all before, had arrived while we had been stalking Horton's remains. Campbell left instructions that the police surgeon was to wait for his arrival before examining the corpse. No one else was to have access to Horton in the interim. 'No next of kin, no priests, most of all no damn reporters—nobody,' he told the uniforms. I got the impression from the insistence of his commands that autopsies in San Francisco could morph into a macabre spectator sport. Were newspaper critics invited to write notices?

I dutifully tagged along with Campbell as we walked down Washington Street towards the Hall of Justice on Portsmouth Square. He was absorbed in his own thoughts. There was something about the final discovery he had made that seemed to bother him even more than Horton's actual death. There was a tightness around his eyes and an urgency in his gait. Had we not been walking downhill, I would have found it impossible to keep up with him. He was pensive and silent. I kept my questions to myself. I was intensely curious, of course, but I had barely been acquainted with Campbell for twenty-four hours. I was reluctant to presume too much on an acquaintance based on the consumption of a dozen bottles of 12% proof beer. He would tell me whatever he wanted to tell me when he was ready to do so.

The police surgeon had been sent for and the autopsy would take place in the bowels of the Portsmouth Square building. Before that happened, however, Campbell was closeted for twenty minutes with Lees. When both emerged from the captain's dingy office, Lees looked apprehensive. Whatever Campbell told him had ruptured his native imperturbability. He patted the detective on the shoulder as they parted. Campbell nodded grimly. As he passed me, he motioned for me to accompany him. From the time Campbell had entered the building, he hadn't spoken a single word to anyone but Lees. He ignored a few barbed pleasantries tossed in his direction by Tracy, who was seated behind the reception desk, bored and in search of amusement. I followed Campbell down two flights of stairs towards a dark basement. As we descended, the aroma of chemicals rose to greet us.

He preceded me into a large room lit only by an elongated narrow window set at street level a few feet above our heads. Two long wooden tables were situated in the centre of the room, which was otherwise unfurnished. On one of the tables was the body of Dan Horton. Campbell closed the door behind us. My eyes roamed about the room. On the empty table, the one closest to us, I noticed small traces of something that reminded me of uncooked chicken breast. Campbell broke the silence.

'Lees says I should fill you in. He seems to repose a lot of confidence in you and thinks you might have some sort of stake in all this. He muttered something about a gentleman called Williamson?'

'Dolly,' I responded, and immediately regretted it. It seemed inappropriate in the neighbourhood of a corpse. Campbell snorted.

'An odd name for a senior policeman. He wouldn't get far in the Barbary Coast.' He paused, probably considering how he might initiate someone whose commanding officer was named after a small girl's toy into the underbelly of San Francisco crime.

'Anyway, be that as it may. You understand that nothing said here today is to be repeated?'

'If you say so, of course.' Behind my back my fingers were crossed, mitigating the flagrancy of the lie.

'Good. Come over here.'

Campbell walked across to the table bearing Horton's body. It was in the brighter corner of the room, directly underneath the street level window. The detective bent down and began opening Horton's shirt again. I was puzzled as to why he had refastened the buttons in the first place. Once again, he gingerly separated both sides of the bloodied garment and exposed the dead man's torso. At Horton's head was a basin and sponge. Campbell took the sponge and carefully began to wash off the blood from wounds caused by the knife that had penetrated Horton's chest. As he did so, I could see the letter 'H' begin to emerge, lividly, on the man's flesh.

'There. You see that?' Campbell pointed to the upper torso. The brand was luridly apparent.

'Lees agrees with me. It's either the work of the Hounds or of someone who wants us to believe it's the work of the Hounds.' I looked at him blankly. 'The Society of Regulators,' he offered impatiently. He made it sound like a firm of accountants. I tried to look even blanker, hoping to extract an explanation.

'Vigilance is mine, saith the Lord,' he intoned, enigmatically. That roused the pedant in me.

'Isn't it "vengeance"?' I suggested.

'It's the same thing in San Francisco. The vigilante is generally looking for revenge of some kind. If you've got a hundred vigilantes, you've probably got a hundred different motives for inflicting pain. The Hounds tarted up their little game by calling themselves 'The Society of Regulators,' but I prefer the more colloquial and evocative 'Hounds' myself. They were forty-niners who preferred running protection rackets to panning dirt for themselves. They didn't approve of anyone who spoke Spanish and who didn't freckle in the sun. So, they beat up Mexicans and stole from them.'

'What happened to them?'

'It was a bit like the old lady who swallowed the fly. She had to swallow a spider to catch the fly, right? The Hounds ran out of Chilenos and Mexicans to rob. When they started harassing pink folks … well, that was a breach of the ten commandments, wasn't it? So, another bunch of vigilante thugs rousted them out. The spider swallowed the fly. The Hounds ended up leaving town with their tails between their legs. Of course, then we had to employ a flock of birds to swallow the spiders.'

'And what has all this got to do with Horton?'

'Since the Hounds left town, legions of devoted admirers have tried to eclipse their noble record. Flattery by imitation. There aren't many Mexicans or Chilenos left to murder, but they have, periodically, taken exception to the presence of the Chinese. When they burn someone out, beat them up, or kill them, they often leave a little calling card, usually the letter 'H'. It's painted on walls, written on a piece of paper, whatever is more convenient, and then tossed beside their handiwork. Just for context, y'all understand. Then, having made their point, they ascend into vigilante heaven, where they are welcomed and waited upon by hordes of ministering white lady angels.'

'Cherubim or Seraphim?' My pedant was fully engorged by now. Campbell just flicked back his floppy fringe and carried on examining the ugly tattoo.

'Perhaps the current generation of the over-privileged is feeling left out and unfulfilled,' he mused. 'They need adventure in their empty lives. Who knows? But this is different, and different is dangerous. Two things here make this …' he pointed at Horton's corpse, '… exceptional. To the best of my knowledge, no one has ever carved the letter 'H' on human flesh before.

'Perhaps they just ran out of paint?'

'That would be a welcome, if unlikely, explanation.'

'What's the other novel feature?'

'The Hounds have never killed a white man before.'

'He's Irish. Are the Irish white?'

'Maybe not in New York or Boston, but around here they are. They got here first. Some of them made a lot of money. If you're rich, you're white.' Muttering to himself he added as an afterthought, 'This is just the kind of trouble we don't need in this city.' He returned his attention to Horton and began sponging again.

'By the way, where were you last night … after we parted company?' he inquired casually. He quietly continued the *postmortem* ablutions while I thought about my answer. That was when we heard the click of a pistol being cocked from the corner of the room. This was followed by a steady, strong, authoritative female voice breaking the silence.

'If you wouldn't mind just putting down that sponge at your convenience. And please step away from my cadaver.'

It had been an interesting first twenty-four hours in San Francisco. Fists, then a knife, now a gun. What next? A howitzer?

Both Campbell and I turned slowly towards the newcomer. She was a young, dark, slim, attractive woman in her mid-twenties, of about average height with luminous brown eyes and an impressive mop of reddish-brown hair as straight as the edge of a safety razor and tied back in a bun, or some other form of confectionery. I'm not very *au fait* with female hairstyles, or baked goods for that matter. But the thing that impressed me most about her at that first meeting was the size of the gun she was holding in her right hand. It was a Smith and Wesson with what looked like a four-inch barrel. It was about the size of my Colt 'Baby Dragoon' and definitely not one of those *bijou* derringer numbers that women seemed to swear by, even though they looked as if they couldn't blow a hole in a fortune cookie. I imagined Bella La Peur offered a home to one or two in her bounteous cleavage. This artillery piece, however, was different. It was a conversation killer.

As the onus was clearly on him, Campbell was the first to respond.

'Your cadaver?'

'Cadaver. From the Latin,' she responded, with more unconcern than I could have mustered under the circumstances. 'Meaning a dead body or a corpse. Is that any help?'

'If you were paying attention, Ma'am I was attempting to emphasise the possessive pronoun. Would you please put down that gun?' Campbell said contemptuously.

'I should warn you that I am an excellent shot. My father taught me well.' She smiled sweetly as she spoke, and her hand was as steady as a Methodist at prayer. Campbell clearly sensed that her estimation of her prowess was no empty boast because he didn't move.

'Who are you anyway?' she asked, amiably enough for someone holding a gun; 'aside, obviously, from being a relic of the old
Confederacy?'

'I am Detective Sergeant Wellington Campbell. At your service,
ma'am. Now could you please lower that weapon?'

Miss Smith and Wesson called to someone waiting outside. 'Rory,
would you come in here for a moment, please.'

Not that I'd ever been in the least bit concerned, you understand,
but I was relieved when my waterfront guardian angel Tracy insinu-
ated his ample frame into the room.

'Who are these people?' Smith and Wesson asked.

'Never seen them before in my life, ma'am,' Tracy responded with
a smirk.

'Tracy!' Campbell's humourless rasp brought the joke to an
abrupt end.

'The gentleman to your left is Sergeant Campbell of the San Francisco Police, the one to your right is Mr. Plantagenet ... is Detective
Sergeant Orpen of the London Metropolitan Police.' Tracy said.

'Is that so? I'm not sure I've ever met a genuine English policeman before, other than the captain,' she remarked.

'You still haven't,' I interjected, marshalling as much asperity as
possible. 'I'm Irish.'

'Oh,' she said, clearly deflated at the news. 'I've met plenty of
them,' she added, eyeing Tracy with a touch of her own asperity. The
Smith and Wesson was uncocked and expeditiously deposited in
some remote province of her dress unknown to fashionable couturi-
ers. I wondered where it could possibly have disappeared to, but I
was unwilling to stare. Tracy withdrew, trying, but unaccountably
failing, to suppress his laughter.

'Are you next of kin?' inquired Campbell. 'I left specific instructions that no relatives were to be allowed near the body. We can do

the formal identification later, thank you all the same. We know who he is. So, now if you wouldn't mind leaving us to do our jobs.'

'Perhaps you'd allow me to do mine. Next of kin I ain't,' she replied cordially, brushing past us and relieving Campbell of the sponge as she did so. He tried to grab it back, but he was too slow.

'There's no call to wash the body yet.' The pitch of Campbell's voice rose by a semi-tone. 'He has to be examined by the police surgeon first.'

'He's about to be.' She held out her hand to Campbell. 'Doctor Ophelia Williams. Police surgeon *pro tem*. Your regular 'sawbones' is on some strange masculine rite of passage in Yosemite. I think he's climbing something. I hope for his sake it's not a brown bear. So here I am.'

I now became less concerned with the tempo and pitch of Campbell's voice and more disturbed by the colour of his face. He had skipped all the customary intermediate shades that signposted resentment and gone straight to puce.

'You cannot be serious,' he growled. 'You're a …'

'Doctor of Medicine. Yes! Class of '81, University of California, San Francisco.'

'… woman.'

'You noticed. You must be such an excellent detective. You don't have much to say for yourself, do you, Sergeant Irish?'

Neither was I given an opportunity to vindicate myself. Campbell was quickly ascending the chromatic scale again, while simultaneously turning the colour of beetroot.

'Just what gives you the right to describe yourself as a doctor?' he barked.

'Five years at Toland Medical School, and 20:18,' she purred.

'Is that some sort of biblical reference?'

'It is to me. Article 20, Section 18,' she responded. 'Don't they teach you the 1879 California State Constitution at Detective Kindergarten?

"No person shall, on account of sex, be disqualified from enter-ing upon or pursuing any lawful business, vocation or profession." Happy?'

Campbell looked about as happy as Robert E. Lee at Appomattox Courthouse. He summoned Charles Dickens to his cause.

'If that is what the 1879 California State Constitution says, ma'am, then the 1879 California State Constitution is an ass, one that would never be allowed to graze below the Mason-Dixon line. More Yankee folly,' he snarled.

'Please don't whip me, Massa Overseer,' Dr. Williams simpered sarcastically, taking off Campbell's drawl with aplomb. 'Now then, Sergeant Stonewall, can you please suspend your manly disapproval for an hour or so and allow me to get on with my work? My corpse is getting warm.'

CHAPTER FOUR

FROM THE MEMOIR OF OPHELIA WILLIAMS

14 October, Basement, Portsmouth Square, Hall of Justice

Let me begin by pointing out that I'm writing this under protest. Orpen can be very persuasive. He can also be calculatedly hazy as to detail but we'll let that go for the moment. I'm seventy-five years old now, an age when most women have turned into their mothers. I don't have time for this and I don't have perfect recall, though I'll take a punt on my memory over Orpen's any day. Nevertheless, I've agreed, so best be getting on with it.

The Southerner, Campbell, who affected the hairstyle of that conceited ass Custer, behaved like a lemon from the outset, so I made lemonade. It wasn't as if I hadn't grown accustomed to wearisome narrow-mindedness. It was just more irritating when it came dressed up in mock-polite Southern inflections. I prefer my misogyny to be chargrilled, not poached. Like the waspish instructor at Toland who proclaimed, the first time he laid eyes on me, that a woman should not be allowed to study medicine until her ovaries had been removed. He flounced out of the room, foaming at the mouth, when I told him that I'd be happy to comply, when all the male students—and their tutors—had sacrificed their testicles. And, since I'd castrated dozens of cattle and horses on my uncle's farm, I even offered to do the job myself.

He, Campbell that is—the Irishman didn't have much to say for himself, though I fancy he enjoyed our little scrimmage—had the brass neck to ask me what my parents made of their daughter practicing medicine. I told him that my father, a San Francisco policeman killed in the line of duty, would probably approve, but that I couldn't be sure about my mother.

'Why is that?' he asked, stepping right onto the dog droppings.

'I haven't seen her for a while. She has been a bit preoccupied with a campaign to have more women admitted to the University of California. But when we next get together, I'll be sure to ask if I have her blessing.'

To his credit, when he finally put two and two together and worked out that I was the daughter of Marcus Williams, he almost managed to contain himself for the duration of the autopsy. Almost.

The other one—his name was Orpen—was about my age and quite good-looking in a juvenile, foppish sort of way. He was one of those muscular Irishmen, the ones who don't look like they've been reared on a diet of potatoes. He was clean-shaven, fair-haired—it was long too, though not as long as Campbell's—with oddly mismatched dark eyebrows and mischievous green eyes. His fringe seemed to be imbued with its own gravitational force. It was constantly attacking his forehead. And, as far as I could tell under that mop of hair, it looked as if he had forgotten to bring one of his ears to California.

When Campbell was at his most annoying—which was for about ninety percent of the autopsy—the Irishman pretended, silently of course, that he was on my side. He would raise his eyebrows—whenever you could see them for the floppy fringe—or roll those fetching green eyes. But he never found it convenient to intervene and tell Campbell that he was being an ass. I had no idea what he was doing there, or why he was being allowed to attend a medical examination six thousand miles from Buckingham Palace. I couldn't be bothered to ask either. I was well used to Irishmen getting under my feet. It seemed like every second San Francisco policeman had a brogue.

The body—which had lain patiently on the gurney all this time waiting for our *tête à tête* to end—was of a white male, probably in his mid-to-late thirties. I suppose I should have been flattered. This was, as it happens, the first time I had even been allowed in the same room as the corpse of a man of European origin. Thus far, in what you could only laughingly refer to as 'my medical career', I had been let loose only on Orientals, mostly the lacerated victims of tong knife fights. Obviously, I didn't share this information with Stonewall Jackson's idiot son.

The victim, an Irishman named Daniel Horton—this information was conveyed lugubriously and reluctantly—seemed to be in good physical condition, other than the inescapable fact that he was dead. He had excellent muscle tone and little or no excess fat.

As I studied the cadaver, I was subjected to a barrage of questions from Campbell. 'Can you tell me when he died?' 'Was he branded before or after he was murdered?' 'Which of the dagger thrusts killed him?' And more besides. He was like a small child demanding his apple pie before eating his vegetables. I ignored him. That only provoked him further. But I had enough serenity for both of us. The lemonade was mouth-watering.

'So, do you want a contemporaneous account of my findings, Sergeant Campbell,' I inquired placidly, 'or would you prefer to read it all in my written report? I'm sure I can have that for you in ... two or three days.'

This unsubtle threat ended the sarcastic comments. I mean his, of course. I always keep mine to hand. Campbell reverted to indecipherable grunts. Orpen was more forthcoming. He nodded enthusiastically and even made notes, but he didn't dare provoke an outbreak of Dixieland wrath by asking any questions.

Although the fatal thrust that killed Dan Horton was to the chest, my attention was immediately drawn to his arms. They had been badly cut, but the gashes were clearly unconnected with his death.

'You'll have noticed the wounds on the victim's right and left arms?' I ventured.

Orpen responded with an energetic nod. Campbell remained in Buddha-like repose.

'These may look like defensive wounds, but they are not. The absence of significant traces of blood indicates that they were administered *postmortem*. Why that should be the case is, of course, up to you to find out. I'm just pointing out that if Mr. Horton tried to defend himself against the dagger that killed him, he didn't use his arms, as someone seems to have wanted to suggest.'

There was a surprisingly high-pitched grunt from Campbell. Was this meant as encouragement, or was it just a snort of derision in the wrong register? I intercepted a pointed look between the two men. There was the shadow of a nod from the Irishman. A palpable hit! I then pointed to Horton's wrists.

'The reason he was unable to use his arms to defend himself is not difficult to determine either. I'm sure you noticed the contusions on his wrists when you examined the body. There is a narrow band of bruising, suggesting that his hands were bound, presumably behind his back. So Mr. Horton was not killed in an altercation. Whoever murdered him was holding him prisoner at the time.'

There was a low rolling guttural grunt, like the premonitory rumbling of a volcano. The tremors suggested that Campbell had not already spotted the bruising on the wrists. Orpen looked intently at his colleague, who declined to reciprocate. I was beside myself with smugness as I continued.

'Now let's look at the torso. The fatal blow was administered … here.' I pointed to an entry wound above the heart, created by a downward thrust. 'What is interesting, however, is the number of similar wounds about the upper body. Mr. Horton was bound and perhaps gagged as well. There appears to be some slight bruising to the corners of the mouth. The condition of the corpse suggests a frenzied attack. This would have been wholly unnecessary. The wound I have just pointed out would have been enough to kill him. Anyone intent on despatching Mr. Horton would have had no difficulty in doing so. So why are there …' I began to count, '… two, three, four, five, stab wounds to the chest and … two more to the stomach? Six of these blows were surplus to requirements. Why such a furious assault?'

Intrigued by the condition of the lower torso, I decided to take a closer look. I inserted the little finger of my right hand, in turn, into two of the wounds. One met with no resistance. The wound was deep. The other, however, was much shallower. The Irishman watched the experiment with awed fascination. Campbell's lip curled in an ostentatious display of feigned indifference.

'These stomach wounds, although only about an inch apart, appear to be of a different depth, as if one of the blows was weaker than the other. But the pattern of the wounds suggests that the same weapon was used in both instances. Why the reduced intensity of some of the thrusts?' There was a gruff, abrupt throaty rumble in response. Derision? Grudging respect? Phlegm?

I then turned to the letter carved on the dead man's chest.

'Owing to your enthusiasm with the sponge, Sergeant Campbell, I can't readily tell you whether the letter 'H', plainly visible on the upper thorax, near the breastbone, was carved onto his chest while the man was still alive or was done *postmortem*. Again, it is for you to divine its significance. That's all I can tell you for the moment. I may have some more information later, if you would now be so good as to remove yourselves from the neighbourhood and allow me to get to work with a scalpel? I'm afraid I haven't quite mastered the skill of cutting into human flesh while indulging in friendly banter.'

The Irishman started. I could see that he had no wish to stick around for the second act. Campbell ignored my instruction and muttered the only three intelligible words he had hazarded since the examination began.

'Time of death?'

Horton looked like he had probably been murdered between eight and eleven o'clock the previous night, but I decided Campbell could wait for that information. I told him jovially, 'It will be in my report.' Anticipating his next question, I added pleasantly. 'Soon!'

That was when I had one of those flashes of inspiration that often enlivened my interactions with the better class of caveman. It occurred to me that I had a weapon to hand with which to provoke our Confederate friend still further. I reached into my medical bag and produced a packet of twenty Duke of Durham cigarettes. They weren't even mine. I'd bought them for my mother, who smoked like the engine of a Southern Pacific train. I lit one and began to smoke it in front of him, trying not to give myself away by coughing up a lung.

For a moment, I thought he was going to explode. Orpen now found it convenient to study an invisible stain on the floor. Sadly, Campbell's genteel ancestors intervened before I could entirely puncture his air of condescension. Generations of Southern breeding—the kind that didn't involve carnal knowledge of terrified slave women—asserted itself. He swallowed hard and everything he had been taught in chivalry class came flooding back. I tried to tighten the screw by offering him one of the cigarettes. He declined gracelessly, and, by way of retaliation, shoved a fat noxious cigar into his mouth as he turned away.

Before I finished the only cigarette I have ever smoked, a pale lanky newcomer arrived. I recognized him as a journalist and lead writer with the *San Francisco Chronicle*, Ross Walsh. I also knew him as a minor poet. Extremely minor. He had one collection to his credit entitled *Asymmetrical Ballads*. The lack of symmetry had, apparently, something to do with the fact that they didn't rhyme. That's not all they didn't do. Mr. Walsh was no Wordsworth, despite affecting a trim goatee beard to make him look more like a man of letters. He was a good reporter though. He mostly covered Chinatown and the city's criminal underworld, so he didn't lack for good subject matter.

Walsh took in the corpse, the two policemen, and me, without even a flicker. He smelt the tension in the room and dismissed it with a shrug. 'What have you got for me?' he brusquely demanded of Campbell.

'Good afternoon to you too, Ross.' Campbell had suddenly recovered his aplomb. ''Tis a sad day for dear old Ireland,' he trilled, mimicking half the San Francisco Police Department. 'Dan Horton has shuffled off his mortal coil.'

'So, I hear,' Walsh deadpanned. 'Aided or unaided?'

'Oh, he had lots of help. By the way …' Campbell indicated Orpen, '… this is Sergeant Robert Orpen, visiting us from the London Metropolitan Police. He's here to learn.'

Walsh looked skeptical as he extended his hand to the Irishman and offered some banal words of welcome. Campbell was now standing with his back to me. He casually flicked his right hand over his left shoulder in my general direction in a simultaneous gesture of introduction and dismissal. 'And that is—'

'Doctor Williams. We meet again,' Walsh said. He approached me good-humouredly with an outstretched hand. Campbell started and looked miffed. 'I didn't think I'd have the opportunity to catch you at work,' Walsh remarked, with enough warmth to light Campbell's cigar.

Campbell turned towards us both with what could only be described as a childish pout. Even if it wasn't fully pouty, it was certainly pout-ish.

'You two are acquainted?' he asked, perplexed that, yet again, a mere woman had scored a home run off his fastball.

'Didn't you read my piece in the *Chronicle* about our first female police surgeon?' Walsh asked. 'The Letters column went apoplectic.'

'You know I never buy that rag,' Campbell grumbled. Now it turned into a cat's arse of a pout. A full-blown sulk was imminent.

'Stuff and nonsense, Campbell. I know for a fact that you imbibe every word I write, along with your morning beverage.'

'Occasionally, but only from a copy purchased by the proprietor of the café.'

'Speaking of proprietors, I imagine mine will be reserving some space in the editorial pages tomorrow to continue his quest for the hides of Tom Newman and Charlie Schroeder. Horton's sad demise gives him a thoroughly excellent pretext. In death, Desperate Dan, will become Honest Horton, knocking at the gates of heaven. Mike will emphatically deny suggesting that Newman had him killed, while making it as plain as possible that Newman had him killed. I intend to stay away from the office for the rest of the day in case he insists that I write his little philippic.'

I was at sea. 'Who's … Mike?' I asked tentatively, just in case I should have known.

'Aha, you are yet to have the incalculable pleasure of meeting one of the princelings of San Francisco. Michael de Young, man about town, Republican, robber baron, owner of the *Chronicle*, and fully paid-up rich bastard. Loathes Democrats in general, Schroeder in particular, and now Newman by extension, as our esteemed former Sheriff snuggles into Charlie's pocket. Any friend of Schroeder's … but let's continue our new acquaintance's education in the Bohemian Club, Campbell. You have so much to learn nice Mr. Metropolitan policeman.' He took a fob watch from his waistcoat pocket and studied it with the intensity of the nearsighted. 'The Bohemian bar should be open. I'm sure Gilsenan, the tavern keeper, has forgotten our little tiff by now. Nobody fights duels these days. Shall we?' Walsh indicated the door with a gesture of impatience. He surveyed me, just a little too despondently, and bowed. 'Sadly, the unenlightened Bohemians do not yet permit the presence of ladies.'

'Or even females,' added Campbell. Walsh looked disapprovingly at his 'source close to the Police Department' but did not demur.

After the three men left together, I turned back to the mortal remains of the late Dan Horton. Just before I continued with my examination, a shiver ran through me. Despite my calling, I am yet to feel entirely comfortable in the presence of the dead.

CHAPTER FIVE

ORPEN

16 October, early morning

For the duration of my highly productive stay in San Francisco, Green Street was my home from home. Like most streets in the city, it was named after a dead war hero, a former President, or a local politician on the make. The estimable Mr. Green—a born huckster if ever there was one—had not even been required to wait for a cortège to carry him off to Boot Hill before the honour was bestowed upon him.

The resourceful Mr. G was set to run for mayor when, one night, he went to a sumptuous ball. There he was spotted and identified by a woman from Philadelphia as a runaway thief who had robbed a Pennsylvania bank. His real name wasn't even Green, it was Geddes. The city fathers never bothered to change the name of the street. Professional courtesy.

In my bawdy house eyrie, I had learned – the hard way I might add – not to dice with Griselda. Granted he was quite the most indolent of cats; in fact, he was the single laziest constituent part of the entire animal kingdom. He would have made a torpid sloth look like a fidgety thoroughbred stallion. Even if a blind, overweight, three-legged mouse paraded right in front of his nose, he wouldn't deign to raise a claw—not even for the sake of ancestral antagonism.

However, that native lethargy did not extend as far as the tolerance of any effort made to remove him from wherever he had chosen to settle. Such an infringement of his dignity, and his right to private property, he would resist like a widow at a Land War eviction. Since he had taken a shine to my bed, I had the scars to prove it. Griselda's philosophy was simple. *J'y suis, j'y reste.*

This sadistic tom cat was the last thing I saw at night and the first sight that greeted me in the morning. The second vision was usually one, or more, of Bella La Peur's employees. They wandered around in scanty clothing that was generally less than opaque. There was a distinct lack of bashfulness when it came to bodily concealment in the precincts of Chez la Peur. To their credit, Bella's ladies, in all the time I spent there, never once propositioned me, though perhaps that is to my debit rather than their credit.

That day Sophie and Marlène were the first housemates I passed on the stairs. I have no idea if those were their real names. Marlène was dark and Hispanic in appearance, while Sophie was a Teutonic blonde. Their accents suggested that both might just as well have hailed from Merced as Marseilles. They greeted me warmly, we flirted for a minute or two, and after a few courteous valedictions, I continued downstairs.

As I passed by what Bella styled 'The Parlour'—a euphemism for the richly brocaded suite where the 'clients' identified the ladies of their choice—I noticed that the piano was free and unlocked. True to Bella's pretensions, it was not a 'honky-tonk' upright, but a baby grand. Every night the sounds produced by a nervous and highly-strung Italian pianist would penetrate to my bedroom. It was a fine instrument, but not in the hands of Signor Fellugio. Some of the girls called him 'Signor Fellatio'; but the more discerning—the ones with some appreciation of musicianship—had nicknamed him 'Banjo'. My Signor Balotelli he was not.

I was tempted and succumbed. I sat down to try a few chords and arpeggios. Then I attempted a few bars of *Für Elise*. The soft and sustain pedals were sticky but matched my performance. My hands felt swollen and disobedient. Signor Fellugio and I were more *sympatico* than I cared to acknowledge. Thoroughly defeated by my own mediocrity I called it a day after the opening refrain and rose to leave. As I did so, I realised that I had drawn a crowd. Sophie and Marlène were smiling approvingly. Two of the pot boys—the term 'boys' was a misnomer; both must have been in their forties—joined the throng. Big John, was *petit* in the extreme, and Hole in the Head, was so called because he still had a cavity in his skull left by a Civil War bullet. Both applauded enthusiastically. I blushed.

'What was that?' Sophie asked.

'*Für Elise*.'

'Elise,' pondered Marlène. 'Doesn't she work at the Roxy on Stockton? You sly dog. You can get it cheaper here you know.'

My blush deepened. I bowed diffidently and left.

I needed a good breakfast. Not that I was going to get one any time soon. They might know something about coffee in San Francisco but what passed for sausages and bacon would have incensed an Irish pig at such a meaningless waste of life. As for the bread? The less said about what they call 'sourdough', the better. It was as white as the bricks on the Roman Catholic Pro-Cathedral in Dublin, and about as appetising.

Campbell was waiting for me outside the Green Street doorway to Chez la Peur—I called it the 'tradesman's entrance' though I think it was used more often for dramatic exits. He was seated on a bench smoking a thinner Cuban cigar than was his custom and enjoying the tepid October sunlight. He had about him little of the air of urgency I might have expected of someone investigating a murder. As I got to know him, I realised that Campbell often lived in a Trappist world of his own devising. It was a comforting realm of *non sequiturs* and vagueness to which he would regularly retreat. Today he greeted me with a pensive smile and a gnomic observation.

'You know,' he said, without explanatory preliminaries, 'the Cheyenne believe there are deities all around us. In the skies and the trees. They're everywhere. There may even be one in this cigar.' He dragged on it in a casual gesture of deicide. He then began to emerge from his cocoon. 'Not that all those Gods ever did the Cheyenne much good, mind you. They live on a filthy reservation. By the way, how do you spell "whatwithal"?'

'What …?'

'… withal. How is it spelled?'

'I have no idea what you are talking about. There's no such word.'

'Of course, there is. If "wherewithal" is a word, then so is "whatwithal".'

Once again, his deadpan expression was either that of the consummate practical joker or of someone who firmly believed that you would find the word 'whatwithal' if you were to search the Oxford English Dictionary under the letter 'W'. I didn't know him well enough to be sure.

'So, does that mean "howwithal" is a word? Or "whywithal"?'.

'Now you're just being obtuse,' he said, with fake, or genuine, severity.

I gave up and spelled "whatwithal" for him.

'Are you certain?' he asked. 'There aren't two 'l's' as in "Humpty Dumpty had a great fall"?'

One of us was looking like a complete idiot.

'No … just one.'

'Heavenly!'

He took a piece of paper from his pocket, unfolded it carefully, added something to it in pencil and replaced it. Finally, he snapped back into life. 'So, are we ready?'

'Ready for what?'

'We are paying a visit to Mr. Thomas Newman. Sadly, our chat will not occur at his place of business. I would have enjoyed a trip to the Emerald Brewery. Instead, we are to be entertained at the headquarters of the illustrious Knights of the Red Branch on Mason and O'Farrell.'

'An elegant title for the local chapter of Clan na Gael.'

'I'm sure both names have some fascinating provenance …'

'The Knights of the Red Branch were …' I began. His expression told me I should have waited for the 'but'.

'Will this be of any practical assistance?' he asked.

'Not in the slightest.'

'So why don't we just skip it?'

Campbell was not someone who felt his way into a conversation.

We walked for a while in mute reverie. As we crossed Broadway heading south-west, he broke his silence. I'd have preferred if he'd broken stride. I was already breathless and falling behind.

'Do try and remember that you are here today merely as an observer. Let us try and keep the meeting as friendly as possible. Bury yourself in that sweet little black notebook of yours.'

'What would you like me to observe?' I asked nervously. It occurred to me that a justifiably vengeful Christopher Riley might be among those present. Unless Doghouse was in the doghouse.

'If that is a serious inquiry, which I doubt, I suggest you concentrate on the hands. The hands are the mirrors of the soul.'

Campbell looked as if he was about to become gnomic again. I brought him back to the here and now.

'I thought that was the eyes.'

'That is what the uninitiated believe, of course, but the eyes lie. The hands are entirely truthful. They have their own independent existence. You can command the eyes but never the hands. There is nothing but duplicity and concealment in the eyes. The hands are open and frank.'

I inspected my own hands but found no obvious evidence of the honesty and sincerity of which he spoke. 'I look forward to your monograph on the subject,' I said.

'A further piece of advice. Have both your own hands ready for use should Mr. Riley happen to be present at the meeting.'

With that he lapsed into an imperious silence. How to disturb the complacency of Sergeant Tranquility, I thought, as we walked along Market towards O'Farrell Street? A recent memory impressed itself on me, one that would surely puncture his equanimity.

'Maybe we should have brought Doctor Williams with us, for protection,' I suggested. He refused to rise to the bait.

'I doubt if her presence would help matters.'

'Her Smith and Wesson might.'

'She might not be able to resist the temptation to use it. Given what Newman did to her father. Allegedly.'

I stopped in my tracks. He went on his way unchecked. I then had to run to catch up with him. He could see that he had my attention, so he continued.

'Marcus Williams was a senior policeman when I started on the force. He had very little time for me, it pains me to admit. This was in the days before Newman managed to get himself elected sheriff by cultivating the dead vote. He ran a lucrative business, selling fire insurance in Chinatown. If you didn't pay your monthly premium … well, I'm sure I don't need to sketch in all the details. Williams had Newman and his thugs in his sights. Then he suddenly disappeared. His body was discovered in a drain in Chinatown a fortnight later. He looked like a pincushion. Newman and Riley—Lord of the Knife— both had solid alibis for every minute of their waking lives to that date. These are busy gentlemen, always in company and always able to account for their whereabouts.'

We had stopped at a large ramshackle wooden building with the initials KRB in green letters displayed over the door. I thought of a young Ophelia Williams. Fathers couldn't all be like mine.

'That information appears to have sobered you,' Campbell observed drily. 'I hope you can maintain that demeanour when we get inside.'

Thomas Newman, in the flesh—of which there was no shortage—inspired several contradictory emotions. For a start, I was disappointed to discover that he was rather more refined than I had expected. I'd been hoping for a Yahoo. He was hardly a Houyhnhnm, but he was reasonably well house-trained. Though fleshy, he still contrived to be dapper. While you were aware that he was someone who could secure a painful and interesting death for anyone who crossed him, he also looked like a man who folded his clothes neatly before retiring for the night. He might even have knelt at the foot of the bed and said his prayers.

He talked like a character in a Henry James novel. I hadn't read any at that point, but I have since. Every sentence was as immaculately composed as if someone was taking notes intended for later inclusion in a memoir.

Newman, as Campbell had suspected would be the case, was not alone. But, to my intense relief, Doghouse Riley, polecat in residence, was nowhere to be seen. The large meeting room in the Knights of the Red Branch building—which, I was unjustifiably flattered to discover, boasted a portrait of my revolutionary namesake on one of its green-painted walls—also sported two small but heavy-set and exceptionally hairy men. Then there was the Gargantua standing directly behind Newman. He was fully a head taller than even the impossibly lanky Haddo. His frame, however, resembled that of the Western Union headquarters, rather than one of its telegraph poles. The giant, it transpired, was an Irishman named Howard, or Howie. I never quite established whether this was his given name or his surname. Aside from his great bulk, the striking thing about Howie was his head. This would have been a phrenologist's delight. The naturally occurring bumps were a map of San Francisco itself: all sweeping hills and majestic ridges. However, I doubt if it was constructed to house a large cerebrum. There was plenty of space available for development. Howie had not been hired to ponder the secrets of the universe and ask the important questions, such as 'Why does no one want the colour grey in their national flag?' He was employed to stand around and look like an imminent threat to life and limb, a skill at which he excelled. A late replacement for Ollie Madden perhaps, the other elephant in the room?

Howie's companions—their names were O'Neill and Byrne—who stood on either side of him, looked like twins, although, apparently, they weren't even related. What made it difficult to distinguish between them, apart from their identical stocky frames—which looked to have been created from the same mould—was their thick, voluminous red beards and the complete absence of a lock of hair north of their eyebrows. Something about their intensity led me to suspect that they lacked the indifference of the casual hireling. I was more comfortable with mercenaries. The hired hand could calculate when an assigned task was above his rate of pay. The ideologue never knew when to shout 'Pax'.

When Campbell introduced himself to Newman, he was largely ignored. Newman brusquely acknowledged his existence with a dismissive 'Campbell, yes, the one they call Dixie. Now I know why.' As Campbell bridled, Newman turned his attention to me. He was ostentatiously courteous and didn't wait to be introduced.

'Mr. Orpen, delighted to meet you at last. Tales of your Irish adventures precede you. News travels fast when an Irishman of Mr. Orpen's stock graces our city,' he explained to Campbell in mock deference. 'I deprecate the Irish fascination with aristocracy myself, but old habits die hard. Welcome to San Francisco, Mr. Orpen. I trust your stay amongst us will be pleasant, and of exceptionally short duration.'

His bonhomie being complete affectation, I affected to ignore him. Fortunately, he didn't extend his hand. I sat to Campbell's right, on the opposite side of a long wooden table to our ostensibly genial host.

'Tea, I think. No reason not to be hospitable. Even to a seasoned *thuggee* like your good self, Mr. Orpen.' Newman began. He called towards the door by which we had entered. 'Rachel...' After a brief hiatus, a young woman popped her head into the room. She was tall and attractive, with a shock of unruly blonde hair, and dressed entirely in black. 'Some tea for our guests if you please, Rachel.' She said nothing, just looked past him at the two 'guests'. Her expression was one of revolted disapproval. I reckoned that the tea, when it arrived, would be strong enough to cause serious injury. She closed the door behind her, and Newman resumed.

'I would ask what I can do for you two gentlemen, but let's not beat about the bush,' he began. 'You are undoubtedly here to inquire where I was on the night of the tragic death of Daniel Horton.' Before Campbell had an opportunity to utter a further word – indeed all he had done so far was to identify himself – Newman continued. 'I think you can vouch for where I was. Howard, tell Constable Campbell.'

'Sergeant! Sergeant Campbell.'

'Really? Apologies. Tell *Sergeant* Campbell.'

Howie smiled, revealing a mouth devoid of at least half its expected retinue of teeth. 'You were here, Boss. Playing bridge. With me, O'Neill and Byrne.' He pointed to the two russet and under-employed goons, who nodded in confirmation. It was probably his choice of fiction that was most galling. Neither Campbell nor I would have credited any alibi contrived by Newman. However, we had no option but to accept the word of three upstanding San Francisco taxpayers, viz. that he had spent the night with them. But bridge! Please! Poker, checkers, even chess. But bridge was gilding the lily, added to the fabrication to accentuate its blatant lack of credibility.

He was rubbing our noses in it. We'd been trumped. Campbell made the obvious response.

'Your companions, I take it, are familiar with the rules of the game, Mr. Newman. We could put that to the test right away if anyone has a deck of cards.' I was about to reach for the pack in my pocket when I realised that such a move might be misinterpreted.

'I fear not,' Newman smiled. 'They are mere beginners. I was teaching them the rudiments of the game at their request. They wish to broaden their horizons. Praiseworthy, don't you agree? But I doubt if much of my tuition stuck, did it, Howard?'

'Not much, boss.' Howie continued smiling, greatly enjoying Newman's little joke. I diverted myself by counting his teeth. I longed for the opportunity to remove some of them, assuming my fist could stretch as far north as his mouth.

'You must have spent most of the evening as dummy, Howard?' I was somewhat taken aback when I heard this tactless jibe, even more so because it had come from me.

'Easy,' muttered Campbell under his breath. Howie's smile vanished. He shifted position. It wasn't exactly a move in my direction, but it was a prelude to one. Newman intervened.

'Thank you, Howard. That won't be necessary.'

Just then Rachel returned with a tray, three cups—two of which looked as if they should have been retired from service shortly before the American War of Independence—and a pot of tea. The two chipped cups were placed in front of Campbell and myself. She poured for Newman, then walked around to our side of the long table, approaching me first. Her countenance suggested that she might be about to empty the scalding contents of the teapot into my lap. Instead, she poured what looked like barely diluted tar into my beaker. Then, putting the pot down on the table, she picked up my cup and spat violently into the brew. With what looked like a grimace, but might, on reflection, have been a self-satisfied smile, she passed it back to me. When I mumbled a stunned—but unfailingly polite—'I won't bother, thank you' under my breath, she affected an exaggerated and scornful curtsy and left. Newman watched as she departed and then flashed a dusty smile.

'An interesting young lady,' he said. I had to agree. 'She has a reputation as a healer.' I looked at my cup and wondered if it was now endowed with miraculous curative qualities. 'She also makes a mean soup,' he added.

I was curious to know what she used for seasoning.

'Was there anything else you gentlemen wanted to discuss?' Newman asked blandly.

Campbell, still transfixed by the generous dollop of saliva floating in my tea, recovered himself.

'Perhaps you could tell us about the state of your relationship with Dan Horton?'

'Daggers drawn would be a good description I think, though probably a shade insensitive given the nature of his demise,' Newman observed urbanely.

'You and he didn't get on?'

'That would be something of an understatement, Sergeant Campbell. We had very serious political differences. Neither of us made any secret of that. But that doesn't give me a motive for killing him. Politics isn't personal.'

'When did you see him last?'

'I think you already know the answer to that question, given that I believe both of you were present at the time. My sincere apologies if I rudely neglected to greet you on that occasion but I did notice you. You may recall that Horton and I had a brief altercation in Ned Allen's place on the afternoon of his demise. Is there anything further you wish to discuss?'

Campbell looked as if he was about to say something and then subsided. Newman turned his attention to me.

'So, Sergeant Orpen … it is Sergeant, isn't it? Another impoverished Irish exile to England,' he remarked disdainfully. 'Tell me, have you been replaced by a cow? According to Mr. Marx, that is the inevitable fate of the Irish emigrant. I assume your ancestry is Scottish, Mr. Campbell. In which case, your people would have given way to a flock of sheep.'

As it happens, I had been replaced by a strapping lad from west Cork, recruited to the Dublin Metropolitan Police from the Royal Irish Constabulary, but I decided that piece of intelligence could not compete with Newman's pointed sarcasm, so I kept it to myself.

'And now here you are. You took instruction from Mr. Greeley, did you?'

'I'm not sure I follow,' I said, feigning lack of interest.

'Go west, young man,' interjected Howie, looking immensely pleased with himself. I assumed he'd been a witness to this line of rhetoric before. He was hardly acquainted with the journalism of Horace Greeley.

'Thank you, Howard,' Newman continued without missing a beat, though clearly displeased by the interruption. The exchange, however, was enough to allow Campbell to recover his equilibrium.

'Speaking of sheep, tell me about your relationship with Charles Schroeder if you would?' he asked, summoning a surprising degree of *faux* ennui to the request. He managed to look as if he wanted to be somewhere else. I certainly did.

Newman looked nonplussed at first but covered his surprise quickly with an unconvincing smile. He turned to his three heavies. His jowls quivered as he moved.

'Observe, gentlemen,' he told them. 'You may learn something about the congenial art of angling. Sergeant Campbell is going on a fishing expedition. My relationship with Mr. Schroeder is hardly germane to our discussion, but you may cast your rod if you wish. What precisely did you want to know?'

Campbell thought for a moment. 'He seems like a strange bed-fellow for someone who, up to very recently, was a Pharoah of The Workingmen's Party.'

Newman cracked a slight smile. 'That displays either a lack of imagination, *a chara*, or a naivety about the realities of our city's pol-itics. Mr. Schroeder and I have discovered, let's say … a confluence of interests. You must understand that, despite the religion of my birth, I don't entirely subscribe to the conciliatory sentiments expressed, so poetically, in the Sermon on the Mount. "Blessed are those who seize their opportunities" was a serious omission in my view. Then there is the Golden Rule of San Francisco politics, "Do unto others before they do unto you". I'm seizing my opportunities and doing unto oth-ers, in tandem with Mr. Schroeder. For the present. Is that a crime?'

Campbell ignored the question. 'And the confluence of interests? That would be the expulsion of the Chinese I presume?'

Newman smiled again. 'We are straying quite a distance from my alibi for the murder of Dan Horton are we not?' He turned to Howie, O'Neill and Byrne. 'I hope you are learning the fundamentals of fly fishing, gentlemen.' Then he returned to Campbell. 'Yes, the Chinese. Our unfortunate oriental neighbours. It might surprise you to know that I have absolutely nothing against the Celestials. They are a fine upstanding, hard-working community. We can learn a lot from them, but I would prefer to do that through a very powerful telescope. I have no need to study their culture, their medicine, their religion, their working methods, or indeed their criminality, up close.'

'You think they should be rounded up and deported?'

'I think they should go home. I think they will be much more content in China and if they have any objection to the current rulers of that fair land, as they appear to do, then they should set about replacing them, just as our Founding Fathers did with Gibbering George, the Mad King of England. And, just as, someday, the Broth-erhood will do to your employers, Sergeant Orpen. Crocker, Stanford,

Huntington and Hopkins brought the Chinese here in the first place, to build their railroad to Utah. Once they built it—from Sacramento mind, not from San Francisco—they had no further need of the Chinese, so they dumped them on the city, and built impressive houses for themselves in the Heavens above. They've never had to observe the result of their handiwork at close quarters. My attitude is readily explained. The Chinese came here to do a job: to build the Central Pacific Railroad. That job is done. They've made a fortune for the Big Four and their heirs, so either the railroaders can house them on Nob Hill, or the Qing Emperor can accommodate them. Is that too much to ask?'

'And despite the fact that Mr. Schroeder lives among the Huntingtons and the Crockers, he shares your philosophy, not theirs?'

'Mr. Schroeder is consistent. He saw what was coming a decade ago and tried to stop it then, but the railroad was too powerful for him. Now the Big Four own California. We might as well change the name of the state to Stanford. The railroad interests have us by the testicles. They set the going rates for everything of consequence. They burn the competition. You try and establish a nickel ferry to Oakland and see how far you get.'

It all sounded well-rehearsed, like a stump speech. Which, of course, it probably was. Like all demagogues, Newman's rhetoric contained a grain of truth, but he exploited that grain like an oyster, not a farmer.

'You are confident that, with Mr. Schroeder's assistance you will win the Third District by-election then?'

I had no idea where, if anywhere, Campbell was going. He was beginning to sound more like his journalist friend Walsh than a police sergeant.

Newman's grin broadened. He turned to his hirsute acolytes. 'We appear to have moved from angling to whaling, so pay close attention, gentlemen.' He addressed Campbell, the response coming out as a long, resigned sigh.

'I'm sure the graves will give up their dead as always, *a chara*, irrespective of what assistance Mr. Schroeder offers. If you're an Irish voter in San Francisco, passing into the next world is no excuse for failure to exercise the franchise. The deceased actually find it easier to cast their ballots here. No one with a club or a bat tries to discourage them. If my opponent manages to recruit more immortal souls to his cause, then he will win. If not ...' He let the idea swing in the air for a while, before chopping it down. 'You could never confuse the politics of this city with Sunday School, could you? Now, if you've had enough political instruction for the day, I have business to attend to.'

Just then a door opened to our left. We had a visitor, and, from my point of view, he was most unwelcome. Doghouse Riley sauntered into the room. His right arm was in a sling, which was a relief. No knife play for him for a while. When Riley saw me, he stopped mid-saunter and bared his teeth. They looked like they were all his own.

'What's that fucking peeler doing here?' He'd looked a bit shifty when he walked into the room but the sight of me energised him. He blossomed, like a carnivorous pitcher plant.

'Good day to you too, Christopher,' Newman responded suavely, never taking his eyes off me. 'These gentlemen are our guests. For the moment. Let's assume that they are here under a flag of truce.'

'And as welcome as the smell of a knacker's yard,' Riley grunted.

'How's the shoulder?' Newman inquired genially, watching for my reaction. 'Does it hurt much?'

'Only when I laugh,' Riley growled.

'Anyone know any good jokes?' I asked.

It wasn't intended as a pleasantry, so I wasn't greatly bothered that it didn't go down well. Only Newman failed to react. Riley almost jumped across the table, in so far as anyone with their arm in a sling is capable of such a movement. The Hairy Ones braced themselves. Acting on Campbell's advice, my hand moved immediately to my pocket. I wasn't reaching for the cards. Riley was quicker. It took him barely half a second to find his knife. Half a second later it was embedded in the wall behind me. I could feel the air parting as it flew between my left ear and Campbell's scalp. When I looked back at Riley, he already had another knife in his hand. His left hand. The duplicitous bastard was ambidextrous.

'That was just a warning to keep your hand out of your pocket, polis-man,' Riley barked. 'If I was ready to kill you, then you'd be dead.'

'That will do, Christopher.' Newman had remained impressively detached and impassive, but even he was starting to look tense. 'We don't want any trouble with the police. Put the knife down.'

'When he takes his hand away from that pocket, I will,' Riley snarled. I could have pointed out that I was merely hoping to return an item of his personal property, but, I reasoned, that might not improve the situation.

'I'm sure Mr. Orpen wishes you no further harm,' hissed Newman. 'Put it down.' Slowly and reluctantly, Riley placed the knife on the table. I became conscious of Campbell's breathing, conscious that I hadn't heard it since the knife had passed between us. I didn't dare look at him. I knew he would not be pleased at my friendly badinage.

'Do you need a receipt for that?' Campbell asked blankly, indicating the knife in the wall behind us.

Newman smiled and relaxed. He then fixed me with a disconcertingly amused gaze. 'So, this is the man who got the better of you, Christopher? He doesn't look very tough. I'm curious. What age are you, Mr. Orpen, as a matter of interest?'

I shrugged. 'Old enough. What about you?'

Riley intervened. 'Don't worry, boss. If you really want to know what age he is, I can cut him off at the neck and you can count the rings.' This was turning into a real party; everyone was doing jokes.

Newman now rose from his seat, revealing, as he did so, his impressive girth. The man didn't have a middle so much as an equator. When he spoke, his voice was pure maple syrup.

'Mr. Campbell and Mr. Orpen were just leaving, weren't you, gentlemen. I think you've got all you need.'

Campbell took the hint. He stood up and motioned for me to accompany him. But I found something about Newman's complacency irksome. And Riley's sneering countenance was galling. I'm not unduly proud of what happened next, but I allowed myself to get the better of me.

'Before we go, can I just ask does anyone here know Ollie Madden?' I heard myself inquiring as we reached the door. I was surprised his name hadn't come up in the conversation. These Red Branch Knights were an unsentimental lot. 'We were great friends in Dublin, you see. Kept an ear out for each other, you might say. I just wanted to look him up. We used to swim together at the Forty Foot. A great bathing spot near Dublin. Very keen swimmer was Ollie.'

There was what could only be described as a primeval roar from Riley. Quick as a flash he picked up his shiv and he was charging at me. I already had his borrowed knife in my hand, eager to complete the job I should have finished on the wharf. This one was going to be for Ophelia Williams and her father, I thought, with specious *noblesse oblige*. But I was to be disappointed. As Riley passed him, Newman stuck out his foot. Riley wasn't expecting any intervention from his allies. He screamed in pain as his injured arm hit the deck.

'Howie,' Newman snapped. 'Smother him.'

Howie obeyed instantly. A second later his knee was in the small of Riley's back. Riley unleashed a torrent of obscenities. I would never have thought a good Roman Catholic was capable of such a churlish display of blasphemy.

Campbell was calmness personified. Calmness with a revolver in its hand, mind you.

'I'm obliged, Mr. Newman,' he said softly. 'I suggest you keep him there until my colleague and I have left, because a single twitch from him and he'll hit that back wall so hard, you'll be able to paint over him.'

That is exactly what he said. Verbatim. Fifty years on and I can remember every comma. The threat was even more effective for being rendered in an indifferent monotone with a Southern inflection. I hadn't discovered it at the time, but Campbell was a keen reader of dime novels. The warning was straight out of the Old Sleuth Library, which he devoured avidly and then tossed aside in contempt as he finished each one. His disdain didn't stop him from spending ten cents on the next issue—or stealing the best lines.

Ignoring this highly derivative threat, as we left the room—backing out of the door—Riley was still screaming imprecations at me, Campbell, Howie, Newman and President Chester A. Arthur for all I know. His mildest profanity was to the effect that Ollie Madden was a better man than any Dublin 'peeler'. There was also a baseless allegation about my mother having ministered to the sexual needs of the entire first *and* second battalions of the Dublin Fusiliers. I let that one go. The man was not to know that my dear mother would never have had dealings with anyone below the rank of captain.

In the hallway, we met the Affable Rachel. She had obviously been listening at the door, though she could probably have heard the din half a mile away without bothering to eavesdrop. As we passed her, the intensity of her stare caused Campbell to shudder involuntarily. Taking this as her cue, she spat viciously in our direction. The woman had a bottomless supply of saliva.

Once outside, Campbell quickly put as much distance between us and the headquarters of the Knights of the Red Branch as possible. In the circumstances I had no difficulty keeping pace with him as we strode along O'Farrell Street towards Market. There is something about headlong flight that opens the lungs most efficiently. Campbell was clearly exasperated and in no mood for conversation. It was not until we reached the corner of O'Farrell and Powell that he stopped abruptly and turned to face me. The rapid walk had, at least, had the effect of soothing him to the level of mere controlled fury.

'You know, I foresee a great future for your pale Irish flesh on the surface of a bass drum if you continue along current lines, my young friend.' The word 'friend' was laced with enough irony to fit out the hulls of a fleet of battleships. 'I may even skin you myself. Shit!'

The oath was not addressed to me. He was looking over my shoulder as he spoke. I turned around to see what had startled him. Less than a block away, and gaining ground rapidly, were Riley, Howie, O'Neill and Byrne. They didn't look as if they had come to apologise.

'Let's pick up this conversation later,' Campbell said. He turned and started to walk at speed – a sprint for any normal human being. I didn't need any encouragement to follow.

Just then a carriage with a familiar driver halted opposite us and I heard a welcome voice call out.

'Are you gentlemen in need of a ride?'

CHAPTER SIX

OPHELIA WILLIAMS

16 October

I admit it was a gesture of bravado belying the metallic taste in my mouth and the heavy weight in the pit of my stomach. What Orpen and Campbell were probably in need of was divine intervention, and my humble carriage wasn't exactly a winged chariot.

I'd spotted the danger before they did. When they emerged from the glorified wooden shack that housed the Shites of the Red Branch, if they had looked uphill towards Geary Street, they would have seen a discreet figure driving a slow-moving buggy and trying not to look Amish. Or conspicuous.

I was there on a whim. I was eavesdropping when I overheard the Hall of Justice Desk Sergeant chatting with the repulsive Thaddeus Kelly—a man who makes even Wellington Campbell look like Sir Galahad. I was passing the desk on my way downstairs to examine one of my stoic Chinese clients. He had expired at the business end of a knife in a melee on Stockton. Kelly, ogling me as I passed, was inquiring about Campbell from Sergeant Major. That is his real name, Sergeant Peter Major. Unfortunate, I know. I doubted if Kelly's interest was merely professional. After his time in charge there, he must have had a lot of treasure buried in Chinatown. Maybe Campbell had been spotted heading out with a pick and shovel!

When the desk Sergeant told him that Campbell and Orpen were meeting Newman in the Red Branch Hall, my curiosity was piqued. I took an intense personal interest every time Thomas Newman belched or broke wind. He was an elusive man, and I wanted a quiet word. I decided, on the spot, that my defunct Celestial could wait for a while. I must admit that I had no clear idea why I was suddenly intent on driving a buggy into one of the less salubrious parts of the city, in dubious pursuit of my obsession with Newman. Was I going to run him under my wheels if the opportunity presented itself? The very idea sent a frisson down my spine. So, I borrowed my mother's rig.

That was why I was touring the seedy Tenderloin in a buggy with a team named Sitting Bull and Crazy Horse. I had no intention of tracking the movements of Campbell and Orpen until I realized they were not alone. I spotted their pursuers as I drove down Mason and recognized one of them instantly. There was no sign of Newman, but here was an equally generous offering, perfectly gift-wrapped. Dogs-hit Riley, presenting an open target. When I reached the next intersection, I noticed a woman emerge from the KRB shack and walk along O'Farrell. She was well-muffled and dressed entirely in black. When one of the trolls turned and looked in her general direction, she ducked into a doorway.

It was apparent that Campbell and Orpen, for at least a block, were unaware of any danger. I was undecided on what I should do. The decision was taken out of my hands when Campbell, for some reason best known to himself, stopped, and turned to give Orpen hell. That was when Dixie-dick realized that they had unwelcome company. The Red Branch goblins twigged they had been spotted and made like an uneducated school of sharks who have just beheld breakfast. I whipped Sitting Bull and Crazy Horse down O'Farrell towards Market, as if they were Preakness thoroughbreds. I overtook the four trolls and as I caught up with the two policemen I slowed down and shouted.

'Are you gentlemen in need of a ride?'

At first both men looked stunned. My presence didn't add up.

'Or maybe you feel lucky?' I suggested.

By now Riley had recognized the danger. When he saw me slow down and lean out of the buggy, he shouted a warning. He and his three fellow primates broke into a run. They could see, like spiders watching a pinioned fly throw off his silky shackles, that if they didn't hurry, they were going to be robbed of their prey.

Orpen jumped on board without further invitation. Both of us looked inquiringly at Campbell. Riley, accompanied by a lumbering giant and two red-bearded leprechauns, had now narrowed the gap to about a hundred yards. Despite the imminent arrival of four highly qualified killers, Campbell stood rooted to the spot. For a second or two I wondered if principled misogyny would trump personal safety. In which case, Orpen would have no alternative but to jump back down and join the donnybrook. So be it, I figured. I had my two good friends, Mr. Smith and Mr. Wesson, on hand. Never again would I get such a watertight pretext to end Dogshit Riley's pointless existence.

Campbell looked like he was actively mulling over that Shakespearean line—the one about discretion and valor. Discretion finally won on points. He leaped up on the buggy. I whipped the horses into action again but, as luck would have it, that was when Riley's travelling zoo caught up with us.

There must have been some sort of hoodlum hierarchy in operation; otherwise, you would have to wonder why it was left to the two smallest members of Riley's goon squad to try and halt the progress of a pair of weighty stallions. The leprechauns tried to grab the bridles of Sitting Bull and Crazy Horse. It was no contest. Both were brushed aside effortlessly by the two big geldings, and I fancy my wheels passed over the leg of the one on Crazy Horse's side, but that might just be wishful thinking on my part. There was a definite bump and a crunch, but O'Farrell didn't have the smoothest of surfaces back then, so it might just have been a pothole. Which would have been a crying shame.

But if Riley was prepared to hang back and let his flunkies take their lumps, I certainly wasn't.

'Here, grab these,' I snapped at Orpen, handing him the reins and the whip. He looked puzzled but obeyed. The London Metropolitan Police had tutored their man to an exceptionally high level in mindless obedience. A second later and the Smith and Wesson was in my hand. Because of my passengers I had to choose starboard instead of port. Reaching around the wrong side of the buggy I was forced to wait until we were well clear before I could get a bead on Riley. We were already passing Grant—I think it was still called Dupont back then—and making a right turn toward Market on one wheel. I still managed to get off two shots, but I completely missed the bastard. Nobody is any good at that range, certainly not with a revolver, and anyone who tells you otherwise is a blowhard. The volley, however, stopped the goblins in their tracks.

'I don't think I've ever seen a more attractive and welcome buggy in my life,' exclaimed Orpen when I took the reins back from him, still cursing my luck. The Irishman's reaction was a clear manifestation of a medical condition I have just invented called 'hyperbolic relief'. It was a tatty old rig, but I suppose he didn't have aesthetics in mind. I turned left off Market and took us north, towards Portsmouth Square. As we drove up Kearny, I dragged on the reins and slowed Sitting Bull and Crazy Horse to a trot. Crossing Geary, I saw the woman in black again. I could have sworn a strained look passed between her and Orpen. He started telling me some fairy tale about the Cup of Tea from Hell. I can't say I paid much heed. It began to rain.

Within seconds it was tossing meatballs, and we were soaked to the skin. The rain rapped off the roof of the buggy, a flimsy covering that offered no protection. Within minutes it seemed as if every street north of Market had water cascading down its gutters and overflowing its picturesque potholes. The carriage almost slowed to a viscous halt. It was like driving over porridge. Except that Riley and his menagerie had already given up the chase, they might well have caught up with us. Oh, what fun that would have been. I still had four bullets left.

Orpen, who was almost embarrassingly grateful for being rescued, was doing all the talking. Campbell was studiously silent as the Irishman chattered. He sat, slumped, on the far side of Orpen, looking like he was facing five years of tax demands. He never even glanced in my direction. When he finally interrupted Orpen's flow, it was like a dam magically materializing at the headwaters of the Colorado river.

'So,' he began slowly. I wasn't sure if it was leading to a question. It was. 'Y'all just happened to be passing?'

'Out on a little joyride. My mother's horses needed to stretch their legs.'

Campbell's eyebrows rose in that universally acknowledged gesture of utter disbelief. 'Do you often exercise your team in the Tenderloin?' he asked sardonically.

The area to the west of Union Square already had a pernicious character and was beginning to acquire its very own name, the Tenderloin. No one really knew why. There was little tenderness in evidence, though loins were certainly overworked after dark. While not yet on a par with the Barbary Coast, its reputation for wickedness was as unsavory as honey dribbled onto a plate of Turkish delight. Virtuous women did not venture too far west of Union Square in those days. Come to think of it, virtuous women did not smoke, or carry guns.

'You wouldn't, by any chance, have been following us, would you?' Campbell asked darkly.

'Don't flatter yourself, Sergeant.'

That was when a ripe idea occurred to me. Chastisement beckoned.

'I'll take you somewhere to dry off,' I said, whipping the team into action again. I knew exactly where to deliver them.

Five minutes later the buggy was drawing up outside the Bull Run bar. When we stopped, Campbell looked puzzled. Orpen merely smiled beatifically. Campbell spoke first. He was impressed despite himself. I had plans to ensure that his favorable opinion would be fleeting.

'An excellent choice,' he muttered, almost inaudibly, 'if somewhat surprising.'

Orpen was charmed. 'Well, well, well. You could almost have been studying our drinking habits,' he trilled. When he heard that, Campbell's features clouded, but he said nothing. I allowed Don Quixote and Sancho Panza to alight from the buggy and made as if to continue on my way. Once they were through the doors of the saloon, however, I tethered the horses and followed them inside. I had a surprise in store for the irascible Campbell.

As I was about to descend from the buggy, I noticed something embedded in its side. It was a bowie knife with a plain wooden handle. I had no doubt about its provenance. I pulled it out of the soft wood and brought it with me.

Campbell was just settling into a seat by the big open fire when he saw me walk into the bar. Not even Rembrandt could have done justice to the intricacy of his emotions as I breezed in. But when Ned Allen greeted me warmly, his face lighting up like a Christmas tree, the portrait of Campbell became pure *chiaroscuro*, his visage barely retaining enough light to emerge from the darkness.

'Miss Williams.'

'Ophelia, please, Ned.'

'Ophelia, welcome back. We haven't seen you here in an age,' Ned enthused, each syllable of friendly greeting a dagger through Campbell's heart. His scowl would have done credit to Moses descending from the mountain with the Ten Commandments, tired and hungry, and beholding the Children of Israel doing unmentionable things to one another while worshipping false gods.

Ned was nicknamed Bull Run, but his face was like a map of the siege of Chattanooga. The union forces were arranged in the trenches across his forehead. The Confederates were south of the tree line formed by eyebrows that never quite separated. Whenever he frowned, a division of the Union army disappeared. When he smiled, the rebels were routed.

'What can I get you?' breezed Ned. 'Not your usual, I presume?'

That would have been a glass of milk. My father would often bring me to the Bull Run as a young girl, when I was left in his charge. It was preferable, he claimed, to watching me cheat at cards back home. We would always end up listening to Ned Allen's tall tales of the Civil War, improbable and self-aggrandizing anecdotes that my father warned me to take with a bucket of salt. While he would sip a beer and express his feigned astonishment at Ned's good fortune in surviving so many full-tilt encounters with murderous rebels, I would drink my milk and draw body parts with the pencil and paper my father always had the foresight to provide. I hadn't been in the Bull Run for at least six years and my 'usual' was the most innocuous drink in a kindergarten, but Campbell wasn't to know that.

'Not today, Ned,' I replied loudly, trying to look as if I had been weaned on neat bourbon. I struggled for a second or two to imagine what tipple Campbell would find most offensive in the hands of a lady drinking in a low dive and settled for a beer. I trusted that Ned's sentimental memories of a personable young lady in her late teens would ensure that I was not dispensed anything too poisonous.

Throughout this performance Orpen smiled cordially if a tad disconcertedly. Campbell remained a dark study, waiting for an idle pre-Raphaelite to come along and capture his lowering countenance. When I sought leave to join them, Orpen politely moved to secure a chair for me.

'Must you?' Campbell asked.

'Must I what?'

'Join us. We were having such an interesting conversation before you … someone who, I am sure, likes to think of herself as a lady … wandered into a saloon of very little distinction and ordered a drink.'

I ignored him and tossed the bowie knife onto the table.

'A gift from Mr. Riley,' I said. Orpen whistled. 'The left side of the buggy took the brunt,' I explained. 'Nothing of much importance there.'

'About an inch from hitting Campbell?' ventured Orpen.

'I rest my case,' I said, meeting Campbell's baleful stare with a well-practiced scowl.

Orpen took up the knife and looked it over. 'I might hang on to this,' he said. 'I already own its twin.' This was followed by an awkward silence. Rather than allow it to ferment Orpen chose to prattle.

'Your name is intriguing, by the way, Doctor Williams. "Ophelia, Ophelia, when sorrows come they come not single spies but in battalions." He waited for a reaction. I didn't give him a nickel. I've had more Shakespeare quoted at me in a short lifetime than Anne Hathaway. After a beat or two I relented, if you can call it relenting.

'You should meet my sister … Salomé' His hand went instinctively to his neck. It was all I could do not to laugh.

Campbell had been watching with little apparent interest. Only when Orpen lapsed into silence, did he intervene.

'Are you a lady who often seeks entertainment in low saloons, Miss Williams?' I granted him the 'Miss' merely because he leaned so excessively on the word 'lady'. We hadn't quite reached the unsightly neighborhood of contempt, but we were adjacent.

'Only ones with beer as excellent as Ned's,' I responded gaily. I hadn't touched mine yet. Since this seemed an apt moment to do so, I raised the glass to my lips. The nauseating aroma announced itself first and the flavor was even more repulsive than the smell. It was like dead cat in cider. It was all I could do to avoid gagging. The slightest tremor on my part would have given the game away and ruined my pleasure in provoking Campbell's lordly disfavor.

'An excellent brew,' I said, quelling the instinct to throw up. While it would have offered momentary satisfaction to have covered Campbell from head to toe in amber-tinted vomit, it would have been far less gratifying than forcing him to behold a 'modern' lady in all her shocking modernity.

I was tempted to use this opportunity to goad Orpen a little as well. He was harmless enough, so I had no intention of seriously embarrassing him. But the previous night, close to my home in North Beach, I had spotted him in the company of a young woman with an impressive mound of blonde hair. I was pretty certain that Orpen had noticed me as well and had taken evasive action to avoid an embarrassing meeting.

I had just decided to reserve all my cartridges for Campbell when he chose that moment to remonstrate with Orpen. I had no idea what had occurred during their visit to Papa Newman and the Knights of the Red Branch, but the Sergeant was obviously not best pleased at the outcome, and he clearly blamed the Irishman.

'You need to learn to keep a civil tongue in your head, boy,' said Campbell tartly, 'Keep that up and you'll be sitting out my interview with Charles Schroeder.'

'You're going to talk to him?' Orpen's interest had been piqued. It was how you punish a small child: hold out the prospect of a trip to the beach and then immediately withdraw it.

'I assume he'll be expecting me. I imagine Newman will report our little exchange to him. But I'll have to run it past Lees, who will probably bring it to Crowley.'

Orpen merely shrugged. I felt sorry for him and decided to call Campbell's feeble bluff. Ignoring the lowering detective, I turned to Orpen. 'Whatever you do, don't antagonize Schroeder's wife. She's performing for me next week.'

'You know her?'

'Well enough to be optimistic that she'll agree to sing at the Disabled Policeman's—'

'If you give me your absolute guarantee,' Campbell interjected tersely, 'that you will assume the demeanor of a Benedictine monk, then I suppose I can take a chance. In the meantime, try and stay clear of Christopher Riley.'

'Can't we arrest him?' he asked. 'He did try to kill us after all.' Orpen picked up the knife. 'Exhibit A.'

'That could have hit the buggy anywhere between Market and here. I'm sure Miss Williams has many enemies.' Campbell's face betrayed the presence of at least one. Orpen replaced the knife resignedly. I let that one go. It was outside the strike zone. I was waiting for a pitch right across home plate. I picked up the knife and began to study it carefully. Best there were no weapons to hand.

'You wouldn't be nervous about trying to arrest Riley, now would you?' I asked, with aggressive innocence. I could almost hear Orpen flinch. Campbell flushed. He dragged on his cigar and blew a mouthful of smoke in my direction.

'An ability to concentrate on matters that concern you would be very valuable in your case, Miss Williams,' he finally hissed. 'Stick to cutting up Chinamen and we will all get along like the Pony Express. It might also serve to keep you out of dens of ill-repute such as this, where only one kind of woman is ever seen.'

He hadn't exactly used the word 'slattern', but he might as well have done. Even Orpen had heard enough. 'Steady on, Campbell. You can't talk to a lady like that.' Campbell inhaled again. As he exhaled, he observed laconically, 'I wasn't aware that I was talking to a lady.'

Orpen suddenly looked like he wanted to be somewhere a lot safer. An active volcano? The womb? My eyes fell on my drink. I really wasn't fond of beer, but I didn't want to see it go to waste. Rising from my seat, I lifted the glass as theatrically as possible and slowly poured the contents over Campbell's head.

On my way out, I flashed Ned my most winning smile. He returned it with interest. Beneath the line of trees, the rebel army was routed.

CHAPTER SEVEN

ORPEN

17 October, mid-morning

During my first few days in San Francisco, my only exercise – other than the lethal tango with Madden – had involved performing card tricks for the female members of Bella La Peur's workforce or trying to keep pace with Wellington Campbell. So, it felt good to be back on the open water in a boat, albeit in wilder conditions than those to which I was accustomed. The difference between the waves of San Francisco Bay and the ripples of the River Liffey, or the Thames, is the difference between a timid lapdog and a slavering wolf. On the lower reaches of the Liffey, near Trinity College boathouse at Island-bridge, your chances of being tipped from a rowing shell into the river by a single-minded wave were far less than than in the spiteful choppy waters of the Bay. Lose control of an oar here, and you were likely to marinade in its icy sauce.

The boat that allowed me to remain in some sort of acceptable physical condition was provided by the South End Rowing Club. Haddo had offered to fix me up with temporary membership of the more aristocratic Dolphin Club, but it was just a bit too caviar for me. The South Enders were more steak and onions. They had what they referred to, tongue in cheek, as a 'clubhouse' at Third and Berry near China Basin. They liked to stick it to the Dolphiniums that South End was four years older. And, sure enough, the clubhouse looked as if it had been built from the boards of the *Nina*, *Pinta* and *Santa Maria* after Columbus had no further need of them.

That day I pulled for an hour against wind, wave, and the most contrary and confusing currents you will find in Neptune's watery kingdom. The China Cove breeze that threatened to capsize my shell had subsided as I walked up Second Street, passing the well-appointed Rincon Hill, and then crossed Market at the bottom of Montgomery.

Here was a street with a multiple personality. It was part whore, part pauper and part merchant, but mostly whore—an unforgiving quicksand that was the purlieu of prostitutes, pimps, footpads, and gamblers. It was far seedier even than its namesake in Dublin. I often wondered who this Montgomery fellow was who had offended the genteel inhabitants of two cities so much that an open sewer had been named after him in each. In Dublin, it was nicknamed 'Monto'. There it was also the favourite haunt of randy military types, and more than a few respectable citizens whose wives would not have approved of their visits to such a depraved neighbourhood. I understand the Monstrous Regimen of Dublin's God Botherers finally closed it down a few years ago.

It was while I was wrapped up in these philosophical musings, on the nature of the human condition and the coincidences of street nomenclature, that I first became acquainted with Bill Briggs. I didn't know anything about him at the time, which made his extravagant behaviour seem very curious indeed. Briggs owned a faro joint that should have been closed down a decade before, after the passage of a well-intentioned city ordnance against gambling.

He operated his tables, with impunity and apparent immunity, behind almost impenetrable, well-barricaded doors, for a decade after every other faro game had been run out of town. But what brought him to my attention that day was his penchant for standing in the middle of the street and tossing coins to waifs. This he did only sporadically, but with just enough frequency to make it worthwhile stalking him if you were less than five feet tall. He would laugh while the urchins grovelled in the gutter and scrambled for his largesse. I only saw him do it once, but he was noted for it. I recall the occasion vividly, because that was when I made my first acquaintance with the Little Bitches.

Briggs was walking towards me, southwards along Montgomery. He was being pursued, at a discreet distance, by a group of hopeful strays, mostly young boys, who all wanted to be in prime position should he choose to divest himself of some of the small change from his faro joint. Near the corner of Montgomery and California he slowed down, put his hand in his right pocket and suddenly wheeled around. With a graceful, almost balletic, motion, he flamboyantly extracted a handful of coins from his coat and threw them, with an audible chuckle, in the direction of his pursuers. They scurried left and right as I watched in amused fascination. It was just as the last rolling coin was being gathered triumphantly by the smallest but fleetest of the tykes that I brushed against someone passing in the opposite direction.

It was a young girl, probably about twelve or thirteen years old, dressed in boy's clothing. Her outfit was topped off with a garishly coloured cloth cap. Some sixth sense caused me to turn and watch her as she, without apology for having walked straight into me, continued her way towards the corner of Montgomery and Pine. There Cloth Cap did something odd. Another girl —this one was probably about sixteen—appeared from nowhere. The first thing you noticed about her was her size. She was exceptionally tall, close to six feet in height, and anything but willowy. She was carrying a small and incongruous basket of flowers. Cloth Cap, in what seemed like a well-rehearsed move, appeared to toss something into the basket. Flower Girl started to cross Montgomery. As she did so, I smelled a rat. I patted my jacket pocket and realised that I'd been relieved of my wallet.

I shouted to Flower Girl, 'Come back here, you little bitch!'

As I did so, her younger accomplice, the actual thief, took off at a run, southwards towards Market. The older girl made it across Montgomery, where I saw her hand off my wallet to a small child, no more than eight or nine years old. She was a patchwork of red hair and freckles, wore a filthy print dress of no discernible colour, and looked as if she hadn't eaten a square meal in her entire life. Flower Girl continued along Pine at a rapid pace and was soon out of sight. I ran across the street and intercepted Freckles. As I approached her, she stopped and put both hands behind her back.

'All right, little lady, give it here,' I demanded.

'Fuck you. What do you want?' Accompanying the invective was a pungent waft of halitosis that came from somewhere beyond the gates of Hell.

'I beg your pardon?'

'You heard me,' she replied vehemently.

She still had both hands locked in place behind her back. I grabbed her spindly left arm with my right hand and dragged it into view. Empty. I spun her around. Her right hand was empty as well. She twisted out of my grip and grinned at me exultantly. Passers-by were beginning to stop and fix me with odd and disapproving looks.

'What were you expecting?' she asked impishly. 'The Crown Jewels? Queen of England's still got 'em. Bye now.'

With that she took off again along Montgomery with all the manufactured guilelessness of an experienced decoy. I looked back down the street for her accomplices. I wanted my wallet back. I didn't mind about the money—I never carried much around with me anyway—but I cared very much about the only picture of my mother that I'd managed to rescue from a photographic inferno staged by my father a few years after she gave up the ghost. There was no sign of either Cloth Cap or Flower Girl. When I looked around for the little redhead, she had disappeared too. I wondered how many other dim-witted dupes they'd managed to take advantage of that day. Judging by the sunken cheeks of the youngest member of the gang, I figured they didn't strike pay dirt too often. This did not improve my mood.

I somehow neglected to mention the incident to Campbell as we walked up Sacramento Street towards Nob Hill a few hours later. That was partly embarrassment, but mostly breathlessness. Campbell couldn't be bothered hanging around for a cable car, so we tackled the forbidding slope on foot. He had managed to convince Lees, who had succeeded in persuading Crowley, that we badly needed to talk to Schroeder.

The land rose gradually as you trudged from Kearny to Stockton, and then precipitously for two blocks, until it flattened out again on reaching the intersection of Sacramento and Mason. I vowed that the next time I made the journey, I would dress like an Alpine climber, bring ropes, and learn to yodel.

It was my first visit to San Francisco's castles in the clouds. This was where the city's nobility resided; hence the abbreviated name given to the area by those less fortunate, i.e., everyone who didn't live there. The Brahmins didn't much like the label 'Nob Hill', but even with their money they couldn't stop the *hoi polloi* renaming their wonderland. Instead, they were forced to huddle together for warmth and protection amongst the buttresses, the granite, and the crenellations of the plush two-hundred-acre plateau they called home. As you walked across this bastion, housing the richest of the rich, it was strange to think that when the earliest dwellings were built on what was then a practically inaccessible hill, the labourers had to hack their way through thick vegetation. Nowadays the foliage was imported and kept well clipped by an army of gardeners.

'Don't breathe too deeply,' Campbell warned, seeing that I was struggling with the incline. 'The air is more expensive up here.' He was taking the hill in his stride. I rationalised. I was suffering from the after-effects of a vigorous session on the water, as well as the sticky sustain pedal of Bella's baby grand.

'Does Schroeder walk up and down this hill every day?' I asked Campbell, doing my best to disguise my breathlessness.

'He has his people do it for him. This is a man who once bought a restaurant just so that he could have the pleasure of throwing out someone who was sitting at his favourite table.'

'Fascinating. Would you be offended if I said I didn't believe a word of it.'

'What if I told you that I was the unfortunate diner?'

'Were you?' I asked, beguiled by his pained expression.

'No.'

We continued in silence.

Schroeder's pile was on California Street, across the way from the huge Gothic monstrosity built for Mark Hopkins, the Railroad King. That was all turrets, twists, ornate reveals, spires, vulgarity, and railway money. It looked as if a dozen architects had contested a design competition and had all jointly been declared the winner. The man who paid for it never even got to see the eyesore completed. Probably just as well.

While Schroeder, as it turned out, was Gothic himself, his mansion was less offensive than that of the late Mr. Hopkins. It could have housed the population of a Dublin street, but at least it didn't look as if it had been dreamed up by Mary Shelley.

We made the mistake of knocking on the front door. As a matter of fact, it was more of a statement on my part, rather than an error. Campbell was undecided whether we should try to gain access via the impressive frontage on California Street. I suggested we brazenly show up at the freeman's entrance rather than cringe with the vassals. I might have implied to Campbell that this could hardly go amiss. It did, and in spades. The pallid flunkey who answered the door looked at us as if we had tried to set fire to the tasseled bell pull.

'State your business,' he said. His bile was corrosive. Not even a 'please' if you please. To make matters worse, he was wearing a morning suit and he'd been imported from England. I could invent a silly moustache but he's not even worth the effort of making something up. Besides which, it would have obscured his thin lips.

My hackles began to rise. Campbell looked at me as if to say 'I told you we should have gone around the back' before remembering that he was a Southern gentleman, and therefore kin to Dixieland royalty. He weighed in with a few ounces of pure disdain. I just waited in reserve. With generations of haughty Orpens at my beck and call, I could easily mop up the stragglers if I was belatedly pitched into the battle.

'Our business is none of your business. We're here to see your employer,' Campbell snapped. I expected him to administer the *coup de grace* with a condescending 'my good man' but he was from Richmond, Virginia not Richmond, Surrey. The butler or valet, or whatever he called himself, was not in the least bit chastened.

'Do you have a card?' he inquired sourly.

'No, and neither do I have very much patience,' Campbell replied acidly. 'He's expecting me: Sergeant Campbell, San Francisco Police.'

'Oh, so you're a policeman?' He pronounced the word as if he was drawing attention to a floating turd in a punchbowl. Blatantly challenged by this display of *hauteur*, Campbell began to warm to the game. He might be wary of the organ grinder, but he was unimpressed by the monkey.

'No, I'm a crazed inmate from a lunatic asylum under the *illusion* that he's a policeman. And this gentleman here …' he pointed to me, 'is Mr. John Wilkes Booth. Furthermore, we're both heavily armed.' To his credit, the flunkey didn't turn a hair. He might not have practised the art of irony himself, but he was capable of recognising an expert.

'Just let us in and go get your boss please,' Campbell concluded, the fire in his eyes dying down.

Thin Lips didn't budge. Campbell's eyes began to flame again.

Just when things were starting to get interesting, someone approached from a corridor off the front door and spoiled the fun. A less pompous factotum, one without a morning suit and lacking the Englishman's air of weary pretentiousness, passed by just as Thin Lips was either going to attempt to dispatch us around the rear, or roll us back down the hill.

'What's going on, Crampton?' he asked. Crampton—a *nom juste* if ever there was one.

'These gentlemen are from the police, Mr. Davies. They claim to have an appointment with Mr. Schroeder,' replied Thin Lips, his expression exhibiting a dangerous lack of respect for Less Pompous Flunkey as he did so.

'It's rather looser than an appointment, Crampton, but they are expected. Come in, gentlemen, please.' He motioned us to enter.

Campbell swanned into the lobby of the mansion as if to the manner born. I glued on a self-satisfied grin as I passed the impassive Crampton and picked an imaginary piece of lint from his immaculate morning suit. He didn't even flinch. Centuries of breeding, or years of training? I shall never know, or care.

Our rescuer introduced himself. 'My name is Evan Davies. I'm private secretary to Mr. and Mrs. Schroeder. And you are …?

'Sergeant Campbell and Sergeant Orpen, San Francisco Police.' Campbell replied. It was the first time I'd been introduced as a San Francisco policeman. I wasn't sure how to take it, but I made no shift to correct him.

Davies didn't exactly look like your average weedy, bespectacled private secretary. He had strapping Welsh sheep farmer written all over his family tree. Probably on both sides. He was small, muscular, clean-shaven, and had about him the air of a man who didn't suffer fools, or affronts to his employers. His handshake—an unexpected move in the circumstances—was resolute and powerful. The purpose, I decided, was to impress on both of us that he wasn't going to be far away and that his musculature was as solid as his grip.

He led us first down a long corridor that reminded me of photographs I'd seen of the Hall of Mirrors in Versailles Palace. It wasn't quite Louis Quatorze, but then this wasn't pre-revolutionary France. We passed an inner courtyard crammed with half-clothed statues of someone's ancestors—probably not Schroeder's—and bubbling fountains. Bedecking the walls, as we turned into a second corridor, were European landscapes, groaning bookshelves, and an occasional mural. Then there were entire dynasties of Roman Emperors, Senators and scribes placed at intervals, heads on plinths. Not a Ming vase in sight mind you. Even in his décor Schroeder was culturally consistent. We'd already made three left turns when we stopped outside an ornate door with two elaborately carved chairs on either side. Up ahead I could see the main entrance again. Davies had taken us the long way around. He meant to impress and overawe. I was suitably overawed. I wondered what Charles Crocker's place, down the street, was like. He was even richer than Croesus.

'I'm sure you will remember not to take up too much of Mr. Schroeder's time, gentlemen,' Davies said, just before he knocked softly on the door and entered without invitation. I was glad to see that he didn't lace the 'gentlemen' with any coded disapproval as, no doubt, Crampton would have done. He returned a minute later and ushered us inside.

I wouldn't do justice to the room, so I won't even bother trying. We certainly had nothing even remotely like it in the Orpen ancestral pile. It was like the corridors, except with a thick pile patterned carpet and three huge bay windows. That will have to do. Schroeder was not alone. Sitting around a small occasional table with him was his wife and one of the stoutest men I have ever seen. Campbell told me afterwards that he was a California State Senator named Cockburn. I imagine he was the sort of politician Julius Caesar had in mind when he expressed a desire to have about him men that were fat. He made Newman look svelte. He was almost perfectly spherical and hadn't enough neck by which you could hang him. His heavy head just sat atop his corpulent body with no intervening buffer zone. You'd have expected something oily to complement the bulk, but he had a chapped look about him. His skin was dry and flaky.

The contrast with the woman who sat across from him was acute. I recognised Caroline Schroeder from our brief encounter of a few days before. Wasp-waisted, she had a brittle elegance, as if she might shatter into dozens of shards at the sound of her own top note. Somewhere in her late thirties, her movements were graceful, her posture was perfection itself. Her blonde hair was pulled tightly off her face. She had that detached look about her that I had noticed before. She looked intensely bored. She and Cockburn rose to leave when we entered. When the portly Senator strayed a little too close to her, Caroline Schroeder flinched and pulled away with an almost imperceptible movement. As she left, she studied Campbell and me without visible interest. Looking at her so closely, the feeling that I had seen her before became even more pronounced. She addressed her husband in a soft, beguiling, English West Country accent, as she rose to leave. The English rose had a burr.

'I'll be back for you in twenty minutes,' she told her husband. 'Don't forget, we're having lunch with Theresa Fair.' And then she seemed to float out of the room.

Schroeder went through some parting pleasantries with Cockburn, whose exit was more conspicuous and less balletic than that of Caroline Schroeder. After his host rose to shake the Senator's hand the man wobbled out of the room like a huge bubble waiting to be burst. Schroeder waited until the door closed behind Cockburn. During this brief lull, I noticed two framed caricatures from the satirical magazine, *The Wasp* on the heavily papered wall behind Schroeder. At the centre of each was a grotesque figure vaguely and cruelly resembling the man sitting in front of us. Although these were clearly barbed attacks on Schroeder himself, in a gesture of vanity or lordly contempt, he had purchased the originals.

When he was certain that we were on our own, Schroeder spoke. He obviously wanted for nothing, other than personal warmth. He had the charm of a rattlesnake poised and ready for his first square meal of the day.

'Now then, gentlemen, state your intentions. Do so without circumlocution, conduct your business expeditiously and leave. Before you begin, be aware that I do not offer inducements to junior officers. My contributions are made much further up the chain of command. If this is some sort of shakedown, you will be disappointed.'

It was a perfunctory and bellicose pre-emptive gambit from a man accustomed to command. A belligerent general dressing down a couple of subalterns. To Schroeder there were two kinds of people: the gods and the soldier ants. The gods—among whom he lived and had his being—disposed, while the soldier ants scuttled to satisfy their dispositions. That was all ye knew on earth and all ye needed to know.

Schroeder was at least a decade older than his wife. He was probably approaching fifty at the time, with all the self-possession and sense of entitlement of someone who was a millionaire many times over. Julius Caesar, however, would not have approved. He was spare, almost ascetic, in appearance. There was little evidence about his actual person that he spent much time revelling in the riches he had acquired. He was certainly more preoccupied with adding to his fortune than enjoying it at the dinner table. The high art *bric à brac* that we had seen on our impromptu tour of the mansion might be *de rigueur* for social acceptance on Nob Hill, but corporeal excess was not a prerequisite, so Schroeder hadn't expanded, like Senator Cockburn.

He had the kind of face you would expect to see among the Roman notaries whose busts proudly lined one side of the long corridor leading to the room in which we stood. He was chiselled marble. It was hard to tell by looking at him whether he was Caligula or Augustus. Probably a little of both. Men who made a fortune in California in those days generally combined political *nous* with criminal ruthlessness.

For someone who was filthy rich, Schroeder didn't look very happy. After tolerating our mute response to his opening salvo for a few seconds, he said impatiently, 'State your business then.'

'May we sit down?' Campbell inquired politely. Schroeder himself remained standing.

'No, you may not. You won't be here long enough to get comfortable.' He then took a seat himself. 'You heard my wife. We have a luncheon appointment with the former wife of a tomcat robber baron. Now get on with it. What do you want?'

'To discuss your relationship with Thomas Newman, sir.' It was the first time I had ever heard Campbell call anybody 'sir'. He didn't even defer to Lees in that way. The poise he had demonstrated in the skirmish with Thin Lips Crampton seemed to have evaporated in the presence of plutocracy.

'And precisely what concern is that of yours?' Schroeder asked curtly.

'We're investigating the murder of Daniel Horton.' It was also the first time I'd heard Campbell refer to our murder victim as 'Daniel'. But he was breathing rarefied air and had to act accordingly. Diminutives were obviously *verboten* in the court of Kaiser Charles.

'Why bother?' asked Schroeder. 'Not much of a loss to society. Go and search among the Irish or the Chinese. But then neither of them is going to give up his killer, are they?' He began to warm to his theme. 'You either deport them all or decide they're not worth the trouble and leave them alone to kill one another. Personally, as you may be aware, we are advocates of the former course of action, but only because decent citizens might suffer in any Irish donnybrook or Chinese tong war.'

'Might I …?' Campbell tried to stem the flow.

Schroeder never even acknowledged the intervention.

'Where the Chinese are concerned, of course, the remedy is simple. Chinatown should be purified by fire and replanted with grass and trees. A razed Chinatown becomes our Central Park. Somewhat hillier, I will concede, than the Golden Gate fields to the west. You might think that too radical an approach, but if we don't opt for a neat solution, then we must settle for a messy one. San Francisco will never achieve the greatness of a New York, or a Chicago, while we must share it with the Celestials.'

Thus spake Schroeder, who, I found out later, was himself the son of German immigrants. A Walt Whitman poem comes to mind, 'Do I contradict myself? /Very well, then I contradict myself/ (I am large, I contain multitudes.)' I obviously didn't think of that at the time. In fact, I'd never even heard of Walt Whitman back then. Not that Schroeder contained multitudes. He might have owned a plethora of material possessions, but he was otherwise quite vacuous.

Schroeder was one of those people who didn't need an interlocutor to conduct a conversation. He supplied both opening and riposte. He liked to verbalise your side of the exchange. It cut out any potential for disagreement. We could have slipped out, done a quick tour of Ancient Rome, and he would have sustained his tirade perfectly well without our presence. Campbell, watching the sand flow through the egg timer, was bold enough to interrupt the millionaire's rant.

'I'm not sure, sir'—He was still proffering the 'sir'—'if you have seen yesterday's editorial in the *Chronicle*. It suggests that you might have had an interest in the death of Daniel Horton. You understand that we are obliged to follow up any possible line of inquiry, however tenuous.'

I waited for the detonation. But the response was surprisingly mild. Schroeder had bigger fish to catch, gut, fry and devour than Wellington Campbell.

'I don't think I've ever been called a "line of inquiry" before. Did I hear you mention that Republican arse rag, the *Chronicle*?'

I didn't think it was possible to spit out a word that didn't contain a single explosive syllable, but he managed it.

'We hold the *Chronicle* in the same regard as the fundament of a sewer rat. Michael Henry de Young is no better than was his late and unlamented brother. Our fervent hope is that he suffers the same fate as his vile sibling at the hands of an equally worthy assassin. De Young the Younger has been grabbing railroad money with both fists, just like his big brother took bribes from the Silver Kings. Hence the fawning love letters to the Big Four in his obnoxious rag.'

I noticed that Schroeder used the word 'we' a lot when he actually meant 'I'. This display of narcissism was accentuated by the fact that he had an eccentric 'w'—either an ancestral affectation or a verbal tic. It came out as something closer to a 'v'.

'As it happens'—Schroeder wasn't finished with the *Chronicle* yet— 'our lawyers have absolute confidence that they will be able to divest the de Young family of its entire fortune in the libel suit that will follow the scurrilous editorial to which you refer. I'm sure George Hearst will be happy to take it off my hands for a few dollars and merge it with the *Examiner*. No doubt it will cause consternation among the *literati* in the Bohemian Club, but we have far too many damned newspapers in this city anyway.'

'Might I ask you again, sir …' intoned Campbell, the 'sir's' now coming thick, heavy and without a trace of insincerity, 'about your association with Thomas Newman. It appears to run counter to your antipathy towards everything Irish.'

'I fail to see, Sergeant—?'

'Campbell … sir.'

'Sergeant Campbell ... I fail to see what my supposed relation-ship with Mr. Newman has to do with your investigation. Neverthe-less, I don't mind saying that, despite his unfortunate origins, he is almost domesticated, and extremely serviceable. At arm's length, of course. Never let the mouse too close to the cheeseboard. We are entirely *ad idem* on the Chinese. Newman had an exemplary record during his term as sheriff when it came to dealing with our Oriental curse. I believe he put the shorn queues of his prisoners to good use as mattress stuffing for the county jail. Very thrifty. It's good to know that our public officials occasionally justify the large sums of money we remit to them in our taxes.'

Which, I was willing to bet, were a fraction of the even larger sums that he, and others of his ilk, remitted in bribes. It was almost as if he read my mind because that was when he noticed me for the first time. 'And who is this?' he inquired waspishly.

'This is Sergeant Orpen from Dublin. Dublin, Ireland that is.' Campbell obliged, careful to lay on my Irishness with a trowel. 'He's with the London Metropolitan Police.'

'An Irishman, eh?' Schroeder responded blandly. Then he sur-prised me. 'Do you speak Gaelic? Say something in Gaelic, why don't you?'

My grasp of the Irish language was rudimentary. Its use wasn't general around our kitchen table. Mother tongue it was not. Still, I had a few choice phrases in my repertoire, picked up from a maid-servant before I was dispatched to Westminster School to have all the Irish beaten out of me.

'If you like,' I responded. '*Go n'iosfaidh an tochas thú.*'

Schroeder looked intrigued. 'What does it mean?'

'It's an old Irish greeting. It means "May the road rise with you"— May you have a safe and secure journey.'

'Excellent. Say it for me again. I might try it out on a Silver King one of these days. I'm sure Mackay would be impressed.'

I obliged him by repeating the phrase phonetically a few times—
'guh neesy on thuccas hu'—until he became palpably bored. I wished
I could be a fly on the wall when he tried it out on an Irish oligarch.

We hadn't got any further than Newman and the de Young family, seed and breed, when there was a knock on the door and Caroline
Schroeder re-entered wearing street clothes. When she had left the
room, she had not been wearing jewelry of any kind. Now she was
bedecked with gems. Highly adorned spouses were plainly obligatory
when affluent he-wolves got together to decide the fate of the world.

'Are we walking or taking the carriage, Charles?' she asked, floating
in much as she had floated out. Her accent was deepest Somerset, yet at
the same time there was a strange familiar flatness underlying it.

'Walk?' Schroeder seemed perplexed, as if the very concept
offended him. 'Why would we walk?'

'Because Theresa Fair lives two blocks away, and it's a beautiful
day.'

'Is it indeed? I hadn't noticed. It looks rather like all the other
days at this time of year. Tell Davies to get the carriage ready,' he
concluded brusquely. Arriving on foot precluded making a magnificent entrance. He dismissed his wife with the sort of gesture you
might reserve for an annoying mendicant monk. An embarrassed
look spread across her face while her husband studied her blankly,
waiting for her to do his bidding. I could see that she was more of an
acquisition than a merger. I had an overwhelming desire to shatter
his smugness, preferably with one of the ornate fire irons perched
beside the inglenook that adjoined the massive fireplace at the centre
of the room. Since nobody else seemed disposed to do anything, I
intervened. I admit that what followed was not my finest hour.

'Might I say that I am a great admirer of yours, Madam. I've
been a fan of opera since I was a small child.' Even I was surprised
at myself for this blatant lie. I found opera tedious, risible, and
mostly conducted in foreign languages with which I had insufficient

familiarity—outside of the scatological. Beethoven had once written an opera, but I could find it in my heart to forgive him. Why Mozart had wasted so much valuable time, in such a short life, writing silly show tunes, I had no idea.

Caroline Schroeder was thrown. So was everyone else, including my good self. In the case of Campbell, his disbelief was laced with glowering disapproval. But having identified myself as a devotee of opera, I was now obliged to deliver on my devotion. The floor was mine, and I needed some immediate inspiration. But I was like a prospector searching for gold in the upper reaches of the American River. It was all panned out. A wise man will advise you that when you find yourself in a hole, stop digging. Instead, I dug some more.

'I saw you in Dublin about ten years ago. You were outstanding.' The hole in which I stood was now rapidly filling with water.

'And you are …?' she inquired. Her tone was not unfriendly, just a trifle bewildered and a little wary.

'Orpen, Robert Orpen, ma'am. Sergeant.'

'Well, Mr. Orpen, Sergeant, I'm obliged to you for your approbation but I'm afraid I am yet to have the pleasure of performing in Dublin. It must have been someone else.'

'Some*where* else perhaps, ma'am. Did I say Dublin? Of course, I meant London. It was in London. Covent Garden I believe. *Rigoletto*. I'm a particular fan of *Rigoletto* – one of Puccini's greatest gifts to the *aficionado*.'

'Really? And how was my Maddalena?'

'Exquisite. Sublime. I was fifteen-years-old at the time. It inspired in me a life-long love of opera.' Unfortunately, I was now starting to grow in confidence. A fatal mistake. Her response was not unkind, considering. She could have hit the lever and opened the trapdoor, but she let me down gently.

'I'm delighted to have been so influential. Though you might need to refresh your memory on the details. The role of Maddelena is taken by a contralto. I'm a soprano. I've played *Rigoletto* in Covent Garden all right, and within the last decade, but always in the part of Gilda.'

Here Schroeder reinserted his oar, but not to come to my rescue. 'Isn't *Rigoletto* by Rossini?'

'Verdi,' his wife corrected, tersely. Schroeder made a face. He obviously did not appreciate being challenged, still less being wrong, even on a subject where his wife patently outmatched him.

'So many Italian operas, so little time,' he said dismissively. 'Is that something French you're wearing, my dear?' he inquired blandly. He turned to us. 'My wife, gentlemen, seems incapable of stepping out without being accompanied by something French, be it a maid, a poodle, or a corsage. I indulge her in these Parisian whims. I would only draw the line at a *gigolo*. Or are they Italian?'

Here was a Leontes who would have preferred his Hermione to remain a statue.

'Now then,' he continued, 'if Sergeant Orpen can contain his admiration, I am obliged to pretend to be fond of Theresa Fair for a tedious hour. In truth I am much more partial to her whoremastering husband, James. Former husband, I should say. She has finally shown him the door.'

Caroline Schroeder looked as if she would like to shove her husband's thin head through one.

The loud metallic sound I heard in my mind's ear was a portcullis coming down on the one-sided conversation. We were left to contemplate the moat. A minute later and we were back in the care of Davies. Campbell maintained a sullen silence, but I thought I might just as well keep excavating. How far could it be to China?

'Have you been with Mr. Schroeder for long?' I asked, as Davies led us past the stone reliquary of the later Roman Empire once again, this time on our way to the rear entrance. The front door was being reserved for the departure of his master and mistress. Davies eyed me quizzically.

'Why do you wish to know?' he asked impassively.

'Idle curiosity. Making conversation. Nothing more.'

'Not long. Since his marriage to Mrs. Schroeder. However, I have been madame's private secretary for a good many years.'

'And bodyguard?' I asked. Davies studied me for a moment, less superciliously this time.

'I have assisted her in a number of ways, including warding off the unwelcome attentions of some extremely persistent enthusiasts.'

Campbell now briefly emerged from beneath his sulk. 'You may have Sergeant Orpen to deal with some day,' he observed petulantly, 'He's a fervent admirer.'

When advocating Shank's mare rather than a draught mare for the short journey to their luncheon date, Caroline Schroeder had pointed out to her singularly unimpressed husband that the weather was eminently suitable for a bit of a ramble. That was certainly the case when she spoke, but by the time Campbell and I reached the back door of the Schroeder mansion the world was as 'tempest-tost' as any of Macbeth's witches could have desired. When it rains in San Francisco, it's not like Dublin. In Dublin, it pours continuously, but politely. In San Francisco, the fog is the climatic equivalent of Ireland's 'soft' weather. When it rains across the Bay – which it doesn't very often – it does so with typical American decisiveness. It descends like a minor waterfall just as it had done on the afternoon of our escape from the clutches of Riley and Emperor Newman's Praetorian Guard.

Davies could have pushed us gracelessly out of the door, to an instant soaking. Instead, he put his head outside, studied the downpour and said 'I'd wait here for a few minutes. It shouldn't last long. I need to go and drum up the carriage' With a not unfriendly nod, he then took himself off to grease the wheels for the Schroeders. As soon as he was out of earshot, Campbell launched his attack on my unprotected flank. The softness of his voice belied the menace of his mission.

'I believe I may have said something about the Benedictines?'

'You did … but—' I felt like an untethered balloon in a hurricane.

'But? There's a "but"?'

The balloon slipped its moorings and floated away. 'No. No "but".'

'So, we understand each other now?'

'We do …' Even though there was another "but" on the tip of my tongue. I swallowed it. Acrid taste.

'Very good. No great damage done I suppose, other than to your prospects of stealing Mrs. Schroeder from her husband.' His voice lost the menacing softness. 'So, what did we learn from that interview?'

'Not a lot,' I observed glumly, 'though I do believe, given the context, that I have finally discovered the meaning of the word "circumlocution".'

'The Gaelic …'—here he made an ineffectual pass at *Go n'iosfaidh an tochas thú*. I repeated it for him. 'Please tell me it has nothing whatever to do with having a safe journey.'

'Not remotely.'

'What does it actually mean?'

'"May the itch devour you".'

Campbell nodded approvingly. 'Heavenly! I do hope he tries it out on Mackay.'

As we waited for the shower to pass, I studied a Flavian, or maybe it was a Vespasian. The strange sightless eyes were unsettling. So was the ostentation.

'Wasn't it Balzac who said, "Behind every great fortune lies a great crime"?' I mused.

'Or a lot of small ones,' said Campbell, before adding, 'who is Ballsack?' I thought about enlightening him but couldn't face the indifference.

'An Inspector in the Metropolitan Police. Quite a comedian.'

'Did you watch Schroeder's hands by any chance?' Campbell asked, returning to his *idée fixe*. The only time I had ever studied anyone's hands was during a session with a three-card trickster at the Curragh racecourse. That hadn't been very informative, and I'd lost my stake. 'Did you notice anything?' he asked eagerly, his own hands resting inexpressively in the pockets of his coat.

I feigned a hatred to disappoint. 'No, I can't say that I did.'

'Perhaps you had just cause on this occasion. They never moved once while we were there.'

'Remained at the end of his wrists you mean?' I knew I wasn't assimilating Campbell's methods with sufficient solemnity, but I still found the idea of the hands as the mirrors of the soul to be patently absurd.

'What I mean, my jocular Irish friend, is that your attention was never drawn to them because they remained entirely immobile during our friendly chat. Mr. Schroeder sat with his elbows on the desk. His hands were splayed and joined at the fingertips. He never once deviated from that posture.'

'Maybe he knew you'd be watching like a hawk, so he glued them together.'

Campbell sighed resignedly. 'Sometimes there is an uppity scepticism about your tone that I really dislike. It was quite a display of self-control on his part. I've never come across anyone whose attention to detail is so highly developed that his hands are as deceitful as his eyes.'

'Was that why you didn't ask him anything about the Hounds?'

'A rather pointless exercise, don't y'all think?' Campbell remarked brusquely. His countenance suggested that, by now, more than my native scepticism was becoming uppity.

'I don't know. I think we had him on the ropes. He might have thrown in the towel.'

Campbell glowered but maintained a dignified silence. I was glad there were no orphan bricks to hand.

As Davies had predicted, it stopped raining as suddenly as it had begun. The rainwater from the guttering above us was rushing noisily through a downpipe as we stepped outside. Someone in a Barbary Coast gutter would be sucking it into their lungs in a few hours. A present from the folks on the Hill.

The architecture of the Schroeder back yard was oddly chaotic. After an indoor glut of pristine marble, it was a surprise to be greeted outside by a landscape of mismatched incongruence. The prevailing impression was of one of the less wholesome precincts of a medieval walled town. Stables, outhouses, and what looked like glorified privies, were arrayed in random order. All it lacked was a portcullis and a grimy citizen with a cart and a bell chanting, 'Oye, oye. Bring out your dead.' It was a debased portfolio from the School of Afterthought. I doubted that the Schroeders spent any time there.

Directly across from the back door, a carriage was waiting, a brougham with two horses patiently standing in the shafts. I was intrigued, once again, by the colourful crest on the door and went to take a closer look. A morose Campbell followed me, allowing himself to be distracted from the dismal failure of our interview with the owner of the carriage. The livery was a genuflection towards Schroeder's Germanic origins. It depicted a monk carrying a red book. This was atop the word 'Munchen' displayed in Gothic lettering.

'Schroeder obviously takes his Teutonic roots seriously,' I observed, running my hand over the crest.

'And "Munchen" means …?' Campbell inquired, with little apparent interest in the answer. I decided that he was going to get the benefit of my Trinity College education, whether he wanted it or not.

'Literally "of monks", but it's also the German word for the city we call Munich. The guilds there …' My pirated treatise, from a dimly remembered medieval European history course given by the great

Lecky himself, came to an early and abrupt end. Just as I was getting into my stride I was rudely interrupted by the arrival of a stout, florid middle-aged man in a top hat—presumably the coachman—who, ignoring our presence, pulled open the door of the carriage and examined the interior. As he did so, his inspection was interrupted by a shrill exclamation from the door of a small lodge beside the imposing back gate of the Schroeder mansion. This came from a handsome woman whose tenderest years were well past. I recognised the accent as pure London. We could have been in the middle of the Covent Garden fruit and vegetable market.

'Oi, you,' she shrieked, 'Where are you 'oppin' off to fat boy? I 'aven't been paid yet.'

Top Hat had his back to us, so the only flesh we could see was his thick neck. This was immediately suffused with a red of the deepest dye. He scuttled back towards the angry she-wolf, leaving the door of the carriage swinging open. As he did so the sun emerged from behind the clouds. It timed its appearance to perfection. Campbell had already turned to leave when I noticed something sparkle under the seat facing towards the front of the carriage. Magpie that I am, my curiosity got the better of me. Checking first to make sure that Davies was still indoors, and that the coachman was settling the bill so volubly presented by his lady friend, I investigated the source of the reflected light. It was a silver cufflink in the shape of a small bird, probably a nightingale. I barely had time to pocket it before the coachman returned, having managed to mollify his creditor. A curt nod from Campbell and we were soon walking through a small gate in the high wall surrounding the Schroeder demesne, and onto California Street.

There we were met by a second surprise, far less welcome than the first. Approaching us on the opposite side of the street were Riley and the hulking Howie. They spotted us the moment we emerged from the rear of the Schroeder mansion. There was a second or two when I thought a battle royal was inevitable and my hand went to my coat pocket for reassurance. It was there all right, ready and waiting.

But my revolver proved to be surplus to requirements. As if they had both seen the same ghost, Riley and Howie stared at us for a few seconds and then, without a word to each other, turned on their heels and shuffled down California Street, before I had even a chance to offer to return one of Riley's daggers. Another opportunity missed. They lumbered towards the Hopkins excrescence without a backward glance. We followed them for a few minutes but with no great urgency. Be careful what you wish for. Had we caught up with them, the result would have been far from a friendly meeting of soulmates. By the time we had descended to Stockton, both men had managed to disappear into Chinatown.

'Newman certainly lacks subtlety,' Campbell said. 'If he wanted to know our business, he might have sent someone less conspicuous than his knifeman and the giant redwood.'

I wasn't so sure. There had been something about the expression on Riley's face that suggested more than mere displeasure at being rumbled. It struck me that he hadn't been expecting to see us, any more than we had anticipated meeting him. Was he following us, or did he have business of his own on Nob Hill?

As we walked past the ramshackle stores along Stockton, with their exotic vegetables and pungent fish adding form to the pavement—I've never been able to call them sidewalks—I put my hand in my pocket and took out my new prize.

'I think this might interest you.' I said, stopping in my tracks as I spoke. Campbell ignored me and kept going. I stood my ground. He had covered half a block before he noticed my absence. He turned, and in a gesture of annoyance motioned me to follow him. From a distance of a hundred yards, I dangled the cufflink between thumb and index finger and waved it slowly from side to side. Intrigued, despite himself, he retraced his steps. At first, he studied the trinket non-committally. Then he took it from me, placed it in his upturned palm and examined it minutely.

'I found it in the coach.' I said, trying not to sound too pleased with myself. To my delight, he whistled.

'Did you indeed?'

'Do you think it's Horton's?' I asked.

'We don't have its brother, so we can't make a match. Our highly methodical killer saw to that. He must have known it was a one in a million chance that the lost cufflink would ever turn up anywhere incriminating, but even at that he didn't like the odds. So, he detached its twin and disposed of it. No loose ends. Which means that what we have here is just a random piece of male ornamentation, found in a random carriage, and we can't prove otherwise.'

'But it could mean that Schroeder's rig was used to move Horton's body.'

'It could mean the Confederacy wins the War Between the States on appeal to the Supreme Court. Or that Los Angeles miraculously becomes something other than a parched sinkhole. Moral certainty is an empowering and immensely comforting state of mind, my friend, but it is not evidence, and evidence is the mother of truth.'

Campbell could sometimes be gallingly pretentious for someone who thought 'whatwithal' was a real word. Pondering the emboldening characteristics of moral certainty, and the nurturing qualities of motherhood, we too blended into Chinatown.

CHAPTER EIGHT

OPHELIA WILLIAMS

17 October

My God-fearing Godfather Lees—who steadfastly refused to allow me to call him Isaiah— always took very seriously the vows he made at the baptismal fount. But after the murder of my father, he became more concerned with my temporal than my spiritual welfare. When I first broke it to him that I was working as a medical examiner, I thought he was going to have an aneurysm. He told me that I had become my father's daughter. I don't think he meant it as a compliment either. But a man in his position could easily have stymied me if he'd wanted to, and he didn't.

We would meet for lunch from time to time. He interrogated me, I teased him. After the renewal of my acquaintance with Ned Allen, I was tempted to take him to the Bull Run Bar, in a mischievous effort to scandalize him. Today he suggested the Tadich Grill on Clay Street, but it was my treat, so we met at the more modest René's on Sutter. After three fires in two years, René had rebuilt in brick. That's the thing about San Francisco. I love it like a brother, but it can be slow on the uptake. The entire city had to burn down seven times before we got a fire department.

René is renowned for the mysterious things he does with fish, but what I love most of all is his bread. There is no substitute for eating sourdough while it is still warm. The smell is intoxicating. Is it any wonder that yeast is such a vital constituent of alcohol? In René's sourdough, it combines with flour and water to produce a crusted poem.

As soon as we sat down, I began to regret my choice of venue. It was lunchtime and Money was on the prowl. Almost every table was occupied by well-dressed women with their heads on a swivel. Whenever the door opened, a dozen hats would turn to see if a Million Dollars or Small Change had walked in. There was plenty of noise, but not many grace notes. I felt like a piccolo that had strayed into a brass band.

My esteemed godfather tried to steer me away from discussing the Horton murder, but I wasn't having any of it. I kept sweetly but determinedly turning it back to the only subject I wanted to talk about. Once he got going it was refreshingly impossible to shut him up on the subject. My own interest had nothing to do with the fact that I had performed the autopsy. I wanted to know why the man who had my father murdered—and got away with it—would now turn on one of his own. I suppose I also wanted him to tell me that, this time, there would be consequences. I had little faith in the ability of the San Francisco Police Department to pin Newman or Riley to the Cross, but I had high hopes that retribution from some of Horton's gorillas would supply the hammer, nails, and executioner.

What he told me was even more encouraging.

'Doghouse doesn't want to be a first lieutenant for the rest of his days, you know,' he remarked, dunking a wall of sourdough into his chowder. 'Make no mistake, he's getting tired of being Newman's bad boy. He got a sweet taste in his mouth as a Deputy Sheriff, and he wants to be King of his own castle. Tsar Newman will never let that happen, so the only alternative is a takeover. Frankly, I won't be losing too much sleep at the notion of Newman and Riley pitching into each other like a pair of cockerels. And if you quote me, I'll deny that I even know you.'

The prospect was not one that was going to have me tossing and turning at night either, but I couldn't help thinking that Riley would be trying to lift a hundred pounds with fifty-pound muscles. My spiritual mentor offered further consolation.

'I've heard talk of Riley tapping into some of Horton's mob, now that they're out of contract, and using that muscle to persuade Newman to devote all his attention to his new supervisor's job. But he'll have to fight for it. Big Tom isn't going to take his snout from the bucket just because he'll be shoving it into the Board of Supervisors' trough as well. It's never 'either/or' with him. He wants it all. Ask Dan Horton.'

'I probably should have done that a few days before carving him up. What, I wonder, does our Irish visitor make of it all?' The question was casual enough, but he looked at me sharply. A spoonful of René's best chowder hovered.

'Why do you ask? Do you find him interesting?'

'In a maternal sort of way.' He looked at me roguishly. 'Well … not maternal—whatever the female equivalent of "avuncular" is. Is he safe to be let out?' I waited for a response while the chowder safely reached its destination.

'Don't underestimate him. He's capable of looking after himself.'

'What does he make of our warring Irish chieftains?'

'You'd have to ask him that yourself. He doesn't take me into his confidence. I caused a bit of a stir in Scotland Yard when I checked his credentials. Apparently, his boss—an old acquaintance of mine named Williamson—had no idea he was in San Francisco. He seems to have just disappeared one day. Puff … gone in a wisp of smoke and didn't even say goodbye. Dolly sent me—'

'Dolly—?'

'Short for Adolphus. He sent me a telegram that would have made your eyes pop. It looked as if they were going to shoot him for desertion the moment they got him back. Then I got a second cable.

This one wasn't quite as full of piss and vinegar. Dolly had obviously been told to mind his own business by one of the big moustaches. So, Sergeant Orpen is ours for a while.'

He paused, distracted by a waiter bending down to pick up an earring that had been shed by Half a Million Dollars nearby. He was handsome. She was drunk, and effusive in her thanks. I assume she had dropped it so that he would have a chance to assess her rolling cleavage. To his credit, and her chagrin, he spurned the opportunity. When the tableau had resolved itself—mightily unsatisfactorily for Mrs. Half a Million—Lees resumed.

'Dolly's cable, the second one, was a bit indiscreet. I'm glad no one else got to see it, and that I didn't have to pay for it out of *my* budget. He went on a bit.'

'About what?'

'It was by way of a warning. He advised me to keep a close eye on our boy. Something about someone Orpen didn't much like, turning up dead in a ditch near his home patch, back in Ireland. It was … considered wise … to get him out of the country. He hasn't been back since.'

'When did this happen?'

'A couple of years ago. I've got Campbell keeping an eye on him. If he's up to anything–and I've no doubt that he is, however ill-informed Dolly might be–our Confederate friend will ferret it out.'

'I don't believe Campbell could find his ear in a fog.'

'Got up your nose already, has he? Shame you can't join the fraternity. We have monthly meetings in the Mechanics' Institute. Campbell could find a way to infuriate Job himself.'

'He doesn't much like women, does he?'

'He doesn't much like anybody. That's what makes him so useful. He's not particular about whom he exasperates. My problem is that includes me. He's the best detective I have, by a distance. But he manages to curdle the milk of human kindness just by walking past the dairy.'

'Couldn't he at least try to be pleasant some of the time? Just to see what it feels like? Useful research?'

'That would probably require an element of trust. That's not his strong point.'

'Meaning—?'

I could see that he was reluctant to elaborate. He'd said too much already. He was debating what, if anything, he should tell me, while playing a nervous arpeggio on the edge of the table. I knew him of old. As long as I kept my curiosity to myself, after the five-finger exercise, he would begin the étude in full. A few more beats and the music began.

'He's told me some things about his past. He didn't have much option at the time. It was either that, or summary dismissal from the force for drunkenness …and worse.'

'Worse?'

He hesitated again, the arpeggio became a drumbeat, but he decided to press on. 'He's had a few adventures with laudanum.'

'And you keep him around? It must have been quite a past. It's all right. You don't have to tell me.'

I didn't mean it of course. Sometimes I think Isiah Lees, a devout Episcopalian, should have been an earnest Catholic with an austere confessor. Instead, he had me. My sympathetic silence was his absolution. I don't know whether he opened up because he wanted me to revise my opinion of Campbell, or because he just wanted to open up. In the way that dying fires often do, this one suddenly crackled into life as a few dry twigs absorbed the heat from their neighbors.

'Have you ever heard of Archie Clement?'

'No. Doesn't ring a bell. Wait … is he prizefighter?'

'You would have been … what … about six or seven years old when he was killed. You've heard of Jesse James of course?'

'Of course. A great lover of the railroads. He'd have fitted in well here.'

'Jesse rode with Clement during the Civil War. They were bushwhackers. There wasn't anything alive they wouldn't kill. If you were a Yankee farmer, they'd slit your pigs' throats first, and then they'd go after your children.'

'What's this got to do with Campbell?'

'He rode with them. He studied under Bloody Bill Anderson and graduated to Clement's academy. Stayed with him even after the war ended.'

'I see.'

'No, you don't. One day he just got sick and tired of gutting Yankees and turned in Clement to the Missouri State Militia. Archie was … "killed while attempting to escape". General Grant didn't send flowers to the funeral. So, there are men, desperate men, who would rip out Campbell's liver and eat it in front of him if they ever found him. That's why he ventured so far west. I suppose the laudanum helps him sleep.'

He didn't need to elaborate. I tried to stave off a mental image of terrified children clutching struggling women while their menfolk were hacked to death. And that was just my imagination. A tame reproduction. For Campbell, the pictures would have been vivid and real, worse than anything I could ever envisage.

' "Campbell" is not his real name. And you know nothing about this. But there will be times, I have no doubt, when you will wonder why I don't gut him myself. I wanted you to understand.'

I understood, although I wasn't altogether happy with the knowledge. Campbell, or whatever his real name was, was still an arrogant misanthrope, albeit one with a harrowing backstory and a lethal drug habit. His was a legal addiction, of course. It was only the smoking of opium—a Chinese leisure activity—that was against the law. Otherwise, all the laudanum swillers on Nob Hill would be felons.

'Here, take these.' He held out a handful of books that he had produced from an old leather bag.

'What are they?'

'Marcus's notebooks. They go back about ten years. You might as well have them. We're supposed to keep them for our records, but I've never known anyone to consult a policeman's notebook once he's … left the force. If I ever need them, I'll know where they are.'

Lees put them on the table in front of me. We stared at them together. Yellowing pages in an indecipherable scrawl that would have embarrassed a drunken spider. Relics of a dead father and an old friend. I put my hand on his. We sat in silence for a few seconds. I thought of Archie Clement and of how much I hoped Newman and Riley would share his fate. I'd be happy to shoot both myself, even if they weren't trying to escape.

When Lees had paid off René—the notion of 'Ophelia's treat' being entirely fictional—we both made our way back to Portsmouth Square. We parted at the entrance. He ascended the staircase to Olympus, I padded towards the entrance to Hades.

I was halted in my tracks by a shout from my single-headed Cerberus, the jovial Rory Tracy. One of his jobs is to stand guard outside the door when I'm performing autopsies. You never know when a corpse will indignantly rise from the dead and take exception to an entry in my notes. So, we've got to know each other quite well. He's not your typical lumbering brain-dead Irish policeman. I've discovered that he reads poetry. I once caught him with a copy of Whitman's *Leaves of Grass*. He swore me to silence and then lent it to me. I haven't given it back yet. I think he's afraid I might return it to him in the corridors of the Hall of Justice, so he hasn't asked where it is.

Tracy had been told to intercept me. 'We have a floater for you, ma'am,' he said gleefully.

'By which elegant expression I take it you mean a recent drowning victim?'

'Not that recent actually, certainly not a candidate for an open casket.' He grinned. I believe Tracy thinks I am as squeamish as he is, and that I prefer my cadavers dapper and well-groomed

'Male or female?'

'Male, ma'am.'

'Does he have a name yet?'

'He certainly does. A big Irish lummox of a lad called Madden. Nasty piece of work.'

CHAPTER NINE

ORPEN

18 October – early afternoon

We were walking south along Montgomery. We paused for a few seconds to investigate a hole being dug in the middle of the road. Not that we got close to it. We were left eyeing the backs of the onlookers who were peering into the hole. I still don't know what attracted the crowd. Had somebody struck gold? Had a body been discovered? Was there a boat race? And, of course, you should never underestimate the capacity of the *hoi polloi* to stand around and just stare at a hole in the ground.

That was when I saw Flower Girl.

My companion—let's just call her Amber for now—was not happy. I had made a distinctly ungentlemanly request of her, at which she baulked. So, I was looking anywhere but at her. That's how I spotted the thief who had walked away with my wallet. She wasn't hard to recognise. She was impossibly large for a young girl and, even though I had barely seen her for ten seconds during our first encounter, you couldn't miss her loping gait.

'I have to go. Sorry,' I told Amber. She looked stunned. Nobody likes being abandoned in mid-rant. She barely had time to mutter a startled 'Where are you off to …?' when, without a backward glance, I quickened my pace until I was about twenty yards behind my immense quarry. My first instinct was to grab her by the arm, haul her into a convenient alley and impolitely demand the return of my property. Not that there was a snowball's chance in hell of getting it back.

But just as I was making up my mind to pounce, I saw a young waif approach us and toss something into Flower Girl's basket. The game was afoot again. I didn't recognise the thief, and I had no idea who the victim was, but I was intrigued. I suddenly developed an overwhelming need to know how this would play out. I wanted to get to the end of Act V. Instead of waylaying Flower Girl, I decided to follow her. It all worked out rather well.

She led me a merry dance, but not because she was trying to shake me off. Unless she had eyes in the back of her head, she had no idea that she was being shadowed. I could out-camouflage a chameleon. She didn't even take the basic precaution of looking behind her every now and then, or of stopping in a doorway to read the 'Wanted' ads. So, no need for me to duck hurriedly out of sight. She headed towards the shoreline through a maze of streets and alleys before walking around the back of a dilapidated warehouse on Battery and Market and pushing open a decrepit wooden door.

When she was out of sight, I followed. The door opened on to a rickety staircase. There was no basement, and the ground floor was deserted. It smelled of hops and dead dogs. The steps looked as if they couldn't possibly take the weight of even a pint-sized adult male, but I reckoned if they could handle the bulk of Flower Girl, they could take anything I threw at them. I reached for Mr. Colt. His cold, inert presence was reassuring as always. That might seem a bit extreme in the circumstances, but I knew my *Oliver Twist*. There might be a Fagin or even a Bill Sykes directing operations. In case both were on duty that day, I had one of Riley's shivs nestling between a sock and my right boot.

I climbed the creaky stairs slowly, trying to make as little noise as possible. There was so much dust that I had to stop myself from sneezing. I could hear a murmur of voices above me. When I got to the top of the stairs, I found myself in a large, badly lit, and smoky room. The windows, all of which seemed to be broken, were covered with hessian, worn linen sheets, and even a voluminous dress that must once have belonged to a lady the size of a small island. A fire, with all the draw of a slow intake of breath, was filling the space with acrid smoke. It was just as well the ceiling was high and that the shattered windows provided some ventilation, or the occupants might have died of asphyxiation.

There were about twenty people in the room. All were young, female—no Fagin or Sykes—and seemed to be talking simultaneously at the tops of their voices. At first, I thought they were having a series of blazing arguments, but as my ears adjusted to the din, I realised that this was just a buzz of ordinary conversation conducted at opera chorus volume. If you wanted to make yourself heard in this company, you had to be a diva.

No one noticed that they had a visitor. They were completely engaged with a dozen different conversations and with sorting through a pile of purloined flotsam. Or maybe it was jetsam; I've never been entirely sure of the difference. They were picking out any items of value: cash, a silver cigarette case, a wallet, a lady's compact. The leftovers were being discarded onto a separate heap. While I stood there undetected, I saw one grimy wizened child of about ten years old, staring curiously at a small bottle of patent medicine. It looked like snake oil. I hoped she wasn't tempted to drink it.

As my eyes became more accustomed to the inky gloom, I noticed some familiar faces. Cloth Cap and Freckles were both squabbling with Flower Girl. They appeared to be the healthiest specimens in a roomful of wraiths. I was sure they were the workhorses. Most of the others looked as if they hadn't seen the light of day in months. Their complexions ranged from pallid to ashen. This place must be a luxury hotel for chronic consumption. Only Goya could have done justice to the attenuated features of the pre-tubercular females who milled around the cavernous space.

I'd say I stood there for fully two minutes and still no one paid the slightest heed to my unauthorised intrusion. It took a bullet into the ceiling to get their attention. As the echo faded, they all turned towards me, slowly and carefully, as if they didn't want to startle a man with a gun by making any sudden movement. I smiled amiably and returned Mr. Colt to my pocket.

'Good afternoon, ladies,' I said good-humouredly. 'Take me to your leader.'

The response was immediate. The bottle of snake oil came hurtling towards me. I caught it neatly with my left hand while my right went back for the revolver. I looked at the label on the bottle. 'Dr. Lavender's Inocuous Remady—the solution to boils, warts and carbuncles.' Dr. Lavender might well have known his way around a verruca, but he obviously couldn't spell.

'Am I supposed to drink it or apply it, do you think?' I inquired genially. 'It doesn't say on the label.'

One of the girls stepped forward into the only shaft of sunlight in the room. It was shining through the window that was half-covered by the impossibly large dress. She was about sixteen years old, dark, and very pretty in a grubby sort of way. She had lifeless brown eyes and was wearing a boy's shirt and men's trousers that were half a dozen sizes too big for her slim frame. She also exuded considerable authority for a young girl. I concluded that this was Mother.

'What do you want?'

Mother was as defiant as it was possible to be while standing unarmed in front of an unknown quantity with a gun. I looked around me. Some of this scrawny cluster–the older ones–were taking up Mother's theme and attempting to look menacing too. The rest slunk into some of the many dark corners of the room and tried to pretend to themselves, and to me, that they were somewhere else.

'I'm looking for a wallet,' I replied.

'We have plenty. Pick one out and go.' She pointed towards a large pile of leather on the floor off to her left.

'It's a particular wallet. It would have come into your possession a couple of days ago. Courtesy of that young lady over there.' I pointed at Freckles. She seemed oddly pleased at being singled out. 'You remember, don't you?' I asked her. She studied me for a moment. Then she smiled in recognition. I could count her teeth. It didn't take long.

'I remember,' she said. Her accent was Irish, something I hadn't noticed when we'd had our difference of opinion. 'You didn't put up much of a fight. Just as well. I'd have screamed like the divil, and Elephant always carries a cosh.' She pointed to Flower Girl. I didn't have to ask how she'd come by her nickname. 'It was black, Cleo, and it had gold letters on it,' continued Freckles. This was addressed to Mother, but there wasn't a flicker in response. Cleo stood, legs apart, arms folded, hostile, dented but steely. I would have felt sorry for her, but I needed to worry about what she might do next. She could have been carrying anything in that enormous pair of trousers.

'Cleo?' I said, 'is that short for Cleopatra?' I take it you're the Pharaoh around here?'

As I spoke, I noticed that Elephant had started to lope across my horizon. She was discreetly trying to outflank me. Not that anyone so large could ever hope to be inconspicuous. A gesture from Cleo, who had spotted her as well, stopped the woolly mammoth in her tracks. Elephant advanced no further but got her message across by other means. She reached into her clothing and pulled out an ugly-looking cosh. She tried it out on the palm of her left hand a few times without once taking her eyes off me.

'Grab what you came for and go.' Cleo said again. I walked slowly towards the uneven pile of brown and black leather wallets. Half-a-dozen young girls, all with frighteningly emaciated features and sunken eyes, stepped aside and allowed me to pass. Freckles, who seemed like an obliging enough sort, joined me. I was grateful but I still stayed upwind of her and avoided conversation. Together we began to search through the batch. After a couple of minutes, we'd got to the bottom of the pile without finding what we were looking for.

'No luck,' Freckles informed the company. There was some movement at the far end of the room and out of the darkness emerged another giant. She was almost identical to the girl Freckles had called Elephant, who was still standing idly by batting her cosh malevolently against her palm. And, believe me, it is possible to be idle and malevolent at the same time. Elephant had perfected the technique.

'Is this what you're looking for?' asked the second mammoth. She tossed me a black wallet with the initials REO in gold lettering on the flap. I inspected the contents. It was empty except for a faded photograph of a courtly but affable woman of early middle age.

'Who is she?' asked Elephant Number Two. 'She looks very sweet. I liked her. That's why I kept it.' Her accent was English.

'Someone very close to me. I wouldn't want to forget what she looked like.'

'The gold letters are lovely too. What do they spell?'

'They're my initials.'

'Thank you, Castle,' Cleo interjected. She turned back to me. 'She can't read. None of them can.'

'Elephant and Castle? Who gave them their names?' I asked.

'I did,' said Cleo. 'They're from London.'

'And where are you from?'

'Haven't a notion. You've got what you want, so you can go now. Don't come back and, if you know what's good for you, you won't tell anyone what you saw here.'

I had got what I came for all right, but now I was curious. I wanted to know more. I offered a trade.

'What happened to my money?' I asked. 'There must have been at least fifty dollars in there.'

Cleo didn't respond. Instead, she took a small notebook out of her pocket and consulted it. Clearly someone had learned to read and write.

'Your memory doesn't serve you very well.' She pointed to an entry in the book. 'Ten dollars, wasn't it, Horsebreath?' This question just had to be addressed to my helpmate Freckles.

'Ten,' Horsebreath agreed.

'Ten dollars is still a lot of money,' I remonstrated, quietly impressed at Cleo's book-keeping skills.

'Think of it as a vigilance tax" she said wearily. 'Or in your case a "lack of vigilance" tax. Rich folks don't like us begging, so we oblige them by stealing instead.' She might have been sixteen, but she could summon up all the bored worldliness of a veteran wine waiter.

'I'd prefer to consider it as a charitable donation. Who *are* you?' I surveyed the room. They were like the members of a skeletal orchestra, under the guidance, not of a conductor, but of an accomplished first violin. 'What *is* this?'

'We're the Little Bitches,' Horsebreath volunteered proudly. 'We look out for each other.'

'So I see. Is this some sort of co-operative?'

'Something like that,' Cleo agreed. Obviously whatever threat I posed had begun to dissipate. Most of the girls, other than Cleo, Horsebreath, and the ever-attentive Elephant, had gone back to whatever they'd been doing before they became aware of my presence. The buzz of high-pitched conversation had started up again. Voices were being raised. I wasn't news anymore.

'Why "Little Bitches"?' I inquired of Cleo. She looked at me impatiently and thought about ignoring the question. But she realised that an answer might get rid of me more quickly.

'When your wallet was stolen, what did you shout after the girl who was running away with it?' I thought back for a moment. I smiled when I remembered.

'That's why,' she said. 'Now will you go?'

'I will. Soon. But there's just one more thing ...'

Half an hour later I was in Union Square. It was a relief to breathe ordinary foggy air again, with just a hint of salt. I was glad to be away from the Lair of the Little Bitches, but it had turned out to be a useful exercise.

As I sauntered across the square, I noticed that Newman's gnomes had gathered for a feast. The great man himself was about to address the *hoi polloi*, and the promise of beer, circuses and bigotry had attracted a receptive multitude. My curiosity got the better of me. I waited to see what was going to happen. I studied the crowd as the candidate railed. It was quite instructive to listen to someone who cherished the sound of his own voice as much as did Thomas Newman. The more enthusiastic supporters—the ones who actually wanted to hear what this nickel demagogue had to say—pressed forward to the front of the crowd and waved their fists devotedly as the temperature rose. The others, the ones who had come to swell the numbers and swill the beer, hung back, and tried to disguise their boredom. Now and again one of them would raise a desultory fist in simulated anger, but the effort usually proved too great, and the clenched hand would quickly return to half-hearted equilibrium. Newman's goons were wandering through the crowd distributing chits of paper—to be redeemed later in beer—encouraging the enthusiasts to raucous excess and upbraiding the apathetic for their lethargy.

On the platform, Newman was doing some upbraiding of his own. The object of his ire on this occasion was, for once, not the members of the Oriental community, but the man he witlessly dubbed 'editor of the *Chinese Chronicle*', Michael Henry de Young. De Young was a dilettante and a charlatan. De Young was a fraud and a sham. De Young was, above all else, a liar and a hypocrite. The *Chronicle* dined at the tables of the rich. The *Chronicle* inserted itself into the colon of the Bohemian Club (raucous laughter at this—the scatological never fails to get a reaction), but, principally, the *Chronicle* published outrageous falsehoods about Thomas Newman. De Young would soon feel the force of the public opinion he daily tried to subvert. De Young would learn the meaning of that most excellent Irish coinage, the 'boycott'. But above all else, de Young would pay for his mendacity and see his empire collapse. I doubted if the candidate had any formal training in rhetoric, though I couldn't help but be impressed by his instinctive grasp of oratory. Everything kept coming in threes, as per the template of Cicero and Demosthenes. The gnomes at the front lapped it up, and their raised fists offered a sustained defiance, not least of the enervating forces of gravity and apathy.

If the mob hadn't already been standing, he would have brought them to their feet when he ended with a poem. There was nothing 'recollected in tranquility' about this verse. It was a big bass drum of a poem that Newman beat with euphoric malice. He dedicated it to Michael Henry de Young. I'll see how much I can remember.

> Dum de dum de dum and envy not
> Those fancy tomtit burlesques of mankind,
> Those witless snobs in idleness who rot …
> Oh, sons of toil, be proud, look up, arise …
> A false society's … something or other … despise.

I don't think it was the first time he had recited the verse. Beside me a raucous citizen, who smelt strongly of soot, mouthed the words along with the candidate.

As I watched Newman rouse himself and the crowd into a minor frenzy, I became conscious of someone standing even closer than the chimney sweep. I presumed I had been seen not to share the rapture and was about to be called ashore. I turned, expecting to behold one of Newman's acolytes urging me into some passionate expression of euphoria for the candidate. But it was Campbell. The man had an insidious talent for suddenly just being there. It was highly disconcerting. He looked at me with what I can only describe as a leer and seemed unsteady on his feet.

'Good to see you communing with your kind, Orpen.' His speech was slow. He spoke as if his tongue was swollen inside his mouth. 'This is what you people do well isn't it? Getting your man elected. That, and eating nettles, or starving to death.'

I had to quell an overwhelming urge to break a few of his teeth. As I allowed my better nature to assert itself Campbell resumed his discourse. 'Mr. Newman will simply need to ensure that he doesn't secure more votes in the contest than there are voters. Such over-en-thusiasm has occasionally been the downfall of ambitious Irishmen. Are you an ambitious Irishman, Sergeant Orpen?'

The urge to punch him wasn't going away. 'Are you drunk?' I asked. It was mid-morning, but the hours immediately after dawn's early light had often been known to accommodate Campbell's sottish habits. In response, he breathed on me ostentatiously. I was glad he paid more attention to dental hygiene than my new friend Horsebreath. There was not even a hint of liquor on the wind, but his eyes were black. Even though it was broad daylight, his pupils were fully dilated. He looked like an Oriental after a particularly stupefying pipe of opium.

'You're coming with me,' I said.

Ned Allen's coffee was almost as strong as his liquor. It was bible black and scalding, with the consistency of quicksand. And just as hazard-ous. After one unforgettable experience that had required medical intervention, I learned to avoid it. Campbell, as a rule, never allowed any non-alcoholic beverage to pollute the temple of his body, but in his condition, there were no rules. Ned and I forced the viscous tar-like substance down his throat.

'You know, you're lucky I didn't flatten you back there,' I told him after three cups of steaming liquid with the consistency of pea soup and the pigmentation of melted tobacco.

'You're lucky you didn't flatten me. I'd have got back up. You mightn't have.'

I let it pass. 'How's your head?' I asked, rather too loudly, I hoped.

'It's not my head I'm concerned about. It's my throat. What is this stuff?'

'It's coffee. Haven't you ever drunk coffee before?'

'Of course, I have, and this is nothing like it.'

I nodded to Ned, who poured Campbell another cup. At least I assume 'poured' is the correct word, but since what emerged from the pot was almost solid, I'm not entirely sure.

'You try it, and then tell me that's coffee,' moaned Campbell. 'I'm choking to death here.'

'I wouldn't know. I was raised on a diet of buttermilk and nettles, wasn't I?'

I reckoned the furtive look Campbell gave me was as close as I would ever get to an apology.

'Take it away, Ned, and bring me a bourbon,' Campbell growled.

'By all means take it away, Ned, but hold the bourbon.'

'Since when did you become my daddy?'

'Since your real daddy started bringing you to opium dens in Chinatown.'

I thought he would take a swing at me. He definitely gave it some consideration. He looked at me with narrowed eyes and raised eyebrows. Try it sometime. It's hard to do, but he managed it. Then he changed the subject.

'We had a shtroke of good luck yesterday.' The 'shtroke of good luck' sounded like a feeble effort to take off my accent. It was better than a fist to the jaw. Once again, I let it go.

'Oh really?' I grunted.

'I sent some worker bees in Yankee uniform out with a rough sketch of the crest of Schroeder's carriage. Someone saw it near Stockton and Washington on Saturday night.'

'Are we going back to Nob Hill for another *tête à tête*?'

'Not immediately, no. Lees suggested we wait until we have something more substantial. They've been playing "pass the parcel". Apparently, Schroeder made his feelings about our last visit known to the Mayor, from whom it descended to Crowley and thence down the food chain ... but I'm sure you follow.'

When we got back to the Hall of Justice, no one seemed to have noticed that Campbell had been AWOL. Or if they did, they didn't make any barbed comments. By the time we entered the station, his eyes had turned blue again, thanks to the therapeutic effect of Ned Allen's pumice and lava coffee. We walked past the three inter-rogation rooms on our way to the Detective Office. They had been dubbed Shadrach, Meshach and Abednego after the pious youths thrown into a furnace by Nebuchadnezzar, King of Babylon. As far as I had been able to make out, the first was for shouting at prisoners. The second was for hitting them. The third, which contained writing material, was for compiling statements and scripting plausible expla-nations to account for what occurred in the first two.

Campbell sat down and briefly surveyed the occupants of the detective room. Satisfied by the inspection, he began to open and close drawers methodically. When he had exhausted his supply, he looked up with a half-puzzled, half-crumpled expression on his face. He spoke almost inaudibly.

'Any idea what I did with that envelope we found on Horton? It's not important but it's in the inventory, so I don't want to misplace it.'

'Sorry. Can't help I'm afraid,' I replied, though why I should have been apologetic I'm not sure.

'Must have left it in my other jacket. I'll find it, don't you worry.' I was happy not to.

On the wall over Campbell's shoulder was a line of photographs of San Francisco policemen, most in the Yankee blue uniforms so despised by the Virginian. Immediately behind his chair was the picture of a chiselled hatless man. He looked vaguely familiar.

'Who's that?' I asked Campbell, pointing at the posed photograph.

'The father of your favourite medical examiner' he snapped, without turning.

'You don't mind him looking over your shoulder?'

'He's earned the right. Although he cordially hated my guts, Marcus Williams was one of the finest policeman I ever knew. One day he would have been Chief of Detectives, maybe even Chief of Police.'

'So why do you loathe his daughter?'

'You've known her for as long as I have, and you need to ask?'

I looked behind him again. The picture was tilted ever so slightly out of plumb. I would fix it later.

Campbell was soon ensconced at his desk laboriously engaged in the torment of composition. Whether it was a laundry list or an investigation report, it was all the same to Campbell. He approached each writing assignment with an air of resigned animosity. He was as antipathetic towards the pen and the blank page as he was towards an overreaching Chinatown tong lord. Despite his natural erudition—he talked like Mr. Micawber—his worldly adventures, exciting as they were, did not seem to have included much of a formal education. The Old Sleuth Library might have been entertaining—though he never admitted as much—but it did nothing for his compositional skills, or his spelling. Campbell, for all I knew, could have had a side-line writing the labels for Dr. Lavender's snake oil. I looked over his shoulder surreptitiously—if he'd realised what I was doing, it would have been pistols at dawn on Angel Island. The first word I saw was 'carridge'. I suppose it was only one letter out.

'Why don't I make myself useful?' I said. 'I'm sure you have better things to do than write boring reports. Let me do it. You can read it over afterwards.'

At first, he looked at me suspiciously, concealing the paper with his arm as he did so. Then, when it was clear that the offer was genuine and not the prelude to a condescending joke, he crumpled up the paper, leapt out of his seat and handed me the pen with a childlike grin.

'You're so right. I've got far better things to do.'

'Like upsetting decent law-abiding citizens?' The ringing inter-ruption came from Thaddeus Kelly, who had just walked into the office and marched straight over to Campbell's desk.

'By the pricking of my thumbs, something wicked this way comes,' trilled Campbell. 'Tedious Kelly. Putty in the hands of anyone with a hand-out.' The last was stated in an undertone but was loud enough for Kelly to hear if he chose to do so. He chose not to.

'What is devouring you this time, oh Sergeant of mine?' Camp-bell continued. 'Has someone been putting too much pepper in your potato soup?'

'You've been to Nob Hill,' barked Kelly, ignoring the slur.

'Indeed, I have.' Here Campbell launched into an execrable imi-tation of Kelly's gruff Cork lilt. 'And sure a fierce pleasant walk 'twas and all. But only in the line of dooty. Don't worry, I didn't catch the gravy train. Must have missed the stop. Your pension is safe.' To his credit—something not often in evidence—Kelly did not allow him-self to be diverted by Campbell's provocation.

'A piece of advice. Keep away from Schroeder. You have no cause to go anywhere near him.'

For a moment Campbell made as if to contemplate Kelly's unsought 'advice'. He stroked his face in a pantomime gesture, and then turned to me. 'Orpen, you've been to school. What's the name of that Greek messenger of the Gods? Begins with a 'P' I think.'

'Pegasus?'

'That's the one. Behold ... Pegasus Kelly, messenger from the Deities of Nob Hill. I trust y'all will be well rewarded for your pains, Kelly.'

'You've been warned, Campbell.'

'Thank you for the good counsel.' And if he'd left it there, everything would have been fine. After a fashion. But Campbell always had to have the last word. Even after having had the last word.

'Next time you take a cruise up Newman's back passage, say hello to Riley for me.' Except he didn't call it a back passage. Then, for good measure, he muttered, 'You dim-witted crooked potato-head.'

'What did you call me?' growled Kelly.

'Let me rack my brains. Yes, I believe it was 'you dim-witted crooked potato-head'. Am I right, Orpen?'

I just scowled at him. He wasn't dragging me in. Kelly, red-faced at the best of times, was rapidly approaching puce. I expected steam to start issuing from his ears.

'That's good,' said Kelly menacingly, 'coming from a dope-head and a Chink-lover who is happy to take it up the arse from any tong lord with the key to an opium den.'

Until that moment I never knew that a silence could have actual weight. This one, brief as it was, you could have put on a set of scales and then sliced into a fruit salad.

Campbell turned to me. His eyes had that lazy, faraway look I would get to know well. It meant he was about to pounce. 'Pray ignore the malicious slanders of our esteemed colleague,' he told me: 'the gargoyle of Nob Hill, ruthlessly inept, except in the prosecution of his own self-interest.'

The last sentence was uttered while he was already in motion. With his head still inclined towards me, he started for Kelly. His right hand got to the Irishman's throat first, rapidly followed by the left. Kelly's own hands were quickly on Campbell's wrists, pulling for dear life as his face passed through the colours of the rainbow. I was first on the scene. The other occupants of the office were rooted, staring in horror at the two warring Sergeants.

I pushed both my hands under Campbell's outstretched armpits and locked them behind his head. I tried to lever him away from Kelly but I couldn't budge him. Another Sergeant, quickest to get over his dazed inertia, came up behind me, put his arms around my waist and pulled. Between the two of us, we slowly managed to disengage Campbell. Kelly gingerly fondled his neck. It was already livid where Campbell's talons had left their mark. As they disengaged, the Irishman aimed a kick at Campbell with his right foot, but before he could make contact, Tracy, lured away from the front desk by the noise, swept Kelly's left foot from under him and sat on him. He then hoisted the stricken Sergeant to his feet and effortlessly frog-marched him out of the office. As Kelly was bundled through the door, Campbell, obviously a rapid learner, shouted after him in passable Irish, 'Go n'íosfaidh an tochas thú!'

After that little music-hall fracas, I was grateful for the society of Kenneth Haddo. He had certain deficiencies of character—one of them being his failure to account for the fifty dollars he still owed me—but just then he had the advantage of not being Wellington Campbell.

My mentor had been unhappy, to say the least, at being restrained while his antagonist was escorted from the Detective Office. So, after Kelly had been removed to a place of safety, Campbell had turned on me instead. He kept his hands to himself but indulged his sharp tongue. To the bemusement of his colleagues, he concentrated his fire on my cultural pretensions, and my abject ignorance of Grand

Opera. I couldn't have been more indifferent. I might have retaliated with a few barbs of my own about the abysmal standard of his spelling, but instead I stepped away. As I made my exit from the office, he was singing an aria at the top of his voice and challenging me to identify it. I began to have some serious doubts about the ingredients of Ned Allen's coffee.

I walked through a chilly October evening mist to the Consulate where I had an appointment to meet Haddo. The gangly Consul General was politeness personified. He seemed a trifle uncomfortable, however. I hoped this was a prelude to some embarrassed reference to my fifty dollars, a temporary shortage of funds, and a solemn promise to return the money as soon as possible. That loan, and the loss of ten dollars to the Little Bitches, had left me short.

But his awkwardness had nothing to do with finance. Haddo was genuinely embarrassed. It turned out that he had been in recent communication with London and was unsure how to broach the subject of Gosselin's unhappiness with my lack of progress. He tried to mitigate the impact of his report with another steaming cup of tea. It was Chinese, not a particular favourite of mine. It helped a little, but it didn't raise my morale. I was forewarned when Haddo used The Gosling's real name, as if he feared even such a remote hint of disrespect would get back to Whitehall and jeopardise his career.

'Sir Nicholas is a little concerned about the fact that a number of extraneous individuals seem to be aware of your presence here.'

'By "a little concerned", you mean "crazy like a grizzly bear", don't you?'

'I wouldn't put it quite like that.'

I would. I saw a copy of the telegram a few months later. The diplomat was being extremely diplomatic in his phraseology. I remember that the word 'imbecile' was used, more than once, and that a substantial sum of money, diligently collected by Her Majesty's Revenue Commissioners, had been expended on superfluous verbiage, all of it abusive. This was in radical defiance of Exchequer standing orders insisting that all international telegraphic communications should be concise. Haddo made it his business to soften the impact of the harangue from London, but I got the message. My spectral superiors were not best pleased with my efforts thus far.

'Sir Nicholas was of the opinion that you might have managed to make contact with Horton,' Haddo observed, reluctant to depress me further.

'Quite challenging … given his sad passing. The Gosling is aware that the man is dead, isn't he?'

'Yes. I think he meant to suggest that you might have had a quiet word *before* his demise.'

'I'm sure that wraith-like God-botherer Anderson has the means to contact him in the afterlife if they need more information,' I remarked morosely. Haddo, bless him, pretended to take my side.

'Undoubtedly. Don't worry about it. No harm done. Have some more tea.'

Not even a premier Darjeeling would have lifted my mood, so I declined any more of his insipid Chinese brew. 'Am I going to be recalled?' I asked self-pityingly. 'Will I spend the next decade trailing pimps in the East End?'

'Absolutely not, old boy. I think I managed to mollify Sir Nicholas with a communication of my own to the effect that you were playing the long game. I believe I implied that while you were carrying out a tactical withdrawal, you had wider strategic objectives justifying the temporary retreat and that the mission would be accomplished soon.'

'You were more concise than that, I trust.'

'Absolutely. Budgets are budgets after all.'

'Did he fall for it?'

'His second cablegram was not quite as testy as his first.' That probably would have been the optimum time for Haddo to request a write-off of the fifty-dollar debt. Instead, he tossed me an entirely different bone of contention. 'How is your accommodation by the way?' Was it possible that this minor matter had been weighing on his mind?

'Sublime!' I replied, opting for the lie expansive. 'Couldn't be better if I was staying with my own family.' That bit was true at least. Accommodation in a whorehouse was immeasurably preferable to lodging with my father. 'Bella has even offered me a job playing piano in the parlour, assuming I can manage a music-hall repertoire.'

'I'm so glad to hear you two are getting along. Bella can be a touch … idiosyncratic. And her cat has a reputation for squalid violence.'

'Really. Can't say as I've noticed.' The exchange of a slight smile was the only acknowledgement that I was lying to spare his blushes. We parted on good terms, with assurances on my side that all was not lost. I appeared more optimistic than I felt, but while Haddo did not have the complete picture he had been right about the long game. I wasn't entirely bereft of ideas.

With a slightly overweight heart, I left the consulate and began to walk north through yet another murky fog–I swear I'm not just inserting them for the sake of atmosphere–towards Green Street and my constant companion, Griselda.

As I approached North Beach, walking along Kearny, I heard footsteps behind me. Acting on the assumption that the owners of the feet craved an audience, I quickened my pace in response. My pursuers now made no attempt to conceal their desire for a meeting. Their eyes must have been more accustomed to San Francisco fogs than mine because I couldn't shake them. As I neared the corner of Green and Grant, from nowhere obvious, a large figure emerged from the mist and blocked my way.

CHAPTER TEN

OPHELIA WILLIAMS

18 October

My day should have been over. Not much of a one as days go. But, like Alice's, it was about to become curiouser. I'd fallen asleep in front of the meager fire and was awoken by the chill when it finally gave up the ghost. I was now wide awake, so I put on my overcoat and reached for some lofty reading material. Just then, it must have been around midnight, a loud banging at the door forced me to abandon my plan to devour the latest Montgomery Ward catalog—educational purposes only, you understand—with a hot water bottle in my lap. The percussion was insistent. The caller was knocking violently with the side of his fist, rather than rapping politely with the knuckles. The effect was that of a booming bass drum. I had strayed into a nocturnal Fourth of July parade. I got up reluctantly to answer the door, taking Messrs. Smith and Wesson with me. I've never met either gentleman, but they always make me feel much safer.

I opened the door a few inches but a solid weight pushing against me pressed it open further. It was the body of a man. My first instinct was to retreat as rapidly as possible but whoever it was didn't look as if he was going to jump up, holler 'Surprise' and skewer me. At first, I couldn't make out who was lying on my doormat. He was face down and it was dark. I tested the recumbent form delicately, with my right foot. There was an answering groan. I managed to turn over the body with some indelicate footwork. It was the Irishman, Orpen. He was clutching his chest in obvious pain, and he grimaced as I twisted him onto his back.

'Would you mind not putting your foot just there,' he gasped. It was hovering over his ribs. 'Stepping out or just stepped in?' he asked, indicating my overcoat.

'Neither. What happened?'

I dropped to my knees to take a closer look. There was no sign of blood, but he was obviously in a lot of pain. He winced as I tried to open the buttons of his coat.

'Mormons,' he wheezed, 'insistent on saving my immortal soul, to the point of violence.' He then lapsed into a coughing fit that brought on a string of curses.

I was unmoved. 'Serves you right for being so amusing.' I managed to get him to his feet, down the corridor and onto my couch. Taking off his coat and jacket was a more difficult proposition. He wanted to keep his left arm entirely to himself. When he moved it even an inch or two, he would unleash a mouthful of curses in at least three languages, one of which I recognized as French. His shoulder was dislocated. There was going to be an unpleasant prolog to any inspection of his ribs. I sneaked my left hand under his jacket. With my other hand, I patted him solicitously on the injured shoulder.

'So where did you learn such colorful language?' I asked. As soon as he began another smart mouth reply, I pushed his upper arm firmly against my right hand. There was a click, immediately followed by another screech, this time of guttural Teutonic expletives. Turns out he could speak German too. The poor soul was going to linguistic extremes to spare my blushes. He needn't have bothered. I'm not much of a blusher.

'If you will keep making jokes ...!'

I was probably a little unsympathetic, but he didn't appear to be too far gone and I had really been looking forward to a long session with Montgomery Ward. Smith, Wesson, and orthopaedic interventions were a poor substitute.

'Now then,' I continued, 'while we're taking off your coat and jacket, very slowly and deliberately I suggest, you tell me what really happened. Mormons only do house calls.'

As we struggled to remove his heavy greatcoat, he described how he had been followed up Kearny Street by at least two men. 'I suppose I should have tried to work my way back to Portsmouth Square … ow … is that really necessary?'

'Yes.' We hadn't even got the right sleeve off. There was worse to come.

'But I got muddled in the fog and kept going north … Jesus wept! SCHEISSE! Could you not find some other way of doing that?'

'Would you prefer me to cut off the sleeves? I'm sure I can find a scalpel around here somewhere.' He thought about this for a moment before fear, or thriftiness, asserted itself.

'No thanks. I like this coat. Keep pulling. Gently does it though. OWWWWWW!' That was after a surprise frontal assault on his left sleeve. It worked a treat. Now we had the coat off. I threw it onto a chair beside the fireplace. A waft of air as it settled on the armrest briefly brought the embers back to life. He pulled away instinctively as I turned back to outflank the jacket.

'Carry on,' I said. 'Last time we talked, you were staggering about in the fog?'

'Long story short, they caught up with me in North Beach. I think another one of them was already waiting for me. Then they gaily gamboled all over me, though they'd left their nice soft dancing pumps at home.'

His right arm was now out of the jacket. He looked warily in my direction and gingerly extracted the left arm himself by bending his upper body towards the floor, though not without suffering in the process. I asked him to lie on the couch. He did so with flinching

reluctance. I pressed his ribcage lightly. You'd have thought I was trying to brand him. He would never have made a Stoic. He sat bolt
upright. The oaths were in French again. I wondered did his Fran-
co-German vocabulary extend beyond the profane. I pushed his head
back down onto the couch and continued to explore his upper torso.

'Two ribs broken, I think. But I'd have to perform an autopsy to
be sure.' He laughed at that, and immediately regretted it. 'Any idea
who they were?' I asked. He had a haunted look about him. I think
he'd begun to realize that keeping up his end of the conversation was
likely to involve considerable pain. I probably should have been more
sensitive. But my empathy deserted me at around the same age as I
lost my capacity to blush.

'They were masked, and they didn't say very much, but one of
them was built like Nelson's Pillar. I think we've met before. You had
a brush with him yourself down on Market Street a couple of days
ago. They call him Howie.'

'I remember—built like a siege train. It was a fleeting acquaintance, thankfully. How did you get away?'

He smiled cheerily. 'Presence of mind.' The smile traveled all
the way to his eyes. 'And presence of this.' He produced a small Colt
revolver from his pocket, one of those police issue models. 'I managed
to get a shot in. It brought down the curtain on the hobnailed ballet.'

I made another move in his direction. He played for time.

'Do you think I could have some water?'

I poured the residue of a pitcher into a chapped cup that was
lying on the mantelpiece over the fireplace. He handed me the Colt
and drank the water avidly. Something bothered me about his gun,
but I wasn't sure what. I put it beside the Smith and Wesson that I'd
left on a small table by the couch. I needed to get him talking again
so that I could examine his ribs more closely.

'Why did they bother trying to beat you up? Why didn't they just
kill you?'

'A question better addressed to— OW! You did that deliberately.'

I had confirmed my original diagnosis. Only two ribs broken. 'You were lucky. You got off lightly,' I observed. He gave me an unappreciative 'try walking in my shoes' sort of look. 'Well, they ran off, didn't they?' I added, by way of explanation. 'Two broken ribs are a lot better than being knifed and dumped in the Bay.'

He smiled again. This one wasn't for my benefit. 'You never know who I might have bumped into there.' It was just a beat and then he was back again. Green eyes with a surprising sparkle. I could see he was regaining his aplomb.

'I don't think my family jewels would agree that I "got off lightly", by the way.'

'I see. Do you want me to examine you … down there?' His default smirk was replaced by a look of sheer horror. He blushed a fetching shade of scarlet. Sometimes I love being a doctor. I shifted the subject away from his genitalia. 'Incidentally, I admire your work.'

'My work?'

'I did an autopsy yesterday. It was on something our friends in blue like to call a floater, to show how grown-up and callous they are.'

'Some … thing?'

'It was a shade too far gone to call it 'someone'. I'd say he'd been about five days in the water. Name of Madden. If he hadn't been hooked, he'd still be down there. The Bay is a tad warmer, but still quite chilly at this time of year, so he could have stayed under for another couple of weeks.'

'Why do you think this has anything to do with me?'

'Because, when someone is drowning, their retina records the image of the last person they see.'

He eyed me with a mixture of disbelief and concern. Mostly concern.

'Is that true?' he asked nervously. Like I said, sometimes I just love being a doctor.

'No. It's an old wives' tale, but I had you worried. Tracy might have mentioned that you and Ollie Madden had a difference of opinion.' He laughed, but it barely reached his cheeks this time. 'You'll need to get your ribs bandaged properly. And that arm should be in a sling for a few days at least. You've dislocated your shoulder.'

'I had some help. What you did ...' his face clouded over as he remembered the 'click,' '... is that called "re-location"?'

'Reduction. So, I guess you've just been reduced.' A vague hope on my part— long odds—prompted another question.

'The men who attacked you. Do you think one of them might have been Christopher Riley?'

'Perhaps. He would certainly be more nondescript in a mask than his friend Howie. And, as I said, they were remarkably uncommunicative.'

The clock on the mantelpiece struck midnight.

'You got off one shot?' I asked.

'I did.'

'Any chance you might have hit him?'

'I don't think so. Maybe a window of the corner house on Green and Dupont, but not Riley. Would it make you feel better if I said I had?'

'I'm just fine. But it would still make me feel better.'

'Campbell told me about your father. I'm sorry.'

My gaze wandered back to the mantelpiece. Beside the clock was a photograph of a kindly, smiling, middle-aged man in a dark blue uniform. Orpen followed my eyes. He stared at the picture for a while.

'What brought you here by the way?'

'The prospect of having my left arm almost ripped from its socket by a real professional.' He winced at the memory.

'Always glad to help. But how did you know where I lived? I don't remember exchanging addresses. Of course, any friend of the high-minded Sergeant Campbell is a friend of mine.' That drew a rueful grin.

'He can be a bit of a trial, can't he?'

'Preferably for a capital offence. But you still haven't told me how you found me.'

'Oh, you know how it is? One hears things. Round and about.'

'Does one?'

'One does.'

Because he hailed from a much older civilization, I was at a disadvantage when it came to jousting. I put down my lance and picked up a scalpel. Here I was on firmer ground.

'I expect you'll have at least one willing female to assist your convalescence, won't you?' I ventured. A sharp look of surprise was followed by a momentary embarrassment, but he quickly shrugged it off. I hope it didn't hurt his shoulder.

'Ah, so you're aware of my singular accommodation on Green Street?' He knew that wasn't what I meant, but I wasn't brazen enough to inquire directly about the woman with the mop of blonde hair.

'One hears things. Round and about,' I prodded.

'Touché. Yes, Bella and her ladies do look after me extremely well. Now then, I've taken up too much of your beauty sleep already. I should be on my way. Thank you for your thoroughly professional and deliciously painful assistance.'

He gathered up his coat and jacket and walked to the door. I followed him.

'Aren't you forgetting something?' I asked. He looked a trifle bewildered. Then his face cleared.

'Ah. I wonder can we leave the matter of your fee till a later date. I came out without my wallet. Just as well really.'

I said nothing, I just handed him the revolver.

'When you are having your ribs bound, you might ask them to check for symptoms of concussion as well,' I suggested. He smiled wanly.

'Goodnight, Doctor Williams.'

'Goodnight, Sergeant Orpen.'

He made as if to tip his hat politely before realizing that he was no longer wearing one. Raising his eyes as if in search of the missing headgear, he turned blithely and walked away. As he did so, I was tempted to bring up the one major issue I had with his story, but I didn't bother.

I've been around guns all my life. I also have an excellent sense of smell. I was certain of one thing; his gun had not been fired.

CHAPTER ELEVEN

ORPEN

19 October 1883—Morning

With a couple of broken ribs, the last thing you want to see when you wake up is the malevolent visage of Beelzebub's pet cat at the foot of your bed. You also need to remind yourself not to make any sudden movement. By sudden movement I really mean movement of any kind. Of course, I forgot to remind myself. I rolled to my right to get out of the bed, as I do every morning, and a dart of pain efficiently restored the memory of my misadventures of the night before.

Griselda didn't appear at all put out by my discomfort. He just lay there with that look of unmitigated contempt that characterised our interactions. I have no doubt that Griselda had, at one point in his life, or maybe in a previous existence, been a prizefighter. His body bore evidence of a career in the ring. His nose was misshapen, and he had lost the business end of his tail. His right ear was at a peculiar angle to his head as if some heavyweight opponent had got a grip of it and refused to let go. A wise move. I doubted if many of his fights had been conducted according to feline Queensberry rules, or if any had gone the distance.

As we eyed each other sullenly, there was a knock on the door. It was one of Bella's girls, Sadie, a good-natured type from Louisiana. I often wondered why she would have seen the need to abandon New Orleans to ply her trade. She must have really annoyed somebody if she couldn't get a job in her chosen walk of life in that Gomorrah. I felt a bit guilty when I saw her. She had been cleaning my room every day, unasked. But when I'd thanked Bella for the great job Sadie was doing, she gave me one of her enigmatic looks. I didn't know at the time that I should have been worried. I made it far worse by trying to explain. It turned out that Sadie was just doing me a favour. Either that, or the state of my room upset her sensibilities—something I can readily understand. 'Neat' is how I take my whiskey. It turned out that tidying up after me wasn't part of the service. Bella said she'd be talking to Sadie, and not in soft words of commendation either. Time spent attending to my neglected housework was time not spent earning her keep. Their little heart to heart had obviously taken place because when Sadie entered, she had a right eye that was changing colour by the minute. Bella was left-handed, so she had clearly administered the punishment herself rather than leave it to underlings.

'There's a polis man downstairs says he wants to see you urgent,' she said shyly.

'What does he look like?' I asked, tensing up in preparation for another visit from Kelly.

'Wild Bill Hickock. Lots of hair. Tall as a redwood.'

I breathed a sigh of relief, although it was probably naïve of me to assume that Kelly would have waited around downstairs while I got dressed. Campbell was a tad more genteel. Or maybe it was prurience.

He was waiting for me on Green Street, but this time he wasn't quietly contemplating nature with the gaze of a philosopher. He was pacing impatiently. When he spotted me, he turned on his heel immediately without even indicating that I should follow. The long coat he was wearing threw up dust on what passed for a pavement as he walked. He looked as if he was moving at the centre of a cloud. I got the distinct impression that he was trying to make an impression.

Today he was playing the role of 'surly and imperious Detective Sergeant' in the Dixie Sleuth library series.

We walked at his pace—which means I never actually managed to catch up with him—until we got to Chinatown. In a three-mile steeplechase, with my two broken ribs, the handicapper would have given him extra weight to carry. We passed a newsstand where the city's dailies were competing for an angle on Thomas Newman's promotion to the Board of Supervisors. He had won the third, either by the power of his rhetoric and the appeal of his agenda, or by hiring goons to beat up Republican voters—it depended on which paper you read. I thought about using this development as a way of striking up a conversation with Campbell but gave up the idea when I realised that I needed all my breath for breathing.

After crossing Broadway, Campbell slowed to an Oriental shuffle and led me up and down a couple of narrow streets before stopping. Then, as an afterthought, he turned around to make sure that I had followed him. Two muscular policemen stood guard over something. I recognised one of them as a bald and leathery desk sergeant named Slyne, who looked odd when removed from his natural habitat. We were still somewhere near Broadway, though I wasn't sure exactly where. Then I spotted what he'd brought me there to see. There was a body propped against a low wall, a neat bullet hole in his forehead. The back of the skull was more disorganised. It looked like the long-range work of a sniper rifle, though that was unlikely in such a tight maze of tall buildings. It took me a while to recognise the victim, followed by a major effort to conceal my delight. Someone had sent Doghouse Riley to the spirit world. There would be no more filleting for Christopher. I was tempted to dance a little jig, but it was just as well I resisted.

'You don't seem too shocked,' Campbell growled.

I shrugged. 'Someday … someone.' I studied the corpse again, more sombrely this time, not to please Campbell but to make sure it wasn't just wishful thinking. No, it was Riley all right.

'I suppose I was wondering when the three days of official mourning begins and where can I sign the book of condolences.'

'Comical! One less Fenian to harass Her Britannic Majesty? Lucky you.'

'Fewer,' and before he could ask, ' ... one *fewer* Fenian. It's nicely alliterative as well, don't you think?' His withering look made it clear that he was in no mood for a tutorial on grammatical solecisms or poetic appreciation.

'Where were you last night?' he barked. I couldn't help noticing that his lips were pursed. I felt like an inebriated husband being called to account by a tetchy wife. The author of the Dixie Sleuth series would not have been impressed at Campbell's thin effeminate lips and would have left out that bit. I pointed to the discoloration beginning to establish sovereignty around my left eye. I'd spotted it in the mirror that morning, all the while monitoring the movements of Griselda behind me. Campbell shrugged and grunted.

'I was being set upon by a thoroughly incompetent group of aspiring assassins.'

He studied me more closely. 'And that's all they managed to accomplish ... before you scattered them in disarray?' The lips unpursed. The brows knitted instead. He didn't sound very compassionate. Or convinced.

'That, and a couple of broken ribs.' I added a wan smile, for effect. He brushed it aside.

'Three misbegotten knaves in Kendal green?' he suggested. If he really knew his Shakespeare, I didn't much like the implication of Falstaffian mendacity.

'More like four rogues in buckram.'

'You didn't happen to recognise any of them, I suppose, so that we can see if they would be willing to confirm your story?'

'It was so dark, Hal, that thou couldst not see thy hand.'

'All right. Enough Shakespeare for now. Did *anyone* see this ... vicious assault?'

'No, but Dr. Williams can vouch for me. She bandaged my ribs.'

'Did she indeed? And you weren't even dead.' He looked at me dolefully, sighed, and reluctantly decided to lock away his suspicions, for the moment at least. I figured he would keep the key close at hand. 'All right. I don't think y'all are stupid or desperate enough to have killed Riley. It was open season on the bastard anyway. I was just making a point. When I drew up my mental *cui bono* list, guess who was right on top?'

'Your suspicious nature does you credit. I'm happy for you, by the way. No knives. You'll be able to enlist the aid of your friend Mr. Vernon.'

'And this time we have the eggs *and* the bacon.' From his pocket, he produced a revolver. It was a brand-new German Mauser with a seven-inch barrel, the 1879 'cavalry model'. In the right hands, and with that much barrel, you might be able to hit a target at up to fifty paces. 'We found it in that alleyway'. He pointed up the hill towards a nondescript lane, less than a hundred yards distant. It was the murder weapon all right. The M1879 was a lovely piece. You wouldn't just toss it away unless you had good cause.

Campbell's bulky form was blocking my view of the body. I ostentatiously craned my neck, stood on tiptoes, and looked over his shoulder. He took the blatant hint and motioned me towards the mortal remains of my former sparring partner. He had a puzzled look. Riley, that is, not Campbell. Campbell was all certainty and taciturnity. Riley had the appearance of someone who had been asked a question to which he had no answer. Other than the pinhole in his forehead the front of his skull was without blemish. Whoever killed him had probably been quite a distance away.

'Excellent shot,' I observed.

'Or lucky.' Campbell countered. 'Either way, he probably wasn't killed from close range. And unless someone else got to him first, he was travelling light too. There's nothing in his pockets. Not even a knife.'

That did surprise me. 'I'd have thought he never left home without one.' I looked around. The low wall against which the body was propped was about ten or twelve yards from the windowless gable end of a tall building. The distance and angles were all wrong. 'He wasn't shot from over there,' I pointed out, nodding towards the gable.

'No. Too close. He was dragged here from the far side of this wall. Look at the tracks. Either he was dumped here by his killer, or he had someone with him when it happened, and he was pulled behind the wall for cover. Either way, he was shot in the street.'

Behind me I could hear raised voices. Slyne was remonstrating with someone. At least that wasn't so unusual. He was a born remonstrator. His ancestors had probably spent their lives arguing with bailiffs and landlords' agents on a meagre holding somewhere in the south of Ireland. The party of the second part was female. Slyne's voice and hackles were raised. The woman's tone was quiet and insistent; that's why it took me a while to recognise it. Campbell's expression as he stared belligerently over my shoulder certainly helped. It was my very own Good Samaritan from the previous night. I had no idea what Ophelia Williams was doing at the scene of a crime.

She clearly hadn't just come upon the tragic tableau by accident. She was dressed for the street; in the overcoat I had seen her wearing the previous night, and carrying her medical bag. She was, it appeared from the tenor of the argument, determined to get access to Riley's body. Slyne was doggedly trying to keep her at bay. He was good at 'dogged', so she wasn't making much headway. But when he trotted out the old saw 'this is no place for a woman', I winced. I wasn't that well acquainted with her, but from what I knew, I didn't think she would sit primly under that sort of provocation. I could see her debating with herself whether to continue the argument or just push the beefy Irishman aside. For the moment, she kept talking.

'Even if that woman is a police surgeon, Sergeant?'

The occurrence of the words 'woman' and 'police' in a single sentence had the same effect on Slyne as if Ophelia Williams had simply shoved him out of the way in the first place. Even from where I was standing, you could hear the gasp. Then he started working up to a 'harrumph'. She took advantage of his perplexity and his loss of faith in moral authority, and just sailed past him. As she did so, she washed up on the treacherous coast of Wellington Campbell, a much rockier proposition than Slyne.

'Good morning, Dr. Williams.' His opening gambit—white pawn to King's Bishop three—seemed affable enough. But there were concealed reefs.

Her response—black pawn to King four—was a polite but non-committal 'Good morning'. That was when Campbell, ill-advisedly, moved a second white pawn to King's Knight four. 'You need to leave immediately,' he instructed, with barely disguised jubilation.

'Do I?' she replied sweetly (black Queen to King's Rook five). 'Not according to your Chief of Detectives. He thinks it's high time police surgeons visited the scene of the crime while the body is still *in situ*. I'm sure you agree that Captain Lees is extremely forward thinking.' White King was stranded. Nowhere to run, block or capture. Fool's Mate.

Despite losing in only two moves, Campbell recovered his equilibrium remarkably quickly. He tried a new opening gambit. 'May I ask how you became aware of the crime? I know that good news travels fast, but it appears to have demonstrated an unusual turn of foot in this case.'

'Jungle drums,' she replied breezily and vaguely.

'I don't hear them.'

'That's possibly because your ears are more attuned to the other-wise inaudible pitch of a dog whistle.'

I decided that this would be a good time to intervene.

'Since you are here, Dr. Williams, perhaps you can confirm to Sergeant Campbell that you assisted me in the small matter of a couple of broken ribs late last night.'

'I can. How are they? Do they hurt much?'

'As someone not far from here once observed, "only when I laugh".'

'Then don't.'

She turned back to her antagonist. 'May I be allowed to do my job, Sergeant Campbell, or should we take it up with Captain Lees?'

Campbell knew when he was beaten. He stood aside and motioned Ophelia Williams towards the corpse with an exaggerated and calculatedly ironic display of graciousness. 'Now I've seen it all,' he told her as she opened her bag: 'medical examiners making house calls. I'm sure we're all very grateful. Are you hoping to make the poor detective entirely redundant?'

'The *poor* detective, yes.' That finally shut him up and he took out his annoyance on Slyne as Ophelia approached the corpse. When she saw who it was her body suddenly seemed to go slack. Her movements slowed down and for a second, I thought she was going to keel over, but she recovered herself and stood for fully half a minute staring at the dead man. Until Campbell became aware of the sudden stillness that had descended on his crime scene.

'This isn't a Chamber of Horrors, ma'am,' he remarked. 'You haven't paid a nickel to come and have a look. And we haven't got all day.'

His gibe seemed to bring her back to the moment. She glared at him scornfully and immediately set about her preliminary examination. Given that she was surveying the body of the man who had probably murdered her father, she seemed unexpectedly dispassionate. Perhaps when she got him back to the Hall of Justice, I thought, she might take unprofessional pleasure in hacking lumps out of the body unnecessarily. Had she been from a different culture, she would have used the opportunity to fashion a bracelet from his ears and make a necklace of his teeth. His penis would probably have ended up in his mouth. I just stopped short of visualising her boiling his decapitated head and sharing it over dinner with her mother.

When she had finished and issued instructions for the body to be moved to Portsmouth Square, Campbell made an extravagant display of not asking her a single question about her findings. He was probably itching to know, at the very least, the approximate time of death, but he wasn't going to give her the satisfaction of his interest until she had performed a formal autopsy. As far as he was concerned, she had defiled hallowed ground, and he wasn't going to reward her blasphemous behaviour.

Just as Ophelia Williams left—and I was curious myself as to how she had found out about Riley's murder so rapidly—Ross Walsh, the *Chronicle* reporter, arrived, summoned either by jungle drums or a dog whistle. He tipped his hat to Ophelia as they passed each other and smiled benignly at her, though his first reaction on seeing her there had been one of surprise. Since she had her back turned to me at the time, I didn't catch her response.

Campbell greeted Walsh warmly. 'You look like animated shit,' he said. He was not far wrong. The *Chronicle* reporter, normally spruce, appeared to have been invaded by Colorado beetle.

'You're not at your dappest, are you?' added Campbell enigmatically.

'Dappest …?' inquired a puzzled Walsh.

'Dap, dapper, dappest,' explained Campbell patronisingly, as if the poverty of the reporter's vocabulary had been exposed. I could see that Walsh was thinking about administering a grammatical beating but decided it would be a pointless exercise.

'A soirée?' inquired Campbell.

'A riot,' said Walsh. 'You can read about it in the late edition. I've filed my copy and now I'm going home. "A baying mob unleashed on Chinatown" was my suggested headline but doubtless that idiot Blighe will go for something more prosaic. And he will manage to bury the lede five fathoms deep. Couldn't sub a birthday card.'

'A riot? Where?' said Campbell.

'Why?' I asked. Walsh looked at both of us quizzically, then rubbed his eyes.

'Geography question first,' he replied, 'It began on Stockton and Broadway and snaked its way to Dupont and Pacific.' He turned to me. 'Why did a mob of masked warriors, and frankly inept arsonists—they couldn't set fire to a cigar covered in whale blubber—pretend to be the reincarnation of the Hounds? I don't know. Boredom? Practice? Perhaps they were all breast-fed by wet nurses rather than Mumsie? Though I suspect it was because they were paid for their exertions. Now, can we get on with this? I got your message and I'm all agog, but I need to get to bed before the Chinese New Year.'

Without even waiting for a nod from Campbell the reporter went to work. He might have been buying a racehorse. The inspection was thorough and involved rather too much poking and prodding for my liking. He twisted and turned the corpse almost as much as Ophelia Williams had done, while Campbell looked on tolerantly.

When Walsh was finished wrestling with the late Christopher Riley, he began writing in a large battered hardback notebook. After scribbling a few sentences, he stepped back from the body, took out a pencil and started to sketch. His head bobbed between notebook and corpse as he made a drawing of Riley's remains. I looped around behind him surreptitiously to see how he was doing. He wasn't much of an artist. Maybe he was drawing it for the delectation of a small child with macabre tastes, because the sketch was not likely to make the front page of the *Chronicle* under the banner headline 'Last agonies of an assassin'. Assuming the pedantic sub-editor, Blighe, whoever he was, would tolerate something so sensational.

When he snapped the notebook shut, it was *quid pro quo* time. Campbell got straight to the point. 'What have you got for me?'

Walsh wasn't in the least fazed. He knew he was not being made privy to information denied every other reporter in San Francisco just because Campbell admired his *oeuvre* or cherished the way the sun played upon his lustrous brown locks as they cascaded across his pale forehead.

'Lots,' he began. 'We've established that our friend Charlie boy has been making a number of property purchases near Chinatown, all going for a song, but he's hiding behind third parties, so we can't prove it.'

Campbell sniffed. 'I can read, you know. *Chronicle*, 17 October, front page. I was hoping for something a bit fresher than two-day-old gruel. Who are these third parties?'

Walsh grinned and pointed at the corpse of Riley. 'That's one of them, right there. And I thought you never read the *Chronicle*?'

Campbell whistled. In spite of himself he was impressed. 'From the Doghouse to the penthouse. So, our Christopher was coming up in the world?'

'And our friend is not after the rent roll either. He means to sell on, and he won't make a profit worth bothering about unless his new real estate isn't next door to Chinatown anymore. Hence the dress rehearsal from the goons last night. That's the real 'why?' Mr. Metropolitan policeman,' he said, turning to me.

'It's Sergeant Metropolitan policeman, actually,' I replied. Walsh sniffed and appeared to address Riley as an alternative to continuing the conversation with Campbell and myself.

'You see Christopher, Charlie isn't rich enough already. He needed to catch up with the Silver Kings and the Big Four to win the respect of his neighbourhood. Though I suppose you know that already. Knew that.'

Despite the interesting intelligence Campbell was getting, just for having allowed a reporter to manhandle a corpse, he looked slightly aggrieved. 'And how is it that *you* know all this, and we don't?'

'Because Schroeder is not doing anything illegal, and because the Police Department doesn't have a Michael Henry de Young who's prepared to foot the bill to bring him down, and Newman along with him. It's personal with young Mike. Schroeder must have stolen his lunch at school or something. He loathes him, just because he can. He's going to keep bankrolling this until he has destroyed Schroeder or goes bust trying.'

'And how does Schroeder intend to get rid of the Celestials? He wouldn't be the first to have tried.'

'Beat 'em and burn 'em. Like the little show last night. He's hoping if he unleashes his hyenas often enough, any Chinese who have managed to make a few dollars will lose heart and just go home. Then if no one is paying the highbinders for protection any longer, the tongs will take lumps out of one another instead, and the whole temple will come crashing down. No more Chinatown. No more deflated prices for the properties next door. And, hey presto, we have a new Emperor of Nob Hill.'

'Where does Newman come into the picture, though I can probably figure that out?'

'Your ten-year-old idiot nephew in Alabama could figure it out. That's where you're from, right? Newman's job is to provide the hyenas. Then he runs a full slate at the next election, wins, and makes things even hotter for the Chinese than Kearney and the WPC did. Kearney was a blowhard. Newman is smarter, and he wants to see Schroeder in the Governor's mansion just as much as Schroeder wants to see *him* in the Mayor's Office.'

'When are you going to publish all this?'

Walsh chortled. I think that was when I discovered what a hollow laugh sounds like. 'Publish? Are you kidding me? Maybe never. We can hint as much as we want—we have been—but if we're going to bury him, then the coffin has to be properly nailed down. Otherwise, Schroeder just calls in Bucher, Gendzel and Spangler, and we are roasted chestnuts.'

'Who are they—German gunmen?'

'Close enough. They're his Dobermans. His legal representatives. Any one of them could stand up in a court of law and get a jury to agree that the square on the hypotenuse is *not* equal to the sum of the squares on the other two sides. Once those gents have got our balls in a vice, we are chop suey.'

'Doesn't your famous First Amendment protect you?' I asked.

Walsh looked at me pityingly. 'I once heard somebody call the First Amendment "a stout oak". To me that just means it doesn't provide much cover in winter.'

Campbell looked at Walsh ruefully. 'I love my job,' he said, 'I get to arrest lots of snakes. But the cross-legged gentleman with the flute always gets away. Just this once. . .'

'That should be the *Chronicle*'s motto. If de Young wasn't such a high-minded Phi Beta Kappa boy, we'd have published what we have long ago. He's vindictive, but he's got scruples.'

Campbell went quiet. He seemed to be staring at Riley's corpse but his eyes were oddly sightless.

Walsh opened his notebook and wrote something. I did what silent observers are supposed to do. My immobility somehow affronted Campbell.

'Are you getting all this?' he snapped.

I nodded. 'If it's any consolation, the same kind of thing happens in London,' I ventured.

'That much I know,' Campbell replied, 'but what was the point of having wasted all that lovely Boston Harbour tea if we can't be any different?'

Walsh put down his notebook. He turned back to me. 'I have something for you as well, *Sergeant* Metropolitan policeman. Where the dead are concerned, thankfully the First Amendment is a pine tree. You can read the *Chronicle* tomorrow for a fuller account, complete with adjectives, but it transpires that Dan Horton's attachment to the 'old sod' was not merely sentimental. He was actively seeking enough dynamite to blow London back to the status of a small town on a river bend.'

'Actively seeking … from who?' I asked.

'I think you mean 'from whom' don't you? That's where it gets really interesting. He was playing footsy with the tongs. The Suey Sing had a more than adequate supply of the stuff and, in return for a few sticks to help 'dear old Ireland' Horton was offering to assist them in their war against the Hop Sing. Now, as you can imagine, that did not go down well in certain parts of Nob Hill, and elsewhere, and may well have contributed to the shuffling off of his mortal coil.'

'Will the adjectives in tomorrow's *Chronicle* make it any more compelling?'

'Not a bit. But my editor is a slave to the qualifier.'

When we got back to Portsmouth Square, Kelly was in his pomp, holding forth at the top of his lungs. If there'd been a chandelier in the office, he would have been swinging from it. His face looked even uglier when it was wreathed in exultant smiles. Despite his obvious elation, the joy still didn't quite make it to his eyes. This left you with the impression of someone who had been looking forward to his own demise and was still smiling when *rigor mortis* set in.

It turned out that Kelly had played a bit part in the capture of a bothersome stagecoach robber known as 'Black Bart'. Kelly's story was that he'd been asked to accompany a Wells Fargo detective named Hume to the boarding house where Bart was hiding away in San Francisco after his most recent attempt at a robbery had gone about as swimmingly as the Charge of the Light Brigade. Bart was supposed to be some sort of English aristocrat, or a member of the British royal family, or at least he'd gone to Eton.

The way Kelly told the story, he had tracked down Bart himself and clapped him in handcuffs after an epic battle of wits across the rooftops of Union Square. We'd brought Walsh with us. He went to work with professional zeal.

'So, what were you doing tagging along with Jim Hume?' Walsh asked.

'I wasn't just tagging along. I was the official representative of the City Police in the arrest.'

'Ah! So, you were along for the ride. How did Wells Fargo find him?'

'How the hell do I know?'

'Was he heavily armed?'

'Not exactly.'

'Not exactly? What does that mean? Was he armed at all?'

'I … suppose not. Jesus, you dogs would take the good out of anything. What are you doing in here anyway? This is no place for reporters. Go on, get outta here.'

Walsh smiled as he closed his notebook and withdrew. He nodded in Campbell's direction and received a sly wink in return. Kelly intercepted it.

'So that's it? Campbell put you up to it,' he snarled. 'I might have known.'

The roomful of detectives collectively tensed. There were slow and wary moves towards both men. No one wanted a repetition of the Strangulation Derby of a few days before. Campbell shrugged nonchalantly. But, if that was supposed to relax me, then it had the opposite effect.

'Bart must have missed this month's payment, so he got no more than was coming to him,' he intoned casually.

There was a solid mahogany desk and three solid mahogany detectives between Campbell and Kelly. The Irishman growled again and looked around for a path to his adversary, but he was hedged in.

'You're doing a great job in Chinatown, Campbell,' Kelly snarled. 'I hear you can't even protect decent citizens from slant-eyed snipers. Good luck finding whoever it was who shot Chris Riley. I look forward to reading your report.'

'You're suddenly very well informed, Kelly. How did you know he'd been shot? Come to think of it, how did you know it was Riley? What if I told you it was Newman and he'd been knifed to death? Would that surprise you?'

Kelly looked nonplussed. But Campbell wasn't finished.

'Or maybe he just died of sheer bliss between your lovely wife's loins. Now that I think of it, that would explain the dirty smile on his face.'

I'd never met Kelly's wife, but I'd been around the San Francisco Police Department long enough to know that she had a reputation for setting aside her marriage vows from time to time. And who could judge her harshly for that? Campbell, however, had just inserted a bayonet in Kelly's ribcage and twisted. Hedged in or not, Kelly blindly and noisily charged like a raging rhino in his direction. He cleared the desk, but the three detectives had already been reinforced and, as he landed on the other side, he was grabbed by at least half-a-dozen men and hauled towards the door.

Campbell, for his part, looked detached and serene, as if he was sipping a cooling mint julep on his mother's porch.

'I'll work on that report,' Campbell called after Kelly. 'And when I finish, I'll roll it up real tight to make it as painless as possible when I shove it up your ass. Good day now.'

I expected that at least some of his colleagues would castigate Campbell for the sheer vulgarity of his antipathy, but no one came forward to protest on Kelly's behalf. The Irishman wasn't popular and Campbell, despite his many flagrant imperfections, was respected by his peers and almost revered by his juniors. Anyone could say pretty much whatever they liked about Sergeant Thaddeus Kelly without fear of reproach, as long as they did it behind his back, but only Campbell was prepared to do it to his face. After a decent interval, to allow Kelly to be escorted by his captors to the nearest bar, Campbell left the office. I saw him talking to Slyne, who had just come back from Chinatown with Riley's body. Ophelia Williams would be getting ready downstairs for the convivial task of cutting open the corpse. After a few minutes, Campbell returned.

'Here's the thing,' he said to me. 'I've just been talking to Slyne. We were the first back from Chinatown.'

'So?'

'Don't you think Kelly seemed to know a lot about the circumstances of Riley's death?' he inquired, with as much patience as he could muster. With Campbell that wasn't much.

'Maybe Dr. Williams was talking to him.' I wondered why I was being Devil's Advocate. It wasn't as if I had any affection for Kelly.

'She's not back yet. Riley is awaiting her attentions downstairs.'

I had taken off my jacket when we got to the station. I started putting it back on.

'Are you going somewhere?' he asked.

'I have to meet someone. I'll see you tomorrow if that's all right?'

Something in my expression tipped him off.

'Well, well, well. Sergeant Orpen is meeting his young lady. Good for you. *Bonne chance, mon ami.* I hear she's a belle.'

This could have been innocent ribaldry. It probably was. But I wondered how much Campbell knew about Amber. I know I haven't been very forthcoming about her. Given the stakes involved, I'm not going to start now.

CHAPTER TWELVE

OPHELIA WILLIAMS

19 October 1883.

I'm not too sure if a job is just supposed to pay the rent, or whether you should expect it to be satisfying. That day mine did both. Cutting into Christopher Riley was positively cathartic. Now I could finally forget about Doghouse. That just left Newman.

I don't know Caroline Schroeder all that well. My relentlessly 'blueblood' mother managed to 'collect' her shortly after she arrived in the city. We were introduced at a *soirée* of some kind in Berkeley and then an 'at home' in Oakland. Tragically, I still can't tell the difference between a *soirée* and an 'at home'. My mother knew all this stuff; she was an East Bay tigress who married beneath her. Grandmother didn't approve of Marcus Williams. In fact, she was scandalized. Which delighted Mother.

I saw enough on both occasions to want to get to know Caroline Schroeder a little better. That was partly because she remembered who I was after the *soirée*. She was intrigued that I was studying medicine, so I must have made an impression. I have no idea when female sopranos took over from *castrati* on the operatic stage, but I'll bet they didn't have to put up nearly as much of a fight as female doctors. I'd have been happy to take on a bunch of men with no testicles rather than the male medical establishment.

Exactly why I agreed to take over the organization of that year's Disabled Policemen's Benefit Concert, I had no idea. All right, I did. It was a bare-faced attempt to ingratiate myself with a hostile peer group. The law enforcement profession is almost as intolerant as the medical fraternity. The Greeks have a word for it: *kudos*. I was blatantly looking for some.

Either way, I thought of Caroline Schroeder first. Through my mother, I asked to meet her. I offered to come and visit her because I was the supplicant, but she wouldn't hear of it and arranged to come to my nest instead. That cost me an entire day. I'm not utterly slipshod when it comes to my domestic responsibilities. It's just that I don't really see them as responsibilities. That's why the word 'chores' was invented. Even though Caroline Schroeder was unlikely to demand to see my bedroom, I cleaned the place from top to bottom. Or more correctly, since I occupy only a single floor, from side to side.

Caroline arrived with her assistant/bodyguard/factotum/manservant/driver; a stocky Welshman named Davies. She was utterly charming—not one of those women whose head was attached to a pivot. No surreptitious and disdainful glances at the dowdy furniture and peeling wallpaper. She sat down, accepted a cup of tea, and we talked animatedly for about twenty minutes while Davies obligingly waited in the hallway. She said she would be very happy to perform at the benefit concert and would not accept a fee of any kind.

I had expected to spend most of the visit sycophantically plying her with questions about her art. This had worried me because I don't know my *Traviata* from my *Trovatore*. In fact, it was the other way around. She wanted to know all about medicine. Not that she was a hypochondriac, or anything like that. She was just intensely curious about how a woman copes in an almost exclusively male profession. 'By wearing a suit of armor' was my answer, 'with a small space provided in the region of the loins so you can still pee sitting down.' Most women either think I'm insane or a dangerous radical. She probably did too, but she disguised it better than most.

We were almost finished when I heard a noise at the front door. Davies was talking to a voice I immediately recognized. It was my distressed patient of the previous night. Since it was broad daylight, I assumed he hadn't been beaten up again. However, in my experience, you can never be that certain with Irishmen. Even ones who sound too much like Englishmen for their own good. Davies knocked gently and put his head in the door.

'Miss Williams has a visitor, ma'am. What do you want me to do?'

'She's "Doctor" Williams, Evan, and since it's her home, hadn't you better put the question to her?' Caroline Schroeder responded tartly.

'It's Sergeant Orpen. The Irish bloke, ma'am,' he said, addressing me.

'What's a bloke? Never mind. Tell him to …' I was about to say 'wait' when Orpen neatly sidestepped Davies and entered the room. What he intended as an ingratiating smile was merely grating. I drew inspiration from the native disposition of my formidable mother, and radiated disapproval.

'Hello there, sorry to breeze in like this,' he began. 'And good afternoon to you, Mrs. Schroeder. I was hoping to speak to Dr. Williams.'

He was as cool as a bucket of ice, despite the absence of his fossilized appendage, Campbell. His self-assurance in the face of my obvious disapproval, and Caroline's bland indifference, was impressive.

'I don't normally do follow up work,' I replied testily, 'my patients rarely require any.'

This drew a chuckle from Caroline Schroeder and a widening of Orpen's emollient grin. I never knew it was anatomically possible to get so much smile on so little face.

'Apologies. Didn't know you were busy. If you're right in the middle of something, I can come back.'

I was about to congratulate him on his acumen when Caroline Schroeder took this as her cue to depart.

'No, no, don't go. We're nearly finished,' she said, rising from her chair.

'Unfortunately, I don't have a Waiting Room,' I observed, assuming Orpen would take the hint and fraternize with Davies in the hallway for a while. Instead, he smiled even more tiresomely and stood his ground. Once it became clear that I was either going to have to tolerate his presence, or ask him directly to remove himself, I turned back to Caroline Schroeder to conclude our business.

If Orpen had managed to stay still, his interruption would not have been quite so irksome. Instead, he began moving about the room in what he obviously took to be an unobtrusive fashion. He quietly, but annoyingly, examined my meager belongings, appraising everything as if he had been invited along to offer a valuation. He eventually fastened on two small busts I had come across in a junk shop in the Mission and was using to weigh down some papers. One was of Abraham Lincoln. He studied this for a moment. Then he picked up its companion.

'I'm sorry for interrupting—' he began.

'Again,' I interjected. There was a pause as he considered lapsing into silence.

Instead of encouraging the notion, I took pity on him. 'Please, carry on.'

'I do apologize. It's just my natural curiosity. Do either of you have any idea who this is?' He brandished the second bust. It was of a gaunt man in his fifties with high cheekbones, a full head of wavy hair and what looked like a small goatee beard. I had never really thought of him as an actual person. He was just a useful gravitational device to keep my papers in one place. Neither of us could help him.

He turned the bust upside down and exclaimed in triumph, 'Ah, here it is. Would you believe it? Jefferson Davies. Staring down Abraham Lincoln. Well, well, well.'

'Fascinating,' I conceded. I would have conceded anything, up to and including the outcome at Gettysburg, to allow us to move on.

'It reminds me'—not even my mother's most intense glare could staunch his flow—'of a bust of Daniel O'Connell in the Reform Club in London. Ever been there? Probably not. You've heard of O'Connell? Great Irish patriot. I've got a brother named after him. As it happens, in the Reform Club, Dan has been placed right opposite a portrait of Oliver Cromwell. I'm sure you've heard of *him*. Not very popular in Ireland. Slaughtered a lot of Roman Catholics in his day. But he and O'Connell have no option but to eyeball each other from now to eternity. Rum situation, don't you think?'

I didn't care, and I hoped my silence and frosty demeanor would convey my manifest indifference. But I clearly need to attend a course in aggressive bodily communication, because Orpen just kept prattling.

'In fact, O'Connell, who was apparently a bit of a ladies' man and fathered several bastards—apologies, pardon *mon français*—also has a full-size statue facing the Rotunda Maternity Hospital at the end of Sackville Street. A constant reminder of his ill-spent youth ... and quite a bit of his middle age, if the stories are true.'

I had had enough. I was about to arrest his flow when Mrs. Schroeder spoke. She got in ahead of me only because I was looking around for the poker. 'Isn't he at the other end of the street? Overlooking the bridge?'

Orpen appeared a bit perplexed, then thought for a moment.

'Do you know. I believe you're absolutely right.' He smiled contritely. 'Rather spoils my story, doesn't it? Ah well. Maybe they'll build a maternity hospital at his end of Sackville Street someday. Please, carry on. Sorry for the interruption.'

We did so, but Theseus continued to stalk the Minotaur in the Labyrinth. When he began picking up some of my medical books and studying the spines, I reached the outer limit of my patience.

'Do you have a particular interest in obstetrics, Sergeant Orpen?' I asked.

He looked at the cover of the volume he was holding and almost dropped it when he saw the title. He quickly replaced *Diagnosis of Ovarian Cysts by Means of the Examination of their Contents* by H.J. Garrigues on the shelf from which he had removed it and, at last, sat down.

Caroline Schroeder took her leave a few minutes later. She nodded politely to Orpen and inquired, with what I can only describe as a wry smile, if he had been to see any interesting operatic performances lately. He responded with what I can only describe as an embarrassed smirk and replied in the negative. I was mystified.

When she and Davies were safely out of earshot, I turned to Orpen, who had begun to show renewed signs of interest in my medical library. He was getting dangerously close to a volume on midwifery. I wanted to save him further embarrassment.

'What can I do for you, Sergeant Orpen? Is it your ribs?'

'No, indeed. It's more about what I can do for you.'

'Really? I wasn't aware that I was in any need of your good offices.'

'It's about your surprise appearance at the scene of the crime today. I was curious as to what exactly you were doing there.'

'My job. Just as I told your friend Campbell, to his delicious displeasure. Captain Lees is a man of progressive ideas who wants to modernize police methods. Today was the first illustration of what will become a permanent fixture in any future murder investigation: the preliminary examination of the body *in situ*. Why? Did you think I was just trying to antagonize Sergeant Campbell? You do me too much honor. That was merely a thoroughly enjoyable aperitif.'

'No. It didn't occur to me that you showed up purely to grig Campbell. My assumption was that you were there to cover your traces.'

I was dumbfounded. 'Cover my traces? What traces?'

'The almost inevitable evidence that any killer will have left behind at the scene of a crime. Traces that can be overlooked by incompetent policemen, or which can lead to the gallows if they come to the attention of a skilled team of investigators.'

I stared at him in disbelief, my gorge rising. The poker was consolingly near at hand.

'Am I to take it that you believe me to have murdered Riley?' I edged towards the fire as I spoke.

'Don't worry. I can provide you with a cast iron alibi.'

'An alibi for what? I don't need an alibi. I didn't do anything.'

'That's normally why people need alibis.'

'You know exactly what I mean. Let me get this right. You're suggesting that after we parted company last night, I managed to procure a rifle, wander into Chinatown, and shoot Christopher Riley from a range of forty to fifty yards? That's absurd. Who do you think I am, Little Miss Sureshot?'

'You're the child of a senior police officer. I suspect he taught you how to look after yourself. That would probably have included instructing you in the use of firearms.'

'As a matter of fact, he did. But, as a senior police officer, he also encouraged me never to break the law.'

'You don't have to convince me. I'm the last person who would want to turn you in.'

'Very well. Let's just assume that you were not as amoral as you appear to be, and that you were here to arrest me. On what evidence would you base your case?'

'It was the overcoat that gave you away. The one you were wearing last night. Either you had just come back from your adventure, or you were on your way out. Your appearance at the scene of the crime in Chinatown this morning was not happenstance. The only way you could have got there so quickly is if you had advance knowledge of the crime. In other words, if you killed Riley.'

'You're very pleased with yourself, aren't you? As it happens, I almost walked straight past you on my way to the Hall of Justice. I was going down Broadway and I saw you, Campbell and that officious uniform—Slyne isn't it—about fifty yards away.' I stared at him as menacingly as I could. But it was like trying to push a log underwater. The moment you turned your back, it just resurfaced.

'That's really quite convincing.'

'But you don't believe it, do you?'

'Not a word of it.'

'What I obviously couldn't do was to identify the victim. I didn't realize who it was until I got past the uniform and Campbell. I was shocked, though not, I admit, unpleasantly.'

'Wonderfully plausible. You get to tie up potential loose ends—though I'm not aware that you'd left any—while making the case that you are expanding the boundaries of criminal investigation.'

I glowered at him. Normally this works quite well, but he failed to wilt. 'I do believe you are either utterly delusional or just as pigheaded as Campbell. Did you breathe it in while swinging from his coat tails or is it some peculiar culture of your own? Very well, have it your way. Your theory is as full of holes as an Emmenthal cheese, but if you persist in clinging to it then I insist that you arrest me and lay your charges before the proper authorities. I'm sure you'll have no difficulty persuading your blood brother Campbell of my guilt, but I don't hold out much hope that you'll manage to convince anyone of even average intelligence.'

'Wouldn't dream of it. I actually came here to thank you for a job well done. If I discover that there is any sort of reward forthcoming from Her Majesty's Government, I'll make sure it comes your way.'

'I'm sure I will be eternally in your debt.'

'And we may be able to pin it all on Kelly! Campbell wouldn't take too much persuasion.'

As our conversation had become more bizarre and unreal, my initial anger began to subside. I adopted the tone of a disappointed school principal upbraiding a wayward student. I was the ghost of Hamlet's father, 'a countenance more in sorrow than in anger.' Somewhere in the background, however, was Lady Macbeth, in case I needed the poker.

'Let me get this straight. You think I'm responsible for the death of that thug Riley, but you are prepared to convince Campbell that the killer is Thaddeus Kelly, who—although he is a rat of the highest order—is entirely innocent?'

'That would be it in a nutshell, yes.'

'I'm sure they must have taught you a lot at Scotland Yard, but didn't they cover ethics?'

'I'm not sure I follow.'

'I'm not sure I'm surprised. Would you mind leaving now? Obviously, I can't guarantee your safety. Given your deeply felt suspicions, I might feel the necessity to kill *you* at any moment.'

He laughed. Which seemed utterly illogical to me. If I was equipped to murder Riley, surely, I was capable of any essential mopping-up operation? However, Orpen wasn't quite finished yet.

'So, you are acquainted with Caroline Schroeder?'

The abrupt change of subject caught me unawares and, instead of simply throwing him out, I responded.

'You didn't believe that either? The Sceptics would have welcomed you to their academy with open arms and placed you on a pedestal. What is your interest in Caroline? Is she also guilty of some heinous crime? It's just as well she's not old enough to have murdered Mr. Lincoln. Should I warn her that you are on her trail?'

'I'm curious about her, that's all. I don't think she likes Irishmen very much.'

'Perhaps *you're* the only one she's ever met. I wouldn't be too curious about her if I were you. Her husband is not nearly as tolerant of people who provoke him as I am, but even *my* patience is not inexhaustible.'

Orpen still didn't budge but he suddenly became earnest and conspiratorial.

'You don't have to answer this question, you know,' he began almost diffidently. 'But I was wondering … how did it feel? Were you close enough to the bastard to see that look in his eye, where they know they are going to die and that they are going straight to hell? There's nothing more satisfying than seeing the tables turned on an assassin, is there?'

That was where I regret to say—or do I?—that I finally lost control. He was immune to logic and sarcasm. I intended to slap him as hard as I possibly could, but a split second before I made contact with his face, the open hand turned into a fist. I blame Lady Macbeth myself. The last thing either of us was anticipating was a punch in the jaw. Orpen staggered back through the open door into the hallway. My fist hurt like hell.

I lashed out again, this time catching Orpen somewhere softer and more amenable. As he tried to get his breath back, I opened the front door and pushed him towards it. He didn't resist.

If he had come back for more, I would have kicked him in the ribs.

CHAPTER THIRTEEN

ORPEN

21 October

I had seen healthier drowning victims than Haddo that morning. He looked as if he had been wheeled in for an autopsy. All the colour had drained from his face. Haddo was haggard. He had no discernible co-ordination in his movements. None of his clothes seemed to fit either, whatever little sense that made. What really drew the eye, however, was a globule of beige-coloured vomit on the lapel of his jacket. The perennially dapper Haddo had obviously admitted himself to the Consulate that morning via some private entrance because, in his current condition, he would never have got past the doorman.

He looked at me imploringly. I was not sure whether he wanted me to finish him off humanely, or to converse in the lowest possible whisper, lest his head should roll off his shoulders and bounce down the baroque staircase that led up to his office. Although I was beginning to have misgivings about the man–I know it's easy to say that now–I did my best to appear sympathetic.

'Are you … unwell?' I inquired, struggling for a suitable euphemism. As I did so, I noticed, for the first time, a grotesque landscape in a hideous frame on the wall behind his desk. Although nature can accommodate all sorts of interesting shapes and angles, there was still a lopsidedness about this panorama that was unnatural. It was also abnormally dark and Gothic. Call it pathetic fallacy if you will, but just at this moment it seemed to chime perfectly with the mood and condition of the man in whose office it was being displayed. I wondered would it brighten up when he was in better form.

'Mnnnn,' he replied. Or at least that is as close as I can approximate, phonetically, to the noise he made in response.

'I'm sorry. I didn't quite catch that.'

Rather than proceed with a tedious outline of the ensuing struggle to bring him to a state of comprehension and cogent expression, I will take a merciful shortcut. Haddo had been gambling. Haddo had been drinking. Haddo had been warding off highbinders, thugs, hoodlums and sundry other reprobates in his efforts to reach the safety of the Consulate with his winnings. Or so he told me.

Now your average San Franciscan gambler would find a way to bet on two horses pissing into a drain. Poker had slowly replaced the roulette wheel as the lottery *du jour* in the city. Some schools seemed to have semesters longer than the University of California. Games could go on for days. Campbell regularly regaled me with stories of epic sessions in upstairs rooms on the fringes of Chinatown. These often culminated in someone having their genitals blown off by a hidden derringer. The talented card sharks could even function while fast asleep, regaining consciousness for long enough to tip their hand and rake in the cash. It seems, despite appearances to the contrary, that Haddo was ahead of the game. One of the games at any rate. The game of poker. Not the other game, the one that involves close attention to personal hygiene and six to eight hours of dreamless sleep per night.

As always, it was the tea that did it in the end. A bracing pot, ordered up from the kitchen three floors below, miraculously transformed the unkempt pile of rubble in front of me into a semi-sentient human being. Gradually, Haddo began to take an interest in the late nineteenth century. He stared for an immeasurably long time at my face. Was he wondering about the bruises, or was he just trying to identify me?

'Been in the wars, have you, old boy?' he finally said. I thought, in the circumstances, the question was a bit rich, coming as it did from someone who looked as if he had just spent a sleepless night wrestling with his own vomit.

'No more than yourself,' I retorted amiably.

'Though your problems don't look as if they were self-inflicted,' he observed.

'They weren't.'

I didn't enlighten him any further. He wasn't that interested anyway. He began to move some papers around on his desk. In the middle of the operation something suddenly distracted him, and he stopped. His right hand then remained suspended over his blotting pad with a sheaf of notes clutched in his fist for a portion of the remainder of our conversation. It was like talking to a human paperweight. During this hiatus, my eyes were drawn back to the evil landscape. I simply had to ask. It would be a source of regret for the rest of my life if I didn't.

'That painting,' I indicated the diabolical pastoral. 'Who is it?'

Haddo started to swivel towards the wall behind him, but since the gesture was both uncomfortable and superfluous, he broke off in mid-pivot.

'An original Haddo. Thank you for noticing.'

If he knew what I thought of it, he wouldn't have been so gracious. 'A night scene,' I observed. 'Daring for a landscape painter.'

He looked grim. Which is to say his face assumed a dour expression on top of his already morose appearance. 'It's not supposed to be. All my landscapes seem to end up like that. It must be the pigments.'

'Do you do portraits as well?'

'No, just landscapes.'

I was glad to hear it. There is only so much Angular Gothic the world can take.

'So, what can I do for you, old chap?' he asked, with surprising breeziness, as if I'd come about a request that he might consider opening a garden fête. I suspected that the display of insouciance took quite an effort.

'I need you to get a message to Gosselin for me.'

There was a dart of panic in Haddo's eyes, as if he couldn't remember who Gosselin was. It passed quickly and was replaced by his customary sang-froid. He noticed the batch of papers he had been clutching and returned them to the desk.

'I have some new information for him about Dan Horton,' I added.

Haddo smiled, a little too superciliously for my liking. He raised a copy of the *Chronicle* to his face and peered at me through a section of an inside page that had been cut out. This, as it happens, was the Ross Walsh special announcing to the newspaper-buying public of San Francisco that Dan Horton, before his untimely demise, had been on the prowl in Chinatown for allies in his insatiable search for dynamite. Horton needed supplies for Emperor Rossa. His old friends in the Safety Nitro Company of San Francisco—who, I suppose, were partly responsible for my (faltering?) mission—had been quietly warned off the course by no less a heavyweight than the State Department and he had been embraced by the Suey Sing tong. Everyone knew that if you wanted dynamite your best bet was a Chinaman, didn't they? The *Chronicle* had opined that Horton's appetite for smooth rounded sticks that went 'boom' in the night posed a threat to an unnamed San Francisco businessman, C*****s S*******r and his Irish political allies.

OK, so Walsh didn't go quite as far as the old asterisk wheeze, but he still made it obvious to whom he was referring, while shying away from a Defamation Derby. You could see Haddo the Hangover blossom into Sir GalaHaddo when he thought he'd beaten me to the punch.

'No need, old boy,' he purred. 'Walsh's piece is already winging its way to the Gosling in the diplomatic bag.'

'Well done. I would have expected no less of you,' I tried to banish the smugness from my tone. 'But that wasn't the information I had in mind.' I was delighted to see the air suddenly drain from his tyres.

'Really?'

'I'm waiting for a suspicion to be confirmed. I'm expecting a visitor.'

'Here? This morning?'

'Yes.' There was a brief silence, during which he replaced the mutilated newspaper and absent-mindedly picked up a paperweight.

'Aren't you curious?' I asked.

He clearly thought about maintaining a dignified indifference and then abandoned the idea.

'Of course, I am,' he grinned. 'I'm just concerned that you'll be obliged to do away with me if you tell me anything confidential.'

'That probably won't be necessary, though I imagine a merciful death might feel like a blessing at the moment.'

Haddo uncurled himself and settled back into his chair.

'Do you believe Walsh's story?' I asked. 'Do you think Horton would throw in his lot with the Chinese?'

'Anything is possible in this city. I saw a man dance with his own wife last week. Distressingly uxorious.' His feigned lack of interest irked me. I skipped past at least half a dozen potential feints and parries and got to the nub of the matter.

'My suspicion is that this alliance has already borne fruit.'

'Succulent or poisonous?' he asked.

'As toxic as bitter almonds. I think the Suey Sing provided Horton with dynamite before he was murdered.'

The old Etonian whistled, unable to maintain his native lassitude. Bliss it was in that dawn to be alive. 'I assume I'm not permitted to inquire where you came by this information?'

I shook my head. He seemed faintly envious of my ability to do so without provoking a splitting headache.

'Am I even allowed to ask where you believe it's being stored?'

'That's what I'm waiting to confirm, although it doesn't take a genius to work it out. Horton ran a large, bonded warehouse south of Market. That's the logical place to deposit the fireworks until Rossa finds a use for them.'

There was a momentary spasm while Haddo dealt with the archer firing arrows inside his skull.

'But do we have anything to worry about? Horton is currently reimbursing the Ferryman. Where is the threat?'

'That comes from Newman.'

Haddo played with this piece of information for a few seconds like a cat with a resourceful rodent. When it kept getting the better of him, he became discouraged.

'No, that doesn't work now does it? With respect, old chap, Newman is not going to allow himself to be distracted from his apotheosis by a few sticks of dynamite for a cause that does nothing to serve his interests.'

'Don't underestimate the Clan in New York. He disposed of their man, after all. He needs to atone. He broke it, so he has to fix it. He may be a milksop Fenian but he's clever enough to know that he is obliged to render unto Caesar the things that are Caesar's.'

Just then the door of Haddo's office opened and a flunkey entered. He was instantly taken aback by the debauched appearance of his superior and by the unsavoury aroma of 'extract of stomach' that assailed his nostrils. But he was a diplomat, so he maintained a diplomatic silence.

'There is a female urchin at the main entrance, sir,' the newcomer advised, after a weighty pause. Haddo did not appreciate the interruption, still less the appraising eye of his subordinate.

'Why are you bothering me with this, Hayes?' he snapped.

To his credit the young man was not in the least cowed. He had considerable presence, was a well-built and self-confident type, and looked like someone who had stroked for Oxford in the Boat Race, before graduating with a double first. His natural composure, and the disheveled appearance of his commissar, conspired to help him stand his ground.

'She's looking for Sergeant Orpen. She says it's urgent.' Hayes responded, with dignity, and not a little dash.

'Is she indeed?' Haddo had noted Hayes's lack of deference and filed it away for later chastisement. He looked at me inquiringly. I nodded. 'Send her up then. No, *bring* her up, there's a good chap.' After Hayes had closed the door behind him, Haddo turned to me for elucidation.

'This will be the news I've been expecting,' I explained.

While we waited, Haddo lapsed into silence and began distractedly moving papers around on his desk to no obvious purpose. I scoured the Haddo landscape again for the least sign of artistic merit and originality but failed to find a screed. He might be a Baliol man, but he would never be a Royal Academician.

When Hayes returned, he was accompanied by the freckled and malodorous Horsebreath. My tiny young friend was curious about, but not in the least overawed by, the magnificence of her surroundings. She looked about her when she entered the room, but only fleetingly. It was an instinctive burglar's appraisal, sensibly truncated in the certain knowledge that she would never have the opportunity to return and pillage. Having delivered his charge, Hayes withdrew and left Haddo and me alone with the multi-talented young brigand. She nodded at me and held out her hand to Haddo.

'Hi, I'm Horsebreath,' she announced proudly. As her native fragrance reached Haddo's nostrils and unerringly confirmed the authenticity of her name, he blanched slightly and reached for a handkerchief in his jacket pocket. I feared the rebel forces in his stomach might finally win the day.

'I say, old chap, does she have to ... ooze so much?' he said, from behind his white linen wall.

'He who is without sin, I think ... old chap,' I replied, pointing to the vomit on his jacket, and at Horsebreath's extended hand. Reluctantly Haddo shook it, before hunkering down behind the handkerchief.

'What have you got for me?' I asked Horsebreath.

She handed me a piece of paper upon which were written the words 'High Explosive' in an uneducated hand. I passed it on to Haddo. Horsebreath informed us that she had transcribed the words—laboriously I had no doubt—from the lid of one of several wooden boxes in the warehouse owned by Horton. I wondered if she knew what they meant. She couldn't read herself, but Cleo could. I had insisted on 'Mother' being there as an overseer.

'Did you have any trouble?' I asked.

She shook her head. 'Elephant and Castle hoisted me in. I did the rest. No one saw us. Or if they did, they didn't try and stop us.'

Haddo was perplexed. 'Elephant and Castle? Is this some sort of rhyming slang?'

'I'll explain later,' I told him, though I never did. I turned back to Horsebreath. 'You covered your traces?'

'Just like you said.'

'Well done. Any other writing on the boxes?'

'Just some funny-looking squiggles.' She reached into her capacious tunic. 'I copied some of them as well.' The script was unintelligible but obviously Oriental. Haddo nodded sagely when I passed the note across to him. He could have been reading it upside down for all either of us knew.

'Looks like you've been vindicated, old boy,' he said, pointing towards Horsebreath, 'though your agent is a shade tender in years. Still, whatever works, I always say. You can win a hand with a pair of knaves just as easily as four aces. What do you want me to do?'

'Call in the Pinkertons. The San Francisco Police are not entirely to be trusted.' I envisioned Kelly passing on the information to his saintly friends the moment he discovered that Horton's cache had been rumbled.

'Hmm,' muttered Haddo. 'I'll see what I can do.'

'See what you can do? What does that mean?'

'It's a budgetary matter I'm afraid. The Pinkertons do an excellent job, but they also have a superior talent for invoicing at imaginative rates. I'll have to pass it up the line.'

'Don't take too long. The bird may be about to fly.'

Horsebreath, ever the adept businesswoman, intervened. 'We can handle it for you. A box of matches in the right place and … boom! Your problems are over.' Cleo had definitely cast her eye over the piece of paper. 'Won't hardly cost you nothing.'

'I'm tempted,' I said. And I was. I didn't understand Haddo's reaction at the time—that would become clear later—and I certainly didn't want Foreign Office bureaucracy getting in the way. 'But, no thank you all the same, Horsebreath. We don't want the entire neighbourhood going up. The Pinkertons will be able to dispose of the goods without an inferno.'

'Suit yourself.' She held out her hand. I shook it. She looked disgusted. I wasn't sure what I'd done wrong.

'Fifty,' she snapped, rubbing her hand on her grubby tunic. 'That was the deal.'

'Of course. I hadn't forgotten.'

I had, but that was partly because I was mentally offsetting part of Horsebreath's reward against the money stolen from my purse. That, however, was not part of the deal. I even toyed with the idea of instructing Haddo to reimburse my loan to him by paying up. In the circumstances I gave that one up as a bad job as well.

I reached into my wallet. I paused at four, but then counted out five ten-dollar bills. She took each one in turn and held it up to the light. I decided not to be offended at this egregious display of bad faith.

'No chance of a receipt I suppose?' I joked. She smiled broadly. No new teeth had appeared since my last impromptu inspection. I advised Haddo that he might be called upon to verify the transaction if my expenses were queried. His head was shaking more than was wise for someone in his condition. Hayes was quickly sent for, and Horsebreath took her leave, pocketing the cash. I say 'pocketing' but the fifty dollars just disappeared somewhere into her clothing like an Arabian footpad into the casbah.

Before departing, I thanked Haddo for his assistance and counselled urgency in the matter of the cache of dynamite. I should probably have warned him against the evils of drinking, gambling, and all-round debauchery as well, but that was a lost cause. 'Happy to oblige, old scout,' he said airily. 'After the Foreign Office wallahs have signed off on it, I'll pop around to the Pinkerton's myself with your commission. I think I'll suggest death by drowning. I'm sure dynamite is far less efficient once it's been immersed in gallons of salt water.'

'Oh, just one more thing,' I said, handing him an envelope. 'Could you cable this to Dublin for me? I'm hoping Mallon can help me with a hunch.'

'How mysterious.' Haddo replied and pretended not to wait for an explanation. This time I had no intention of elaborating.

'It concerns a lady.'

'Ah, *cherchez la femme*. In that case, mum's the word. I'll see that it finds its way to the Castle.'

As the oversized mahogany door of the Consulate closed behind me, the first thing I saw was Cleo loitering on the opposite side of the street. I looked about me to see if she was conducting Little Bitches' business or just savouring the fifty dollars Horsebreath had handed her. I hailed her and crossed the street.

There was something we had to discuss.

CHAPTER FOURTEEN

SAN FRANCISCO CHRONICLE

22 October 1883. Page three.

'Horton Warehouse destroyed by explosions and fire'

Last night a large, bonded warehouse on the corner of Mission and First was destroyed by an intense fire. The conflagration was preceded by several huge explosions. Were it not for the prompt action of the San Francisco Fire Brigade, the fire might well have spread to other businesses in the area. Arson is strongly suspected.

The warehouse was rented in the name of the late Mr. Daniel Horton, murdered some days ago in an internecine Irish feud. The police and fire brigade have uncovered evidence in the wake of the fire that the premises were being used to store high explosives. As a bonded warehouse, the building was normally devoted to the stocking of whiskey and other spirits.

It is also reported that, but for outside interference, the officers of the Fire Department might well have prevented the worst of the damage. When tenders arrived at the scene, the fire had not yet taken hold, but firemen came under a hail of missiles from a large group of children—all of whom, according to witnesses, appeared to be young girls—and were forced to withdraw temporarily.

The Police Department was last night unwilling to speculate as to the use to which they suspected the high explosives were to be put, but the theory, advanced to them by a *Chronicle* reporter, that the explosives were destined for Fenian dynamitards in England, was not denied.

CHAPTER FIFTEEN

ORPEN

23 October

I had plenty of time to chew on my own thoughts and take in my surroundings as I walked along Montgomery with Campbell. He wasn't being very communicative. I ambled along silently beside him, preparing for the arrival of the first non sequitur of the day. It was a chilly morning; winter was more than just a whisper on the wind.

We passed a building on fire. Charred sheaves of paper, blown by the stiff breeze, were floating northwards, and spreading ash as they floated by. Montgomery Street was an excellent tunnel for a zephyr and was being exceptionally accommodating in spreading the flames. Some of the muscular employees of the Fire Department were shepherding young ladies down the fire escape of the smoking building. In San Francisco fire escapes did exactly what the name suggested. Mostly made of wood, they allowed any decent fire to escape and burn down the neighbouring properties as well. For the moment at least, the firemen seemed to be more interested in the distressed females they were rescuing than in controlling the flames. Their interest was reciprocated. Call me bitter and twisted, but I have always resented the fact that firemen are much more attractive to the opposite sex than policemen. I didn't hold out much hope for the burning building.

Suddenly, Campbell broke his silence. As it turned out, it hadn't been worth waiting for, but at least he was talking again.

'Why isn't there a word for something that's not natural, but not quite supernatural either?' he asked abstractedly.

'There is,' I informed him. 'Preternatural.'

'You don't say? How is it that I've never heard of it?'

'Probably because you've never asked the question "why isn't there a word for something that's not natural, but not quite supernatural" before now.'

Faced with such immutable logic, he lapsed into another engrossed silence. He didn't bother to explain the reason for his interest in the preternatural. We turned right on California Street and I idly tried to wind back Campbell's thought process, just to see if I could return to his first premise. Why was he looking for an alternative word to 'supernatural'? Was he mulling over Riley's everlasting soul? Did he suspect some preternatural force to have been responsible for the Irishman's murder? I gave up after a few minutes of reflection. That way lay madness.

As we approached Stockton Street, the rising ground, and Campbell's habitual pace, were taking the chill out of the day. I saw a group of young Chinese men studying an impressive notice pasted to a wide gable end. I couldn't read a word of the Oriental script but wondered if it was a *chun hung,* a public notice offering rewards for the death of certain individuals. If you owed money in Chinatown, it was often cheaper to have someone killed than to repay the debt. The *boo how doy*, the tong hatchet men, were only too willing to oblige. Then something occurred to me.

'What if the Suey Sing felt an obligation to revenge Horton's murder?' I ventured. Campbell wasn't listening. 'Maybe it was an honour thing,' I added half-heartedly. I hadn't been in San Francisco for long, but even I knew that the tongs avoided killing whites, except in self-defence, or when under the most severe provocation. Sometimes when you articulate a passing thought, it takes the lustre off.

An empty cable car trundled past. Out of the blue, Campbell jumped on board, and I followed him. He motioned me to the front, away from the brakeman. As we settled into our seats, with no explanation on his part, I spied the reason for the sudden move. We were not alone. Perched beside the brakeman, having followed us onto the car, was the large, ungainly, but threatening figure of Newman's gorilla, Howie. I made a mental note to scourge myself later that night for not having spotted that we were being followed by someone almost as large as a circus elephant. Instinctively my hand went to my right pocket. It wasn't an elephant gun, but it was enough to stop Howie in his tracks.

But Howie had come in peace. He was not carrying a white flag, but he patted his pockets and held up his hands to indicate that he wasn't armed. I produced my pistol, and waved it around, to alert him to the fact that I was. Campbell turned towards me and shook his head. Obligingly, but with some misgivings, I returned the gun to my pocket. Campbell motioned Howie to join us. As the cable car rumbled up California towards Nob Hill, he lowered himself into a seat opposite, managing to look both furtive and nervous. Campbell took out an enormous Cuban Corona Grande.

Though Howie obviously hadn't come to chat with me, I opened proceedings with a personal beef. 'Thank you for the broken ribs, by the way.'

Howie feigned surprise. 'I don't know what you're talking about.'

The pain in my chest urged me on, though I already sensed Campbell's impatience. 'Who sent you? Not that I really need to ask.'

'Then don't bother. Am I supposed to have beaten you up or something?' He shrugged and wiped his mouth. 'Not that you don't richly deserve a drubbing, but I had nothing to do with it. If it had been me, you wouldn't be walking.'

Campbell intervened. 'What do you want?' he snapped.

'This conversation never took place—' Howie began.

'This conversation isn't going to take place if you don't get on with it.'

'I have some information.'

'So do I. For starters, I know that I've got a big ugly Irish lug sitting in front of me into whose custody I would not confide a Yankee nickel.'

'Amen to that brother,' Howie retaliated, 'because I wouldn't trust you with a Confederate dollar.'

First round to the heavyweight Irishman. While my heart didn't exactly swell with national pride, I wondered if I'd misjudged the man. I had Howie down as someone who still needed rudimentary instruction in how to breathe correctly. Campbell took refuge in a jaded grunt.

'State your damn business.'

'I was following Riley.'

'Were you, indeed?' Campbell was unimpressed. 'Are you some sort of disciple?'

'OK then. I was stalking him.'

'When?'

'The night he was killed.' As we waited for more, Howie looked around him nervously. 'Newman's orders. I wasn't happy about it, but he gave me guff about someone squealing on us. He said he wanted me to follow Riley around for a bit to see if he met up with any Peelers.'

'And what, pray tell, is a Peeler?'

'You are.'

'Am I?' He looked at me for confirmation. I nodded. 'I'll add it to my lengthy list of qualifications. Why weren't you happy about your mission?'

'Because it was bullshit. If any of our boys had gone to the Peelers, Kelly would have fed it right back to Newman.'

'I'll ignore the fact that you have just impugned the reputation of a fine police officer.' Even Howie looked perplexed. I searched Campbell's face. Not a flicker. He would have made a far better poker player than Haddo.

'Go on,' he said.

'Newman was right to be suspicious of Riley, but not because he was peaching to the Peelers.' Howie paused to gauge Campbell's reaction. The cable car had reached the corner of Mason and California. Campbell put away the Corona and casually lit a cigarette. If Howie had been hoping for some dry-mouthed excitement on our side of the aisle, he was disappointed.

'Riley was fed up playing second fiddle,' he continued. 'He talked to me about scraggin' Newman, but I wasn't keen.'

'In line for a reward from the new Supervisor, were you? Third District dogcatcher?'

'The likes of you wouldn't understand loyalty.'

'I'm a secessionist. Try me.'

'Riley thought Newman had forgotten about where he came from.'

'So that was why Riley, the pea-green patriot, sliced up brave Daniel Horton? Mother Ireland must despair of her sons.'

'Riley had nothing to do with that. Neither did Newman.'

Campbell exploded in a mirthless laugh. Howie was unabashed at Campbell's derision. He made a 'take it or leave it' face.

'Let's get to the History section, shall we?' said Campbell. 'I'm finding Fiction a bit thin. Move it along to where our hero—that's you by the way—stalks Riley with a heavy heart. What did Christy Our Redeemer get up to during his final tour of Chinatown? Did he rescue any Celestial slave girls? Did he bring nourishing broth to the dope addicts in the opium dens?'

Ignoring Campbell's sarcasm, Howie produced his showstopper.

'He spent most of the night with Davies, Schroeder's bagman.' Despite himself, Campbell was suddenly interested.

'Did he indeed? Were they intimate?'

'They were go-betweens, so they had to get together from time to time.'

'To discuss what? The wrong-headed tactics of General Lee at Gettysburg? Astonish me! What did these two intellectual giants have to talk about?'

'When Schroeder wanted someone dealt with, he sent Davies to talk to Riley.'

Campbell favoured Howie with a cloud of acrid blue smoke.

'Ah, now we appear to be getting somewhere,' Campbell drawled. 'We're back on Plausibility Street. I feared we were trapped forever on Fantasy Avenue without a hansom in sight. Your employer offered that invaluable service to his betters, did he? Did Newman ever force you – reluctantly I'm sure – to "deal with" any of Herr Schroeder's irritants personally?'

'I'm hardly going to admit to something like that now, am I?'

Campbell stubbed out his cigarette on the floor of the cable car. I wasn't sorry to see it die. The state of my ribs made coughing painful.

'Your circumspection becomes you, sir. I'll take that as a "yes". Carry on. Your narrative was just beginning to get interesting, though it's still quite a distance from "compelling".'

'That's all I have to say. I don't have any proof of anything, and I didn't follow them for long. I bailed out early and told Newman that I'd lost him.'

Campbell suddenly looked bored. The cable car was descending from the heights of Nob Hill. The conversation with Howie had never quite soared, but it too was on a downward trajectory. As we passed Leavenworth, the brakeman stopped to let on some passengers. Campbell motioned Howie across to our side of the aisle. I noticed that he smelt of fried bacon fat. It was preferable to one of

Campbell's cigarettes. The remainder of the conversation was barely conducted above a whisper. It was like the intimate transaction that I'm told takes place between a Roman Catholic priest and a parishioner in the confessional. I found it increasingly difficult to hear what passed between the two men but thought it might be a bad idea to ask them to speak up.

'And why, pray tell,' Campbell asked, as we took off for Van Ness again, 'do you think Davies might have chosen to shoot Riley in the middle of an otherwise pleasurable stroll through Chinatown?' He made no effort to conceal his scepticism.

Howie, whether honest or just well-schooled, was prepared for that one. 'If Boss Newman looked after the German's little problems from time to time, maybe Schroeder was doing the same for the Sheriff.'

In the circumstances, it sounded odd to be conferring Newman with his former title.

'I see,' said Campbell, showing some interest again. 'A convenient reciprocal arrangement. And might I inquire as to why you're telling me all this?'

'Riley was a good friend of mine.' His voice quavered ever so slightly. He was either genuinely upset, or a gifted actor. I doubted it was the latter.

'And, as a decent law-abiding citizen, you want to see justice done. Am I right?'

Howie said nothing in response to Campbell's transparent contempt.

'I should applaud your public spirit,' Campbell went on, 'in bringing this matter to my attention.' He pinned Howie to his seat with a leery stare. 'You could have pursued justice yourself. Instead, you have chosen to step off the merry-go-round. I will be recommending you for a Good Citizenship Award, sir, and I will fight like a tiger to ensure that the mayor himself bestows it upon you.'

Howie had had enough. 'Look, Dixie boy. I don't give a rat's ass whether you believe me or not. And if I was going to be sticking around, I'd deal with Davies myself.'

'Please don't tell me you're leaving us, Howard. Not before you get the Freedom of the City, surely?'

'I'm moving out, for the good of my health. Riley had takeover plans, and I was too close to him.'

'Take my *bon voyage* with you,' Campbell continued airily. 'Your friendship and loyalty to Mr. Riley brings a lump to my throat.'

'Just one more thing,' Howie added. 'I read the *Chronicle*.'

'An excellent choice of newspaper. Do your lips move as you read?'

Howie ignored the gibe. 'Tell your friend Walsh to mind how he goes. Horton's boys didn't appreciate being fingered for killing Riley. Riley was close to recruiting them. They wouldn't have touched him.'

'Is that one of those medieval things? You kill the warrior in single combat and possess yourself of his army?'

'I'll just say it one more time. Riley didn't kill Horton. He had a bullet in his shoulder. Ask your friend there.' Suddenly I was back in the conversation. I could have used my *entrée* to point out that, technically, the bullet had been extracted, but that would have been splitting hairs.

'That one doesn't float, friend Howard,' said Campbell. 'I have personal experience of his ambidexterity. If there is such a word.' I reached into my pocket.

Howie looked on warily as I produced a bundle of cards. With the faces down I fanned out the pack. 'Pick one,' I urged.

'Are you serious?'

'Do as the gentleman says,' Campbell interjected.

Reluctantly Howie chose a card from the middle of the pack. He studied it for a second before tossing it in disgust on the floor of the cable car. The Joker.

We had now reached Van Ness, the end of the line. The brakeman had alighted to spin the car around for its homeward journey. Beyond the turntable I could see an argument beginning between two hansom cab drivers. One of them had an Irish accent, so it was bound to develop into a fistfight. My money was on the Irishman, but there's never a bookmaker around when you need one.

When I looked back, Howie was gone. He could move very stealthily for such a large man. If his story was true—if— it was a quality that might well stand him in good stead over the next few days. Campbell and I stayed on the California Street car for the return trip to Market. I had my own ideas about our heart-to-heart with Howie, but I waited for him to break cover first. Not for long though. My natural impatience got the better of me again. There was a hiatus—like that beat in a Strauss waltz where, just for a split second, nothing is happening.

'Informant or emissary?' I asked, to get the dance started.

'Pithy!' Campbell did that trick with the match and the sole of his shoe again. After he'd lit another foul Turkish cigarette, he spoke.

'Not even the presence of stigmata would convince me of Howie's veracity.'

'To be fair to the man—and I have no reason to be—he's not exactly claiming to be the risen Christ.'

'I don't believe he's about to be crucified either, do you?' He let that one sink in for half a block before he elaborated. 'Think about it – if you wanted to track Riley, would you send someone like Howie into the field? Divided loyalties, and enhanced visibility, wouldn't you say?'

His expression hinted that to claim otherwise was cloth-headed folly. From nowhere a pigeon settled on the railing behind the brakeman and peered through the window at us. He seemed to be eyeing me with intellectual disdain. While I might have taken it from an eagle or a hawk, I wasn't going to put up with the value judgment of a rodent with wings. I made a threatening gesture in his direction, and he took off for the Tenderloin. Unaware of this skirmish, Campbell warmed to his theme.

'I'm not entirely clear what Newman has against Davies, but I'll figure it out.'

I was about to say something when he put a finger to his lips. The car was beginning to fill up with passengers. My Socratic contribution to the Howie debate would have to wait.

As we exited on California and Stockton, Campbell stubbed out his cigarette on the discarded Joker.

Half an hour later we were ensconced in the Bull Run Bar with our noble proprietor preparing two hot whiskies. The day had turned chilly. Night was beginning to press against the window. Although the liquor in question, at Campbell's insistence, was Tennessee bourbon rather than good Irish whiskey, it would be very welcome indeed. Campbell exchanged pleasantries with Ned about the woeful inadequacy of all Union commanders above the rank of Corporal. He was obliged to except Grant and Sheridan and reserved his particular venom for Sherman. Ned had heard it all before and had other customers to attend to. We were soon left to our own devices and two steaming hot whiskies.

'I think you have the floor,' Campbell began.

'Before I start, I have one question.'

'Be my guest.'

'What you said about Kelly the other day—are you morally certain you told him nothing about how Riley was killed?'

'Don't introduce morality, please. We're talking about Kelly. The only confidence I would ever share with that cockroach was if I had sexual congress with his mother.'

'It could have been an inspired guess.'

'Kelly hasn't been inspired since he worked out how to stuff a ballot box before he was tall enough to reach the slot. Forget about Kelly for the moment. His black soul is as constant as the Northern Star. Let's concentrate on the variables. Where do you stand on the *bona fides* of our oversized friend?'

I chose Devil's advocacy. 'Why couldn't he be telling the truth?'

'To Howie's kind, the truth is something you clutch at arm's length while holding your nose.'

'That's as may be but hear me out anyway.'

Campbell lapsed into an attentive silence. I really did have the floor. I took a nervous gulp from the glass and burnt my tongue. When Ned Allen made a hot whiskey, he didn't stint on the heat.

'For the purposes of this exercise, and this is all hypothetical, let's assume Howie is telling the truth, the whole truth and nothing but the truth,' I began.

'So help me God if you don't get on with it, I swear I will break the rest of your ribs.' It was said without obvious malice, but I toned down the rhetoric just in case.

'What if Howie is right and Schroeder was returning a favour by getting Davies to kill Riley? Does that stretch credibility too far?'

'No, but you are straying perilously close to the edge of plausibility. If Newman had commissioned the murder of his lieutenant, why send out Howie to witness the event? That makes no sense. And brings us back to the more comforting likelihood of Newman dispatching his household giant to try and take me for a sucker.'

He had the smug air that I imagine Euclid must have projected after yet another *quod erat demonstrandum*. Then he relented. 'But we'll go and have another chat with Mr. Davies anyway. Just to be on the safe side.'

I returned to my whiskey more contentedly. This time I sipped cautiously.

CHAPTER SIXTEEN

ORPEN

23 October

I have never really appreciated the camaraderie or the discipline of a team. That was one of the few things Campbell and I had in common. He was a loner too and I could see that his patience with me was wearing thin. It was like that famous line in Hardy's *Far from the Madding Crowd* when the shepherd Gabriel Oak tells the alluring Bathsheba, 'And at home by the fire, whenever you look up, there shall I be, and whenever I look up there shall you be.' But Campbell wasn't a lovelorn herdsman and I wasn't a rustic beauty with a biblical name. I was just *there*. All the time. I once suggested that he could always tie me up in a bag and deposit me on someone else's desk if I became a distraction.

'I'd really hate you to believe that I haven't thought about it. But you appear to be well-connected,' he responded lugubriously. Like it or not, for the moment we were joined at the ankle, like two warring harpies in a three-legged race.

That day we were returning to the palaces of Nob Hill. Campbell had decided not to walk this time, so we were back on the obliging California Street cable car. I didn't miss Howie's company. He was either still ensconced in the bosom of Family Newman, or on his way into exile with the Mormons in Utah or the Pennsylvania Amish. No one would follow him to either destination and it could only exalt his inner life.

The weather had changed suddenly, and it was like a spring day— summer if you were Irish. But this time we weren't going to arrive at the Schroeder fortress in a lather of perspiration. Campbell wanted to be fresh before tackling Davies and there was always the passively belligerent Crampton to negotiate as well. As the brakeman took us ever upwards towards the Mason Street intersection, I rummaged for my inner aristocrat, polished the shoes and buttons, clipped the vowels to a fine point, and I was ready for the Satyr.

I needn't have bothered. Neither my metaphorical military grade pike, nor my more patrician épée was required. Campbell just used a mallet instead. When Crampton opened the front door in response to his confident knock, Campbell brushed past him with a curt 'Get Davies now.' The flunkey thought about protesting but detected just enough early Stonewall Jackson in Campbell's manner to think better of it. He padded off down the long marble corridor without dissent. I fancied one or two of the haughty Roman emperors were impressed as well. The temperature in that echo chamber of a lobby was mer- cifully mild, which was helpful while we cooled our heels. Campbell paced impatiently as we waited. For artistic reasons, I affected a con- trasting stillness. Some of the Emperors looked disapprovingly at our presence but most retained their stony indifference.

Crampton didn't come back with Davies; he'd obviously decided that he had suffered enough indignities for one day. The Welshman materialised himself, as if by magic, from a panel in the wall to our left which neither of us had noticed on our previous visit. An open- ing suddenly appeared behind Vespasian or Tiberius, or one of those post-Republican types, and there he was. In spite of myself, I was intrigued. Campbell's only response was a non-committal grunt, but it was a tenor grunt, so perhaps he was impressed as well.

'Somewhere private,' Campbell growled, without preliminaries. Davies, who had looked unflustered by our arrival, darkened. He pushed open the panel behind him and motioned us to follow. We entered a dimly lit narrow corridor that broadened out into an unpretentious and far less resonant lobby. To our right was an open door. We followed Davies through. The room was an office of some kind. Davies closed the door, seated himself behind a desk uncontaminated with papers or much else, and indicated the settee opposite. I sat; Campbell stood. I don't think he had any aesthetic motive in mind.

'What can I do—' began Davies.

Campbell cut him short. 'I want to know about your movements two nights ago, on the nineteenth of October.'

Davies was taken aback by the directness and specificity of the question. He paused, mulling over his response. This allowed Campbell to follow up his exploratory left jab with a right uppercut.

'You shouldn't have to think about it. Where were you?'

'I was here,' Davies replied calmly.

'All night?'

'I would say so, yes.'

'You would say so? Were you, or weren't you, here all night?'

'Yes, I was here all night.'

'Will Mr. or Mrs. Schroeder verify that?'

'I hope we won't need to drag them into this.'

'I'm sure we won't.'

'I'm relieved.'

'Because you're lying.'

Davies didn't look quite so relieved any more, but he still took it without flinching. The fingers of his right and left hand had been entwined since he'd sat down. The only obvious sign of emotion was when his right and left thumb began to rotate in opposite directions.

Maybe Campbell had a point about the hands being mirrors of the soul. Or perhaps I'd just spent so long as his hostage that I was beginning to think like him.

Davies didn't respond. A pair of bushy raised eyebrows invited his accuser to continue.

'I have two witnesses who saw you last Friday night strolling in Chinatown with Christopher Riley.'

I wondered where the second informant had come from. Had Campbell taken one of Howie's ribs and, Godlike, created another eyewitness? It seemed to be the only plausible explanation.

'Is it a crime to walk in Chinatown these days?' Davies inquired blandly. You had to admire the man's composure. And his expertise as a sniper, assuming he was guilty. If he survived the noose, there was bound to be some nasty little war where his marksmanship would prove useful.

'Do I take it that you no longer cling to the fiction that you were here all night?' Campbell's delivery had now slowed down to his customary drawl.

'I may have stepped out for a while,' Davies conceded.

'Alone, or in the disagreeable company of Mr. Riley?'

'I was with Riley for a time, yes.'

'Good. We're getting somewhere. Can you tell me what you two gentlemen discussed on this friendly ramble?'

Davies had a look of someone who wasn't quite with us anymore. 'This and that?' he replied at last.

'Really? Can you be more specific? I abhor vagueness.'

'Like I said. Just—this and that. Nothing of any substance.' Davies was now staring intently at the door. Campbell didn't seem to notice that he was losing his audience.

'This is how it works: either you enlighten me *here* as to the details of your conversation and your activities, or I ask you to join me in the Hall of Justice in Portsmouth Square. There I may be compelled to introduce you to *my* friends … this' here he closed his right hand and presented a fist, '… and that.' He repeated the movement with his left. Campbell paused to allow his melodramatic gesture to take effect. Davies looked up for a moment, dumbly registered the empty theatrics and resumed his liaison with the door.

Campbell changed tack. 'Perhaps we should discuss your movements with your employer?' Unlike the threat of physical violence, this suggestion provoked an instant reaction. Davies jumped slightly in his seat. At the same time the pitch of his voice climbed towards an emotional falsetto.

'No, no …' he began. Then, for emphasis, he added a third and fourth 'no'. Campbell waited as the negatives accumulated. Davies finally ended the sequence. 'We're not going near Mrs. Schroeder with this.'

'I was actually referring to her husband.' Campbell said.

'Nor him.' Suddenly Davies stood. I thought he was going to launch an ill-advised attack on Campbell, and I braced myself. But Davies ignored both of us, walked quickly and quietly to the door, and pulled it open with a swift jerk. He stepped out into the dark lobby and spoke.

'Thank you, Crampton. That will be all.'

From where I was sitting, I couldn't see the plump Satyr, but I was aware of him beating a hasty retreat. How much had he heard? What would he tell Schroeder? I assumed the answer to both questions was 'everything'. Davies appeared more put out than at any time since our conversation began. As soon as Crampton was safely out of earshot, he addressed himself to Campbell.

'Is that invitation to the Hall of Justice still open?' he asked.

Campbell nodded. Davies took a set of keys from the top left-hand drawer of the desk. With one of these he opened a small safe in a corner of the room. He took something out. I didn't see what it was; the desk got in the way.

As we left, via the front door this time, Caroline Schroeder was walking down the long corridor populated by the sculpted spawn of Octavian. When she saw us leaving with Davies in tow, her pace quickened. She approached us and was about to say something when an almost undetectable shake of the head from the Welshman silenced her.

Davies looked ill at ease in his new surroundings. His native jauntiness had deserted him. While there was no actual trace of bloodstains on the walls of the interview room—it was cleaned regularly—he must have been conscious that dialogues there could often become discourteous. Our guest—it was too early to call him a prisoner—had remained thoughtful and silent on the ten-minute walk from Nob Hill. When we got to Portsmouth Square Campbell had had a quick word with Lees before shepherding Davies towards Shadrach. We settled ourselves as comfortably as the forbidding suite permitted.

'Unburden yourself, Mr. Davies.' Campbell spread his arms expansively and became a non-conformist preacher. 'Speak the truth and your soul shall be healed.'

Davies appeared understandably hesitant. Campbell, despite the redemptive gesture, was a dubious confessor. Davies looked around him nervously before he began to speak.

'I met Riley at his own request,' he began.

'Sent in his card, did he? Or a billet-doux?'

Davies wisely chose to skate over Campbell's sham jocularity. 'I had no idea what he wanted. He spent ten minutes beating about the bush and walking me towards Chinatown. I don't know exactly where we were when he sprang at me, but it was dark and there was no one around.'

Here Campbell contented himself with nodding approvingly, encouraging Davies to continue. I doubt if the Welshman even noticed the gesture. He was somewhere in Chinatown watching an expert assassin preparing to kill him. Remembering. Or imagining.

'He came at me with a knife. I was lucky. He was too cocksure. I got in one swift kick to his groin and fled. The place was a maze of alleys, so I lost him easily enough. I probably threw him by heading uphill.'

'Towards heaven, and home. And that was it?'

Campbell's palpable cynicism had the same effect on Davies as if he'd rudely whipped out a toothpick and started working the gaps for rotting food.

'What do you mean?' the Welshman asked guardedly.

'Having slipped the clutches of Demon Riley, you ascended unto Nob Hill without a care in the world?'

'No. As a matter of fact I assembled the artillery piece in my jacket pocket, lay in wait, and killed him. Is that what you want to hear?'

'I'd imagine it's closer to the truth than the Aesop's fable of the deadly hare and the resourceful tortoise. Highly entertaining though. Would you happen to have any injuries about your person that might serve to corroborate this exhilarating tale?'

'Not a scratch. Should I have pounded my head against a brick wall to throw you off the scent?'

'Did you manage to dispossess him of his knife? Because none was found on his body?'

'Can't say that I even tried.'

'Did you happen to inform the police of this ... murderous assault?' Campbell's whole attitude was freighted with disbelief. He was a cargo train of incredulity. Suddenly Davies laughed. His hilarity was genuine, not ironic.

'Do you know, I haven't quite managed to find the time to report an attack commissioned by someone who is well protected by the guardians of the law.'

Campbell was all injured innocence. 'I'm shocked at this egregious slander on such a fine body of men, sir.'

'Your outrage becomes you, Sergeant. I'm sure you are the only good apple in the barrel.'

Campbell moved in for the finishing coup. 'Can I ask one further question, though I do admit it's unlikely to stop at one? Where were you on the night of the thirteenth of October last?'

Now Davies looked genuinely puzzled.

Campbell enlightened him. 'Perhaps I can jog your memory? It was the night of the murder of Mr. Daniel Horton, late of this parish. Does that help?'

A momentary flicker of panic passed across Davies's face. It was brief but it was unmistakable. Campbell might have had no success on the Comstock lode but sometimes his haphazard panning paid dividends. I risked a look at my colleague and was rewarded with an almost imperceptible smirk in return.

'Have I said something to disturb you, Mr. Davies?'

'N-not at all,' the Welshman responded, 'You'll need to give me a second or two. It was a while ago.'

'Take your time, take your time. We don't want you to make an unfortunate error, now do we?'

Davies found it difficult to conceal the fact that he was having what I like to call a moment of fecal catharsis.

'I remember now. I was in Sacramento on an errand from Mr. Schroeder.' He paused to gauge the reaction to this piece of information. Campbell was impassive.

'Go on.'

'I was visiting Senator Cockburn. I remained in Sacramento overnight.' I had a vivid image of trembling flesh and a missing neck. Senator Cockburn was a hard memory to shake off.

'And I'm sure the Senator will verify the date and time of your visit?' asked Campbell mockingly. Given that Cockburn—despite his continental bulk—fitted neatly into Schroeder's pocket, I expected an enthusiastic affirmative from Davies. So, I was puzzled by his response.

'There might be a problem there.'

'Might there now?'

'He could be … reluctant to confirm the meeting because of the nature of the transaction between us,' continued Davies.

'Indulge me. What was the precise character of your business together?'

An almost theatrical display of reluctance now slowed proceedings to a crawl. 'I was sent to Sacramento to hand over a large sum of money to the Senator.'

'To what end, might I ask?'

Davies mulled over that one for a few moments as well. It was almost as if he was counting down the seconds. You had to give him credit for nerve, and timing. When he spoke, the hesitations were almost perfectly symmetrical. It was as impressive a display of mendacity as I think I have ever seen.

'He was expected to use the funds … to bribe a number of State Senators into voting for a land zoning measure in Sonoma County… which would be very much to Mr. Schroeder's financial benefit.'

'Your boss needed some more pocket money, did he?'

Davies ignored the taunt. The feudal spirit was strong in Wales. 'So, I suspect the Senator would not be anxious to confirm my presence in Sacramento for fear that there might be some awkward follow-up questions.'

I never got to hear what Campbell thought of that, because just then the door of the room burst open, and Thaddeus Kelly loomed large in the entrance with his arms folded and his legs apart. His rodent eyes went from Campbell to Davies and back.

'What the hell is going on here?' he asked belligerently.

Campbell uncurled himself from his seat and responded coolly, 'It's called "police work", Sergeant Kelly, I'm not surprised you don't recognise it.' He turned back to Davies. 'Apologies for the intrusion.

This is Sergeant Kelly. He has an unequalled talent for fundraising, but he often forgets his manners.'

If the level of our prisoner/guest's anxiety could be calculated on a graduated scale, it had just risen from a five or a six to a solid ten. Campbell and I should probably have felt slighted.

'What's *he* doing here?' Davies demanded of Campbell.

Campbell maintained his detachment. 'He was obviously misinformed as to the reason for your presence and just thought he would bring the collection box here, for your mutual convenience.'

'That's enough, Campbell,' rasped Kelly. 'You have no right to interrogate this man. He's out of your jurisdiction.'

'Whatever gave you the impression, Sergeant Kelly, that this was an interrogation? Mr. Davies came here of his own volition. We're just having a friendly chat. Aren't we …eh … Evan?'

The Welshman was white-faced. He stared at Kelly like a Spanish heretic watching Torquemada pay a flying visit to the dungeons.

'Do you both take me for a fool?' Davies asked. 'I wasn't around for the fitting, but I can see I'm going to be forced into the suit.'

Just then there was a second interruption. A policeman named Lowry stuck his head in the door. 'Lees wants to see you,' he told Campbell. 'Him too,' he added, pointing at me. Before we could question the messenger, Lowry had disappeared. Campbell looked uneasy. Davies rose from his chair.

'I came here voluntarily, so now I guess I can leave,' he said.

'You're free—' Campbell began.

'Not just yet,' Kelly interjected. 'You and I have a few matters to discuss first.'

Davies looked as if he did not relish the prospect of a chat with the Weasel, but he would have to wait and shift for himself until we got back. With obvious misgivings, we both left a clearly unnerved Davies behind and made our way to the captain's office. There weren't many people around. The chorus of good-natured abuse that normally greeted Campbell as he walked through the detective office was strangely muted. We knocked on Lees's door and entered. His reaction made me instantly uneasy. I got the distinct impression that he hadn't been expecting us.

'Finished already?' he asked.

'Far from it,' answered Campbell suspiciously.

'Then why are you here? I don't need to see you until you're—' Before he could finish the sentence, he was interrupted by the report of two gunshots in rapid succession. Campbell was the first to move. He sprinted back through the office. I tried to keep pace. My uneasiness had given way to the conviction that we were going to be too late.

The shots had attracted half-a-dozen policemen, and most of those drawn to the scene were armed. Campbell roughly pushed his way past several wary uniforms on their way to the interview room with cocked handguns. Although he must have known what he would find, he was cautious enough to stop outside the door. No point in giving Kelly a pop at *him* as well.

'Who is in there? Identify yourself,' he shouted.

'Lowry here, Sergeant Campbell.' It was the messenger.

'You know damn well I'm in here, Campbell,' snarled Kelly.

Campbell pulled a revolver from his pocket, cocked it, and pushed open the door with his foot. The smell of gunpowder grew stronger in the hallway outside. 'I'm coming in,' he barked. As he stood in the entrance to the room, he said, 'Don't either of you move. Don't even twitch.' When he turned back to me, he was pale. 'Orpen, come here. I need you to check for a pulse.'

Davies lay on the floor without moving. As I bent over him, I could see that the right half of his head was a bloody pulp. Searching for a heartbeat was a formality. Campbell followed me into the room cautiously. There was a small knife lying beside the man's body. It looked familiar. The last time I'd seen one like it, Ophelia Williams

had been tossing it onto a table in the Bull Run bar. Campbell kicked
it away while keeping his gun trained on the two policemen.

'Captain,' he called out, without looking around. Lees appeared
behind him and started at the sight of the Welshman's body.

'What the hell happened here, Sergeant?' he asked Kelly. In
response, the Weasel raised his revolver and aimed it at Campbell.

'First tell that dope-head to put down his gun.'

'Both of you lower your weapons immediately,' Lees snapped.
The two men did so with glacial speed, each shadowing the movements of the other, vying to be the last to return their revolvers to
the vertical. I began to rummage through Davies's pockets. I found
something interesting, but that's for another day.

'Explain yourself, Sergeant Kelly,' Lees demanded.

'Not much to explain, captain. I was questioning this man, his
name is Davies, when Constable Lowry returned. Without any warning Davies jumped up, took out that knife, and held it to Lowry's
throat.'

'Is this true, Lowry?' Lees asked.

''Tis indeed, Captain. Right at my throat he was.' My attention
was immediately drawn to Lowry's Adam's apple. It was vast. If I ever
intended to knife him—and I was sorely tempted to do so now—that
is exactly where I would have been drawn.

'I was lucky, sir—' the Constable continued.

'Thank you, Constable,' rasped Lees. 'Where did the knife come
from?' he asked Kelly.

'He just produced it from his pocket. I assumed he had been
properly searched by Sergeant Campbell, who was interrogating him
before I came on the scene.'

'You murdering Irish viper,' roared Campbell. One or two of the
uniforms, all too familiar with the history between the two men,
moved into position to restrain him. 'He came here of his own free
will. Why the hell would he be carrying a weapon?'

'You'd have to ask *him* that, wouldn't you, Sergeant?' Kelly was fighting to suppress a smirk. 'Maybe he didn't trust you, though I can't for the life of me think why.'

'That's enough, Kelly.' Lees said. 'What happened after he grabbed Constable Lowry?'

'He started to back out the door with one arm around Lowry's chest, holding the knife to his throat. But he had to stop and lean away from Lowry for a second to open the door. That's when I shot him. I got off two. Missed with the first.'

'For which I'll always be thankful, Captain. Sergeant Kelly will be in me prayers tonight,' piped up the curiously unmoved Lowry. He might have been extraordinarily cool and courageous, or he might just have been in shock. But I doubted if either was the case. He wasn't even in mild surprise, although his Adam's apple was bobbing around like a stray balloon heading out to sea.

'You are prepared to verify all this, are you, Lowry?' asked Lees, making no effort to conceal his disbelief.

'Verify, sir?' Lowry now looked like the unread son of a Tipperary farmer that he was. For someone who was supposed to have been inches away from an exploding skull, he seemed as if he had just stepped out of a soothing bath.

'Is he telling the truth?' barked Lees.

'The whole truth and nothin' but the truth, sir. That's exactly how it was. I think Sergeant Kelly should be gettin' a medal.'

That was when Campbell finally combusted. He had been inert for the duration of the charade being played out in front of him. His stillness lulled his self-appointed guards into a false sense of safety. They weren't ready for him when he suddenly leaped on top of Lowry, grabbed him by the collar, and brought his forehead down violently onto the bridge of the man's nose. He then pushed Lowry into the corner of the room and threw himself at Kelly, pummelling the Weasel's torso with both fists. Kelly, taken aback by the onslaught, could only shout 'Will someone get this bastard off me?' In my considered opinion, Isaiah Lees was culpably slow to intervene, bless him.

'That's enough,' he snapped, but only after Campbell had landed a few heavy blows, including one well below the belt. Lees motioned to some of the uniforms—one of whom was the Archangel Rory Tracy—to separate the two men. As they pulled Campbell and Kelly apart, the Weasel managed to get in his first blow, a punch to the right kidney, as soon as Campbell's back was turned. Before Campbell could respond, Tracy had swung a roundhouse punch that connected with the very fetching cleft of Kelly's chin and sent the Weasel staggering, eyes rolling, to the corner of the room where he hit the back wall and slid to the floor. I kept a close eye on Lowry but he was crumpled in the other corner trying to stem the stream of blood pouring from his nose.

When some semblance of order had been restored, Lees took control again. The room and the corridor outside were now full of uniforms and detectives.

'Were there any other witnesses?' Lees asked loudly. No one came forward.

'Right,' he said to no one in particular. 'Get Kelly and Lowry out of here and somebody fetch Doctor Williams. I want her to examine the body before it's moved. And I want a guard on this door.' He pointed at a stray uniform. 'You'll do. Stand outside until I tell you otherwise. Nobody gets in here other than the police surgeon. Is that clear?'

The Chosen One nodded apprehensively.

As Kelly and Lowry stumbled out, Lees stopped them. He stood in the doorway and pointed towards each in turn. 'I'm suspending you both pending a full investigation. I don't want to see either of you within a hundred yards of each other until this is over, though it sounds like you've already got your stories nicely cooked. Now get the hell out of here.' As he left, Kelly was clutching his jaw and glowering at Tracy. Lowry exited with his nose held high in the air, a crimson trail following him into the corridor outside.

The door closed, leaving the three of us together; four if you include Davies, I suppose. Lees sighed. He gazed at Campbell solicitously but helplessly. He didn't try and hold Campbell's eye for long. You don't readily exchange glances with a basilisk. It was Campbell who broke the silence. He raised his arm and pointed at the captain like a Shakespearean ghost.

'If you let that Irish dungbeetle away with this, I'll hang him myself.'

'No, you won't. You're not riding with Archie Clement now, Campbell.'

I had no idea what Lees was talking about, but Campbell's visage darkened, and he looked as if he was about to pounce on the Chief of Detectives. I knew the warning signs by now. It wasn't my fight, but then I've never been shy about sticking my elbows between two flaming red faces. However, I've long since worked out that in cases like these it's always better to pick a side than have both parties wanting to disembowel you. Before Campbell could even think about covering the distance between himself and Lees, my Colt was out and the muzzle was caressing his forehead.

'You'll thank me for this later,' I told him, for want of anything more compelling to say. He looked as if he couldn't have agreed less. His eyes crossed as he tried to get the muzzle of my gun into focus. For a second, I was reminded of the late lamented Oliver Madden. I cocked it just in case he thought I was still playing the Joker. I backed him towards the door. As I was about to reach for the handle, it opened from the outside. Ophelia Williams entered in a rush. She looked at the three of us in turn, saying nothing, but breathing heavily.

In the circumstances I figured there was only one thing I could do. I pointed to Davies's body— the head was now bathing in a pool of blood—and said, 'I think I owe you a profound apology, ma'am'.

CHAPTER SEVENTEEN

ORPEN

24 October

It was probably a sign of the advance of the cancer of gentility across San Francisco. Ned Allen, heretofore a mastodon of philistinism, had installed a painting on his wall, though it may well have been intended to cover the pattern left behind by a shotgun blast. It adorned an establishment that was otherwise embellished only by mirrors, most of them bearing advertisements for brands of liquor.

It would, however, be a misnomer to glorify the daubing as 'art'. It was a reclining nude, female, painted in oils. Lots of oil had been required. She was bulky, large-breasted and with a full pale stomach that I imagined would quiver at the slightest touch. All she wore was an enigmatic Mona Lisa smile, a silver tiara and a diaphanous shard of chiffon draped expertly across her pudenda. I found her as alluring as a duck-billed platypus. It was School of Haddo, though brighter, and more technically accomplished.

When I walked into the Bull Run Bar, Ned was proudly straightening his new purchase on the wall. He nodded in the direction of a crumpled form in a dark corner of the dingy saloon. He needn't have bothered. Campbell was the only customer. It was shortly after ten o'clock in the morning, but it was almost pitch dark. Natural light was disobeying every known law of physics—as it tended to do around the Bull Run— and giving the place a wide berth.

Word had reached me that Campbell was on a monumental bender. I was getting ready to return to London, but I felt some misguided sense of responsibility or loyalty towards the man. In my youth, I had been one of those scrupulous boys who, any time anything untoward happened, assumed that I had been solely and personally responsible. My brother's chickenpox, the death of my mother, and the Franco-Prussian War were all tragic events in which I supposed myself to have played an active but unfathomable role.

In the case of the disintegration of my former colleague, I was a *bona fide* dweller on the threshold. While it might have been fanciful to imagine myself having contributed to the defeat of Napoleon III and 100,000 Frenchmen at Sedan, I had certainly played at least a peripheral role in the current malaise of Wellington Campbell. I owed him a sobering experience at least.

Mademoiselle Reclining Nude certainly did nothing whatsoever for Campbell, who, although contiguous, was oblivious of this historic breakthrough in the cultural life of the city. His whole aspect reeked of defeat, while his immediate environment stank of the crescent of drinks laid out on the table around him. I was impressed. They appeared to have been arranged alphabetically, from absinthe to whiskey. When Campbell drowned his sorrows, he did so methodically. He did not have the demeanour of a man who had just successfully concluded a double murder investigation, but then I couldn't see his face because it was pressed into the table. For all I knew it might have been wreathed in a triumphant smile.

He was snoring impressively when I shook him. The snoring abated and he began to twitch. At least that's what I thought it was. But it turned out to be his right arm winding up for a badly aimed swing at my jaw. The blow looped harmlessly in the direction of my shoulder before missing land altogether. The abortive haymaker caused Campbell to slump from his chair on to the floor. I bent down and gingerly restored him to his former position. As I did so, he opened one eye, looked at me lethargically and slurred a surprisingly friendly 'It's an illusion.' Then his lolling head bounced off the table and he promptly fell asleep all over again.

I'd never been able to shake off a childhood puritanical streak, so I took each of the glasses of assorted liquor and poured them, in turn, over his head. We went through the alphabet as far as 'rum' to no discernible effect. I was reluctant to proceed beyond the letter 'r'. Ned had included a glass of his good Cork whiskey and I didn't want to waste that on the back of Campbell's head. Instead, I took my revolver from my pocket and pointed it at the ceiling. A raised eyebrow of inquiry in Ned's direction elicited a nod of permission and I fired. Campbell jerked into consciousness. To guard against instant and overpowering retaliation, I pointed the gun at him. It was becoming a habit.

As he slowly returned to his senses, I pressed the whiskey into his hand. He swallowed it in one gulp and regarded me from under heavy eyelids.

'So, what are we celebrating?' I asked breezily.

The eyelids drooped for a moment, teetered briefly, toying with slumber again, and then disappeared.

'What are you doing here?' he rasped. The greeting was not nearly as promising as the amiable 'It's an illusion.' I rationalised. I had just poured absinthe, brandy, gin, port and rum over him, in that precise sequence, so what did I expect? I reminded him—as politely as one can while staring down the sight of a gun barrel— that I too was a regular patron of the Bull Run saloon.

Suddenly his mood changed. 'Join me so.' He waved an arm— the one that had recently been employed to poleaxe me—towards an empty chair. I accepted the invitation, trying to disguise my reluctance. I had a long train journey in prospect. The aftereffects of a belly full of Bull Run's finest can be prolonged and I didn't especially want to spend the entire trip throwing up onto the tracks from the rear deck. I also kept the revolver close by just in case Campbell's disposition reverted to cranky polecat. He effected not to notice.

'Delirium tremens, Ned,' Campbell grunted, 'by two.' It was now ten minutes after ten o'clock in the morning. It would be almost another two hours before the sun was over the yardarm. But I saw no alternative.

'So why the merrymaking?' I asked innocently. I wondered would he notice the empty glasses, or the fact that he was moist and stank of liquor. My hope was that he would assume he'd drunk the entire cocktail himself.

'Haven't you heard? I solved two murders.'

'Is that a fact? You don't seem too convinced.'

'Chief Crowley patted me on the back. So, I must have done.'

The two DTs arrived. Campbell attacked his. I sipped mine like a Dowager Duchess, and a coy Dowager Duchess with a distaste for strong liquor at that. Silence descended on our compact and happy throng. From outside the sounds of the street percolated through. Ned busied himself washing glasses, but not too thoroughly. An ungodly crowd, his clientele objected to manifest cleanliness. The silence remained unbroken as Ned set about piecing together a couple of chairs that looked as if they had succumbed to a heated argument the night before.

In truth I had one or two ulterior motives for this rendezvous with Campbell. We had not parted on the best of terms the day before, but I was keen to pick my companion's brain on a couple of outstanding matters. Representatives of Her Majesty's Government, eagerly awaiting my return to London, would be anxious for certain items of information. While Campbell wasn't exactly omniscient, he was my safest bet.

But I wasn't anxious to appear too curious. Campbell could essay a passable imitation of a clam when he chose to remain mute.

I mulled over the many ways in which I might approach the subject obliquely before impatience overpowered me and I just broke cover.

'So, you got your man?' I ventured, trying to sound more confident and disengaged than I felt.

'Did I?' He'd been staring at his empty glass, willing it to replenish itself, or for Ned Allen to minister to it. Now he turned to me and looked into my eyes with a peculiar intensity. I felt I was about to share the experience of the guest at the wedding feast, the one seized by the emaciated hand of the Ancient Mariner. I wanted to clear up a few minor points all right, but his eyes heralded a full postmortem. I sipped my DT with even less energy and enthusiasm.

'I got *a* man all right. And I've been advised to take one or two leaps of faith, all the credit for a thorough investigation, and a week's vacation. So here I am … vacating. Not a pretty sight, is it?'

I owned that it was anything but attractive.

'Did I ever tell you, by the way, that I used to be a pacifist? When the War between the States began, I told them that if they made me fight, I'd aim to miss. They put me in a uniform anyway. My tenderness and sympathy didn't last long when the shooting started. The battle plan isn't the only thing that doesn't survive the first encounter with the enemy.'

That Ancient Mariner gleam in his eyes was getting stronger. I hadn't expected our discourse to go all the way back to the first verse—'the ship was cheered, the harbour cleared'. I had to get him to the part where 'all the boards did shrink' as quickly as possible. Or at the very least to the bit where he shoots the albatross.

'And your point is …?' I interjected. He looked offended at my brutal indifference to his tragic reminiscence. I felt slightly guilty, but only slightly.

'That I used to have ideals,' he snarled.

'Didn't we all?'

'Thus spaketh the Irishman in the pay of Her Britannic Majesty.' It was an entirely valid point, so I didn't argue. He resumed the breast-beating where he had left off. 'Now I just hold my nose and grovel,' he continued.

'That sounds like one of those fraternity initiation rituals.'

'Indeed, it is, my young friend, a rite of abasement. I'm sure you have more than a passing acquaintance with it yourself. The alternative is to grease the cheeks of your arse and await the pleasure of whomever it is they send to mount you.'

I dismissed the image as quickly as possible. I was, after all, a reluctant graduate of the English public school system.

'Do I take it, from your self-pitying diatribe, that you are unconvinced about the guilt of Evan Davies? You have some doubts … regrets perhaps?'

In response, he just shrugged. I would have thought the allegation of abject defeatism alone would have provoked a stronger reaction. It was half a DT—Ned had been busy replenishing our stock—before he spoke again.

'A man is murdered. Society requires a measure of revenge. A plausible suspect dies in police custody. *Ipso facto*, he must have been guilty. Is there enough incriminating evidence? Can we keep our betters out of it? Yes, on both counts. Mission accomplished. QED. Everybody is happy. Roll over and go back to sleep. Or take a vacation and forget about it. That's how it is you see. Will that be all?'

'What about the awkward crumbs? The bits that don't fit. The arrows that point in the wrong direction?'

'And what would they be? Astonish me with something that defies rationalisation.'

'Well, for example, why would Davies, if he shot Riley, divest himself of his gun but double back and steal a dead man's knife?'

'Is that the best you can do? No need for him to double back. Riley used his weapon of choice in all sorts of ways. As I recall, you even have some experience of his ballistic artistry yourself. Simple. He threw it after a retreating Davies and missed. Davies picked it up, turned around and shot him. Covered! You see what I mean by rationalisation? That's how it is.'

'And then he kept the knife with him just in case he might need to hold it to the throat of a policeman with the biggest Adam's apple I've ever seen?'

'There's no accounting for human nature is there? Perhaps he felt he would mystically possess himself of Riley's manic energy if he held on to something so personal? Either way it magically materialised at the scene of his untimely death, and the received wisdom—after a long and exhaustive internal investigation of course—is that no member of the San Francisco Police Department could conceivably have deposited it there. This, despite my subtle hints to the contrary. That's how it is. So, you noticed the huge Adam's apple as well?'

'Completely spoils the line of his neck. Very well. Let's give them Davies for the public-spirited culling of Riley. I've already set in train the process of a posthumous knighthood, by the way. Services to Her Majesty's government. He's probably still a British citizen. Furthermore, let us assume—despite the din of inescapable logic and natural prejudice—that Kelly is entirely unconnected with the alleged appearance of the knife at Lowry's enormous appendage. But who killed Horton? What do the Gods of Received Wisdom have to say about that?'

'Little enough. The fact that the incorruptible Senator Cockburn refused to admit that Davies had been suborning him in Sacramento at the strategic moment, weakened our hero's case. The Tablets of Stone that have been passed down—when translated from the original hieroglyphics—inform us that Davies was Riley's accessory on that occasion. He borrowed the Schroeder coach—without permission of course—for nefarious purposes. Who am I to fly in the face of the stern Gods of Received Wisdom? Ironically, I enhanced the credibility of that dumbass theory myself when I submitted the orphan cufflink as evidence.'

He reached into his pocket and produced Exhibit A. He handed it to me.

'Here, you might as well have it as a *memento mori*. No one in Portsmouth Square appears to want it.'

As I accepted the unexpected gift I yawned involuntarily. It was a symptom of nothing other than near exhaustion. Naturally Campbell chose to misinterpret.

'Am I being tedious? Should I truncate? Would you prefer a précis?'

'Please, not on my account,' though I hoped he wouldn't take me too literally. I had an eastbound train to catch sometime over the next forty-eight hours. 'I have another question.'

'Then I suppose we might as well proceed with the mutual self-flagellation.'

'Why—according to the Angel of Expediency—would Davies have offered an alibi that no self-respecting Senator, spectacularly on the take, was ever going to confirm?'

'Ah. An excellent question. Double bluff.'

'Double bluff?' I scoffed.

'Remember, I am merely the messenger of the Gods ...sorry, I've forgotten his name again.'

'Pegasus.'

'Thank you. I Pegasus ... you Mortal! Spare me your naïve scepticism. Double bluff. Davies had no one to support his alibi, so he offered an explanation that had no chance of confirmation, but still had the ring of authenticity. You will recall that I mentioned something about leaps of faith?'

'So, logically, Cockburn's denial should make no difference to Davies's credibility.'

'Your reasoning is a tad too subtle, and Crowley no longer chooses to operate above a ground-floor level of logic. In the past, he might quietly have accepted Davies's word against that of a crooked politician. Now, sadly, it is no longer politic for him to do so. If Cockburn says Davies was not offering him inducements on behalf of Charles Schroeder on the day Horton was murdered, then we must accept the good Senator's sanctified word. In addition to which, even to whisper the name of the 'Man Who Would Be Governor' causes spasms of anxiety in the colon of our Chief of Police. Am I painting a rosy picture? Well, that's how it is.'

It was becoming a refrain. He looked wretched and defeated. This was a new experience for me. I had never seen anyone take a preordained *fait accompli* so personally. It was just as well he wasn't working for the London Metropolitan Police, Special Irish Branch. The Gosling abhorred the concept of a personal conscience.

'So that's the official sequence of events, is it?' I asked. 'Riley and Davies killed Horton in tandem and then Davies murdered Riley all by himself? None of this was done at the behest of others? Both men nurtured fierce animosities in their bosom which drove them to kill?'

'Crowbar seems to like it. Lees is less sanguine, but he isn't allowed an inconvenient opinion until he gets the top job himself. And when he does, I have no doubt that he too will go the way of all flesh. Putty can be moulded into many shapes. *C'est la vie*, my Irish friend.'

'So, that's it? The hawk on Nob Hill is to be allowed to hover above it all?'

'Haven't you noticed how we Americans cherish our birds of prey? This is the Land of the Bald Eagle.'

'Everyone is happy?'

'Everyone, except the enchanting Sergeant Kelly. Lees appears to have conjured a vacancy in the Barbary Coast detail, where the kickback regime is just not up to scratch. Sergeant Kelly has turned into a frog and he must wait for the kiss of a beautiful Princess to restore him to his kingdom.'

'Other than Kelly?'

'The only losers appear to be Messrs Horton and Riley, though their names will live for evermore in the hearts of Irish-America. Adequate reward I'm sure. As for the rest of us—no disrespect to your estimable nation—but two less Irishmen ... apologies, two *fewer* Irishmen ... here or there doesn't even constitute a bump in the road.'

'Shall we drink to that, so?'

'I thought you'd never ask. Ned, two more DTs.'

I raised a glass and intoned. 'May the itch devour you, sir.'

'To the bone.'

'The marrow.'

'And may you find comfortable lodgings in hell before the devil knows you are dead.'

Reader, I caroused him.

What else could I reasonably do? He needed to still a beating conscience and I was a master of that particular art. We traded DTs like merchant princes. We cursed the rich, their capacity for deceit, and the studied ease with which they managed to avoid the consequences of their depravity. We toasted the South and Good Old Ireland. We poured scorn on Yankee and Saxon alike. We drank, with little hope of satisfaction, to the horribly painful ill-health of Thomas Newman and Charles Schroeder. We wished Thaddeus Kelly well in the shithole of his own making. Only when Campbell was close to oblivion again did I propose a toast to Dr. Ophelia Williams. There were no takers.

As the daylight dimmed, Campbell lit one of those unspeakable cigars and asked sottishly, with an unbecoming lump in his throat almost as pronounced as Lowry's Adam's apple, how he would survive in this vale of tears without me. I told him he would manage. It was all conviviality and bibulous bonhomie, not at all like the meeting of two men who had been at opposite ends of a cocked and loaded revolver twice in the last forty-eight hours. Such is the mutual respect of the mercenary.

The reclining nude watched with a jaundiced eye, but after a few drinks I had the measure of her. When I finally abandoned Wellington Campbell, he was as I had found him. Face down. The man could never hold his drink.

So, the curtain fell. That curtain at any rate. The real finale would be conducted backstage.

CHAPTER EIGHTEEN

OPHELIA WILLIAMS

24 October

To describe a camel as a horse designed by a committee does scant justice to both quadrupeds. No committee I've ever sat on would have had the unity, or firmness of purpose, to create something as efficient as a dromedary. Take the claque behind the Disabled Police Benefit Concert. The program for the evening, staged in the California Theatre on Bush Street, was not the result of intelligent design. Neither had it evolved organically. It was mostly arrived at by a process of unnatural selection which brought together the sublime and the outlandish. At the two extremes were Caroline Schroeder, *diva extraordinaire*, and the Dancing Heifer, doyenne of the Barbary Coast.

The latter was the sister, and former terpsichorean partner, of the (sadly retired) Galloping Cow. She moved like the grass-fed animal after which she was named, in an act that made the late louche Lola Montez look like a sophisticate. To lovers of poetic movement, it was an abomination. But then, I suppose, the joke was on them. My escort for the night certainly appreciated the humor. Orpen had been so abjectly apologetic for accusing me of murder that I indulged him when he hinted that before returning to England he would love to see a performance in one of our 'wonderful old theatres'. They weren't that old, but I didn't contradict him. Besides, I had an ulterior motive in inviting him, something we needed to discuss. He spent the

Heifer's entire performance in paroxysms of life-threatening laughter. His enthusiasm nettled some of our stuffier patrons. Reluctant to
witness the onstage shambles itself, they decided to be offended by
his enjoyment of the spectacle.

If he was disconsolate at the interval, when I broke it to him that
the Dancing Heifer would not be regaling us during the second half
of the evening, he was utterly crestfallen when he discovered that
the final hour would be consumed by operatic recitals. Not that I
was a passionate champion of the form myself, but what did he have
against opera?

'The predictability. There is always a cheeky manservant, an
ingénue played by a soprano in her forties, a thigh-slapping drinking companion, mistaken identity—twice—a strawberry birthmark,
gypsies, and a young lover played by an overweight tenor, to complement the soprano in her forties.' It was pithy, I'll give him that.

So, I felt a small glow of triumph when, after witnessing a mas-
terful performance of a selection of popular arias from Caroline
Schroeder, he was so dazzled with her artistry and talent that he
almost begged me to be allowed to meet her backstage. I temporized
and bantered for a while, before giving in.

As we crossed the dress circle foyer, Charles Schroeder was herd-
ing the occupants of his box towards a table, where a magnum of
champagne and six glasses awaited their pleasure. When he saw me,
he bowed with just a little too much contrived unctuousness.

'Miss Williams,' he purred. I didn't bother to mention that I prefer 'Doctor' Williams. After a six-year testicular-dogged struggle, I
think I've earned it. 'Congratulations on an excellent evening. And I
thought it was all over after the Fat Lady danced.' His prattling companions thought this was sidesplittingly funny, so it was clear who
was paying for the overpriced champagne. I was being patronized by
a true professional, but since he was the husband of the biggest draw
of the evening, I overlooked the condescension.

'I'm just popping in to thank your wife on behalf of the committee,' I said politely. 'I promise I won't keep her long.'

'Take your time. I imagine the theatre will not run out of champagne, so we should be here for a while.' He was already tipsy and set on finishing the job. He was surveying Orpen with curiosity. 'And who is this gentleman?'

'A visitor from London,' I explained vaguely. Schroeder studied Orpen intently.

'Haven't we met?' he asked.

'No, sir. We have not had the pleasure. Darcy Plantagenet is the name. Delighted to make your acquaintance.'

'I thought as much. Rarely forget a face,' Schroeder remarked, with scant logic, before turning back towards his guests. We were dismissed from the presence. As we descended the stairs towards the backstage dressing rooms, I asked Orpen about the mysterious Darcy Plantagenet.

'Oh, Darcy would have been in his element tonight, though I suspect he would find Herr Schroeder a trifle gauche. Darcy has standards.'

My knock on Caroline Schroeder's dressing room door was answered quickly from within.

'Come in; it's open.'

She was alone. The gratitude of our camel having extended to only a single bouquet of flowers, the room was almost entirely bare but for her dress and cape, hanging from a rail. She seemed pleased enough to see Orpen, and I must give him credit, he fawned exquisitely.

'What a magnificent performance, Mrs. Schroeder,' he gushed. 'The world of opera lost an incomparable jewel when you retired from the stage.' I thought this was a tad rich given his diatribe during the interval.

'Why thank you, Mr. Orpen,' she responded graciously. 'If I'd known you were in the audience, I would have chosen an aria from

Rigoletto.' Was our diva flirting with my escort? She was certainly teasing.

'Could I beg a favor?' Orpen continued. 'You have already plumbed the depths of my own ignorance of opera, but I have an older brother who is quite an *aficionado*. He would never forgive me if I came back from San Francisco without having secured your autograph. Would you mind?' He proffered a piece of paper and began searching in his pockets for a pen. When he found one, she accepted both.

'Perhaps you could sign it to him personally? His full name is Daniel O'Connell Orpen.'

'Ah, the famous patriot who spoiled your story about the maternity hospital?'

'The very same,' he acknowledged. She duly obliged him and handed back the signed sheet. Rather than putting it straight into his pocket he, rather cheekily, read aloud what she had inscribed. He looked elated, like a little boy who has been patted on the head by a favorite aunt.

'"To Daniel O'Connell Orpen, who needs to educate his younger brother, Caroline Schroeder-Edwards"' he read amusedly. 'I fully intend to immerse myself; I promise.'

It was all getting a shade too cozy, so I interjected. 'You've changed your tune, Orpen.'

'And how is that, pray tell?'

'Based on your critique during the interval. Don't you remember your little tirade against operatic plotting?'

'A small child, and a rather dim one at that, could eclipse the efforts of most librettists when it comes to plot. I dare say even I could outdo them.'

'That's a bold assertion, Sergeant Orpen,' Caroline exclaimed.

'Allow me to prove it to you then, ma'am. As it happens, I've been mulling over a storyline of my own devising for a while now. I think it would make an excellent opera. It's full of deceit, passion, melodrama ... and murder. Would you like to hear it?'

He stared at Caroline. She returned his gaze, quizzically at first, but then began to wilt as she perceived a new energy in the man. I looked uneasily from one to the other. I sensed a sudden change of atmosphere in the room. Orpen appeared to grow and Caroline to shrink. Neither, for very different reasons, seemed disposed to break the leaden silence. I had become accustomed to Orpen in the guise of attendant lord, a Rosencrantz or a Guildenstern at best. Now he was suddenly holding the stage with the unabashed confidence of a lead tenor. A disquieting thought assailed me. Had he been masquerading all along?

'I'm sure Caroline has better things to do,' I suggested.

When he turned to me it was with an expression of barely concealed resentment. It was as if he'd forgotten about my existence. When he spoke, his voice was both compelling and peculiarly inexpressive.

'I think it might be in your best interests, Mrs. Schroeder, if Doctor Williams were to absent herself from this narrative.' I would have scowled dismissively but I turned instead to the diva.

'I'm not sure why that should be necessary, Sergeant Orpen,' she replied, with a mixture of mild astonishment and irritation.

'It would perhaps be for the best,' he insisted. During this exchange, he didn't look once in my direction. My gorge was rising. I could taste the bile.

'Doctor Williams is here as my guest. As are you, Sergeant Orpen. When she is quite ready to leave, I'm sure she will do so.'

'Aside from which, I wouldn't dream of deserting my escort for the night,' I added sardonically, already regretting the moment of weakness that had prompted me to invite him in the first place.

Orpen bowed slightly. 'As you wish.' He paused, like someone about to make an entrance, and then continued. 'Shall I?'

'Orpen, I hardly think—'

'No, please, be my guest,' said Caroline with more grace than I could have mustered. The timbre of her voice combined curiosity with a strange apprehension. 'Should I take notes?' I asked testily. He looked straight through me and carried on.

'Act One. The curtain rises. The story begins in Dublin, about a decade and a half ago. That is when an aspiring soprano—whom we will call Elizabeth Bird—meets a handsome, plausible young man, let's call him—Daniel Horton. She is an impressionable young lady, and he cuts quite a dashing figure. He has the added romance and mystery of being an Irish revolutionary. A Fenian; a member of the Brotherhood. She makes the mistake of agreeing to marry him. He turns out to be a brute, who is little more than an unsuccessful petty criminal.'

Bar the melodramatic opening, this had little of the feel of Grand Opera about it. It was more like a violin concerto, with Orpen as the soloist. He had paused, for effect, or to gauge our reaction. His only reward was a slight movement from Caroline Schroeder. She picked up a brush and methodically combed her long golden locks. For my part, although I had only a dim understanding of where this was leading I did not like the direction of travel. Orpen looked slightly miffed at our apathetic response to his virtuosity. Somewhat abashed, he approached his first cadenza more diffidently. He began patrolling the room at an unhurried pace.

'Her husband's true character quickly becomes apparent to Elizabeth. This is after several particularly violent beatings, one of which comes to the attention of the Dublin Metropolitan Police. Elizabeth, however, foolishly declines to press charges, much to the chagrin of the DMP who are not overly fond of her revolutionary spouse. After months of relentless mistreatment, all without legal consequences for Horton, she manages to flee to sanctuary in London. A short while later, before he can pursue her, her tormentor is himself forced to escape to America when he is implicated in the murder of an IRB informer. How do you like it so far?'

This was addressed to Caroline. He had not taken his eyes off her since the beginning of his performance. She had resolutely avoided his gaze. Occasionally she would glance in my direction as if she was looking for some sort of cue from me. I felt like a particularly hapless conductor. All I could do in the circumstances was to follow the soloist. Then, just as Orpen was cranking up for the adagio, she intervened.

'Might I suggest a refinement?' she asked. 'Why not have the tormentor—Horton—insist that, after they are married, in addition to her musical career, Elizabeth will supplement their income by working as a prostitute, with him as her pimp.'

Orpen, taken aback at her frankness, responded warily. 'I'm sure I can work that into the plot.'

An eerie stillness now descended on the room. I noticed for the first time the ticking of the dressing room clock. Caroline had barely shifted in her chair since the start of Orpen's narrative. The narrator himself ceased his own slow and deliberate movements. I felt like an unwelcome eavesdropper listening at the door.

'Do you want me to leave?' I asked Caroline. She glanced up at me with a haunted look in her eyes. She shook her head. It was already too late for that.

'Shall I continue?' Orpen asked her. He was enjoying himself far too much. I wanted to slap him as hard as I could, but, to my shame, I also wanted to get to the denouement. Caroline nodded.

'Released from any further peril,' he resumed, 'by the news of the exile of her former lover, the young soprano feels it is safe to return to her chosen profession in London and is quickly identified as an outstanding talent. But she does so under the pseudonym of Caroline Edwards. Elizabeth Bird is dead. She builds a successful international career. She is lauded by critics and adored by fans. When performing in New York, she receives a proposal from a wealthy Californian with political ambitions. We can call him Schroeder. She succumbs to his advances and moves west. She soon realizes, to her horror, that she has settled in the same city as her former tormentor. Horton is well established, quite respectable, and relatively prosperous.

'Act three of the opera opens with the former diva at her wit's end. The man who has cruelly abused her in the past, and to whom she is still legally married, now threatens her future. He has the capacity to destroy her and will have no qualms about taking advantage of that power. Egged on by those demanding twins, Revenge and Self-Protection, she devises a plan with her inevitable faithful retainer, a loyal and willing accomplice. Let's call him Davies. The retainer succeeds in enticing Horton to Elizabeth's new and imposing home. On arrival, her erstwhile tormentor is seized by the loyal retainer, bound, dragged into one of the many outbuildings to the rear of the Schroeder mansion, confronted with his past sins, and stabbed to death. Later, such is the fury and the loathing of our heroine for Horton, that she frenziedly attacks the corpse of her former lover, postmortem. A suitably *grand guignol* interlude, don't you think? The faithful retainer then carves the letter 'H' on the chest of the dead man, in the hope of convincing the authorities that Horton has been the victim of a vigilante murder. He then makes the potentially fatal mistake of using his employer's distinctive carriage to transport Horton's body to the location where it is later discovered. Because of the divisive nature of the victim's personality, the murder is widely accepted as an act of political revenge. The conspirators appear to have escaped the consequences of their crime. Shall I continue?'

Here he paused again. He had executed the tricky adagio with considerable composure. I took a deep breath. If I had been the object of this *roman à clef*, I would, at this point, have been begging him to stop. Caroline Schroeder merely nodded again, almost absently.

There was no attempt at denial or self-justification. You could see that Orpen was relishing the rousing finale to come.

'However, Nemesis is at hand. Her husband, piecing together information from a variety of sources—including a conniving valet and, I regret to say, a corrupt agent within the police department—discovers what has happened and is angered at this un-businesslike procedure. He is also incensed that his wife has left a hostage to fortune in the form of her accomplice's intimate knowledge of what has taken place. Schroeder seeks to clean up this mess by engaging the services of an ally—we can call him Newman—to arrange the murder of Caroline's co-conspirator, Davies. That plan, however, goes awry. The assassin deployed to kill the loyal retainer fails in his task. Davies turns the tables by shooting dead the man who has been assigned to murder him.'

Caroline had retained some semblance of calm up to this point, but now she grew suddenly pale and became agitated. I offered to fetch her a glass of water. She merely shook her head and resumed the mechanical combing of her hair. There was a knock at the door. We all ignored it. Orpen resumed his monologue.

'Later, however, because he is still a potential threat, her retainer is arrested on the basis of information supplied, through Newman, to the police. He is taken in for questioning and dies at the hands of a co-operative policeman on the express orders of her husband. A suitably sanguinary conclusion to the melodrama, don't you think? The opera ends unhappily, with the flawed heroine in the clutches of her ambitious and ruthless husband, mourning the death of her loyal retainer. I hope I'm not imposing too much on your patience or your credulity, ma'am. I'm nearing the end of my libretto.'

Whoever was outside knocked again. Soon they were bound to become discouraged and leave.

'Allow me, however, to crave your continued indulgence because there is room for one final twist. The loyal retainer has lived up to his job description. He has retained a keepsake by way of insurance. He possesses himself of something that had once belonged to their victim, a silver cufflink in the shape of a nightingale—a signature gift from the young and gullible Elizabeth Bird to Daniel Horton in better times. It is one of a pair worn by Horton for the visit to his former lover's home, perhaps as a sentimental gesture to past affection, perhaps as a visual reminder of his power over her. When the police arrive to take him away for questioning, the resourceful Davies—I fancy he's probably the principal tenor— brings this trinket with him, just in case.'

He reached into a jacket pocket, withdrew a small silver cufflink with great delicacy and dangled it before Caroline's eyes. He studied it himself for a moment, shook his head, and then returned it to his pocket.

'No, on second thoughts, no need to complicate the plot. Let it stand without the cufflink. On its own it counts for nothing anyway.'

Orpen then stretched out his right hand towards Caroline's left temple, with a flick of his wrist he produced the cufflink from behind her ear and handed the tiny silver nightingale to the diva. For the first time, I saw some color return to her cheeks. She glanced at me again as if looking for guidance. As I was having trouble finding my place in the score, I had no help to offer. When she spoke, her voice was dull and lifeless.

'Shall we just abandon your central conceit, Sergeant Orpen, and acknowledge what it is we are discussing here?' She still avoided eye contact with her accuser.

'Very well, ma'am. By the way, you may want this as well.' He reached into his pocket and removed a small white envelope. The name 'Daniel Horton' was written clearly on the front in a female hand.

'Mr. Davies was loyal, but he was cautious. This was left in the dead man's pocket—the accompanying card removed—as another piece of insurance. The police were intended to find it and place no significance on it unless he required them to do so.'

'How do you know this is my handwriting?'

'I could just ask you for a sample to support my theory. But there is no need.' He reached into his pocket again and made an ostentatious display of bringing out the paper that she had just autographed. With an unnecessary flourish, he underlined the word 'Daniel'.

'The Liberator actually betrayed you twice,' he remarked. 'A few days ago, you displayed a detailed knowledge of the statuary of a city you claim never to have visited. You corrected my deliberately erroneous assertion that Daniel O'Connell was to be found overlooking the Rotunda Hospital.'

'I could not allow *that* falsehood to stand. I was born there, and my mother was a Rotunda midwife.' She paused and seemed to drift away. For just a moment she was shining a light into a corner of an erased past. Then she shook herself and looked directly at Orpen for the first time since he had begun to unravel that past.

'I take it then that your brother is not an aficionado of opera after all?'

'Since it has nothing whatever to do with foxhounds or the Meath Hunt Ball, I'm afraid not.'

'May I have my autograph back, in that case?' She held out her hand. It was steady and insistent.

'Certainly. It would be pearls before swine.' He returned the paper to her.

'Have we got to the point where you walk away and leave me with a loaded gun?' she asked. Her voice was now regaining some of its resolve.

'No need for histrionics, I think.'

'Isn't that what the English do in circumstances like these?'

'As I'm constantly having to remind people, I'm not English.'

'Can we stop dancing around the mulberry bush? What are your intentions?' she demanded. Orpen took a step backwards in surprise.

'I intend to catch a train to New York tomorrow and after that to sail for England.' He waited for this to sink in before continuing. 'It's a question of jurisdiction really. Well, that's not entirely true. It's also a question of national interest. You, and the late Mr. Davies, have done the state some service. Not this state, of course … although that's a moot point as well. Naturally any sort of formal recognition from Her Majesty's Government would be inappropriate and inadvisable. Obviously, HMG does not condone murder. I'm obliged to mention that, but don't take it too much to heart.'

As he spoke, the realization of her deliverance began to dawn slowly on Caroline Schroeder. Instead of looking grateful or reassured, she appeared to be stunned and bewildered.

Orpen saw no purpose in gilding the lily. He had made his point. He bowed.

'I bid you good day, ma'am, and I do hope our paths cross again. I was sincere in my approbation of your talents, and sincerity is not my long suit. You have quite converted me.' He turned and made to leave the room. I touched his arm gently as he opened the door.

'Wait for me outside,' I whispered.

I had a coda of my own in mind.

CHAPTER NINETEEN

OPHELIA WILLIAMS

24 October – approaching midnight

I parted company with a pensive Caroline Schroeder as speedily and politely as I could. The time for sycophancy had long passed. The best I could do was thank her *pro forma*, as if nothing had happened. It was all rather perfunctory, and it was the coward's way out. It was also pointless because I don't believe she heard a word I said. She looked like someone who had just awoken from a coma.

I caught up with Orpen in the hallway. He was lounging with his back to the wall staring at a floor-to-ceiling mirror opposite. I had the feeling that I'd interrupted him as he was about to take a bow.

'That was a bravura performance,' I remarked, trying to disguise a mixture of irritation and admiration with non-committal flatness.

'Always a delight to win your approval. Though I should acknowledge the critical assistance of Superintendent Mallon of the Dublin Metropolitan Police, and that most excellent invention, the telegraph. With John Mallon's help, a patchwork of hunches became a formidable tapestry.'

'Good of you to share the credit.'

'We are a band of brothers—.'

'—and native to the soil.'

'You've lost me,' he seemed genuinely perplexed.

' "Fighting for the property we gained by honest toil"? The 'Bonnie Blue Flag'? The original banner of the Confederacy? Campbell must have been getting into your head and you weren't even aware of it.'

'I believed I was misquoting *Henry the Fifth*.'

'Subliminal self-deception.'

'Hardly deception,' he said, like a small boy affronted at being blamed for someone else's peccadillo.

'You speak as if you are wholly unfamiliar with the art. You wouldn't even be here tonight if you hadn't deceived me into inviting you.'

'A small and necessary transgression I'm afraid. I do apologize. But you were excellent company.'

'I'm flattered. By the way, as we're devising operatic scenarios, do you mind if I take my turn?'

'Sally forth. It's a highly diverting parlor game, isn't it?'

'Quite so. But before I begin, you don't have any misgivings whatever about your … small sin of omission back there?'

'Which was?'

'Isn't it called "misprision of felony"? Failure to report a crime?'

'Is denying the State of California the opportunity to hang a woman a sin?'

'It's certainly a crime, or a misdemeanor at least. And I guess, technically, that's a sin, isn't it?'

'I'm afraid I'm not an authority on these matters. When one hasn't had much evidence of the existence of a deity, one doesn't give much consideration to the fear of offending him. I merely truncated the judicial process. Or perhaps 'abrogated' might be the *mot juste*. I took it upon my own shoulders and commuted her sentence. Her punishment—and I'm not sure she deserves any—will be the wrath and contempt of her wrathful and contemptible husband. There are worse fates, I suppose. I'm not sure that being hanged by the neck until death is one of them. But we're straying off the point, aren't we?'

'Shall we walk?'

'If it helps your creativity.'

'It does.'

The California Theatre was on Bush Street, three blocks west of its intersection with Market. Without any definite plan or destination in mind, we started walking eastward. Silences can be disconcerting. I conjured one, intrigued to see for how long Orpen would allow it to linger. He broke quickly.

'You had an operatic plot in mind, I think?' he said, making another of those irritating sweeping gestures, of mock obeisance, and then slipped his hands into his pockets. 'The floor is yours.'

I wound up the metronome and began.

'*My* plot begins in London. The tenor, who is naturally our hero—'

'Naturally. Not too overweight I hope.'

' … is a young Irish police officer, to be called, for want of a better name … Orpen.'

'You couldn't want for a better name.' His tone was still flippant but edged with a new wariness.

'Am I to be constantly interrupted?' I asked, with mock truculence. He shrugged apologetically and lapsed into a simulated sulk.

'He is dispatched by his government to a thriving American west coast city. Orpen, despite his apparent affability, charm, occasional haplessness, and air of wide-eyed innocence—'

'I like him already,' he interjected. I unleashed my best scowl. 'Sorry.' He subsided.

'… is extremely capable and utterly ruthless. A killer if needs be.'

This time there was no facetious interruption. I wouldn't exactly say that Orpen began to look uncomfortable, but he was suddenly a lot less garrulous.

'He is tasked with nullifying the activities of a prominent Fenian in this unruly western city. Horton … for want of a better name. Horton has been making a nuisance of himself with gifts of dynamite, frankincense and myrrh to Rossa the Redeemer, a sort of Irish demigod. Opera isn't really opera without a god or two. Interesting word "nullify" don't you think? I use it in the sense of "to neutralize" as you would an acid with something alkaline. But in my scenario Orpen's superiors hold open the possibility of another interpretation. The choice is left to him. He can be a humble alkali, or he can act like a demi-god himself, with the power of life or death over Horton.'

Orpen, consciously or otherwise, was mimicking Caroline Schroeder's reaction to his own monologue. He was looking at the revelers on Bush, and the prostitutes on Montgomery. He was looking anywhere but at me. Even a lengthy pause, which I tried to charge with meaning—without the requisite skill to achieve such an effect—elicited no response whatever. I resumed my narrative.

'Orpen has the luck of the Irish.'

'There's no such damn thing,' I heard him mutter. I could see his breath in the cold late October air. At least he was listening attentively.

'Somebody beats him to the punch. Horton is murdered, allegedly by a rival Irish warlord. But, of course, this conspiracy is hydra-headed—always good to get a bit of mythology in as well, don't you think? The removal of one dynamitard results in his immediate replacement. A power struggle amongst the professionally Irish of this west coast city throws up a potential successor … Riley, for want of a better name. This man—obviously played by an accomplished *basso*—is a ruthless, cold-blooded killer. Orpen finds himself back in the tradition of Thomas Hobson. He must make a choice: nullification or assassination, assuming there's a difference. What is it to be? What do you think he should do?'

At least this drew a glance. It was a searching, impassive look. Neutral, if you will. He was torn between a desire to bring the conversation to an abrupt end, and curiosity to hear how much I had managed to work out.

'Very well. I'll decide, shall I? I'll play God instead. Even though he is my very own artistic creation, I have no love for Riley, so why don't we have Orpen ambush him. A single shot to the head and Riley is despatched. After Orpen's brief turn as a malign *deus ex machina*, he jettisons his weapon—not his standard issue pistol by the way—and manufactures an alibi. He administers a few blows to his head and ribs and shows up at the door of an acquaintance, an accomplished young female doctor—here's the glamorous soprano lead I think, well under the age of forty—with a story about having been assaulted. He claims to have managed to scatter his assailants with a single gunshot. Yet the doctor, who has some knowledge of such matters, notices that his revolver has not been fired.'

That was what finally drew first blood. He winced.

'Ah, yes,' he sighed. 'The very reason for my rapid return visit. I made the mistake of over-elaboration during our first soirée. The sequel was a misdirected piece of attempted misdirection. My impeccable rationale was that if you felt the need to convince me of your innocence, you would not question mine. I presume I only succeeded in making you even more suspicious?'

'Let's just stick with my libretto, shall we? Upon examining her surprise patient's wounds, the accomplished young female doctor finds they are not nearly as severe as he has suggested. Perhaps he has a low pain threshold, but she is now finding it difficult to believe his story.'

'Have we reached your finale yet?'

'Not quite.'

'Might I suggest a refinement?'

'By all means.'

'Rather than have "Orpen" inflict the injuries on himself, why not have him employ the services of two of the most physically imposing members of a young female street gang whose acquaintance he has made. They offer all sorts of promising choral possibilities. To account for the unconvincing nature of the injuries, it might be the case that one of the females in question was so reluctant to perform the appointed task that the injuries inflicted would not bear too close an inspection.'

'A dramatic and poignant—if somewhat implausible—modification.'

We were still walking quite briskly and had almost reached Market by now. Orpen had long since removed his hands from his pockets. They were making urgent and precise movements, clasping, and unclasping rhythmically.

'What's next?' he asked.

'Time for the comic interlude now. In this digression from the main plot, Orpen tries to persuade the young doctor that she has murdered Riley herself. Or at least he tries to convince her that he thinks she has done the dastardly deed. He posits as a motive, the revenge killing of the man who murdered her father, with a suspicious overcoat as Exhibit A for the prosecution. But never fear, he will protect her from the callous forces of law and order by remaining silent. However, it's all a bit too clever by half.'

He had the decency to look abashed. He was right, as a piece of gratuitous window dressing it had prompted me to ask myself some awkward questions. Awkward for him that is.

'Despite some obvious reservations, I wasn't entirely averse to having you in the audience just now, you know,' he observed.

'You were hoping I might finally succumb to your version of events? Gratified that I was no longer the object of your suspicions?'

'Something like that. A forlorn hope. You are a mite too clever. Smarter than the good Sergeant Campbell anyway.'

'If you are hoping to flatter me, you can do better than that.'

This was followed by another hiatus. An understandable awkwardness had settled upon our conversation. This will happen when you accuse someone of being a professional assassin. We were on

Market now, headed east. I admired, for the umpteenth time, the impressive architecture of downtown San Francisco. Orpen studied his boots. A chilling mist swirled around us as we neared the Embarcadero. It was Orpen who broke the silence.

'Have we got to the point where you walk away and leave me with a loaded gun?'

'I don't expect I will. As you keep reminding me, you're not English.'

'The Irish believe in the notion of honor too.'

'But their sense of it is not quite as highly developed, is it?'

'I suppose not. Irish notions of chivalry have more to do with shooting someone else at ten paces than doing away with oneself when caught red-handed.'

The fog was thickening as we approached the Bay. There was little point in holding back now and there was something I wanted from him.

'Why do you do what you do?' I asked suddenly. I was hoping for an answer I could comprehend. 'Is it a cause?' I prodded. His laugh was calculatedly mirthless.

'Hardly. I'm a committed non-believer.'

'In what?'

'In anything.'

'So … why do you do what you do?'

'Because I am who I am.'

'Don't be flippant.'

He thought for a moment. 'You're a medical person. Think of me as a vaccine rather than a prophylactic. That might help. Or a catalyst who has sold his inertia to the highest bidder. Is that too glib?'

'A little.'

'Well then, it's a job. Like any other. And I have debts to pay, like everyone else.' He shrugged. It was the gesture of a man who thought he had said enough.

'So, no gun then?' he asked.

'No gun. I couldn't be sure you wouldn't use it on me. Besides, I'm very fond of my Smith and Wesson. This one.' I produced it and pointed it at him in case he thought I lacked gravitas. We hadn't been acquainted for long, but I think he knew me well enough to be certain that I would use it if I had to. He glanced behind me. It was quite a childish gesture really. An amateur conjuring trick, and I wasn't about to be bamboozled. Then, almost imperceptibly, he shook his head. If he was trying to get inside mine, it was starting to work. I shifted position, moving to my left. He was still in my sights but out of the corner of my eye I could cover the ground to my right. About thirty yards away from where we were standing were two young women, probably not much more than girls really. One stood out even in the gathering mist because of her enormous bulk. She was walking backwards slowly, watching us carefully as she began to disappear into the fog. She had something in her right hand. She was gently patting her left palm with it. The other girl, smaller, dark and pretty, stood her ground. She stared at Orpen as if seeking some instruction in his face. I looked at him quizzically.

'Some allies. Recently added to the retinue,' he said cheerily. "We few, we happy few." Tomorrow is St. Crispin's Day after all. Don't worry, they know they won't be needed.'

'But they won't be far away?'

He shrugged again. This time it was the gesture of a man who knows nothing about such things. 'So, is this where I extend my wrists and you produce the manacles?'

'Not unless you particularly want to be handcuffed on the first leg of your journey to New York.'

'Chains tend to be an inconvenience on trains. They rattle, and inevitably excite comment in the second-class carriages.'

'You're not travelling first-class then?'

'My travel plans appear to be entirely up to you. You're the one with the gun.'

Maybe it was a trick of the light, or an illusion fostered by the mist that was enveloping us, but I could have sworn that I saw my father just then. Marcus was standing under a streetlamp, in uniform. He was smiling. His smile was that special one he reserved for me. My eyes welled up, but I managed to smile back. We gazed at each other for what seemed like an age. Should I warn him about the large female presence looming somewhere in the mist nearby? Probably no need. When the reverie ended, I wondered how long Orpen had been waiting for his answer.

' "Misprision" is such an odd word,' I said. 'It's hard to take it seriously. I mean if I did decide to overlook the fact that you cold-bloodedly murdered a cold-blooded murderer would I be "misprising" your felony?'

'As with sin, I'm afraid I'm not an authority in these matters.'

'Will you ever come back to San Francisco do you think?'

His face relaxed. Until then I hadn't realized his expression had been strained. Now that he had his answer, he began to search his jacket. I raised the revolver a few inches, just in case.

'No need for that,' he said. 'I just wanted to give you something.' From an inside pocket he produced a silver cufflink, an exact replica of the one he had returned to Caroline Schroeder. With a ceremonial flourish, he handed it to me.

'I was going to keep this for myself, but you are the Victrix Ludorum and this is your laurel crown. As it happens, the one I presented to Mrs. Schroeder was a sentimental parting gift from Campbell. This is its twin, purloined from the pocket of Evan Davies a few minutes before you began your examination of his corpse.'

'You stole evidence from under the noses of Campbell and Lees? Priceless. I do so look forward to my next luncheon date with my Godfather.'

'I know it sounds like my customary depravity, but Davies had no further use for it, and there was already another in circulation. I merely preferred to retain the one acquired by my own efforts. Now it's yours. Please accept it with my gratitude and admiration.'

How could I say no? I took it from him, fully intending, at some point, to reunite it with its twin.

'You haven't answered my question. Will you ever come back to San Francisco?'

'Perhaps. I could be tempted by an invitation to the impending nuptials of Sergeant Wellington Campbell, bachelor, and Doctor Ophelia Williams, spinster.'

Someone walked on my grave, and I grimaced. 'Not for a lease on the entire Comstock lode. Not even if the failure to procreate with that misogynistic bigot spelled the end of humanity itself.'

'Probably not then. But you never know. Is the gun still necessary?'

'Probably not. Just a precaution. Like your friend … St. Crispin.'

'Can I ask you something?'

'If you like.'

'Do you really have a sister called Salomé?'

I had been prepared for anything. This was disappointing. It was like a condemned man demanding bread and butter as his last meal. Not even a plea for some strawberry jam.

'Yes. I do.'

'Heavenly.'

We had reached Market and Battery by now. The fog had concentrated as we neared the bay, and the chill was eagerly exploring every pore and orifice. From somewhere off to our left came the sound of a scuffle. This was followed by a pained and drunken caterwauling. Momentarily distracted, I turned in the direction of the noise, but I could see nothing in the gathering mist. I hoped it wasn't my father coming to grips with St. Crispin. When I turned back, Orpen had gone.

He wasn't taking any chances. He could hardly be blamed for that.

CODA

TO: The Home Secretary, Sir William Harcourt
FROM: Sir Nicholas Gosselin
DATE: 6 December 1883
RE: Operation Yerba Buena

I am happy to report, as per our verbal briefing, that the above operation has been successfully concluded.

Sergeant Robert Orpen of the London Metropolitan Police, seconded to the Special Irish Branch, was dispatched in October of this year to the city of San Francisco. His mission was (a) to ascertain the status of Daniel Horton *vis à vis* his erstwhile collaboration with Her Majesty's Government and, depending on his findings, to come to terms with, or eliminate same; (b) to interdict the movement of dynamite from San Francisco for the use of various Irish nationalist factions in the bombing of targets in Britain.

Sergeant Orpen was permitted to enlist the aid of Rachel Courtney, codenamed 'Amber', the principal agent of HMG in the city. She has succeeded in insinuating herself into the employment of the main Clan na Gael/IRB 'front' organisation in San Francisco, the Knights of the Red Branch.

Sergeant Orpen's mission was compromised (see below) before his arrival in San Francisco. Through the good offices of the city's

Captain of Detectives, Isaiah Lees—a friend of Scotland Yard—Orpen was fortuitously seconded to the San Francisco Police Force and assigned to a Sergeant Wellington Campbell. HMG had no prior information on this officer.

Sergeant Orpen quickly established, with the assistance of 'Amber'/Rachel Courtney, that Daniel Horton had terminated his temporary collaboration with HMG, posed a significant threat to HMG, and was involved in supplying dynamite to the O'Donovan Rossa faction. However, before he could remove Horton, Sergeant Orpen was pre-empted by the murder of same by a person or persons unknown.

Based on intelligence received, and acting on his own initiative, Sergeant Orpen subsequently deemed it necessary to eliminate one Christopher Riley, who, he considered, posed a threat to HMG as a potential successor to Horton. This was achieved by the procurement by 'Amber' (under protest) of a suitable weapon, by the shadowing of Riley, and by his removal in the Chinatown district of the city.

It is with regret that I must inform you, Home Secretary, that we have now established beyond reasonable doubt that the source of the information, which led to Operation Yerba Buena being compromised from the outset, was the Foreign Office diplomat Kenneth Haddo, HMG Consul General in San Francisco. Other than Orpen, Sir Robert Anderson, and myself, Haddo—who was vulnerable due to the accumulation of unpaid gambling debts—was the only person who had any foreknowledge of the existence of the operation. Haddo has been recalled, on the orders of the Foreign Secretary, but has, so far, failed to report to the Foreign Office in London. It is assumed that he has taken flight. Sir Robert Anderson and I have thus been vindicated in our absolute refusal to reveal the identity, or even the very existence, of 'Amber' to the Foreign Office. To have done so, it is now clear, would have risked her identification by Haddo to the

Knights of the Red Branch, as our agent, with the obvious consequences which would have resulted from that exposure.

I wish to commend Rachel Courtney for her invaluable contribution to Operation Yerba Buena. She undertook several hazardous
tasks on behalf of HMG, as she has often done in the past. It is fortunate that she can continue as an asset to HMG in the future. I am
happy to endorse the payment to her of the additional sum of $200,
as recommended by Sergeant Orpen, on the successful conclusion of
his operation.

May I be permitted to reiterate the point made to you in our
private briefing concerning the potential reputational risk to HMG
inherent in this operation. The San Francisco Police Department is
entirely satisfied that the killer of Horton and Riley has been identified. There should be no repercussions for HMG from the elimina-
tion of the latter.

It is regrettable that operations such as that codenamed 'Yerba
Buena' should have to be carried out on the soil of a friendly power
such as the United States of America and should involve the liquida-
tion of any American nationals (formerly citizens of the United Kingdom). However, this is an unavoidable consequence of the refusal of
the State Department of the United States to countenance the extra-
dition of those who are responsible for both seditious provocation
and murderous attacks against the people of the United Kingdom.
Should this attitude persist, it will undoubtedly prove necessary in
the future to authorise the neutralisation of several other threats to
the safety and security of Her Majesty's subjects.

In conclusion, I am confident that with Mr. Thomas Newman
now in complete control of the IRB/Clan operations in San Francisco, the interests of HMG are well served. Newman's preoccupation
is with his own political advancement rather than with foment-
ing revolution in Ireland. He would be loath to allocate time and

resources to anything that did not advance his personal objectives and promote his desire for pre-eminence in local politics. The threat of sanctions or direct action against him from the IRB/Clan in New York is a remote prospect. Newman is too well ensconced in his own bailiwick.

I am aware of your prior concerns at my choice of agent for this operation, based on Orpen's history. However, it was this very history which, in my estimation, made him the ideal choice. Despite his regrettable nationalist leanings, he has an uncompromising aversion to outrage and to its perpetrators. That this may have led to Sergeant Orpen taking questionable measures in the past is unfortunate. But it has, thus far, redounded to the benefit of Her Majesty's Government.

I therefore recommend that, in due course, Sergeant Orpen should be promoted to the rank of Inspector.

ABOUT MYLES DUNGAN

Myles Dungan is a writer, lecturer and broadcaster who currently presents the weekly RTÉ Radio 1 programme *The History Show*. He is an Adjunct Lecturer in the UCD School of History and is the recipient of two Fulbright Awards. He has taught Irish history in UCD, Trinity College and the University of California, Berkeley. He holds a PhD from Trinity College, Dublin (2012) and is the author of more than a dozen books on Irish and American history (including *Four Killings, Conspiracy: Irish Political Trials, Irish Voices from the Great War, How the Irish Won the West, The Captain and the King: William O'Shea, Parnell and Late Victorian Ireland* and *Mr. Parnell's Rottweiler*). He is also the author of two works for children, *The Great Irish History Book* (shortlisted for an Irish Book Award) and *The Forgettables*. His latest work for adults, *Land is all that matters: the struggle that shaped Irish history*, was published in May 2024 and was shortlisted in the Best Irish History Book category in the 2024 Irish Book Awards. *The Red Branch* is his first solo novel (he was the co-author with Jim Lusby of the detective novel *Snuff* in 1992).

Books from Etruscan Press

Zarathustra Must Die | Dorian Alexander

The Disappearance of Seth | Kazim Ali

The Last Orgasm | Nin Andrews

Son of a Bird | Nin Andrews

Drift Ice | Jennifer Atkinson

Crow Man | Tom Bailey

Coronology | Claire Bateman

Viscera | Felice Belle

Reading the Signs and other itinerant essays | Stephen Benz

Topographies | Stephen Benz

What We Ask of Flesh | Remica L. Bingham

The Greatest Jewish-American Lover in Hungarian History | Michael Blumenthal

No Hurry | Michael Blumenthal

Choir of the Wells | Bruce Bond

Cinder | Bruce Bond

The Other Sky | Bruce Bond and Aron Wiesenfeld

Peal | Bruce Bond

Scar | Bruce Bond

Until We Talk | Darrell Bourque and Bill Gingles

Big Time | Rus Bradburd

Poems and Their Making: A Conversation | Moderated by Philip Brady

Crave: Sojourn of a Hungry Soul | Laurie Jean Cannady

Toucans in the Arctic | Scott Coffel

Sixteen | Auguste Corteau

Don't Mind Me | Brian Coughlan

Wattle & daub | Brian Coughlan

Body of a Dancer | Renée E. D'Aoust

Etruscan Press Is Proud of Support Received From

Wilkes
University

 Ohio Arts COUNCIL

The Stephen & Jeryl Oristaglio Foundation

[c|mp]

 NATIONAL ENDOWMENT FOR THE ARTS

Drs. Barbara Brothers & Gratia Murphy Endowment

Founded in 2001 with a generous grant from the Oristaglio Foundation, Etruscan Press is a nonprofit cooperative of poets and writers working to produce and promote books that nurture the dialogue among genres, achieve a distinctive voice, and reshape the literary and cultural histories of which we are a part.

Etruscan Press

www.etruscanpress.org

Etruscan Press books may be ordered from

US/Canada: Consortium Book Sales and Distribution

800.283.3572

www.cbsd.com

UK/Europe: Script Books

Tel: +44 (0)1226 734350

Email: orders@scriptps.co.uk

Etruscan Press is a 501(c)(3) nonprofit organization.
Contributions to Etruscan Press are tax deductible
as allowed under applicable law.
For more information, a prospectus,
or to order one of our titles,
contact us at books@etruscanpress.org.

www.ingramcontent.com/pod-product-compliance
Lightning Source LLC
Chambersburg PA
CBHW031108030726
47496CB00002BA/443